The critics on Lawrence Block

'Scudder is one of the most appealing series characters around'   *LA Times*

'Bull's-eye dialogue and laser-image description . . . any search for false notes will prove futile . . . [Block's] eye for detail is as sharp as ever, and characters almost real enough to touch abound'   *New York Times Book Review*

'Fast-paced, insightful, and so suspenseful it zings like a high-tension wire'   Stephen King

'Outstanding . . . excellent . . . smoothly paced, deftly plotted, brightly phrased study of perversity'
Chicago Tribune

'One of the very best writers now working the beat'
Wall Street Journal

'Cries out to be read at night . . . First class . . . Tough and sharp . . . It would be hard to find a better mystery'   *People*

'Absolutely riveting . . . Block is terrific'
Washington Post

'What he does best – writing popular fiction that always respects his readers' desire to be entertained but never insults their intelligence'   *GQ*

'There with the best . . . The real McCoy with a shocking twist and stylish too'   *Observer*

Lawrence Block is a Grandmaster of the Mystery Writers of America, and has won a total of fourteen awards for his fiction, including one Edgar Award and two Shamus Awards for best novels for titles in the Matt Scudder series. He is also the creator of other great characters such as Bernie Rhodenbarr, Evan Tanner and Chip Harrison, and has written dozens of award-winning short stories. Lawrence Block lives in New York City.

EVEN THE WICKED

A MATT SCUDDER MYSTERY

Lawrence Block

ORION

An Orion paperback
First published in Great Britain by Orion in 1996
This paperback edition published in 2000 by
Orion Books Ltd,
Orion House, 5 Upper St Martin's Lane,
London WC2H 9EA

A CIP catalogue record for this book
is available from the British Library

ISBN 0 75283 450 9

Typeset by Deltatype Ltd, Wirral
Printed and bound in Great Britain by
Clays Ltd, St Ives plc

For Bill Hoffman

with thanks, variously, to
Joan Acocella, Ron Brogan and
Memphis Jim Evans

'Even the wicked get worse than they deserve.'

Willa Cather, *One of Ours*

ONE

On a Tuesday night in August I was sitting in the living room with TJ, watching two guys hit each other on one of the Spanish language cable channels, and enjoying the fresh air more than the fight. A heat wave had punished the city for two weeks, finally breaking over the weekend. Since then we'd had three perfect days, with bright blue skies and low humidity and the temperature in the 70s. You'd have called it ideal weather anywhere; in the middle of a New York summer, you could only call it a miracle.

I'd spent the day taking advantage of the weather, walking around the city. I got home and showered in time to drop into a chair and let Peter Jennings explain the world to me. Elaine joined me for the first fifteen minutes, then went into the kitchen to start dinner. TJ dropped by just around the time she was adding the pasta to the boiling water, insisting that he wasn't hungry and couldn't stay long anyway. Elaine, who had heard this song before, doubled the recipe on the spot, and TJ let himself be persuaded to take a plate and clean it several times.

'Trouble is,' he told her, 'you too good of a cook. Now on, I wait to come by until mealtimes is come and gone. I don't watch out, I be fat.'

He has a ways to go. He's a street kid, lean and limber, indistinguishable at first glance from any of the young blacks you'll see hanging around Times Square, shilling for the monte dealers, running short cons, looking for a way to get over, or just to get by. He's

I

much more than that as well, but for all I know there may be more to many of them than meets the eye. He's the one I know; with the others, all I get to see is what's on the surface.

And TJ's own surface, for that matter, is apt to change, chameleon-like, with his surroundings. I have watched him slip effortlessly from hip-hop street patter to a Brooks Brothers accent that would not be out of place on an Ivy League campus. His hair style, too, has varied over the several years I've known him, ranging from an old-style Afro through assorted versions of the high-top fade. A year or so ago he started helping Elaine at her shop, and on his own decided that a kinder, gentler 'do was more appropriate. He's kept it cropped relatively short ever since, while his dress ranges from the preppy outfits he wears to work to the in-your-face attire they favor on the Deuce. This evening he was dressed for success in khakis and a button-down shirt. A day or two earlier, when I'd seen him last, he was a vision in baggy camo trousers and a sequined jacket.

'Wish they was speakin' English,' he complained. 'Why they got to talk in Spanish?'

'It's better this way,' I said.

'You tellin' me you know what they sayin'?'

'A word here and there. Mostly it's just noise.'

'And that's how you like it?'

'The English-speaking announcers talk too much,' I said. 'They're afraid the audience won't be able to figure out what's going on if they're not chattering away all the time. And they say the same things over and over. "He's not working hard enough to establish the left jab." I don't think I've watched five fights in the past ten years when the announcer hasn't observed

2

that the fighter should be using the jab more. It must be the first thing they teach them in broadcasting school.'

'Maybe this dude sayin' the same thing in Spanish.'

'Maybe he is,' I agreed, 'but since I don't have a clue what he's saying it can't get on my nerves.'

'You ever heard of the mute, Newt?'

'Not the same. You need the crowd noise, need to hear the punches land.'

'These two ain't landin' many.'

'Blame the one in the blue shorts,' I said. 'He's not working hard enough to establish the left jab.'

He did enough to win the four-round prelim, though, getting a decision and a round of perfunctory applause from the crowd. Next on the card was a ten-round welterweight bout, a classic match-up of quick light-hitting youth against a strong puncher a couple of years past his prime. The old guy – I think he was all of thirty-four – was able to stun the kid when he landed a clean shot, but the years had slowed him some and he missed more often than he connected. In return, the kid peppered him with a barrage of blows that didn't have much on them.

'He pretty slick,' TJ said, after a couple of rounds. 'Too bad he doesn't have a punch.'

'He just keep at you, wear you down. Meanwhile he pilin' up the points. Other dude, he be tirin' more with each round.'

'If we understood Spanish,' I said, 'we could listen to the announcer saying pretty much the same thing. If I were betting this fight I'd put my money on the old guy.'

'Ain't no surprise. You ancient dudes has got to stick together. You think we need any of this here?'

'This here' was the line of goods in the Gehlen catalog. The Gehlen Company is an outfit in Elyria,

3

Ohio, offering electronic espionage equipment, gear to bug other people's phones and offices, gear to keep one's own phones and offices bug-free. There's a curiously bi-polar quality to the whole enterprise; they are, after all, promoting half their lines as a defense against the other half, and the catalog copy keeps changing philosophical horses in midstream. 'Knowledge is power,' they assure you on one page, and two pages later they're championing 'your most basic right – the right to personal and corporate privacy'. Back and forth the argument rages, from 'You have a right to know!' to 'Keep *their* noses out of *your* business!'

Where, you have to wonder, do the company's sympathies lie? Given that their namesake was the legendary German intelligence chief, I figured they'd happily sell anything to anybody, committed only to increasing their sales and maximizing their profits. But would any of their wares increase my sales or boost my profits?

'I think we can probably get by without it,' I told TJ.

'How we gonna catch Will without all the latest technology?'

'We're not.'

''Cause he ain't our problem?'

'Not as far as I can tell.'

'Dude's the whole city's problem. All they talkin' about, everywhere you go. Will this and Will that.'

'He was the headline story in the *Post* again today,' I said, 'and they didn't have any news to back it up, because he hasn't done anything since last week. But they want to keep him on the front page to sell papers, so the story was about how the city's nervous, waiting for something to happen.'

'That's all they wrote?'

'They tried to put it in historical context. Other

4

faceless killers who've caught the public imagination, like Son of Sam.'

'Be a difference,' he said. 'Wasn't nobody cheerin' for Son of Sam.' He flicked a finger at an illustration in the Gehlen catalog. 'I like this here voice-changin' telephone, but you see them all over now. They even got them at Radio Shack. This might be a better one, the price they charge for it. Ones at Radio Shack is cheaper.'

'I'm not surprised.'

'Will could use this here, if he was to start makin' phone calls 'stead of sendin' letters.'

'Next time I see him, I'll pass along the suggestion.'

'I almost bought me one the other day.'

'What for? Haven't you got enough of a repertoire of voices?'

'All I got is accents,' he said. 'What this does is change the pitch.'

'I know what it does.'

'So you can sound like a girl, or a little kid. Or if you was a girl to begin with you can sound like a man so's perverts won't be talkin' dirty to you. Be fun to fool around with somethin' like that, only be like a kid with a toy, wouldn't it? One, two weeks and you used up all the newness out of it and be tossin' it in the closet and askin' your mama to buy you somethin' else.'

'I guess we don't need it.'

He closed the catalog and set it aside. 'Don't need none of this,' he said. 'Far as I can see. You want to know what we need, Reed, I already told you that.'

'More than once.'

'A computer,' he said. 'But you don't want to get one.'

'One of these days.'

'Yeah, right. You just afraid you won't know how to use it.'

'It's the same kind of fear,' I said, 'that keeps men from jumping out of planes without parachutes.'

'First thing,' he said, 'you could learn. You ain't that old.'

'Thanks.'

'Second thing, I could work it for you.'

'A passing ability with video games,' I said, 'is not the same thing as being computer literate.'

'They ain't necessarily that far apart. You 'member the Kongs? Video games is where they started at, and where they at now?'

'Harvard,' I admitted. The Kongs, their real names David King and Jimmy Hong, were a pair of hackers devoted to probing the innards of the phone company's computer system. They were high-school students when TJ introduced them to me, and now they were up in Cambridge, doing God knows what.

'You recall the help they gave us?'

'Vividly.'

'How many times have you said you wished they's still in the city?'

'Once or twice.'

'More'n once or twice, Bryce. Whole lot of times.'

'So?'

'We had us a computer,' he said, 'I could get so I could do the same shit they did. Plus I could do all the legit stuff, diggin' out trash in fifteen minutes that you spend a whole day findin' in the library.'

'How would you know how to do it?'

'They got courses you can take. Not to teach you to do what the Kongs can do, but all the rest of it. They sit you down at a machine and teach you.'

6

'Well, one of these days,' I said, 'maybe I'll take a course.'

'No, *I'll* take a course,' he said, 'an' after I learn I can teach you, if you want to learn. Or I can do the computer part, whichever you say.'

'I get to decide,' I said, 'because I'm the boss.'

'Right.'

I started to say something more, but the veteran fighter picked that moment to connect with an overhand right lead that caught the kid on the button and took his legs away from him. The kid was still unsteady on his pins after an eight count, but there was only half a minute left in the round. The older fighter chased him all around the ring and tagged him a time or two, but the kid managed to stay on his feet and weather the round.

They didn't break for a commercial at the bell, electing instead to keep the camera on the younger fighter's corner while his seconds worked on him. The announcers had a lot to say about what they were showing us, but they said it in Spanish so we didn't have to pay any attention to it.

'About that computer,' TJ said.

'I'll think about it.'

'Damn,' he said. 'Had you the next thing to sold on it, and the old man there had to land a lucky punch and break the flow. Why couldn't he wait a round?'

'He was just one old guy looking out for the interests of another,' I said. 'We old guys are like that.'

'This catalog,' he said, brandishing it. 'You happen to see this here night-vision scope? Came from Russia or some such.'

I nodded. It was Soviet Army issue, according to the Gehlen people, and would presumably enable me to

7

read fine print at the bottom of an abandoned coal mine.

'Can't see what we'd need it for,' he said, 'but you could have fun with something like that.' He tossed the catalog aside. 'Have fun with most of this shit. It's toys, is all it is.'

'And what's the computer? A bigger toy than the others?'

He shook his head. 'It's a tool, Buell. But why do I be wastin' my breath tryin' to get through to you?'

'Why indeed?'

I thought we might get to see a knockout in the next round, but it was clear halfway through that it wasn't going to happen. The kid had shaken off the effects of the knockdown, and my guy was slower, having a hard time getting his punches to go where he wanted them. I knew how he felt.

The phone rang, and Elaine picked it up in the other room. On the TV screen, my guy shook off a punch and waded in.

Elaine came in, a hard-to-read expression on her face. 'It's for you,' she said. 'It's Adrian Whitfield. Do you want to call him back?'

'No, I'll talk to him,' I said, rising. 'I wonder what he wants.'

Adrian Whitfield was a rising star, a criminal defense attorney who'd been getting an increasing number of high-profile clients in the past couple of years, and a corresponding increase in media attention. In the course of the summer I'd seen him three times on the TV screen. Roger Ailes had him on to discuss the notion that the jury system was outmoded and due for replacement. (His position was a tentative maybe in the civil courts, a flat no in criminal cases.) Then he was on

Larry King twice, first to talk about the latest star-spangled homicide case in Los Angeles, and then to argue the merits of the death penalty. (He was unequivocally against it.) Most recently I'd seen him along with Raymond Gruliow on Charlie Rose, all three of them caught up in an earnest discussion of the question of the lawyer as popular celebrity. Hard-Way Ray had put the issue in historical context, telling some wonderful stories about Earl Rodgers and Bill Fallon and Clarence Darrow.

I had done some work for Whitfield on Ray Gruliow's recommendation, running checks on witnesses and potential jurors, and I liked him well enough to hope to do more. It was a little late for him to be calling me on business, but the nature of the business is such that you get calls at all hours. I didn't mind the interruption, especially if it meant work. It had been a slow summer thus far. That wasn't all bad, Elaine and I had been able to get away for some long weekends in the country, but I was beginning to get rusty. The signs were there in the way I read the morning papers, obsessively interested in the local crime news and itching to get mixed up in it.

I took the phone in the kitchen and said, 'Matthew Scudder,' announcing myself to whoever had placed the call for him.

But he'd made it himself. 'Matt,' he said. 'Adrian Whitfield. I hope I didn't get you at a bad time.'

'I was watching two fellows hitting each other,' I said. 'Without much enthusiasm, on my part or theirs. What can I do for you?'

'That's a good question. Tell me something, would you? How do I sound?'

'How do you sound?'

'My voice isn't shaky, is it?'

9

'No.'

'I didn't think it was,' he said, 'but it ought to be. I got a phone call a little while ago.'

'Oh?'

'From that idiot with the *News*, but perhaps I shouldn't call him that. For all I know he's a friend of yours.'

I knew a few people at the *Daily News*. 'Who?'

'Marty McGraw.'

'Hardly a friend,' I said. 'I met him once or twice, but neither of us had much of a chance to make an impression on the other. I doubt he'd remember, and the only reason *I* remember is I've been reading his column twice a week for I don't know how many years.'

'Isn't he in there three times a week?'

'Well, I don't usually read the *News* on Sundays.'

'Got your hands full with the *Times*, I suppose.'

'Full of ink, generally.'

'Isn't that something? You'd think they could print the damned newspaper so it doesn't come off on your hands.'

'"If they can put a man on the moon . . ."'

'You said it. Can you believe there's a newsstand in Grand Central sells disposable white pliofilm gloves to wear while you read the damn thing?' He drew a breath. 'Matt, I'm avoiding the point, and my guess is you already know what the point is.'

I had a pretty good idea. 'I suppose he got another of those letters. From Will.'

'From Will, yes. And the subject of that letter?'

'It would have to be one of your clients,' I said, 'but I wouldn't want to try to guess which one.'

'Because they're all such estimable men?'

'I just wouldn't have a clue,' I said. 'I haven't

followed your cases that closely, except for the couple I've worked on. And I don't know how Will's mind works, anyway.'

'Oh, it's an interesting mind. I would say it works very well, certainly well enough for the purpose at hand.' He paused, and I knew what he was going to say an instant before he said it. 'He wasn't writing about one of my clients. He was writing about me.'

'What did he say?'

'Oh, lots of things,' he said. 'I could read it to you.'

'You've got the letter?'

'A copy of it. McGraw faxed it to me. He called me first, before he called the cops, and he faxed me a copy of the letter. That was actually damned considerate of him. I shouldn't have called him a jerk.'

'You didn't.'

'When I first brought his name up, I said –'

'You called him an idiot.'

'You're right at that. Well, I don't suppose he's either one, or if he is he's a considerate specimen of the breed. You asked what Will said. "An Open Letter to Adrian Whitfield." Let's see. "You have devoted your life to keeping guilty men out of prison." Well, he's wrong about that. They're all innocent until proven guilty, and whenever guilt was proved to the satisfaction of a jury, they went to prison. And stayed there, unless I could get a reversal on appeal. In another sense, of course, he's quite correct. Most of the men and women I've represented did what they were accused of doing, and I guess that's enough to make them guilty in the eyes of Will.'

'What's his beef with you, exactly? Doesn't he think the accused are entitled to a defense?'

'Well, I don't want to read you the whole thing,' he said, 'and his position's hard to state with precision, but

11

you could say he takes exception to the fact that I'm good at what I do.'

'That's all?'

'It's funny,' he said. 'He doesn't even mention Richie Vollmer, and that's what got him started.'

'That's right, you were Vollmer's attorney.'

'I was indeed, and I got my share of hate mail when he managed to dodge the wheels of justice, but there's nothing in here about my role in getting him off. Let's see what he says. He says I put the police on trial, which is hardly unique on my part. Our mutual friend Gruliow does that all the time. It's often the best strategy with a minority defendant. He also says I put the victim on trial. I think he's talking about Naomi Tarloff.'

'Probably.'

'It might surprise you to know I've had some second thoughts about that case. But that's neither here nor there. I defended the Ellsworth boy the best I knew how, and even so I didn't get him off. The jury convicted the little son of a bitch. He's up state serving fifteen-to-twenty-five, but that's nothing to the sentence our friend Will has imposed. He says he's going to kill me.'

I said, 'I assume McGraw went straight to the cops.'

'With the briefest pause to ring me up and then fax me the thing. As a matter of fact he made a Xerox copy and faxed that. He didn't want to screw up any physical evidence by running the original through his fax machine. Then he called the cops, and then I heard from them. I had two detectives over here for an hour, and I can call them idiots without regard to the possibility that they're friends of yours. Did I have any enemies? Were there clients who were bitter about my efforts on their behalf? For Christ's sake, the only embittered clients I've got are the ones behind bars, where nobody has to worry about them, least of all myself.'

'They have to ask.'

'I suppose so,' he said, 'but isn't it fairly obvious that this isn't a guy with a personal motive? He's already killed four people, and he nailed the first one because Marty McGraw told him to. I don't know what earned me a place on his shit list, but it's not because he thought I charged him too much for keeping him out of jail.'

'Did they offer you protection?'

'They talked about posting a guard in my outer office. I can't see what good that's going to do.'

'It couldn't hurt.'

'No, but it couldn't help all that much either. I need to know what to do, Matt. I've got no experience in this area. Nobody ever tried to kill me. The closest I've come to this was five or six years ago when a man named Paul Masland offered to punch me in the nose.'

'A disaffected client?'

'Uh-uh. A stockbroker with a snootful. He accused me of fucking his wife. Jesus, I was one of the few men in western Connecticut who hadn't had a shot at her.'

'What happened?'

'He swung and missed, and a couple of guys grabbed his arms, and I said the hell with it and went home. The next time I ran into him we both acted like nothing had ever happened. Or maybe he wasn't acting, because he'd been pretty drunk that night. It's possible he didn't remember a thing. You think I should have told the two detectives about Paul?'

'If you think there's a chance he could have written that letter.'

'It'd be a neat trick,' he said, 'because the poor

bastard's been dead for a year and a half. A stroke or a heart attack, I forget which, but he went in a minute, whichever it was. Son of a bitch never knew what hit him. Not like our friend Will. He's a fucking rattle-snake, isn't he? Warning you first, letting you know what's coming. Matt, tell me what I should do.'

'What you should do? You should leave the country.'

'You're not serious, are you? Even if you are it's out of the question.'

That didn't surprise me. I said, 'Where are you? At your office?'

'No, I got out of there once I got rid of the cops. I am at my apartment. You've never been here, have you? We always met downtown. I live at . . . Jesus, I was wondering if I should say it over the phone. But if he's got the phone tapped he'd have to know where it's installed, wouldn't you say?'

Early on, he'd asked if his voice was shaky. It hadn't been and it still wasn't, but his anxiety was apparent in the way his conversation was becoming increasingly disjointed.

He told me the address and I copied it down. 'Don't go anywhere,' I said. 'Call your doorman and tell him you're expecting a visitor named Matthew Scudder, and not to let me up until after I've shown him photo ID. And tell him I'm the only visitor you're expecting, and not to let anybody else up. And tell him that includes the police.'

'All right.'

'Let your machine screen your phone calls. Don't pick up unless you recognize the caller. I'll be right over.'

By the time I was off the phone there were two different fighters in the ring, a pair of sluggish

14

heavyweights. I asked how the other bout had turned out.

'Went the distance,' TJ said. 'Check it out — for a minute or two I thought I knew how to speak Spanish.'

'How's that?'

'The ring announcer. He's talkin' away, and I'm understandin' every word, and I'm thinkin' it's a miracle and next time you gonna see me's on "Unsolved Mysteries".'

'The fight's being held in Mississippi,' I said. 'The ring announcer was speaking English.'

'Yeah, well, I knows that. It slipped my mind is all, hearing all that Spanish from the announcers. And then when I did hear the English, I just thought it was Spanish and I was understandin' it.' He shrugged. 'Young dude got the decision.'

'It figured.'

'These two don't look to be in a hurry. They just takin' their time.'

'They'll have to do it without me,' I said. 'I have to go out for a while.'

'Some kind of business?'

'Some kind.'

'Want me to tag along, maybe watch your back?'

'Not tonight.'

He shrugged. 'You be thinkin' 'bout that computer, though.'

'I'll give it some thought.'

'Ain't got much time, if we's gonna join the twentieth century.'

'I'd hate to miss it.'

'That's how they gonna catch Will, you know. Computers.'

'Is that a fact?'

'Put all the letters the fool writes into the computer,

15

press the right keys, an' it'll analyse the words he uses and tell you the sucker's a forty-two-year-old white male of Scandinavian ancestry. He be missin' two toes on the right foot, an' he a big Jets and Rangers fan, an' when he a child his mama whupped him for wettin' the bed.'

'And they'll get all this from the computer.'

'All that an' more,' he said, grinning. 'How you think they gonna get him?'

'Forensics,' I said. 'Lab work at the crime scenes and on the letters he writes. I'm sure they'll use computers to process the data. They use them for everything these days.'

'Everybody does. Everybody but us.'

'And they'll follow up a ton of leads,' I said, 'and knock on a lot of doors and ask a lot of questions, most of them pointless. And eventually he'll make a mistake, or they'll get lucky, or both. And they'll land on him.'

'I guess.'

'The only thing is,' I said, 'I hope they don't let it go too long. I'd like to see them hurry up and get this guy.'

TWO

One newspaper column started the whole thing.

It was Marty McGraw's, of course, and it ran in the *Daily News* on a Thursday in early June. McGraw's column, 'Since You Asked', appeared in that newspaper every Tuesday, Thursday, and Sunday. It had been a fixture in New York tabloid journalism for ten years or more, always with the same title, though not always on the same days, or even with the same paper. McGraw had jumped ship a few times over the years, moving from the *News* to the *Post* and back again, with an intermediate stop at *Newsday*.

'An Open Letter to Richard Vollmer', was what McGraw called this particular column, and that's what it was. Vollmer was an Albany native in his early forties with a long sheet of arrests for minor sex offenses. Then a few years back he'd been sent away for child molestation. He did well in therapy and his counselor wrote a favorable report for his parole board, and Vollmer returned to society, sworn to behave himself and devote his life to helping others.

He'd been corresponding with a woman on the outside. She'd answered a personal ad of his. I don't know what kind of woman thinks it's a good idea to exchange letters with a convict, but God seems to have made a lot of them. Elaine says they combine low self-esteem with a Messiah complex; also, she says, it's a way for them to feel sexy without ever having to put out, because the guy's locked away where he can't get at them.

Frances Neagley's pen pal did get out, however, and there was nothing in Albany he wanted to get back to, so he came to New York and looked her up. Franny was a thirtyish nurse's aide who'd been living alone on Haven Avenue in Washington Heights since her mother died. She walked to work at Columbia Presbyterian, volunteered her services at church and block-association fundraisers, fed and fussed over three cats, and wrote love letters to upstanding citizens like Richie Vollmer.

She abandoned her correspondence when Vollmer moved in with her. He insisted on being the only felon in her life. Before long she didn't have much time for the church or the block association. She still took good care of the cats. Richie liked the cats, and all three of them were crazy about him. Franny said as much to a co-worker who'd been alarmed at her friendship with an ex-prisoner. 'You know cats,' she crowed, 'and what a good judge of character they are. And they absolutely love him.'

So did Franny, who was about as good a judge of character as her cats. Remarkably enough, jailhouse therapy hadn't changed her man's sexual orientation, and he went right back to the seduction of the innocent. He started by luring teenage boys to the Haven Avenue apartment with the promise of sex with Franny, showing them nude Polaroids of her as an enticement. (There was a slump to her shoulders and a bovine cast to her features, but otherwise she was a not unattractive woman, with large breasts and generous hips.)

She gave the boys what Richie had promised them, whether grudgingly or enthusiastically. Some of her guests were very likely enthusiastic themselves when Richie joined the party and sodomized them. Others

18

were not, but what recourse did they have? Richie was a hulking, powerful man, physically capable of taking what he wanted, and afterward the boys were compromised by having been eager participants in the first stage of the proceedings.

Things escalated. Franny emptied her savings account and bought a van. The neighbors grew used to the sight of Richie washing and polishing it on the street in front of the apartment house, clearly proud of his new toy. They didn't see how he'd tricked it out on the inside, with a mattress on the floor and restraints attached to the side panels. They would drive around town, and when they got to a likely spot, Franny would drive while Richie lurked in the back. Then Franny would find a child and persuade him (or her, it didn't matter) to get into the van.

They would let the kids go when they were finished. Until one day there was a little girl who wouldn't stop crying. Richie found a way to stop her, and they left the body in a thickly wooded section of Inwood Hill Park.

'That was the best ever,' he told Franny. 'That rounds it out, it's like dessert after a meal. We should have been finishing them off all along.'

'Well, from now on,' she said.

'The look in her eyes right at the end,' he said. 'Jesus.'

'Poor little kid.'

'Yeah, poor little kid. You know what I wish? I wish she was alive so we could do her all over again.'

Enough. They were animals — a label we affix, curiously enough, to those members of our own species who behave in a manner unimaginable in any of the lower animals. They found a second victim, a boy this

19

time, and dumped his corpse within a half mile of the first one, and they were caught.

There was no question of their guilt, and the case should have been solid, but piece by piece it fell apart. There was a ton of evidence the jury didn't get to see, testimony they couldn't hear, because the judge threw it out for one reason or another. That might not have mattered, because Franny was set to confess and testify against Richie – they weren't married, there was no cloak of privilege to preclude her doing so.

When she killed herself, that ended that.

The case against Richie did go to the jury, but there wasn't much to it and his lawyer, Adrian Whitfield, was good enough to punch holes in it big enough for him to walk through. The judge's charge was the nearest thing to an order of dismissal, and the jury took a scant hour and a half to come back with an acquittal.

'It was awful,' one juror told a reporter, 'because we were all dead certain he did it, but the prosecution didn't prove it. We had to find him not guilty, but there should have been a way to lock him up anyway. How can someone like that be released back into society?'

That's what Marty McGraw wanted to know. 'You may not be guilty in the eyes of the law,' he thundered, 'but you're as guilty as sin in my eyes, and the eyes of everybody I know, outside of twelve men and women forced by the system to be as blind as justice herself . . .

'There are too many like you,' he went on, 'falling through the cracks of the system and making the world a bad place to live. And I've got to tell you, I wish to God there were a way to get rid of you. Lynch law was a hell of a way to run things, and only a fool would want to go back to vigilante times. But you're a powerful argument for it. We can't touch you, and we've got to let you live among us like an ineradicable virus. You're not going to change. You're not going to get help, and guys like you are beyond help anyway. You nod and shuffle and con therapists and counselors and parole boards, and you slither out onto the streets of our cities and go back to preying on our kids.

'I'd kill you myself, but it's not my style and I haven't got the guts. Maybe you'll step off the pavement and get hit by a bus. If you do, I'll gladly kick in for the bus driver's defense fund, if they're crazy enough to charge him with anything. They ought to give him a medal – and I'd kick in for that, too, with pleasure.

'Or maybe, for once in your awful life, you'll be a man and do the right thing. You could pick up a cue from Franny and put yourself out of everybody's misery. I don't suppose you've got the guts, either, but maybe you'll summon up the courage, or maybe somebody'll give you a hand. Because no matter what the nuns at St Ignatius taught me, I can't help it: I'd give a lot to see you with a rope around your neck, hanging from a tree limb, twisting slowly, slowly in the wind.'

It was classic McGraw, and very much the sort of thing that kept the tabloids hiring him away from one another at ever higher salaries. His column was, as somebody had said, one of the things that made New York New York.

He'd tried his hand at other tasks over the years, and not without some success. He had published several books of non-fiction over the years, and while none had been a big seller they'd all been respectfully received. A couple of years back he'd hosted a talk program on a local cable channel, giving it up after a six-month run and a series of arguments with the station management. A while before that he'd written a play and actually had it produced on Broadway.

But it was with his column that he made his mark on the city. He had a way of articulating the anger and impatience of his readers, putting better words to it than they would have chosen yet sacrificing nothing in the way of plain-spoken blue-collar fury. I remember reading the column he wrote about Richie Vollmer, and I remember more or less agreeing with it. I didn't much care for frontier justice, but there were times it seemed better than no justice at all. I'd hate to see a lynch mob marching down the street, but if they stopped in front of Richie Vollmer's house I wouldn't have run out there and tried to talk them out of it.

Not that I gave a lot of thought to the column. Like everybody else, I nodded from time to time in agreement, frowned now and then at this oversimplification or that infelicitous turn of phrase, thought to myself that it would not be a bad thing at all if Richie was found dangling from a limb or a lamp post. And, like everybody else, I turned the page.

Almost everybody else.

The column ran on Thursday, with the paper's Bulldog edition on the street late Wednesday night. In addition to eight or ten letters to the editor, two of which were later excerpted in 'The Voice of the People', five letters came in Friday and Saturday addressed to McGraw personally. One, from a Catholic layman in Riverdale, reminded McGraw that suicide was a mortal sin and urging another to commit such an act was sinful as well. The others all expressed agreement with the column, to one degree or another.

McGraw had a stack of printed postcards: 'Dear—, Thanks for taking the time to write. Whether you did or didn't care for what I had to say, I'm grateful to you for writing, and pleased and proud to have you as a reader. I hope you'll keep reading my stuff Tuesday, Thursday, and Sunday in the *Daily News*.' Not everyone who wrote would include a return address – some didn't even sign their names – but those who did got postcards in reply, with their first names written in after 'Dear' and a hand-written comment at the end – 'Thanks!' or 'You said it!' or 'Good point!' He'd sign the cards and mail them off and forget the whole thing.

One of the five letters gave him a moment's pause. 'Your open letter to Richard Vollmer is sharply provocative,' it began. 'What are we to do when the system fails? It is not enough to walk away, congratulating ourselves on our commitment to due process even as we wring our hands at the incident's unfortunate outcome. Our criminal justice system requires a back-up, a fail-safe device to correct those mistakes that are an inevitable outcome of a flawed system.

'When we send a rocket into space, we build it with components designed to back up other components which might fail. We allow for the possibility that some unforeseen factor will nudge it off course, and build in devices to correct any such deviations as occur. If we routinely take such precautions in outer space, can we do less on the streets of our cities?

'I submit that a back-up system for our criminal justice system exists already in the hearts and souls of our citizens, if we have the will to activate it. And I believe we do. You're a manifestation of that collective will, writing the column you write. And I, too, am very much a manifestation of that will, the will of the people.

'Richard Vollmer will be hanging from that tree soon. It is the people's will.'

23

The letter was more literate than most, and it was typed. McGraw's readers were not all clowns and morons, scrawling their approval in crayon on brown paper bags, and he had received typed and well-phrased letters before, but they were invariably signed and almost always bore return addresses. This one was unsigned and there was no return address, not on the letter itself, not on the envelope it had come in, either. He made a point of checking, and the envelope bore his own name and the newspaper's address. Nothing else.

He filed it and forgot about it.

The following weekend, two Dominican kids on mountain bikes came tearing down a steep path in Inwood Hill Park. One of them cried out to his friend, and they both braked to a stop as soon as they got to a spot that was level enough. 'Joo see that?' 'See what?' 'On that tree.' 'What tree?' 'Was a guy hanging from that tree back there.' 'You crazy, man. You seeing things, you crazy.' 'We got to go back.' 'Uphill? So we can see some guy hanging?' 'Come on!'

They went back, and the boy had not been seeing things. A man was indeed hanging from the stout limb of a pin oak ten or fifteen yards off the bike path. They stopped their bikes and took a good look at him, and one of the kids promptly vomited. The hanging man was not a pretty sight. His head was the size of a basketball and his neck was a foot long, stretched by the weight of him. He wasn't twisting slowly in the wind. There wasn't any wind.

It was Richard Vollmer, of course, and he'd been found hanging not far from where both of his victims had been found, and McGraw's first thought was that the misbegotten son of a bitch had actually done what he'd told him to do. He felt a curious sense of unsought power, at once unsettling and exciting.

But Richie had had help. Asphyxiation had caused his death, so he'd been alive when the rope went around his neck, but he'd probably been unconscious. An autopsy disclosed that he'd been beaten severely about the head, and had in fact sustained cranial injuries that might have proven fatal if someone hadn't taken the trouble to string him up.

McGraw didn't know how he felt about that. It certainly appeared as though a column of his had led some impressionable yahoo to commit murder; at the very least, the killer had looked to McGraw for the murder method. That disgusted him, and yet he could hardly bring himself to mourn the death of Richie Vollmer. So he did what he had grown in the habit of doing over the years. He talked out his thoughts and feelings in a column.

'I can't say I'm sorry Richie Vollmer is no longer with us,' he wrote. 'There are, after all, a lot of us left to soldier on, eight million and counting, and I'd be hard put to argue that the quality of life will be a whole lot worse with Richie in the cold cold ground. But I'd hate to think that I, or any reader of this column, had a part in putting him there.

'In a sense, whoever killed Richie Vollmer did us all a favor. Vollmer was a monster. Is there anyone who seriously doubts he'd have killed again? And aren't we all justified now in feeling relieved that he won't?

'And yet his killer did us a disservice at the same time. When we take the law into our own hands, when we snatch up in our own hands the power of life and death, we're no different from Richie. Oh, we're a bunch of kinder, gentler Richie Vollmers. Our victims deserve what they get, and we can tell ourselves we've got God on our side.

'But how different are we?

'For wishing publicly for his death, I owe the world an apology. I'm not apologizing to Richie, I'm not for one moment sorry he's gone. My apology is to all the rest of you.

'It's possible, of course, that the person or persons who took Richie out never read this column, that they did what they did for reasons of their own, that they were old foes of his from his days in prison. That's what I'd like to believe. I'd sleep better.'

McGraw had a visit from the cops, predictably enough. He told them he'd had a batch of letters agreeing and disagreeing with his column, but that no one had specifically offered to see that his wishes were carried out. The cops didn't ask to see the letters. His column ran, and the next day's mail brought a second letter from Will.

'Don't blame yourself,' McGraw read. 'It might be interesting to discuss the extent to which your column prompted my action, but a search for the ultimate cause of any phenomenon is ultimately fruitless. Can we not say with more assurance that Richard Vollmer, by his monstrous actions, caused you to write what you wrote even as it caused me to do what I did? Each of us responded – promptly, directly, properly – to an insupportable state of affairs, i.e. the continuing capacity of a child-murderer to walk free among us.

'Or, to put it another way, each of us embodied for a moment in time the collective will of the people of New York. It is the ability of the public to work its will that is, when all is said and done, the genuine essence of democracy. It is not the right to vote, or the several freedoms provided by the Bill of Rights, so much as it

26

is that we are governed – or govern ourselves – according to our collective will. So don't hold yourself accountable for the timely execution of Richard Vollmer. Blame Vollmer himself, if you wish. Or blame or credit me – but when you do, you are only blaming or crediting

The Will of the People

One of the cops had left his card, and McGraw dug it out and reached for the phone. He had the number half-dialed when he broke the connection and started over.

First he called the City Desk. Then he called the cops.

RICHIE'S KILLER GOES PUBLIC, the next day's headline screamed. The lead story, under McGraw's byline, reproduced Will's letter in full, along with excerpts from the first letter and a report on the progress of the police investigation. Sidebar stories included interviews with psychologists and criminologists. McGraw's column ran on page four, with the title 'An Open Letter to Will'. The gist of it was that Will may have been justified in what he'd done, but all the same he had to turn himself in.

But that didn't happen. Instead Will was silent, while the police investigation proceeded and got nowhere. Then, about a week later, McGraw's mail included another letter from Will.

He'd been expecting more from Will, and had been keeping an eye out for a long envelope with a typed address and no return address, but this time the envelope was small and the address hand-printed in ballpoint, and there was a return address as well. So he went ahead and opened it. He unfolded the single sheet of paper, saw the typeface and the signature in script type, and dropped the letter like a hot rock.

'An Open Letter to Patrizzio Salerno,' it began, and McGraw went on to read a virtual parody of his own open letter to Richie Vollmer. Patsy Salerno was a local mafioso, the head of one of the five families, and the elusive target of a RICO investigation who had survived innumerable attempts to put him behind bars. Will detailed Patsy's various offenses against society. 'Your own cohorts have tried repeatedly to rid us of you,' he wrote, referring to the several attempts on Patsy's life over the years. He went on to suggest that Patsy perform the first public-spirited act of his life by killing himself; failing that, the letter's author would be forced to act.

'In a sense,' he concluded, 'I have no choice in the matter. I am, after all, only

The Public's Will

The story sold a lot of papers. Nobody managed to get an interview with Salerno, but his attorney made good copy, describing his client as an innocent businessman who'd been persecuted by the government for years. He saw this latest outrage as further persecution; either 'Will' had been launched on his crackpot crusade by the lies the government had spread about Patrizzio Salerno, or in fact there was no Will, and this was an elaborate federal effort to uncover or fabricate new evidence against Patsy. He advanced the latter possibility while declining on his client's behalf an NYPD offer of police protection.

'Imagine the cops protecting Patsy,' the *Post* quoted

an anonymous wise guy as saying. 'Make more sense to have Patsy protecting the cops.'

The story got a lot of play locally, in the papers and on TV, but after a few days it began to die down because there was nothing to keep it going. Then on a Sunday Patsy had dinner at a restaurant on Arthur Avenue in the Bronx. I don't remember what he ate, although the tabloids reported the meal course by course. Eventually he went to the men's room, and eventually someone went in after him to find out what was taking him so long.

Patsy was sprawled out on the floor with a couple of feet of piano wire around his neck. His tongue was hanging out of his mouth, double its usual size, and his eyes were bulging.

Of course the media went crazy. The national talk shows had their experts on, discussing the ethics of vigilantism and the particular psychology of Will. Someone recalled the number from *The Mikado*, 'I've Got a Little List,' and it turned out that everybody had a little list of 'society offenders who might well be underground', as the Gilbert & Sullivan song had it. David Letterman was on hand with a Top Ten list for Will's consideration, most of the entries overexposed showbiz personalities. (Rumor had it that there was a good deal of backstage debate about the propriety of putting Jay Leno at the top of the list; in any event, Letterman's late-night rival went unmentioned.)

There were more than a few people who claimed to be Will, and tried to take credit for his acts. The police set up a special phone number for calls relating to the case, and they got the predictable glut of false claimants and confessors. Open letters to various citizens, purportedly by Will, flowed to the *News* offices in a great stream. McGraw got a couple of death threats: 'An Open Letter to Marty McGraw . . . You started this, you son of a bitch, and now it's your turn . . .' A lot of people, in public and private, were moved to guess who Will's next target might be, and offered their recommended candidates.

Everyone was sure of one thing. There would be a third. Nobody stopped at two. One maybe, three maybe. But nobody stopped at two.

Will didn't disappoint, although his next pick may have surprised a lot of people. 'An Open Letter to Roswell Berry', was his heading, and he went on to identify the city's leading anti-abortion activist as an unindicted murderer. 'Your rhetoric has provoked violent action on the part of your followers time and time again,' Will asserted, 'and on at least two occasions death has been the direct result. The bombing at the 137th Street clinic, the assassinations of the nurse and physician on Ralph Avenue, were wanton acts of murder. Both times you have talked out of both sides of your mouth, disassociating yourself from the act but all but applauding it as a means to an end, and a far lesser evil than abortion . . . You champion the unborn, but your interest in a fetus ends at birth. You oppose birth control, oppose sex education, oppose any social program that might lessen the demand for abortion. You are a despicable human being, and seemingly unpunishable. But no one can hold out for long against

The Will of the People

Berry was out of town when the letter landed on Marty McGraw's desk. He was in Omaha, leading a massive protest against an abortion clinic. 'I am doing God's work,' he told the TV cameras. 'It's His will that

I continue, and I'll stack that up against the so-called will of the people any day.' He told another interviewer that whatever business Will had with him would have to wait until he returned to New York, and he expected to be in Omaha for some time to come.

God's will. In AA, we're advised to pray only for knowledge of His will, and the power to carry it out. My sponsor, Jim Faber, has said that it's the easiest thing in the world to know God's will. You just wait and see what happens, and that's it.

It may indeed have been God's work that Roswell Berry was doing, but it evidently wasn't God's will that he continue. He stayed in Omaha, just as he said he would, but when he returned to New York it was in a box.

The maid found him in his room at the Omaha Hilton. His killer, not without a sense of humor, had left him with a coat hanger wrapped around his neck.

It was the Omaha Police Department's case, of course, but they welcomed the two NYPD detectives who flew out to consult with them and exchange information. There was no evidence to link Berry's murder with the killings of Vollmer and Salerno, none aside from Will's having singled him out in his open letter, and this left room for speculation that some native Omahan, spurred perhaps by Will's suggestion, had handled the matter on a local level.

Will's next communication – sent, like all the others, to Marty McGraw – addressed that notion. 'Did I go off to Omaha to settle accounts with Mr Berry? Or did some citizen of Omaha, outraged at having to put up with Roswell Berry's disruption of that fair city's urban equilibrium, take matters into his own hands?

'My friend, what on earth does it matter? What

difference can it possibly make? I myself am nothing, as someone is purported to have said in a slightly different context. It is the will of the people that acts through me. If indeed another pair of hands than mine stuck the knife in Roswell Berry's pitiless heart before girdling his neck with a coat hanger, it is as moot to ponder my own responsibility in the matter as it is to wonder how much your own writing gave rise to my actions. Each of us, alone or in concert, helps to express

The Will of the People

It was cleverly done. Will wouldn't say whether he'd gone to Omaha, arguing that it didn't matter one way or another. At the same time, he pretty much settled the matter by alluding to the fact that Berry had been stabbed. The Omaha authorities had suppressed this. (They would have liked to suppress the coat hanger as well, but it leaked, and the symbolism was just too good to expect the press to keep it under wraps. It was easier to hold back the knife work, because it hadn't shown up until they had Roswell Berry on the autopsy table. He'd been killed with a single stab wound to the heart, inflicted with one stroke of a narrow-bladed knife or dagger. Death was virtually instantaneous and there was no bleeding to speak of, which is why the stabbing wasn't noticed at first, and why it managed to stay out of the papers.)

Roswell Berry had looked like a difficult target. He'd been more than halfway across the country, staying in a hotel with a good security setup, and escorted at all times by a cadre of loyal bodyguards, broad-shouldered young men in chinos and short-sleeved white shirts, with buzz haircuts and unsmiling faces. ('Thugs for Jesus,' one commentator had styled them.) There was plenty of speculation as to how Will had managed to slip through their ranks and get in and out of their leader's hotel room.

WILL O' THE WISP? the *Post* wondered on its front page.

But if Berry was a hard target, Will's next pick was clearly impossible.

'An Open Letter to Julian Rashid' was the heading on his next letter to McGraw, mailed some ten days after his ambiguous response to Berry's death. In it, he charged the black supremacist with fomenting racial hatred for purposes of self-aggrandizement. 'You have created a fiefdom of a people's discontent,' he wrote. 'Your power feeds upon the hatred and bitterness you create. You have called out for violence, and the society you vilify is at last prepared to turn that violence upon you.'

Rashid first landed in the spotlight as a tenured professor of economics at Queens College. His name back then was Wilbur Julian, but he dropped the Wilbur and tacked on the Rashid around the time he began formulating his theories. The name change was not part of a conversion to Islam, but merely represented his admiration for the legendary Haroun-al-Rashid.

His theories, which he expounded in the classroom in spite of the fact that they had little demonstrable connection to economics, contended that the black race was the original human race, that blacks had founded the lost civilizations of Atlantis and Lemuria, that it was this race of black men who were the elders revered in the prehistory of societies throughout the world. They were the builders of Stonehenge, of the heads on Easter Island.

Then white men had arisen as some sort of genetic

33

sport, a mutation of the pure black race. Just as their skins lacked melanin, so were their spirits lacking in true humanity. Their bodies were similarly stunted; they could not run as fast or as far, could not jump as high, and lacked that primal connection to the very pulse of the earth, which is to say that they didn't have rhythm. Perversely, however, they were able to prevail because of their inhuman nature, which led them to overwhelm and betray and subvert the black man whenever the two races met. In particular, it was a late offshoot of the white sub-race whose special role it was to serve as architects of the white subjugation of the black race. These mongrel dogs at the heart of it all were, surprisingly enough, the Jews.

'If it turns out there's life on Saturn,' Elaine said, 'and we go there, we'll find out that they've got three sets of eyes, and five sexes, and something against the Jews.'

Whenever he was given the opportunity, according to Rashid, the black man showed his natural superiority – in track and field, in baseball and football and basketball, and even in what he labeled 'Jewish' sports – golf and tennis and bowling. (There were few great black equestrians, he explained, because that too involved subjugation and domination, of the horse by the rider.) Chess, for which he apparently had a passion, provided further proof of black superiority; a game of the intellect, it was studied out of books by the Jews and their followers, while black children took to it naturally and played it well without having to study it.

It was now the black man's burden – his phrase – to separate himself entirely from white society, and to establish his innate supremacy in every area of human endeavor, exerting dominion over and, yes, enslaving whites if need be, in order to usher in the new

34

millennium with the black-run human civilization that was essential if the planet itself was to survive.

Predictably enough, there was a strong move to oust him from his sinecure at Queens College. (Ray Gruliow represented him in his successful battle to hang on to his academic tenure, and insisted that he liked Rashid personally. 'I don't know how much of that horseshit he believes,' he once told me. 'It hasn't kept him from hiring a Jewish lawyer.') He won in court, then resigned dramatically and announced he was starting his own academic institution. His supporters had managed to get title to a full square block in the St Albans section of Queens, and there they constructed a walled compound to house the new black university and the greater portion of its students and faculty.

Julian Rashid lived there, with his two wives and several children. (Although the inevitable rumors had circulated of a passion for white women, both wives were dark-skinned, with African features. They looked enough alike, in fact, to give rise to another rumor to the effect that they were sisters, or even twins.) A guard was posted around the clock outside of Rashid's living quarters, and a phalanx of armed men in khaki uniforms accompanied him whenever he left the compound, which in turn was fortified and guarded twenty-four hours a day.

At a press conference shortly after the news broke of Will's latest open letter, Rashid announced that he welcomed the challenge. 'Let him come. It is true that he embodies the will of his people. They have always hated us, and now that they can no longer dominate us they wish to annihilate us. So let him come to me, and let the will of the white race break itself upon the rock of black will. We shall see whose will is stronger.'

Nothing happened for a week. Then the police were

summoned to the St Albans compound where they had never previously dared attempt entry. A group of his followers, some of them members of the uniformed bodyguard, others weeping youths and children, led the way to Rashid's private quarters and into his bedroom. Rashid was in his bed, or rather his body was. His head had been placed upon a small devotional altar he had built at the far end of the room, and stared out from among a group of wooden carvings and strings of trading beads. He had been beheaded, a medical examination determined, with a single stroke of a ceremonial axe, itself a highly-prized artifact of the Senufo tribe of Ivory Coast.

How could Will have managed it? How could he penetrate the compound's airtight security, slipping in and out like a ghost? Theories abounded. Will was black himself, one contingent maintained, and a comparative linguistics graduate student at Columbia was quick to buttress that argument with an analysis of Will's letters, purportedly proving an African origin for their author. Someone else suggested that Will had disguised himself as a black man, darkening his face like a player in a minstrel show. The political rectitude of each position was held up to scrutiny. Was it racist to assume the killer was white? Was it more racist to assume he was black? The Senufo axe was not the only one around; everybody, it seemed, had an axe of his own to grind.

The debate was just warming up when the police announced the arrest of Marlon Scipio, a trusted associate of Rashid's and a member of his inner circle. Scipio (né Marlon Simmons; Rashid had suggested the change with a nod to Scipio Africanus) had broken down under police interrogation and admitted he'd seized the opportunity of Will's open letter to right a longstanding injury. Apparently Rashid's libido had not been slaked by his two official wives, sisters or twins or whatever they were, and he'd had a fling with Scipio's wife. Scipio only had one wife, and he'd taken this the wrong way. When his chance came around, he took the Senufo axe down from the wall and made Rashid a head shorter.

Will was so pleased you'd have thought he did it himself. His next letter, posted hours after Scipio's arrest and confession became public knowledge, restated the theme of his letter upon the death of Roswell Berry. The people's will had found expression. What did it matter who swung the axe?

And there he'd let it lie for the ten days or so since. There were other voices – letters and phone calls purporting to be from Will, but clearly not, a couple of anonymous bomb threats, one of which cleared a midtown office building. McGraw got a handwritten letter, 'An Open Letter to the So-Called Marty McGraw', whose semiliterate author blamed him for Will's reign of terror. 'You'll pay for this in your own blood, asshole,' the letter concluded, and it was signed with a large red X that covered half the page. (A lab analysis quickly established that the X was not in fact blood, but red Magic Marker.)

It took the cops just two days to pick up Mr X, who turned out to be an unemployed construction worker who'd written the letter on a dare and then boasted about it in a saloon. 'He thinks he's hot shit,' he said of McGraw, but outside of that he didn't really have anything against him, and certainly planned him no harm. The poor son of a bitch was charged with menacing and coercion in the first degree, the latter a

Class D felony. They'd probably let him plead to a misdemeanor and my guess was he'd get off with probation, but in the meantime he was out on bail and not feeling terribly proud of himself.

And the city went on speculating about Will. There was a new joke about him every day. (Publicist to client: 'I've got good news and bad news for you. The good news is you're the subject of a column in tomorrow's *Daily News*. The bad news is Marty McGraw's writing it.') He kept winding up in your conversation, as had happened at least once that very evening, when TJ assured me that computers would ultimately reveal Will's true identity. There was, of course, no end of guesswork about the sort of person he was and the sort of life he was likely to be leading. There was guesswork, too, as to who would next draw his attention. One shock jock had invited his listeners to submit names for Will's consideration. 'We'll see who gets the most votes,' he told his unseen drive-time audience, 'and I'll announce your top choices over the air. I mean, who knows? Maybe he's a listener. Maybe he's a big fan.'

'If he's listening,' purred the fellow's female sidekick, 'you better *hope* he's a fan.'

That was on a Friday. When he returned to the air on Monday morning he'd had a change of heart. 'We got lots of letters,' he said, 'but you know what? I'm not announcing the results. In fact I'm not even tabulating them. I decided the whole thing's sick, not just the poll but the whole Will fever that's gripping the city. Talk about everybody's baser instincts. You wouldn't believe some of the jokes that are going around, they are truly sick and disgusting.' And, to prove the point, he told four of them, one right after the other.

The police, of course, were under enormous pressure to find the guy and close the case. But the sense of urgency was very different from that surrounding Son of Sam, or any of the other serial killers who had cropped up over the years. You weren't afraid to walk the streets, not for fear of Will stalking you and gunning you down. The average person had nothing to fear, because Will didn't target average people. On the contrary, he took aim only at the prominent, and more specifically at the notorious. Look at his list of victims — Richie Vollmer, Patsy Salerno, Roswell Berry, and, if indirectly, Julian Rashid. Wherever you stood in the social and political spectrum, your response to each of Will's executions was apt to be that it couldn't have happened to a nicer guy.

And now he'd set his sights on Adrian Whitfield.

THREE

'I'll tell you,' he said. 'I just don't know what to make of it. One minute I'm laughing over the latest Will joke. Next thing you know I find out that *I'm* the latest Will joke, and you want to know something? All of a sudden it's not so funny.'

We were in his apartment on the twenty-first floor of a pre-war apartment building in Park Avenue and 84th Street. He was a tall man, around six-two, lean and firm, with patrician good looks. His dark hair had gone mostly gray, and that just enhanced the commanding presence that stood him in good stead in a courtroom. He was still wearing a suit but he'd taken off his tie and opened his collar.

He was at the serving bar now, using tongs to fill a tall glass with ice cubes. He added club soda and set it down, then dropped a couple of ice cubes in a shorter glass and filled it with a single-malt Scotch. I got a whiff of it as he was pouring it, strong and smoky, like wet tweed drying alongside an open wood fire.

He gave me the tall glass and kept the short one for himself. 'You don't drink,' he said. 'Neither do I.' My face must have shown something. 'Ha!' he said, and looked at the glass in his hand. 'What I mean to say,' he said, 'is that I don't drink like I used to. I drank a lot more when I was living in Connecticut, but I think that's because everybody in that crowd used to hit it pretty good. One small Scotch before dinner is generally as much as I have these days. Tonight's an exception.'

'I can see why it would be.'

'When I left the office,' he said, 'after I got rid of those cops, I stopped at the bar down the block and had a quick one before I went and hailed a cab. I can't remember the last time I did that. I never even tasted it. I threw it down and walked right on out again. And I had another when I walked in the door, I went over and poured it without thinking about it.' He looked at the glass he was holding. 'And then I called you,' he said.

'And here I am.'

'And here you are, and this will be my last drink of the night, and I'm not even sure I'll finish it. "An Open Letter to Adrian Whitfield." You want to know the most distressing thing about it?'

'The company you're in.'

'That's it exactly. Now how the hell did you know I was going to say that? That's the clarity of club soda talking.'

'It must be.'

'Vollmer and Salerno and Berry and Rashid. A child-killer, a mobster, an abortion-clinic bomber and a black racist. I graduated from Williams College and Harvard Law School. I'm a member of the bar and an officer of the court. Will you please tell me how I can possibly belong on the same list with those four pariahs?'

'The thing is,' I said, 'Will gets to decide who's on his list. He doesn't have to be logical about it.'

'You're right,' he said. He went over to a chair and sank into it, held his glass to the light, then set it down untasted. 'You said something earlier about leaving the country. You were exaggerating to make a point, right? Or were you serious?'

'I was serious.'

'That's what I was afraid of.'

41

'If I were you,' I said, 'I'd get the hell out of the country, and I wouldn't wait, either. You have a passport, don't you? Where do you keep it?'

'In my sock drawer.'

'Put it in your pocket,' I said, 'and pack a change of clothes and whatever else will fit into a bag you can carry onto the plane. Take whatever cash you've got around the house, but don't worry if that's not very much. You're not a fugitive, so you'll be able to cash checks and use credit cards wherever you wind up. You can even get cash. They've got ATMs all over the world.'

'Where am I going?'

'That's up to you, and don't tell me. Some European capital would be my suggestion. Go to a first-class hotel and tell the manager you want to register under another name.'

'And then what? Lock myself in my room?'

'I don't think you'd have to do that. He followed Roswell Berry to Omaha, but he didn't have to do any detective work. Berry was right there on the evening news every night, throwing cow's blood on doctors and nurses. And you don't need a passport to go to Nebraska, either. My guess is if you leave the country and don't make it too obvious where you've gone, he'll find it a lot simpler to dash off an open letter to somebody else than to knock himself out tracing you down. And he can always tell himself he won the game by scaring you out of the country.'

'And he'd be quite right about that, wouldn't he?'

'But you'll be alive.'

'And a little tarnished around the image, wouldn't you say? The fearless defense attorney who skipped the country, rousted by an anonymous letter. I've had death threats before, you know.'

'I'm sure you have.'

'The Ellsworth case brought a whole slew of them. "You son of a bitch, if he walks you're dead." Well, Jeremy didn't walk, so we'll never know.'

'What did you do with the letters?'

'What I've always done with them. Turned 'em over to the police. Not that I expected a lot of sympathy from that quarter. There weren't a lot of cops pulling for me to get Jeremy Ellsworth acquitted. Still, that wouldn't keep them from doing their jobs. They investigated, but I doubt they pushed it too hard.'

'They'd have dug a lot deeper,' I said, 'if you'd gotten killed.'

He gave me a look. 'I'm not leaving town,' he said. 'That's out of the question.'

'It's your call.'

'Matt, death threats are a dime a dozen. Every criminal lawyer in this town's got a desk drawer full of them. Look at Ray Gruliow, for God's sake. How many death threats do you suppose he's received over the years?'

'Quite a few.'

'He got a shotgun blast through his front windows on Commerce Street one time, if I remember correctly. He said the shooters were cops.'

'He couldn't know that for sure,' I said, 'but it was a logical guess. What's your point?'

'That I've got a life to live and I can't let something like this make me run like a rabbit. You've had death threats yourself, haven't you? I'll bet you have.'

'Not that many,' I said. 'But then I haven't had my name in the papers all that much.'

'But you've had some.'

'Yes.'

'Did you pack a bag and hop a plane?'

43

I took a sip of club soda, remembering. 'A couple of years ago,' I said, 'a man I'd sent to prison got out determined to kill me. He was going to start out by killing the women in my life. There weren't any women in my life, not at the time, but his definition turned out to be broader than mine.'

'What did you do?'

'I called an ex-girlfriend,' I said, 'and I told her to pack a bag and leave the country. And she packed a bag and left the country.'

'And lived to tell the tale. But what did you do?'

'Me?'

'You. My guess is you stayed around.'

'And went after him,' I said. 'But that was different. I knew who he was. I had a fair shot at getting him before he got me.' I frowned at the memory. 'Even so, I came awfully close to getting myself killed. Elaine came even closer. She got stabbed, she had her spleen removed. She almost died.'

'Didn't you say she left the country?'

'That was another woman, a former girlfriend. Elaine's my wife.'

'I thought you didn't have any women in your life at the time.'

'We weren't married then. We'd known each other years previously. Motley brought us together again.'

'Motley was the guy who wanted to kill you.'

'Right.'

'And after she recovered – Elaine?'

'Elaine.'

'After she recovered you resumed seeing each other, and now you're married. A good marriage?'

'A very good marriage.'

'My God,' he said. 'Maybe if I stick around and see this thing through I'll wind up back in Connecticut

44

with Barbara. But it's hard to imagine her without her spleen. It's the key element of her character.' He took a drink. 'In the meantime, my friend, I've got a law practice to run and a case to try. Tempting as it may be to fly off for a couple of weeks in Oslo or Brussels, I think I'll stick around and face the music. But that doesn't mean I want to get killed, nor do I think it makes much sense to leave the task of protecting me to the NYPD. I'm safe here –'

'Here?'

'In this apartment. The building has good security.'

'I don't think Will would have much trouble getting in here.'

'Didn't the guy on the desk make you show ID? I told him to.'

'I flashed a card at him,' I said. 'I didn't give him time to look at it, and he didn't insist.'

'I'll have to speak to him about that.'

'Don't bother. You can't expect very much from the building personnel. The elevator's self-service. All anybody has to do is take out the doorman and he's in.'

'Take him out? You mean kill him?'

'Or just slip past him, which wouldn't be on the same level with getting into Fort Knox. If you want a good shot at getting through this alive, and if you won't leave town, you need bodyguards around the clock. That means three shifts a day, and I'd recommend you employ two men per shift.'

'Would you be one of those men?'

I shook my head. 'I don't like the work and I don't have the reflexes for it.'

'Can you supply bodyguards?'

'Not directly. I'm a one-man operation. There are people I can call for back-up, but not as many as you'd need. What I can do is recommend a couple of agencies who can be counted on to furnish reliable operatives.'

I took out my notebook, wrote down the names of two firms, along with a phone number for each and a person to ask for. I tore out the page and handed it to Whitfield. He read it, folded it, and tucked it in his breast pocket.

'No point in calling now,' he said. 'I'll call first thing in the morning. If Will lets me live that long.'

'You've probably got a few days. He'll wait until the story runs, and until you've had time to worry about it.'

'He's a real prick, isn't he?'

'Well, I don't suppose he's on the short list for the Jean Hersholt Humanitarian Award.'

'Not this year, but then he's got a lot of competition. Ah, Jesus, you think your life's in order and then something like this comes at you from out of nowhere. Do you worry a lot?'

'Do I worry a lot? I don't know. I don't think so.'

'It seems to me that I do. I worry about a stroke or a heart attack, I worry about prostate cancer. Sometimes I worry about having some bad gene that'll have me coming down with one of those rare diseases. I can't think of the word I want and I start to worry about early-onset Alzheimer's. You know something? It's a big fucking waste of time.'

'Worrying?'

'You said it. You never worry about the right thing. I never worried about this son of a bitch, I'll tell you that, and now he's got me on his list. Tell me what else I can do. Besides hiring guards. You must have a few ideas on the kind of routine I should follow, the precautions I ought to take.'

By the time I was done suggesting ways he could

increase the odds of his staying alive, he'd made a pot of coffee and we were each working on our second cup. He talked about a current case of his, and I talked about a piece of work I'd wrapped up a month previously.

'I want you to know I appreciate all this,' he said. 'I'd tell you to send me a bill, but a man on Will's list ought to keep his accounts current. What do I owe you? I'll write you a check.'

'There's no charge.'

'Don't be silly,' he said. 'I dragged you out of your house in the middle of the night and got two solid hours' worth of your professional expertise. Go ahead and put a price on it.'

'I have a vested interest in your survival,' I told him. 'If you stay alive, there's a chance you'll throw some work my way.'

'I'd say you can count on it, but you still ought to get paid for tonight.' He patted the pocket where he'd put the slip I gave him. 'Will you get a referral fee from these guys?'

'It depends which one you call.'

'Only one of them'll pay you for a referral?'

'I do a certain amount of per diem work for Reliable,' I said, 'and Wally Donn pays me a commission on anything else I happen to steer their way.'

'Then why'd you put down the other agency as well?'

'Because they're good.'

'Well, I'll use Reliable,' he said. 'That goes without saying. And I'd still like to pay you for your time tonight.'

'There's no need.'

'In that case, I've got a better idea. I'd like to hire you.'

'To do what?'

'To go after Will.'

I told him all the reasons why it didn't make sense. Half the police force was already assigned to the case, and the cops had access to the available data and evidence along with the scientific apparatus to learn something from it. On top of that, they had the manpower to knock on every door and run down every lead and phone tip that came their way. All I could do was get in their way.

'I know all that,' he said.

'So?'

'So I still want to hire you.'

'Why? As a way of paying me for this evening?'

He shook his head. 'I want you on the case.'

'What for?'

'Because I think there's a chance you'll make a difference. The first time I hired you, you know, was on Ray Gruliow's recommendation.'

'Yes, I know.'

'He said you have a good mind and caught on fast. "Give him the first sentence and he's got the whole page," that's what he said.'

'He was being generous,' I said. 'Sometimes I move my lips.'

'I don't think so. He also said good things about your character and personal integrity. And he said something else, too. He said you were dogged.'

'It's a nicer word than pigheaded.'

He rolled his eyes. 'You're a hard man to compliment, aren't you? Matt, offense is the best defense. That's true in the courtroom and it's true on the street. I don't know what the hell you can do that the cops can't, but the one thing I don't have to worry about these days is money, and if I can throw a little of it your way I can tell myself I'm doing something to see that

Will gets nailed before he nails me. Now why don't you just say you'll take the case so I can write you out a check?'

'I'll take the case.'

'See? You're stubborn, which may be part of the job description for what you do. But I'm persuasive, which is very definitely part of my job description.' He went over to the desk, got out his checkbook and wrote me a check, tore it out and handed it to me.

'A retainer,' he said. 'Good enough?'

The amount was $2000. 'That's fine,' I said.

'You have anything else you're working?'

'Not at the moment,' I said. 'I don't know what I'm going to do, but I'll start doing it in the morning.'

'And I'll call Donn at Reliable and see about getting my body guarded. What a thing to have to do. Can I tell you something? Don't repeat this, but until this afternoon I sort of liked Will.'

'You did?'

'Let's say I had a grudging admiration for him. He was a kind of urban folk hero, wasn't he? Almost like Batman.'

'Batman never killed anybody.'

'Not in the comic books. He does in the movies, but Hollywood'll fuck up anything, won't they? No, the real Batman never killed anybody. Listen to me, will you? "The real Batman". But when you grew up on the comic book that's how it seems.'

'I know.'

'For Christ's sake,' he said, 'I'm Adrian Whitfield, I'm a fucking lawyer. That's all I am. I'm not the Joker, I'm not the Penguin, I'm not the Riddler. What's Batman got against me?'

FOUR

Elaine was still up when I got home, watching a wildlife documentary on the Discovery channel. I joined her for the last ten minutes of it. During the credit crawl she made a face and switched off the set.

'I should have done that when you came in,' she said.

'Why? I didn't mind watching.'

'What I have to learn,' she said, 'is always to skip the last five minutes of those things, because it's always the same. You spend fifty-five minutes watching some really nice animal, and then they ruin the whole thing by telling you it's endangered and won't last out the century. They're so determined to leave you depressed you'd think they had Prozac for a sponsor. How was Adrian Whitfield?'

I gave her a summary of the evening. 'Well, he's not depressed,' she said. 'Bemused, it sounds like. "Why me?"'

'Natural question.'

'Yeah, I'd say. How much did you say the retainer was? Two thousand dollars? I'm surprised you took it.'

'Cop training, I guess.'

'When somebody hands you money, you take it.'

'Something like that. He wanted to pay me for my time, and when I turned him down he decided he wanted to hire me. We can use the money.'

'And you can use the work.'

'I can, and maybe I'll be able to figure out something to do. I just hope it won't involve buying a computer.'

'Huh?'

'TJ. He was on my case earlier. When did he leave?'

'Half an hour after you did. I offered him the couch, but he didn't want to stay over.'

'He never does.'

'"What you think, I's got no place to sleep?" I wonder where he does sleep.'

'It's a mystery.'

'He must live somewhere.'

'Not everybody does.'

'I don't think he's homeless, do you? He changes his clothes regularly and he's clean about his person. I'm sure he doesn't bed down in the park.'

'There are a lot of ways to be homeless,' I said, 'and they don't all involve sleeping on the subway and eating out of Dumpsters. I know a woman who drank her way out of a rent-controlled apartment. She moved her things to a storage locker in Chelsea. She pays something like eighty dollars a month for a cubicle eight feet square. That's where she keeps her stuff, and that's where she sleeps.'

'They let you sleep there?'

'No, but how are they going to stop you? She goes there during the day and catches four or five hours at a time that way.'

'That must be awful.'

'It's safer than a shelter, and a lot more private. Probably cleaner and quieter, too. She changes her clothes there, and there's a coin laundry in the neighborhood when she needs to do a load of wash.'

'How does she wash herself? Don't tell me she's got a shower in there.'

'She cleans up as well as she can in public rest rooms, and she's got friends who'll occasionally let her shower at their place. It's hit or miss. A shower isn't necessarily a daily occurrence in her life.'

'Poor thing.'

'If she stays sober,' I said, 'she'll have a decent place to live sooner or later.'

'With a shower of her own.'

'Probably. But you get a lot of different lifestyles in this town. There's a fellow I know who got divorced six or seven years ago, and he still hasn't got his own place.'

'Where does he sleep?'

'On a couch in his office. That'd be a cinch if he was self-employed, but he's not. He's some kind of mid-level executive at a firm with offices in the Flatiron Building. I guess he's important enough to have a couch in his office.'

'And when somebody catches him sleeping on it —'

'He yawns and tells them how he stretched out for a minute and must have dozed off. Or he was working late and missed the last train to Connecticut. Who knows? He belongs to a fancy gym two blocks from there, and that's where he has his shower every morning, right after his Nautilus circuit.'

'Why doesn't he just get an apartment?'

'He says he can't afford it,' I said, 'but I think he's just being neurotic about it. And I think he probably likes the idea that he's getting over on everybody. He probably sees himself as an urban revolutionary, sleeping in the belly of the beast.'

'On a leather sofa from Henredon.'

'I don't know if it's leather or who made it, but that's the idea. In the rest of the country people with no place to live sleep in their cars. New Yorkers don't have cars, and a parking space here costs as much as an apartment in Sioux City. But we're resourceful. We find a way.'

In the morning I deposited Adrian Whitfield's check and tried to think of something I could do to earn it. I spent a couple of hours reviewing press coverage of the case, then spoke to Wally Donn and checked the security arrangements they'd made. Whitfield had called first thing in the morning, but not before Wally'd seen a paper, so he'd known right away what the call was about.

'Let me get your thinking on this,' he said, 'since you know the guy and steered him over here, which incidentally I appreciate. We're basically looking at him in three places, the courtroom and his home and his office. In court it's a crowded public place, plus you have to go through a metal detector to get in.'

'Which doesn't mean somebody couldn't wheel in a howitzer.'

'I know, and this is a guy who walks through walls, right? Has he used a gun yet? He mostly goes for the throat. He strung up Vollmer and garotted Patsy S. and what was it the right-to-lifer got, a coat hanger around the neck?'

'First he'd been stabbed.'

'And what's-his-name got his head chopped off, the black guy. Except that doesn't count on account of his own man did it. Skippy, whatever his name was.'

'Scipio.'

'Anyway, no guns. The point is he's not afraid to work close, and he always manages to get the vic in private. Which means Whitfield's gonna have men around him all the time but he's especially not walking in anywhere by himself. Like the john in the Criminal Courts Building, for example. That's where he got Patsy, isn't it? In a toilet?'

'That's right.'

'His MO's all over the place,' he said, 'which is a

pain in the neck. You're right about the abortion guy, he got stabbed first, and Vollmer pretty much got his head beat in, if I remember correctly. So the point is he's not married to a single way of doing it, which means you can't rule out a rifle shot from across the street.'

'That's hard to guard against.'

'It's close to impossible,' he agreed, 'but there's still precautions you can take. I got him wearing a Kevlar vest, which won't stop everything but it's still a lot more protection than he was getting from his Fruit of the Looms. For transportation he's getting an armor-plated limo with impact-resistant glass all around. He's got two men with him at all times, plus the driver who never leaves the vehicle.'

He went on to run it all down for me. I couldn't think of a way to improve it.

'He's never the first to walk through a door,' he said. 'Makes no difference if it's a room that got checked ten minutes ago. Before he walks in, somebody checks it again.'

'Good.'

'This fucker's spooky, Matt. "The People's Will." Thinks he's Babe Fucking Ruth, calling his shots and then hitting the ball out. And he's batting a thousand, too, the son of a bitch. This time we're gonna strike him out.'

'Let's hope so.'

'Yeah, let's. Personal protection work's supposed to be boring. If you do it right, nothing ever happens. But it generally doesn't come with front-page headlines attached to it. "WILL TAKES AIM AT LEGAL WHIZ." And everywhere you go with the guy, there's reporters and film crews, jokers sticking a mike in his face, other jokers pointing a video cam at him.'

'Now you know what the Secret Service goes through.'

'I do,' he said, 'and they're welcome to it. I never cared for Washington anyway. The streets go every which way, and the fucking summers there are enough to kill you.'

I found things to do over the next several days. I saw Joe Durkin at Midtown North, and he made a couple of phone calls and confirmed that the open letter to Adrian Whitfield had been written by the same person (or at least laid out in the same fashion and printed in the same typeface) as Will's earlier correspondence. I'd assumed as much, just on the basis of literary style, but it was something I'd wanted to confirm.

Even so, I spent a little time looking for someone with a personal reason to want Whitfield dead. He'd been divorced twice, and was presently married to but legally separated from his third wife, who continued to live in Connecticut. Each of the marriages had produced children, and I remembered that one son (the eldest, it turned out) had been arrested two years previously for selling a few hundred dollars' worth of Ecstasy to an undercover police officer. Charges had been dropped, evidently in return for his rolling over and giving up his supplier. That looked promising, but it didn't seem to lead anywhere.

I liked the idea of someone with a private grudge. It wouldn't be the first time someone had concealed a personal motive behind the smokescreen of serial murder. Sometimes an opportunist would disguise his own solitary act of homicide to look as though it was part of somebody else's string – I'd had a case like that once, the killer used an icepick and so did the imitator. And I'd known of cases where the killer committed several purposeless murders at random to establish a pattern of serial murder, then struck down someone he had reason to kill as part of that same pattern. It was a way to divert suspicion from oneself when one would otherwise be the first and most obvious suspect. But it didn't work, because routine police work sooner or later led someone to take a look at everybody with an individual motive, and once they started looking they always found something.

If this was a smokescreen, Will was certainly blowing a lot of smoke. Writing letters to newspapers and knocking off a batch of public figures was a long way from strangling a string of housewives so that you could wring your own wife's neck without being obvious about it.

But maybe he just plain got into it. That happens. The man who did the housewives killed four of them before he left his own wife with her pantyhose knotted around her neck. And he went on to do three more before they caught him. I can't believe he went on that long just to make it look good. My guess is he was enjoying himself.

The good weather held into the weekend. Sunday it was supposed to rain, but it didn't, and by late that afternoon it was hot and hazy. Monday was worse, with a high of 92 and the air like wet wool. Tuesday was more of the same, and that afternoon I got a phone call that diverted my attention from Will for the time being.

The caller was a woman I knew named Ginnie. She said, 'God, I'm so upset. You've heard about Byron?'

'I know he's ill.'

'He's dead.'

I knew Ginnie from AA. She lived at 53rd and Ninth

and came to meetings at St Paul's. Byron was a friend of hers, and I'd met him a few times at meetings, but he lived in the Village and mostly attended meetings down there. He came into the program because he couldn't stop drinking, but some years before that he'd been a heroin addict, and he'd shared needles, and shortly after he got sober he had the antibody test and turned out to be HIV-positive. You'd think people would react to such news by saying the hell with it and going out and getting drunk, and I suppose some of them do, but a lot don't.

Byron didn't. He stayed sober and went to meetings, and he took the drugs his doctor gave him, along with a nutritional regimen designed to strengthen his immune system. This may have done him some good, but it didn't keep him from coming down with AIDS.

'I'm sorry to hear that,' I said. 'The last time I saw him would have been in March or April. I ran into him at a meeting in the Village. I think it was Perry Street.'

'That's where he mostly went.'

'I remember noticing that he didn't look well.'

'Matt, AIDS would have killed him but it didn't get the chance. Somebody shot him.'

'Somebody —'

'Pointed a gun at him and pulled the trigger. Now why in God's name would anybody do a thing like that?'

Gently I said, 'Ginnie, he'd be the one with the best reason.'

'What?'

'Maybe he did it himself.'

'Oh, Christ,' she said, impatient with me. 'He was in a public place, Matt. You know that little park across the street from his building?'

'I don't know where he lived.'

'Horatio Street. Not the Van Gogh but the pre-war apartment building next door to it. There's a little park across the street. Abingdon Square? No, that's the other one.'

'Jackson Square.'

'I guess so. He was sitting there this morning with a cup of coffee and the morning paper. And a man walked up to him and shot him dead.'

'Did they catch the shooter?'

'He got away.'

'But there were witnesses.'

'There were people in the park. It was early, so it was still comfortable. It's an oven out there now.'

'I know.'

'Thank God for air conditioning. Byron should have stayed in his own air-conditioned apartment, but he liked the sun. He said he'd spent his whole life staying out of it, but now he seemed to get energy from it. Solar energy. He said one good thing about being HIV-positive is you didn't have to worry about skin cancer. You didn't know him well, did you, Matt?'

'Hardly at all.'

'You know how he got the virus.'

'Sharing needles, as I understand it.'

'That's right. He wasn't gay.'

'I gathered as much.'

'Living in the Village and having AIDS, it'd be natural to assume that he was. But he was straight. Very much so.'

'Oh?'

'I was sort of in love with him.'

'I see.'

'What do you do when you fall in love with somebody and he's HIV-positive?' She didn't wait for an answer, which was just as well, because I didn't have

58

one. 'Gay men have to face that all the time, don't they? I guess they practice safe sex, or else they just don't date across HIV lines. If they're virus-free they don't let themselves get involved with anybody who's not.' She was silent for a moment. 'Or they just go ahead and take chances.'

'Is that what you did?'

'Oh, no. Me? What makes you say that?'

'Something in your voice.'

'It's probably envy. Sometimes I wish I were the kind of person who can act on that kind of impulse. I never was, not even in the bad old days. I liked Byron a lot and I had this kind of yearning for him, but his status put each of us off-limits for the other. We had one conversation about it, how if things were different we'd do something about it. But things weren't different, things were the way they were. So we stayed friends. Just friends, as the saying goes, but what's the word "just" doing in there? Friendship's pretty rare, don't you think?'

'Yes.'

'I learned so much from him. He treasured each day. Do you think they'll get the man who killed him?'

'It sounds likely,' I said. 'He was killed in a public place with witnesses around. And that's the Sixth Precinct, it's not a high-crime area so it won't get written off as drug-related. The odds are they'll have somebody in custody by the end of the week.'

'They might think it's drug-related.'

'Why?'

'He used to be a junkie. It'll be on his record, won't it?'

'If he was ever arrested.'

'A couple of times. He never had to go to prison, but he told me he'd been arrested a few times.'

'Then it'd be on his record, yes.'

'And there's drug-dealing that goes on in that park. It's not swarming with dealers like Washington Square, but Byron told me how he would sit in the window and look out at the street and watch people cop.'

After a moment I said, 'He didn't go back to using dope, did he, Ginnie?'

'No.'

'Then they won't think the killing was drug-related, unless they figure it for a case of mistaken identity, and maybe that's what it was. It doesn't matter. Either way they'll handle it by the book and run down whatever leads they've got. My guess is they'll find the shooter and close the case.'

'I hope so. Matt? Why should it matter to me? It's not going to bring him back.'

'No.'

'And it's not like I've got this thirst for revenge. I don't hate the man who killed Byron. For all I know he did him a favor. He was at peace, Matt. He treasured each day, but I already said that, didn't I?'

'Yes.'

'He was still able to get out of the house. He could still go to meetings. He had to use a cane, but he would walk the few blocks to Perry Street, and there was always somebody who would give him a seat. That was the other good thing about AIDS, he said. No worries about skin cancer, and you didn't have to get to Perry Street an hour early to get a good seat. He could joke about it, all of it. I guess it's bad when you can't.'

'I guess so.'

'There was a friend of mine at work. When he couldn't come to work anymore I used to visit him. Until I couldn't take it anymore. It destroyed his mind, but not all at once. He would go in and out of dementia. I couldn't bear to be around him. It's not as though I was deserting him, he had a lover who was taking care of him, and dozens of friends. I just knew him casually, from the office. Listen to me, will you? Always having to explain myself.' She stopped to draw a breath. 'I found myself looking for signs of dementia with Byron. But he was spared that.'

I read the coverage in the newspapers, and I was watching New York One, the local news channel, when Melissa Mikawa did a stand-up in Jackson Square in front of the very bench where Byron Leopold was shot to death. The cameraman provided a shot of his apartment building directly across the street, and Mikawa pointed as the camera panned to indicate the killer's escape route.

Then she went on to something else, and so did I. I could hardly claim close ties with Byron, I hadn't even known his last name, and the apprehension of his murderer was the responsibility of the fellows at the Sixth Precinct. They could handle it just fine without any help from me.

Except they didn't, not right away, and I found myself being drawn in for no good reason. On Thursday, two days after the murder, I realized in my wanderings that I was a five-minute walk from the murder scene. I went over there and sat on a park bench for half an hour. I got into a couple of conversations, then went over and exchanged a few words with the doorman at Byron's building.

Saturday afternoon there was a memorial service for him at St Luke's on Hudson Street. People who had known him during the years he was sober shared reminiscences. I listened as if for clues.

Afterward I had a cup of coffee with Ginnie. 'It's

funny,' she said. 'I keep having the feeling that I ought to hire you.'

'To find the guy who shot Byron? The cops can do a better job of that than I can.'

'I know. The feeling persists all the same. You know what I think it is? I'd be doing something for him, Matt. And there's nothing else I *can* do for him.'

Later that day I had a call from Adrian Whitfield. 'You know what?' he said. 'I've figured out how the son of a bitch is going to get me. He's fixing it so I die of boredom.'

'You hear about people dying of boredom,' I said, 'but you don't see it listed as "cause of death" on a whole lot of autopsy reports.'

'It's a cover-up, like the Catholics do with suicide. People who die of boredom can't be buried in hallowed ground. Did you ever know a fellow named Benedetto Nappi?'

'I think I saw a couple of his paintings at the Frick.'

'Not unless there's a side to the man that I don't know about. Benny the Suitcase is what they called him, although I couldn't tell you why. The story goes that he had a job starting Tony Furillo's car. He'd warm up the engine, and then if there was no explosion that meant it was safe for Tony to go for a ride.'

'Like a food taster.'

'Exactly like a food taster. You turned the key in the ignition and when nothing happened you went back home and watched cartoons. Benny did this for a couple of months and then quit. Not because he couldn't take the pressure. I don't think he noticed any pressure. "Nothing ever happens," he complained. Of course if anything ever did happen you'd have had to pick him up with a sponge, but all he knew was the boredom was too much for him.'

'And you know how he feels.'

'I do, and in point of fact I've got less right to complain than Benny ever had. I could gripe about having to wear body armor during a heatwave, but the truth of the matter is that I go from an air-conditioned apartment to an air-conditioned limo to an air-conditioned office. It's hotter than hell on the street, but I don't get to spend enough time out there to matter.'

'You're not missing a thing.'

'I'll take your word for it. I don't know that Kevlar flatters my figure much, and it's not the last word in comfort, but it's not like a hair shirt. So here I am living my life and waiting for the bomb to go off, and when it doesn't I start feeling cheated. What about you? Are you getting anywhere at all?'

'As a matter of fact,' I said, 'I've been thinking about sending you your money back.'

'Why's that?'

'Because I can't think of a good way to earn it. I've put in some hours, but I don't think I've learned anything I didn't already know, and I'm certainly in no position to improve on the official investigation.'

'And?'

'I beg your pardon?'

'There's something else, isn't there?'

'Well, there is,' I said, and I told him about Byron Leopold.

He said, 'He's what, a friend of a friend?'

'Essentially, yes. I knew him, but just to say hello to.'

'But not so closely that you can't sleep as long as his killer walks the streets.'

'I'm surprised there hasn't been an arrest by now,' I

said. 'I thought I'd give it a couple of days, but I've already got a client.'

'You've never worked more than one case at a time?'

'Occasionally, but —'

'But you think I'll feel cheated. I'm walking around under sentence of death and you ought to be earning the money I paid you, not moonlighting while the sun shines. The friend wants to hire you?'

'She mentioned it. I wouldn't take her money.'

'You'd be working pro bono.'

'You lawyers and your Latin phrases.'

'A man sits on a bench in a pocket park with a cup of coffee and the *New York Times*. Another man walks up, shoots him, runs off. And that's it, right?'

'So far.'

'Victim had AIDS. What is it, homophobia?'

'Byron was straight. He used to shoot dope, he got AIDS sharing needles.'

'So maybe the killer was an ill-informed homophobe. Or it's the other way round, some kind of mercy killing. Is that how you're thinking?'

'Those are some of the possibilities.'

'Here's another. You figure there's any possible connection between this incident and our friend Will?'

'Jesus,' I said. 'That never crossed my mind.'

'And now that it has?'

'Crossed it and kept right on going,' I said. 'If there's a connection, I can't say it leaps out at me. He didn't announce it first or claim credit for it afterward. And the victim was the farthest thing from a public figure. Where's the connection?'

'It's so random,' he said. 'So pointless.'

'So?'

'Whereas Will's hits are all very specific. He

addresses his target directly and tells him why he's got it coming.'

'Right.'

'His official hits, that is.'

'You think he's doing some unannounced killing?'

'Who knows?'

'What would be the point?'

'What's the point of any of it?' he said. 'What's the point of killing me, for God's sake? Maybe he likes killing and he can't get enough of it. Maybe he's planning to shoot me and he wants to practice on an easy target, somebody who's not expecting it and isn't surrounded by bodyguards. Maybe the little *pas de deux* in Jackson Square was a dress rehearsal.'

It was an interesting idea. It seemed farfetched, but it was sufficiently provocative so that I found myself suggesting other possibilities. We kicked it around for a few minutes, and then Whitfield said, 'I don't think there's any connection and neither do you. But I don't see why you can't spend a couple of days looking for one. Don't send me my money back. You'll find a way to earn it.'

'If you say so.'

'I say so. What I'm paying you is small change compared to what Reliable's getting from me for guarding my body. Forty-eight man hours a day, plus the limo and the driver, plus whatever extras get tacked onto the bill. It doesn't take long to add up.'

'If it keeps you alive –'

'Then it's worth it. And if it doesn't, then paying the tab becomes somebody else's headache. What a deal, huh? How can I lose?'

'I think you're going to be all right.'

'Tell you something,' he said. 'I think so, too.'

FIVE

The next day was Sunday, and I didn't have a hard time talking myself into taking the day off. I watched an hour or so of pre-season football on television, but my heart wasn't in it, which gave me something in common with the players.

I have a standing dinner date on Sundays with Jim Faber, my AA sponsor, but he was out of town for the month of August. Elaine and I caught a movie across the street from Carnegie Hall, then had dinner at a new Thai place. We decided we liked our regular Thai place better.

I got to bed fairly early, and after breakfast the next morning I went down to the Village. My first stop was the Sixth Precinct station-house on West Tenth, where I introduced myself to a detective named Harris Conley. We wound up having coffee and Danish around the corner on Bleecker Street, and he told me what he knew about the murder of Byron Leopold.

From there I went to Byron's building on Horatio, where I once again spoke with the doorman. He'd been on duty when the shooting occurred, and he was thus able to tell me more than the man I'd exchanged a few words with earlier. He couldn't let me in, but he summoned the building superintendent, a stocky fellow with an Eastern European accent and the stained fingers and strong scent of a heavy smoker. The super listened to my story, looked at my ID, and took me up to the fifteenth floor, where he opened Byron's door with his passkey.

The apartment was a large studio with a small bathroom and a Pullman kitchen. The furniture was sparse, and unexceptional, as if someone had chosen it out of a catalog. There was a television set, books in a bookcase, a framed Hopper poster from a show a year ago at the Whitney. There was a hardcover book, a post-Cold War spy thriller, on the round coffee table, with a scrap of paper tucked in to mark his place. He'd got about a third of the way through it.

I picked up a little elephant, brass or bronze, from its own small wooden stand on top of the television set. I weighed it in my hand. The super was across the room, watching me. 'You want it,' he said, 'put it in your pocket.'

I put the little fellow back on his stand. 'I think he's already got a home,' I said.

'Not for long. All this stuff gotta go out of here. Who's it belong to now, can you tell me that?'

I couldn't. I told him I was sure somebody would be in touch with him.

'Co-op board's gonna want to put this on the market. He was a tenant, Mr Leopold. He didn't buy when he had the chance, so the apartment ain't his no more. Clothes and furniture'd go to his family, if he had one. Somebody's gotta come around, say, "All this here is mine now." Nobody shows up, where it all goes is the Salvation Army.'

'I'm sure they'll make good use of it.'

'Anything real good, the drivers got dealers they call, tip 'em off. Then the dealer snaps it up and slips 'em a few bucks on the side. I saw you lookin' at that book. You want, pick it up, take it home with you.'

'No, that's all right.'

I went to the window, looked out at the park across the way. I poked through the closet.

'Cops been through here a couple of times,' he said. 'One of 'em took things. Thought I didn't notice. I notice plenty.'

'I'll bet you do.'

'Pills from the medicine chest, a watch from the table next to the bed. Wasn't a cop, he'd make a good thief. One of the other cops, he didn't want to touch anything. Walks around like this.' He stood with his arms folded and pressed snug against his chest. 'Thinks he's gonna catch it if he touches anything. Catch it from breathing the air. Stupid bastard. That ain't how you catch it.'

On the last morning of his life, Byron Leopold breakfasted on half a cantaloupe and a slice of toast. (They'd found the melon rind in the garbage, the melon's other half wrapped in plastic in the refrigerator, the dishes he'd used stacked in the sink.) He made a pot of drip coffee and filled a lidded plastic cup, then collected his home-delivered copy of the *Times* from the mat in front of his door. With the paper tucked under his arm, the coffee cup in one hand and his rubber-tipped cane in the other, he rode the elevator downstairs and walked through the lobby.

This was his usual routine. On cold or rainy mornings he stayed in his apartment and sat at the window while he drank his coffee and read his newspaper, but when the weather was good he went out and sat in the sun.

He was sitting down, reading the paper, with his cup of coffee on the bench beside him. Then a man had approached him. The man was white, and the eyewitness consensus seemed to be that he was neither old nor young, neither tall nor short, neither stout nor lean. He was evidently wearing light-colored slacks, although one witness recalled him in jeans. His shirt was either a T or a short-sleeved sport shirt, depending whose word you took. My sense was that nobody paid any real attention to him until they heard the gunshot. At that point the few who weren't diving for cover tried to see what was going on, but by then the shooter was showing them his heels, and not much else.

He said something to Byron. A couple of people heard him, and one said he called Byron by name. If that was true it meant the killing was other than wholly random, but the cop I talked to at the Sixth hadn't placed much faith in that particular witness. He was a neighborhood street person, I was given to understand, his consciousness generally under the sway of one chemical or another, and apt to see and hear things imperceptible to you or me.

Two shots, almost simultaneous. No one actually saw the gun. One witness remembered him as carrying a paper bag, and maybe he was, and if so he could have had the gun concealed in it. Both slugs entered the victim's chest, and were evidently fired from a distance of five to ten feet. The gun was a .38 revolver, more than powerful enough for the task at hand, though hardly a high-tech armor-piercing weapon. If Byron had been wearing the Kevlar vest that Adrian Whitfield was griping about, he'd have lived to tell the tale.

But he wasn't, and the bullets entered side by side, one finding his heart and the other an inch or so to the right of it. The pain and shock must have been something beyond description, but they couldn't have lasted long. Death was pretty close to instantaneous.

Two shots, and the shooter was off and running before the light died in Byron's eyes. He was lucky. He could have tripped and gone sprawling, he could have run around a corner and right into a cop. Or, failing

69

that, he could have rushed past somebody who managed to get a good look at his face.

Didn't happen. He got away clean.

That afternoon I beeped TJ, and he met me at a coffee shop a couple of blocks from there. 'We been here before,' he said. 'Fixed the place up since then. Looks nice.'

'How's the cheeseburger?'

He considered the question. 'Fulfillin',' he said.

'Fulfilling?'

'Be fillin' me full,' he said, pushing his plate away. 'What kind of work you got for me?'

'Nothing we could use a computer for,' I said, and told him what I knew about Byron Leopold and the manner of his death.

'Legwork time,' he said. 'Knockin' on do's and talkin' to ho's.'

'That's the idea.'

'We on the clock?'

'You are,' I said.

'Means you payin' me, but who be payin' you?'

'Peter's paying me,' I said, 'while I try to find out what happened to Paul.'

'Think you lost me 'round the turn, Vern.'

'I have a client,' I said. 'Adrian Whitfield.'

'Lawyer dude. Got hisself on Will's list.'

'That's right.'

'How's he hooked up with Byron?'

'He's not,' I said, and explained Whitfield's theory.

'Thinks Will's runnin' warm-up sessions,' he said. 'Make sense to you?'

'Not really.'

'Me neither,' he said. 'What for's he need to practice? He doin' fine.'

Suppose Byron Leopold's murder was a street crime. Maybe he'd been killed out of anger at something he'd said or done. Maybe he'd witnessed a crime, maybe he'd seen something from his window or heard something from his park bench. Maybe he'd been mistaken for somebody who'd burned the shooter on a drug sale, or made a pass at the shooter's lover.

If it was anything of that sort, there was a chance the word would get around on the street, and I sent TJ off to look for it. He could get more that way than I could.

Meanwhile, I could look for the motive in Byron's life.

I picked up the phone and called Ginnie. 'Tell me about him,' I said.

'What do you want to know?'

'There are things that don't add up. He was a rent-stabilized tenant with a decent apartment in a good building that went co-op a little over twelve years ago. It was a non-eviction plan, which meant the tenants could either buy in at the insider's price or stay on as rental tenants. That's what he did, he went on paying rent.'

'He was shooting half a dozen bags of heroin at the time,' she said. 'Junkies don't generally make the best investment decisions. He said he wished he'd bought the apartment when he had the chance, but it never even seemed like an option at the time.'

'What's surprising,' I said, 'is that he managed to keep the place at all. If he was a junkie '

'He had the habit but not the lifestyle, Matt. He was a Wall Street junkie.'

'You don't mean he was addicted to the stock market.'

'No, he was addicted to heroin and alcohol. But he worked on Wall Street. It was a low-level position, he

71

was some sort of order clerk in a brokerage house, but he put in his nine-to-five and didn't take too many sick days. He kept his job and he paid his rent and he never lost his apartment.'

'I know there are people who manage to pull that off.'

'Drunks do it all the time. When you hear the word heroin you automatically think of criminals.'

'Well, buying it's a criminal transaction to start with.'

'And a heavy habit costs more than most junkies can earn legitimately. But if you've got a decent job and your habit's not a monster, you can maintain.'

'I know there are middle-class people who use it,' I said. 'There was that woman last month, a magazine editor married to a tax lawyer. Of course she didn't use a needle.'

'Not in the age of AIDS. Byron wouldn't have used a needle either, if he'd started a few years later than he did. But it's still heroin even if you snort it. You get high if you use it and dope-sick if you don't. And if you take too much it kills you. The reason we know about the magazine editor is that she died of an overdose.'

We talked about that, and then I said, 'So he kept the same job all those years.'

'He kept it until he got sober. Then he lost it when his firm was swallowed up in a merger, but I don't think he was out of work for more than two months before he found something very much like it with another firm. And he kept *that* job until he had to quit for health reasons.'

'And how long ago was that?'

'I think six months, but it may have been longer than that. Yes, it was, because I remember he had stopped working before the holidays, but he went back to the office Christmas party.'

'Always a comfortable place for a sober alcoholic.'

'He was depressed afterward, and I don't think it was from being around all the drinking. Although that might have been part of it. I think it was from knowing that part of his life was over. He'd never be able to go back to work.'

'Some people would call that one of the good things about AIDS.'

'Like not having to worry about skin cancer? I'm sure you're right. But Byron wasn't like that. He liked having a job to go to.'

'He had money in the bank,' I said. 'Close to forty thousand dollars.'

'Is that how much it was? I knew he didn't have to worry about money. His health insurance was in force, and he said he had enough money to last him. To see him out, that was the expression he used.' She was silent for a moment. 'This past winter he said he thought he had about a year to go, two years at the outside. Barring a miracle drug, or some other kind of miracle.'

'I understand there was a will,' I said. 'Simple and straightforward, he used a printed form and had two of his neighbors witness it. He left everything to a couple of AIDS charities.'

'That's what he told me he was going to do.'

'Was he ever married?'

'For about a year, right after he got out of school. Then they got divorced, or maybe it was an annulment. I think that's what it was.'

'No children, I assume.'

'No.'

'Any family?'

'A broken home, and both parents were alcoholic.'

'So he came by it honestly.'

73

'Uh-huh. They both died, his father many years ago and his mother sometime after he got sober. One brother, but nobody's heard from him in years, and Byron thought he was probably dead. There was another brother, and he'd been dead for some years. Byron said he died of an esophageal rupture, so I guess he must have been an alcoholic, too.'

'All happy families are alike,' I said.

'God.'

'Where do you figure the forty thousand came from? And it must have been more than that to start with, if he stopped working before last Christmas. Even if he started putting something aside each week when he sobered up, that's a lot of money to have saved in such a short amount of time.'

'Life insurance.'

'He was somebody's beneficiary?'

'No, he had a policy on his own life. He took it out years ago because somebody convinced him it was a good investment.'

'And maintained the coverage all those years?'

'He said it was the luckiest thing that ever happened to him. There were stretches when he didn't have the money or he forgot to send in the premiums, but they were automatically paid by loans against the cash value. So when he got sober it was still in force, and he went on paying the premiums.'

'Who was his beneficiary?'

'I think it was probably his wife originally. Then for years he had his mother as beneficiary, and then when she died –'

'Yes?'

'I'm sorry, it's hard to get the words out. I didn't know it at the time, but as it happens he listed me as the beneficiary. I guess he had to put someone.'

'You said you were close.'

'Close,' she said. 'You know how I found out? I had to be notified when he cashed in the policy. The company had a requirement to that effect, so that was a paper I had to sign. I didn't have to consent to it, but he was required to notify me.'

'A lot of them have that rule,' I said. 'In case the insured is required to maintain coverage, say as part of the terms of a divorce settlement.'

'He was almost apologetic, Matt. "I'm afraid you're not going to be a rich lady after all, Ginnie. I'm going to need the money myself".'

'How much was the policy for?'

'It wasn't a fortune. If I remember correctly it was eighty thousand dollars.'

'And what did he get for surrendering it?'

'Less than that, obviously. I think it was somewhere between fifty and fifty-five.'

'Thousand.'

'Of course.'

'That seems high,' I said.

'It does? It was all he had in the world, for God's sake, and it had to last him the rest of his life.'

'That's not what I meant. It seems like more than the cash surrender value of an eighty-thousand-dollar policy, that's all.'

'Oh,' she said. 'Well, I wouldn't know anything about that.'

'I don't know much about it myself, but it seems to me it's based on what you've paid in premiums over the years. You gradually build up a cash value for the policy, depending on the type of policy you've got. With straight life you pay high premiums and your policy's cash value builds up gradually over time. With term coverage your premiums are lower but you don't build up any cash value. And there are some intermediate categories, too.'

'I don't know what kind he had.'

'It couldn't have been term,' I said, 'because you can't borrow against term insurance. That's how his coverage stayed in force when he stopped paying premiums.'

'There were loans against the cash value, yes.'

'So you said. But it seems to me that the cash surrender value never adds up to that high a percentage of the death benefit. And of course the cash value's reduced by any outstanding loans against the policy.'

'He would have paid those back, though. Wouldn't he?'

'Not necessarily. The interest rates are very low, since what you're essentially doing is borrowing your own money. Say you've borrowed a couple of thousand dollars that way. Why pay it back out of your own pocket? What's the incentive? If you just put it off they'll deduct whatever's outstanding from the death benefit when you die. Your beneficiary'll get less than he would otherwise, but you won't be around to hear him whine about it.'

'Well, I don't know how much Byron's loans amounted to,' she said, 'or if he paid it back. I don't really know very much about life insurance.'

'Neither do I,' I admitted. 'But it seems to me he couldn't get as much as he did by surrendering the policy.'

'I'm sure you're right. He probably had some other investments that he sold. Or I may have got the numbers wrong. I have a terrible memory for that sort of thing. Oh, and that reminds me. Did you say you were actually inside his apartment? You didn't happen to see a little brass elephant, did you?'

76

She'd given it to him back when they were both getting sober. His memory had been unreliable then, as is not infrequently the case in early sobriety. He could never remember phone numbers, or where he put his keys. This is the elephant that never forgets, she'd told him, and it had become a running gag between them.

'I'd like to have it,' she said. 'It's not worth anything, and it wouldn't mean a thing to anybody but me.'

'It must have meant something to him,' I said. 'He didn't have a lot in the way of knickknacks, and he gave it a place of honor on top of the TV. I'm sure that's why I happened to notice it. The super told me to put it in my pocket.'

'And did you?'

'No, dammit, I put it back where I found it. It's funny, too, because I had the impulse to take it. I'll go back and get it.'

'I hate to ask you to make a special trip.'

'I'm two blocks from his building,' I said. 'It's no trouble at all.'

The hard part was finding the super. He was fixing a leaky faucet on the seventh floor, and it took the doorman a while to track him down. This time I didn't linger long in Byron's apartment. It seemed to me that the scent of AIDS was more palpable on my second visit. There is a particular musky odor that seems to be associated with the disease. Earlier I'd noticed it when I'd looked in his closet – clothing holds the smell – but this time the entire apartment was full of it. I took the little elephant and left.

SIX

Forty-eight hours later I'd made two more visits to the Horatio Street apartment building. I'd knocked on a lot of doors and talked to a great assortment of people. The police had already spoken to most if not all of them, but that didn't make them unwilling to talk to me, even if they didn't have much to tell me. Byron was a good neighbor, he mostly kept to himself, and as far as they knew he didn't have an enemy in the world. I heard a host of different theories about the killing, most of which had already occurred to me.

Wednesday afternoon I met TJ and compared notes, and was not too surprised to learn that he wasn't doing any better than I was. 'Elaine wants me to work tomorrow,' he said, 'but I told her I got to check with you first.'

'Go ahead and mind the shop for her.'

'What I thought. We gettin' noplace on the street.'

I rode the Eighth Avenue bus uptown and got off when it got mired in traffic around Fortieth Street. I walked the rest of the way home, and I was across the street in my office when Ray Gruliow called.

'Why, you son of a gun,' he said. 'I understand the self-styled Will of the People knows he's licked now that you're on the case.'

Ages ago, when I turned in my gold shield and moved out on my wife and sons, I took a room at the Hotel Northwestern on West Fifty-seventh Street just east of Ninth Avenue. I've come a long ways since then in certain respects, but geography is not one of them.

The Parc Vendôme, where Elaine and I have our apartment, is on the downtown side of Fifty-seventh, directly across from the hotel. I kept my room when we moved in together, telling myself I'd use it as an office. I can't say it gets much use. It's no place to meet clients, and the records I keep there would fit easily in a closet or cupboard across the street.

'Adrian Whitfield,' Ray Gruliow said. 'I ran into him downtown earlier today. As a matter of fact I found myself at loose ends, so I sat down and watched him at work. He's trying a case, as I'm sure you know.'

'I haven't spoken to him in a couple of days,' I said. 'How's he holding up?'

'He doesn't look so hot,' he said, 'but it could be that he's just plain exhausted. I can't turn on my television set without seeing him. If they're not sticking a mike in front of his face outside of the Criminal Courts building, they've got him in a TV studio somewhere. He was on Larry King last night, doing a remote from their New York studio.'

'What did he talk about?'

'Moral aspects of the adversary system of criminal justice. To what lengths can a lawyer go, and to what extent do we hold him accountable? It was starting to get interesting, but then they took questions from listeners, and that always reduces everything to the lowest common denominator, which is generally pretty low.'

'And dreadfully common.'

'All the same, he was hell on wheels in court this morning. You know what Samuel Johnson said. "When a man knows he is to be hanged in a fortnight, it concentrates his mind wonderfully".'

'Great line.'

'Isn't it? I'm surprised the capital punishment people

haven't dragged it out as evidence of the efficacy of their panacea for the world's ills.'

'I hope you're not getting ready to make a speech.'

'No, but I might haul out Dr Johnson next time I do. Our boy Adrian seemed pretty well bodyguarded. Your doing, I understand.'

'Not really. I made a couple of strategic suggestions and gave him a number to call.'

'He says he's wearing body armor.'

'He's supposed to be,' I said, 'and I wish he'd keep his mouth shut about it. If a shooter knows you're wearing it, he'll go for a head shot instead.'

'Well, Will's not going to hear it from me. Of course we don't know who Will is, do we?'

'If we did,' I said, 'he'd cease to be a problem.'

'For all you know,' he said, 'I could be Will myself.'

'Hmmm. No, I don't think so.'

'What makes you so sure?'

'His letters,' I said. 'They're too elegantly phrased.'

'You son of a bitch. He does have a way with words, though, doesn't he?'

'Yes.'

'Almost makes a man want to get a letter from him. Here's something I'm not proud of. You know my immediate reaction when I saw the open letter to Adrian?'

'You figured it should have been you.'

'Now how the hell did you know that? Or am I more transparent than I ever thought?'

'Well, what else would you be ashamed of?'

'I didn't say I was ashamed. I said I wasn't proud of it.'

'I stand corrected.'

'It's true, though. You remember how many actors it takes to change a light bulb?'

'I heard it but I forget.'

'Five. One to climb the ladder and four to say, "That should be me up there!" Trial lawyers aren't all that different. In this case, my friend, you could say I've been auditioning for the part my whole professional career. Who's the most hated man in New York?'

'Walter O'Malley.'

'Walter O'Malley? Who the hell ... oh, the cocksucker who moved the Dodgers out of Brooklyn. He's dead, isn't he?'

'I certainly hope so.'

'You're an unforgiving son of a bitch, aren't you? Forget Walter O'Malley. Who's the most hated lawyer in New York?'

'If that's another joke, the answer is they all are.'

'The answer, as you well know, is Raymond Gruliow.'

'Hard-Way Ray.'

'You said it. I'm the one with the most loathsome clients, the ones you love to hate. Wasn't it Will Rogers who said he never met a man he didn't like?'

'Whoever it was, I'd say he didn't get out much.'

'And he never met my list of clients. Arab terrorists, black radicals, psychotic mass murderers. Warren Madison, who only shot half a dozen New York police officers. Who did Whitfield ever defend who can compare to Warren Madison?'

'Richie Vollmer,' I said. 'For openers.'

'Warren Madison's as bad as Richie Vollmer. You blame the system for Vollmer's acquittal. For Warren, you have to blame the lawyer.'

'"He said humbly."'

'Forget humble. Humility's no asset in this line of work. You know the Chinese curse, my friend? "May you be represented by a humble attorney." You think our friend Adrian's going to be all right?'

'I don't know.'

'Will's taking his time. This is the longest he's let it slide, isn't it? Between the open letter and the payoff. Maybe it's because Adrian's better protected, harder to get to.'

'Maybe.'

'Or he could be tired of the game. Or for all we know he could have stepped in front of a bus.'

'Or he could have been sitting on a park bench,' I said, 'and somebody could have shot him by mistake.'

'Somebody who didn't even know who he was.'

'Why not?'

'Why not indeed? He could have died some kind of anonymous death, and we'll never know who he was. Be a hell of a thing for Adrian, wouldn't it?'

'How do you figure that? He'd be off the hook.'

'Think about it.'

'Oh.'

'You're only off the hook if you know you're off the hook. How long before you let the bodyguards go? How much longer before you can really relax?'

I thought about Whitfield, and after dinner I gave him a call. I left a message on his machine. It was nothing urgent, I said, and evidently he took me at my word, because I didn't hear from him.

I saw him on the late news, though. There'd been no developments, but that wouldn't stop them from pressing him for comments. It was the same principle that kept Will's name on the front page of the *Post*.

He was on the news again the following evening, but this time there was a story to go with it. His trial, due to go to the jury in a week to ten days, had been abruptly settled, with his client agreeing to plead to a lesser charge.

I went to a meeting at St Paul's. I was still carrying the little elephant around with me, and Ginnie showed up so I gave it to her. I was going to leave on the break but I'd been doing that a lot lately, so I made myself stay to the bitter end. It must have been around ten-thirty when I got home, and I was pouring a cup of coffee when the phone rang.

'Matthew Scudder,' he said. 'Adrian Whitfield.'

'I'm glad you called,' I said. 'I saw you a couple of hours ago on the news.'

'Which channel?'

'I don't know, I was watching two or three of them at once.'

'Channel-surfing, eh? A popular indoor sport. Well, I think we'd have won if it went to the jury, but I couldn't advise my client to roll the dice. He's essentially getting off with time served, and suppose the jury should wind up seeing it the wrong way?'

'And there's always that chance.'

'Always. You never know what they're going to do. You may think you know, but you can never be sure. I thought they were going to convict Richie Vollmer.'

'How could they? The judge's instructions ruled that out.'

'Yes, but he stopped short of a directed verdict of acquittal. They wanted to convict, and more often than not a jury will do what it wants to do.'

'A conviction wouldn't have stood up.'

'Oh, no way. Judge Yancey could very easily have thrown it out on the spot. If he'd let it stand I'd have knocked it out on appeal.'

'So Richie was going free no matter what they did.'

'Well, not right away. What *I* thought would happen – do you want to hear all this?'

'Why not?'

'I thought Yancey would let it stand, knowing the appeals court would reverse it. That way he wouldn't be the man who put Richie on the street. And I thought Richie'd go off to prison, where some public-spirited psychopath would kill him before his appeal could go through. Like the fellow in Wisconsin. Well, it amounts to about the same thing, doesn't it? Except the psychopath who actually did kill Richie isn't a convict, and it turns out he's a serial killer himself.'

'How are you holding up, Adrian?'

'Oh, I'm all right,' he said. 'It takes some of the pressure off to know I don't have to go to court tomorrow. At the same time there's the bittersweet feeling you get whenever something ends. A trial, a love affair, even a bad marriage. You may be glad it's over, but at the same time you're a little bit sorry.' His voice trailed off. Then he said, 'Well, nothing lasts forever, right? What goes up comes down, what starts stops. That's the way it's supposed to be.'

'You sound a little blue.'

'Do I? I think it's just that I'm running out of gas. The trial was keeping me going. Now that it's over I feel like a puppet with the strings cut.'

'You just need some rest.'

'I hope you're right. I have this superstitious sense that the trial was holding Will at bay, that he couldn't take me out as long as I had work that had to be done. Now all of a sudden I've got a bad feeling about the whole situation that I never had before.'

'You just didn't allow yourself to feel it before.'

'Maybe. And maybe I'll feel better after a good

night's sleep. I know goddam well I'll feel better after a drink.'

'Most people do,' I said. 'That's why they put the stuff in bottles.'

'Well, I'm going to uncap the bottle and let the genie out. It'll be the first one today. If you were here I'd pour you a club soda.'

'I'll have one here,' I said, 'and think of you.'

'Have a Coke. Make it a real celebration.'

'I'll do that.'

There was a pause, and then he said, 'I wish I knew you better.'

'Oh?'

'I wish there were more time. Forget I said that, all right? I'm too tired to make sense. Maybe I'll skip that drink and just go to bed.'

But he didn't skip the drink.

Instead he went into the front room, where one of his bodyguards was posted. 'I'm going to have a drink,' he announced. 'I don't suppose I can talk you into joining me.'

They'd gone through this ritual before. 'Mean my job if I did, Mr Whitfield.'

'I wouldn't tell anybody,' Whitfield said. 'On the other hand, I want you razor-sharp if our boy Will comes through that door, so I shouldn't be pushing drinks at you. How about a soft drink? Or some coffee?'

'I got a pot brewing in the kitchen. I'll have some after you turn in. Don't worry about me, Mr Whitfield. I'll be fine.'

Whitfield took a glass from on top of the bar, went into the kitchen for ice cubes, came back and uncapped the bottle of Scotch. He filled the glass and put the cap on the bottle.

'Your name's Kevin,' he said to the bodyguard, 'and I must have heard your last name, but I don't seem to remember it.'

'Kevin Dahlgren, sir.'

'Now I remember. Do you like your work, Kevin?'

'It's a good job.'

'You don't find it boring?'

'Boring's just fine with me, sir. If something happens I'm ready, but if nothing happens I'm happy.'

'That's a healthy attitude,' Whitfield told him. 'You probably wouldn't have minded starting Tony Furillo's car.'

'Sir?'

'Never mind. I ought to drink this, wouldn't you say? I poured it, I ought to drink it. Isn't that how it works?'

'Up to you, Mr Whitfield.'

'Up to me,' Whitfield said. 'You're absolutely right.'

He raised the glass in a wordless toast, then took a long drink. Dahlgren's eyes went to the bookcase. He was a reader, and there was a lot to read in this apartment. It was no hardship, sitting in a comfortable chair with a good book for eight hours, helping yourself to coffee when you wanted it. It was nice to get paid for something you'd do on your own time.

That's what he was thinking when he heard the man he was guarding make a sharp sound, a sort of strangled gasp. He turned at the sound and watched Adrian Whitfield clutch his chest and pitch forward onto the carpet.

SEVEN

'It's like he saw it coming,' Kevin Dahlgren said. He was a tall, broad-shouldered man in his early thirties, his light brown hair cropped close to his broad skull, his light brown eyes alert behind his eyeglasses. He looked at once capable and thoughtful, as if he might be a studious thug.

'I was the last person to talk to him,' I said. 'Except for yourself, of course.'

'Right.'

'He was tired, and I think that soured his outlook. But maybe he had a premonition, or just some sense that he'd reached the end of the line.'

'He offered me a drink. Not that I even considered taking it. On the job, and a bodyguard job at that? They'd drop me like a hot rock if I ever did anything like that, and they'd be right to do it. I wasn't even tempted, but now I'm picturing what would have happened if I said yes. We clink glasses, we drink up, and boom! We hit the deck together. Or maybe I'd have been the first to take a drink, because he was sort of stalling. So I'd be dead and he'd be here talking to you.'

'But that's not how it happened.'

'No.'

'When you met him and entered the apartment . . .'

'You want me to go over that? Sure thing. My shift started at ten p.m., and I reported to the Park Avenue residence, where I met up with Samuel Mettnick, who was sharing the ten-to-six shift with me. We stationed ourselves downstairs in the lobby. The two fellows on the previous shift brought Mr Whitfield home in the limo and turned him over to us at ten-ten. Sam Mettnick and I rode upstairs with Mr Whitfield, observing the usual security procedures as far as entering and exiting the elevator, and so forth.'

'Who opened the door of the apartment?'

'I did, and went in first. There was a whistle indicating the burglar alarm was set, so I went to the keypad and keyed in the response code. Then I checked all the rooms to make sure the place was empty. Then I returned to the front room and Sam went downstairs and I locked the door and made sure it was secure. Then Mr Whitfield went off through his bedroom to use the bathroom, and I guess stopped in his bedroom and used the phone before returning to the front room. And you know the rest.'

'You'd been in the apartment before.'

'Yes, sir, for several nights running. From ten o'clock on.'

'And you didn't notice anything out of place when you entered.'

'There were no signs of intrusion. Anything like that and I'd have grabbed Mr Whitfield and got him the hell out of there. As for anything out of place, all I can say is everything looked normal to me, same as on previous nights. The thing is, I'd been relieved at six that morning, so my counterpart on the six a.m. to two p.m. shift would have been the last person in there. Whether anything had been moved around since he and Mr Whitfield left to go to the court, that's something I couldn't say.'

'But there was nothing about the appearance of the room that drew a comment from Whitfield.'

'You mean like, "What's this bottle doing over

here?" No, nothing like that. Though to tell you the truth I'm not sure he would have noticed. You know the mood he was in.'

'Yes.'

'He seemed abstracted, if that's the word I want. Sort of out of synch. Right before he took the drink –' He snapped his fingers. 'I know what it reminded me of.'

'What's that, Kevin?'

'It's a scene in a movie I saw, but don't ask me the name of it. This one character's an alcoholic and he hasn't had a drink in, I don't know, months or years, anyway a long time. And he pours one and looks at it and drinks it.'

'And that's how Whitfield looked at his drink.'

'Kind of.'

'But he had a glass of Scotch every night, didn't he?'

'I guess so, I wasn't always there to see him have it. Some nights he was already home when my shift started, so I would just come up and relieve the man from the earlier shift. Other times he'd already had his drink before I got him. As far as being an alcoholic, I'd say he was anything but. I *never* saw him take more than one drink a night.'

'When I talked to him,' I said, 'he said he was about to have his first drink of the day.'

'I think he said as much to me. I wasn't with him earlier, but I can testify he didn't have it on his breath.'

'Would you have noticed it if he had?'

'I think so, yes. I was standing right next to him in the elevator, and I've got a pretty good sense of smell. I can tell you he had Italian food for dinner. Plus I hadn't had anything to drink all that day, and when you're not drinking yourself it makes you much more aware of the smell of alcohol on somebody else.'

'That's true.'

'It's the same thing with cigarettes. I used to smoke, and all those years I never smelled smoke on anybody, me or anybody else. I quit four years ago, and now I can just about smell a heavy smoker from the opposite side of an airport. That's stretching it, but you know what I mean.'

'Sure.'

'So I'd guess it was his first drink of the night. Jesus.'

'What, Kevin?'

'Well, it's not funny, but I was just thinking. One thing for sure, it was his last.'

I didn't have to take Kevin Dahlgren's word about the acuity of his sense of smell. He'd proved it shortly after Adrian Whitfield collapsed. Dahlgren's immediate assumption had been that he was in the presence of a man having a heart attack, and he reacted as he'd been trained to react and began performing CPR.

At the onset of the procedure, he had of course smelled alcohol on Whitfield. But there was another odor present as well, the odor of almonds, and while Dahlgren had never smelled this particular almondy scent before, he was sufficiently familiar with its description to guess what it was. He picked up Whitfield's empty glass from where it had fallen and noted the same bitter-almond scent. Accordingly, he discontinued CPR and called the Poison Control number, although his instincts told him there was nothing to be done. The woman he spoke to told him essentially the same thing; about the best thing she could suggest was that he try to get the victim breathing again, and his heart beating. He took a moment to call 911, then resumed CPR for lack of anything better to do. He was still at it when the cops got there.

That was shortly after eleven, and New York One

was on the air with a news flash well before midnight, beating Channel Seven by a full five minutes. I didn't have the set on, however, and Elaine and I went to bed around a quarter of one without knowing that a client of mine had died a couple of miles away of the ingestion of a lethal dose of cyanide.

Sometimes Elaine starts the day with 'Good Morning America' or the Today show, but she's just as likely to play classical music on the radio, and when I joined her in the kitchen the next morning she was listening to what we both thought was Mozart. It turned out to be Haydn, but by the time they said as much she had left for the gym. I turned off the radio — if I'd left it on I'd have heard a newscast at the top of the hour, and Whitfield's death would have been the first or second item. I had a second cup of coffee and the half bagel she had left unfinished. Then I went out to get a paper.

The phone was ringing when I left the apartment, but I was already halfway out the door. I kept going and let the machine answer it. If I'd picked it up myself I'd have received word of Whitfield's death from Wally Donn, but instead I walked to the newsstand, where twin stacks of the *News* and the *Post* rested side by side on adjacent upended plastic milk crates. LAWYER WHITFIELD DEAD cried the *News*, while the *Post* went right ahead and solved the crime for us. WILL KILLS #5!

I bought both papers and went home, played Wally's message and called him back. 'What a hell of a thing,' he said. 'Personal security work's the most clearcut part of the business. All you have to do is keep the client alive. Long as he's got a pulse, you did your job right. Matt, you know the procedures we set up for Whitfield. It was a good routine, and I had good men on it. And there's cyanide in the fucking Scotch bottle and we come off looking like shit.'

'It was cyanide? The account I read just said poison.'

'Cyanide. My guy knew it from the smell, called Poison Control right away. A shame he didn't sniff the glass before Whitfield drank it.'

'A shame Whitfield didn't sniff the glass.'

'No, he just knocked it right back, and then it knocked him on his ass. On his face, actually. He pitched forward. Dahlgren had to roll him over to start CPR.'

'Dahlgren's your op?'

'I had two working. He's the one was upstairs with Whitfield. Other guy was in the lobby. If I'd of put them both upstairs . . . but no, what are they gonna do, sit up all night playing gin rummy? The procedure was the correct one.'

'Except the client died.'

'Yeah, right. The operation was a success but the patient died. How do you figure poison in the whisky? The apartment was secure. It was left empty that morning and the burglar alarm was set. My guy swears he set it, the one who picked Whitfield up yesterday morning, and I know he did because my other guy, Dahlgren, swears it was set when he opened up last night. So somebody got in there between whenever it was, eight or nine yesterday morning and ten last night. They got through two locks, a Medeco and a Segal, and bypassed a brand-new Poseidon alarm. How, for Christ's sake?'

'The alarm was new?'

'I ordered it myself. The Medeco cylinder was new, too, on the top lock. I had it installed the day we came on the job.'

'Who had keys?'

'Whitfield himself, of course, not that he needed a key. Coming or going, he was never the first one to go through the door. Then there were two sets of keys, one for each of the men on duty. When they were relieved they passed on their keys to the next shift.'

'What about the building staff?'

'They had keys to the Segal, of course. But we didn't give them a key to the new lock.'

'He must have had a cleaning woman.'

'Uh-huh. Same woman's been coming in and cleaning for him every Tuesday afternoon for as long as he's had the apartment. And no, she didn't get a key to the Medeco, or the four-digit code for the burglar alarm, and not because I figured there was much chance of Will turning out to be a nice old Polish lady from Greenpoint. She didn't get a key because nobody got one who didn't need one. On Tuesday afternoons one of our men would meet her there, let her in, and stick around until she was done. He's sitting there reading a magazine while she's vacuuming and ironing and on her hands and knees scrubbing out the bathtub, and you know his hourly rate's three or four times what she's getting. Don't you ever let anybody tell you life is fair.'

'I'll remember that,' I said.

'Let me answer a question or two before you ask it, because the cops already asked and I already answered. The alarm's not just on the door. The windows are also wired in. That was probably excessive, since there's no fire escape, and do we really figure Will to be capable of doing a human fly act, coming down from the roof on a couple of knotted bedsheets?'

'Is that what flies do?'

'You know what I mean. I been up all night talking to cops and not talking to reporters, so don't expect me to sound like Shakespeare. It doesn't cost that much more to hook up the alarm to the windows, so why cut corners? That was my thinking. Besides, if this guy could get Patsy Salerno and Whatsisname in Omaha, who's to say he can't walk up a brick wall?'

'What about a service entrance?'

'You mean the building or the apartment? Of course there's a service entrance for the building, and a separate service elevator. There's also a service entrance for the apartment, and nobody went in or out from the time we got on the case. One of the first things I did was throw a bolt on it and keep it permanently shut, because as soon as you got two ways in and out of a place you've got the potential for headaches from a security standpoint. Sooner or later somebody forgets to lock the service door. So I had it all but welded shut, and that meant Mrs Szernowicz had to take the long way around when she took the trash to the compactor chute, but she didn't seem to mind.'

We talked some more about the security at the apartment, the locks and the alarm system, and then we got back to the cyanide. I said, 'It was in the whisky, Wally? Do we know that for sure?'

'He drank his drink,' he said, 'and flopped on the floor, so what could it be but the drink? Unless somebody picked that particular minute to plink him with a pellet gun.'

'No, but –'

'If he was drinking tequila,' he said, 'and he was one of those guys goes through the ritual with the salt and the lemon, takes a lick of each after he does the shot of tequila, then I could see how we could check and see if the lemon's poisoned, or maybe the salt. But nobody drinks tequila that way anymore, at least nobody I know, and anyway he was drinking Scotch, so where the hell else would the poison be but in the whisky?'

94

'I was at his place once,' I said. 'The night he got the letter from Will.'

'And?'

'And he had a drink,' I said, 'and he used a glass, and if I remember correctly he had ice in it.'

'Aw, Jesus,' he said. 'I'm sorry, Matt. I was up all night, and it's shaping up to be a bitch of a day. Could it have been in the glass or the ice cubes? I don't know, maybe. I'm sure they're running an analysis of the booze in the bottle, if they haven't done it already. Dahlgren smelled cyanide on the guy's breath, and I think he said he smelled it in the glass, or maybe on the ice cubes. Did he smell what was left in the bottle? I don't think so. It was on top of the bar and he was on the floor with Whitfield, trying to get him to start breathing again. Neat fucking trick, that would have been.'

'Poor bastard.'

'Which one, Whitfield or Dahlgren? Both of them, I'd have to say. You know, I was concerned about food in restaurants. You remember that case where there was poison in the salt?'

'I must have missed that one.'

'It wasn't local. Miami, I think it was. Mobbed-up businessman, he's having dinner at his favorite restaurant, next thing you know he's face down in his veal piccata. Looks like a heart attack, and if it happened to Joe Blow it would have gone as that, but this guy's the target of an investigation so of course they check, and they establish that cyanide killed him and find cyanide on the food that's left on his plate, and there's a surveillance tape, because this is the restaurant he always goes to and the table he always sits at, the dumb bastard, and the Feds or the local cops, whoever it was, were set up to tape it. And the tape shows this guy come over to the table and switch salt shakers, but you can't be absolutely certain that's what he's doing, and anyway they didn't find any cyanide in the salt shaker, because evidently somebody switched them again afterward. So they couldn't get a conviction, but at least they knew who did it and how it was done.' He sighed. 'Whitfield never sat down to a meal without one or two of my guys at the table with him, primed to make sure nobody switched salt shakers. It's like generals, isn't it? Always preparing for the last war. Meantime, somebody got in his house and poisoned his whisky.'

We were on the phone for quite a while. He anticipated most of my questions, but I thought of a few others as well, and he answered them all. If there was a weak link in the security he'd set up for Adrian Whitfield, I couldn't spot it. Short of posting a man full-time in the apartment itself, I didn't see how it could have been rendered more completely secure.

And yet someone had managed to get enough cyanide into Whitfield's drink to kill him.

It was late afternoon by the time I got to talk with Kevin Dahlgren, and by then I'd been interrogated myself by two detectives from Major Cases. They'd spent close to two hours learning everything I could tell them about my involvement with Adrian Whitfield, from the cases I'd worked on for him to the contact I'd had with him since he was the target of Will's open letter.

They found out everything I knew, which wasn't much. It was more than I learned from them. I didn't ask many questions, and the few I asked went largely unanswered. I did manage to learn that cyanide had been found in the residue of Scotch left in the bottle, but I'd have learned that shortly thereafter anyway by turning on the television set.

I was worn out from my session with the two of them, and what I went through was nothing compared with what Dahlgren had to undergo. He'd been up all night, of course, and had spent most of the time either answering questions or waiting for them to get around to interrogating him some more. He managed to get a couple of hours' sleep before I saw him, and he seemed alert enough, but you could tell he was pretty well stressed out.

He was a suspect, of course, along with the several other men who'd had access to Whitfield's apartment in their capacity as bodyguards. Each of them was subjected to an intensive background check and interrogated exhaustively, and each voluntarily underwent a polygraph examination as well. (It was voluntary as far as the police were concerned. It was compulsory if they wished to remain employees of Reliable.)

Mrs Sophia Szernowicz, Whitfield's cleaning woman, was interrogated as well, though not subjected to a polygraph test. They talked to her more to rule out the possibility of anyone else having visited the apartment while she was cleaning it than because anyone thought she might be Will. She'd been there on Tuesday afternoon, and he'd swallowed the poisoned Scotch Thursday night. No one could testify with absolute certainty that Whitfield had poured a drink from that bottle on either Tuesday or Wednesday evening, so the possibility existed that the cyanide could have gone into the bottle during her visit.

She told them she'd seen no one in the apartment while she cleaned it, no one except for the man who'd let her in and out, and who'd sat watching talk shows on television all the time she was there. She could not recall seeing him anywhere near where the bottles of liquor were kept, although she couldn't say what he'd done when she was in one of the other rooms. For her part, she had been at the bar, and might even have touched the bottle while dusting it and its fellows. Had she by any chance sampled it, or any of the other bottles while she was dusting? The very suggestion outraged her, and they were a while calming her down to the point where they could resume questioning her.

The only fingerprints on the bottle were Whitfield's. All that suggested was that the killer had wiped the bottle off after adding the cyanide, and one could hardly have assumed otherwise. It also implied that no one but Whitfield had touched the bottle after its contents were poisoned, but, as far as anyone knew, no one but Whitfield had laid a hand on that particular bottle since it had come into the house.

It had been delivered two weeks before. Will mailed his threat against Whitfield to Marty McGraw. A liquor store on Lexington Avenue had delivered the order, consisting in all of two fifths of Glen Farquahar single malt Scotch whisky, one quart of Finlandia vodka, and a pint of Myer's rum. The rum and vodka remained unopened, and Whitfield had worked his way through one bottle of the Scotch and was a third of the way into the second bottle when he drank the drink that killed him.

'You don't drink,' he'd said to me. 'Neither do I.' He'd been enough of a drinker to order two bottles of his regular tipple at a time, but a light enough hitter that it had taken him over a month to drink as much as he had. A fifth holds twenty-six ounces, or something like eighteen drinks if you figure he poured approximately an ounce and a half of Scotch over his two ice cubes. Eighteen drinks from the bottle he'd finished, another six or so from bottle #2 – I decided the math worked out right. There were nights when he had his drink before he came home, and other nights when he evidently didn't drink at all.

That night Elaine and I walked over to Armstrong's for dinner. She had a big salad. I had a bowl of chili and stirred a large side order of minced Scotch bonnet peppers into it. It must have been hot enough to blister paint, but you couldn't have proved it by me. I was barely aware of what I was eating.

She talked some about her day at her shop, and about what TJ had said when he dropped by to jive with her. I talked about my day. And then we both fell silent. Classical music played over the sound system, barely audible through the buzz of conversations around us. Our waiter came around to find out if we wanted more Perrier. I said we didn't, but he could bring me a cup of black coffee when he had a moment. Elaine said she'd have herb tea. 'Any kind,' she said, 'Surprise me.'

He brought her Red Zinger. 'What a surprise,' she said.

I tried my coffee, and something must have shown in my face, because Elaine's eyebrows went up a notch.

'For an instant there,' I said, 'I could taste booze in the coffee.'

'But it's not really there.'

'No. Good coffee, but only coffee.'

'What they call a sense-memory, I guess.'

'I guess.'

You could say I came by it honestly. Years ago, before Jimmy lost his lease and relocated a long block to the west, Armstrong's had been situated on Ninth Avenue around the corner from my hotel, and it had functioned for me almost as an extension of my personal living space. I socialized there, I isolated there, I met clients there. I put in long hours of maintenance drinking there, and sometimes I did more than maintain and got good and drunk at the bar or at my table in the back. My usual drink was bourbon, and when I didn't drink it neat, the way God made it, I would stir it into a mug of coffee. Each flavor, it seemed to me then, complimented and enhanced the other, even as the caffeine and alcohol balanced one another, the one keeping you awake while the other softened the edges of consciousness.

I have known people who, when quitting smoking, have had to give up coffee temporarily because they so strongly associate the two. I had problems of my own getting sober, but coffee was not one of them, and I have been able to go on drinking it with pleasure, and apparently with impunity, at an age when most of my contemporaries have found it advisable to switch to decaf. I like the stuff, especially when it's good, the way Elaine makes it at home (although she hardly ever has a cup herself) or the way they brew it in the Seattle-style coffee bars that have sprouted up all over town. The coffee's always been good at Armstrong's, rich and full-bodied and aromatic, and I took a sip now, savoring it, and wondered why I'd tasted bourbon.

'There was nothing you could have done,' Elaine said. 'Was there?'

'No.'

'You told him he ought to leave the country.'

'I could have pushed a little harder,' I said, 'but I don't think he would have done anything differently, and I can't blame him for that. He had a life to live. He took all the precautions a man could be expected to take.'

'Reliable did a good job for him?'

'Even in hindsight,' I said, 'I can't point to a thing they did wrong. I suppose they could have posted men around the clock in his apartment, whether or not there was anybody in it, but even after the fact I can't argue that that's what they should have done. And as far as my own part in all this is concerned, no, I can't see anything I left undone that might have made a difference. It would have been nice if I'd had some brilliant insight that told me who Will was, but that didn't happen, and that gives me something in common with eight million other New Yorkers, including however many cops they've got assigned to the case.'

'But something's bothering you.'

'Will's out there,' I said. 'Doing what he does, and getting away with it. I guess that bothers me, especially now that he's struck down a man I knew. A friend, I was going to say, and that would have been inaccurate, but I had the sense the last time I spoke with him that Adrian Whitfield might have become a friend. If he'd lived long enough.'

'What are you going to do?'

I drank the rest of my coffee, caught the waiter's eye and pointed to my empty cup. While he filled it I thought about the question she'd asked. I said, 'The funeral's private, just for the family. There'd be a crowd otherwise, with all the headlines he's getting. I understand there'll be a public memorial service sometime next month, and I'll probably go to that.'

'And?'

'And maybe I'll light a candle,' I said.

'It couldn't hoit,' she said, giving the phrase an exaggerated Brooklyn pronunciation. It was the punchline to an old joke, and I guess I smiled, and she smiled back across the table at me.

'Does the money bother you?'

'The money?'

'Didn't he write you a check?'

'For two thousand dollars,' I said.

'And don't you get a referral fee from Reliable?'

'Dead clients don't pay.'

'I beg your pardon?'

'A basic principle of the personal-security industry,' I said. 'Someone used it for the title of a book on the subject. Wally took a small retainer, but it won't begin to cover what he has to pay in hourly rates to the men he's had guarding Whitfield. He's legally entitled to bill the estate, but he already told me he's going to eat it. Since he'll wind up with a net loss, I won't be picking up a referral fee.'

'And you're just as glad, aren't you?'

'Oh, I don't know. If he'd made money on the deal I'd have been comfortable taking a share of it. And if the two grand Whitfield paid me starts bothering me I can always give it away.'

'Or try to earn it.'

'By chasing Will,' I said, 'or by hunting for the man who shot Byron Leopold.'

'On Horatio Street.'

I nodded. 'Whitfield suggested there might be a link, that maybe Will killed Byron at random, more or less for practice.'

'Is that possible?'

'I suppose it's possible. It's also possible Byron was gunned down by an extraterrestrial, and every bit as likely. It was his way of telling me to keep his money and investigate whatever the hell I wanted to investigate. It made as much sense for me to be working one case as the other. Either way I wasn't going to accomplish anything, was I?'

'That's it, isn't it? That's what's making you taste

alcohol that isn't there. That you can't accomplish anything.'

I thought about it. I sipped some coffee, put the cup in the saucer. 'Yeah,' I said. 'That's it.'

Outside, I took her hand as we waited for the light to change. I glanced at the building diagonally across the street, and my eyes automatically sought out a window on the twenty-ninth floor. Noticing my glance, or perhaps just reading my mind, Elaine said, 'You know what that shooting in the Village reminds me of? Glenn Holtzman.'

He'd lived in that twenty-ninth floor apartment. His widow, Lisa, had gone on living there after his death. She hired me, and after I was through working for her I continued to return occasionally to her apartment, and to her bed.

When Elaine and I were married we went to Europe for a honeymoon. We were in Paris, lying together in our hotel room, when she told me that nothing had to change. We could go on being ourselves and living our lives. The rings on our fingers didn't change anything.

She said this in a way that made the unspoken subtext unmistakable. *I know there's someone else*, she'd been saying, *and I don't care.*

'Glenn Holtzmann,' I said. 'Killed by accident.'

'Unless Freud's right and there's no such thing as an accident.'

'I thought about Holtzmann when I was poking around the edges of Byron's life. The idea of someone killed by mistake.'

'It's bad enough being killed for a reason.'

'Uh-huh. Somebody heard the shooter call Byron by name.'

'Then he knew who he was.'

'If the witness got it right.'

We walked the rest of the way home, not saying much. Upstairs in our apartment I put a hand on her shoulder and turned her toward me, and we were in each other's arms. We kissed, and I put a hand on her hindquarters and drew her against me.

Nothing has to change, she'd told me in Paris, but of course things change over time. We have been many things to each other over many years, Elaine and I. When we met I was a married cop and she was a sweet young call girl. We were together, and then we were apart for years, until the past drew us together again. After a while she quit hooking. After a while we found an apartment together. After a while we got married.

Passion, after all those years, was different from what it had been when I'd made those first visits to her Turtle Bay apartment. Then our desire for each other had been fierce and urgent and undeniable. Now it had been tempered by time and custom. The love, present from the beginning, had grown infinitely broader and deeper with time; the delight we had always taken in each other's company was keener than ever. And our passion, if it had grown less furious, was richer as well.

We kissed again, and her breath caught in her throat. We moved to the bedroom, shed our clothes.

'I love you,' I said. Or maybe she said it. After a while you lose track.

'You know,' she said, 'if we keep on like this, I can see where we might acquire a certain degree of proficiency.'

'Never happen.'

'You're my bear and I love you. And you're about to drop off to sleep, aren't you? Unless I keep you awake by glowing in the dark. I almost could, the way I feel.

Why does sex wake women up and put men to sleep? Is it just bad planning on God's part or does it somehow contribute to the survival of the species?'

I was turning the question over and over in my mind, trying to form an answer, when I felt her breath on my cheek and her lips brushing mine.

'Sleep tight,' she said.

EIGHT

The big news over the weekend had to do with the results of the autopsy performed on Adrian Whitfield. The cause of death was no surprise. It had been confirmed as having resulted from the ingestion of a dose of potassium cyanide which, according to the *Post*, would have been enough to kill a dozen lawyers. (Monday night Leno read that item in his opening monologue, rolled his eyes heavenward, and got a laugh without saying a word.)

What the autopsy also established was that Will had done little more than anticipate Nature. At the time of his death, Adrian Whitfield had already been stricken with a malignant tumor that had metastasized from its initial site on one of the adrenal glands and invaded the lymph system. Will had cheated him, at most, out of a year of life.

'I wonder if he knew,' I said to Elaine. 'It would have been largely asymptomatic, according to the story in the *Times*.'

'Had he been to the doctor?'

'His doctor's out of town. Nobody can get hold of him.'

'Doctors,' she said with feeling. 'He never said anything?'

'He said something. What was it?' I closed my eyes for a moment. 'The last time I talked with him, right before he drank the poison, he said something about wishing we'd had more time. To get to know each other, was what he meant. Or maybe he meant he wished he'd had more time in general.'

'If he knew –'

'If he knew,' I said, 'maybe he's the one who put the cyanide in the Scotch. That would explain how Will managed to walk through walls and get in and out of a burglar–proof apartment. He was never there at all. Whitfield killed himself.'

'Is that what you think happened?'

'I don't know what I think,' I said, and got up to answer the phone.

It was Wally Donn, with the same question. 'The son of a bitch was dying,' he said. 'What do you figure, Matt? You knew him pretty well.'

'I hardly knew him at all.'

'Well, you knew him better than I did, for Christ's sake. Was he the type to kill himself?'

'I don't know what type that is.'

'The most I can get out of Dahlgren is he was moody. The hell, I'd be moody myself if I got a letter from Will. I'd be twice as moody if I had what Whitfield had.'

'If he knew he had it.'

'For that you'd need his medical records, and his doctor's out of town for the weekend. They'll be getting in touch with him tomorrow and we'll know a little more. I'm just picturing this son of a bitch, deliberately taking poison right in front of a young fellow who's getting paid to protect his life.'

'You know,' I said, 'you're calling him a son of a bitch, but if it wasn't suicide . . .'

'Then I'm maligning a man after I already failed to protect him, and that makes me the son of a bitch.' He sighed. 'The world's a confusing fucking place to be in, and don't let anybody tell you different.'

'I wouldn't dream of it.'

'What'd he be doing, anyway, committing some Polish version of suicide? Trying to disguise it, make it look like murder?'

'Usually it's the other way around.'

'Guys killing people, trying to fix it so it looks like they killed themselves. Why would you turn it around? Insurance?'

'That would only make sense if there's a policy he took out recently. The clause that excludes suicide only applies for a certain amount of time.'

'Usually a year, isn't it?'

'I think so. It's to prevent a person from deliberately bilking them by taking out a policy with the intent of killing himself. But when you've got a policy-holder who's been paying premiums for twenty years, you can't weasel out of your obligation to him just because he got depressed and took a dive in front of the F train.'

'I don't know,' he said. 'We've done enough insurance work over the years to convince me they'll weasel out of anything they can. They're the worst when it comes to questioning items when we bill them for our services. Force of habit, it must be.'

'Speaking of bills, if it turns out he did it himself –'

'What, I can bill the estate? We signed on to protect him and we couldn't even protect him from himself? I'd rather eat it than try to collect it.'

When there's enough media attention, you can't find a place to hide where somebody won't come after you. Will seemed to be managing so far, but Philip M. Bushing, MD, didn't have an equal talent for conceal-ment. He'd gone fishing in Georgian Bay, and some enterprising reporter had managed to track him down.

Bushing was Adrian Whitfield's physician, specializing in internal medicine – a term, Elaine pointed out, that you would think ought to cover just about everything but dermatology. He evidently confined doctor-patient privilege to those patients who were still breathing, and so felt free to disclose that he had diagnosed Adrian Whitfield's illness in the spring, and had had the sad task of communicating that fact to the patient.

Whitfield had taken it well, Bushing recalled, ultimately treating the physician as a hostile witness. He'd forced Bushing to admit that neither surgery nor chemotherapy offered any prospect of curing his condition, and got him to estimate how much time he had left. Six months to a year, Bushing told him, and referred him to an oncologist at Sloan-Kettering.

Whitfield called that man, a Dr Ronald Patel, and made and kept an appointment with him. Patel confirmed Bushing's diagnosis and proposed an aggressive protocol of radiation and chemotherapy, which he felt might win the patient another year of life. Whitfield thanked him and left, and Patel never heard from him again.

'I assumed he wanted another opinion,' Patel said.

If he wanted an opinion on anything, he was in the right town for it. Everybody had one, and by Tuesday morning I think I'd heard them all. The general consensus seemed to hold that Whitfield's death was suicide, and one authority on the topic described it as an opportunistic act of self-destruction. I knew what he meant, but it struck me as a curious phrase.

More than a few people were bothered by the method he chose, regarding it as showing little consideration for others – or, for that matter, for Whitfield himself. Cyanide brought an end that was a long way from painless. You did not drift off dreamily into that sleep from which there was no awakening. All that was to be said for it, really, was that you went fast.

'Still,' I told Elaine, 'there aren't that many gentle paths out of this world, and a surprising number of people pick a rocky road for themselves. Cops eat their guns with such regularity you'd think the barrels were dipped in chocolate.'

'I think it makes a statement, don't you? "I'm using my service revolver, therefore the job killed me."'

'That fits,' I agreed, 'but by now I think it's just part of the tradition. And it's quick and it's certain, unless the bullet takes a bad hop. And the means is close at hand.'

A local television personality quoted Dorothy Parker:

> Razors pain you,
> Rivers are damp,
> Acids stain you
> And drugs cause cramp;
> Guns aren't lawful,
> Nooses give,
> Gas smells awful –
> You might as well live.

This brought a rejoinder, predictably enough, from a spokeswoman for the Hemlock Society, who felt the need to point out just how far we'd come since Parker wrote those lines. There were, she was pleased to report, several carefree ways one could do away with oneself, and the two of which she seemed fondest consisted of gassing yourself in the garage with carbon monoxide or suffocating yourself with a plastic bag.

'Unfortunately,' she said, 'not everybody has a car.'

'Sad but true,' said Elaine, talking back to the

television set. 'Fortunately, however, just about every-body has a plastic bag. "Dad, can I borrow the car tonight? No? Well, can I borrow the plastic bag?"'

The real victim, someone else maintained, was Kevin Dahlgren, who'd been subjected to no end of stress by virtue of the fact that Whitfield had been inconsiderate enough to drop dead in front of him. At least one talk show included a psychologist and a trauma expert talking about the possible short- and long-term impact of the incident upon Dahlgren.

Dahlgren ducked most interviews, and acquitted himself creditably when he was cornered. He had, he said, no opinion as to whether we'd witnessed an act of suicide or murder. His only regret was that there'd been nothing he could do to save the man's life.

If Dahlgren didn't want the victim role, a man named Irwin Atkins was eager to snatch it up for himself. Atkins was Adrian Whitfield's final client, the brawler who'd decided to plead guilty to a misde-meanor assault charge just hours before Adrian Whit-field went off to argue his own case before a higher court. Building on the speculation that Whitfield had felt free to end his life once the case had been disposed of, Atkins served notice of his intention to file an appeal on the grounds that he'd been improperly served by counsel.

'He's got two arguments,' Ray Gruliow told me. 'One, Whitfield deliberately talked him into pleading because he was in a rush to go home and drink rat poison, or whatever the hell it was. Two, Whitfield's suicidal state of mind impaired his judgment and rendered him incapable of furnishing sound legal advice. He could buttress his second argument by pointing out that Whitfield was sufficiently unbalanced to take on a mutt like him for a client.'

'You think it'll work?'

'I think they'll let him withdraw the plea,' he said, 'and I think he'll regret it, the silly son of a bitch, when his retrial ends in a conviction.'

'And will it?'

'Oh, I'd say so. You pull something like that, withdraw an eleventh-hour plea, and you invite the widespread perception that you're a pain in the ass. I think it's all a load of crap anyway. Adrian didn't kill himself.'

'No?'

'I'd never argue it'd be a bad choice, or that it isn't his choice to make. And I think he might have done it sooner or later. He could very well have been contemplating the act, might even have had it on his mind while he poured himself that drink. But I don't believe he had the faintest idea there was anything in that bottle but good Scotch whisky.'

'Why?'

'Because what in the hell is the point? If Adrian was going to kill himself he'd damn well leave a note, and I wouldn't have put it past him to get the document notarized. Anything else would have been inconsistent with the man.'

I'd thought as much myself.

'I'm not saying he lacked a sense of the dramatic. He was a trial lawyer, after all. If we didn't like to be in the spotlight we'd spend our lives writing briefs in back rooms. I can imagine Adrian killing himself, and I can even see him doing it in front of witnesses. Remember Harmon Ruttenstein?'

'Vividly.'

'Invited some friends over, sat them down, gave them drinks, and told them he wanted them around so there wouldn't be any horseshit about what happened.

And then he took a header out the window. I'm committing suicide, he was saying, and I want you fellows here to attest to it. That's completely different from what they say Adrian did.'

'He made it look like murder.'

'Exactly, and why? That's the question nobody bothers to ask, maybe because nobody can answer it. Because there's a stigma attached to it? Adrian wasn't raised Catholic, and as far as I know the only thing he believed in absolutely was collecting fees in advance in criminal cases. Because he didn't want to invalidate his insurance policies? They keep floating that in the press and on television, as if suicide automatically had that effect.'

'I was talking about that the other day,' I said. 'It's a pretty common misconception.'

'And of course it doesn't apply, because Adrian's coverage consisted entirely of policies which had been in force for years. He hadn't applied for additional coverage since the doctor gave him the bad news. This all came out yesterday, but they're still prattling about insurance. I just heard a new wrinkle. Double indemnity.'

'For accidental death?'

'Right. As far as the insurance companies are concerned, murder is an accident. It qualifies in that respect if the policy contains a clause specifying a two-hundred-percent payout for accidental death. Stupid clause, incidentally. You're buying financial protection, what the hell's the difference if you fall out of the hay loft or flake away with terminal psoriasis? If anything, you'd think it should be the other way around. It's slow natural deaths that run up the costs for the family, so that's when they'd need extra protection.'

'I gather suicide's not considered accidental.'

'Well, you can't argue it's natural death, either, but it's excluded from double-indemnity coverage in every policy I ever heard of. So it's within the realm of possibility that a man would be sufficiently moved by consideration of his family's financial wellbeing to commit suicide in such a manner as to resemble accidental death.' He took a breath. 'Whew. Did you hear that? I sounded like a goddam lawyer.'

'You did at that.'

'But,' he went on, 'there's an easy way to do that, and it's done all the time, and not necessarily to defraud an insurance company. All you have to do is get in your car and drive into a bridge abutment. I don't know what the best guesses are as to percentages, but the conventional wisdom holds that a whole lot of unwitnessed single-car accidents are nothing but suicide, whether pre-planned or spontaneous. It's a foolproof method for killing yourself and being buried with the full rites of the Catholic church, and it would be just as effective in getting double payment from John Hancock and his friends.'

I thought of the earnest lady from the Hemlock Society. 'And for city dwellers who don't have cars —'

'There's always the subway. You lose your balance and fall in front of it. Here's the kicker, though. Say you're determined to make it look like murder. Unless your name is Ed Hoch or John Dickson Carr, you're not going to turn it into a fucking locked-room murder, are you? Because that's what this is. The security's so tight, between the bodyguards and the burglar alarm, nobody can figure out how the hell Will got in there to drop the poison in. It's so obviously impossible that half the city's convinced Adrian must have done it himself, which is just what he's supposed

114

to have attempted to conceal. Does that make any sense to you?'

'Wherever Adrian is now,' I said, 'if he needs an attorney, I think he ought to pick a guy named Gruliow.'

'I'm right, though, wouldn't you say? Makes no sense.'

'I agree.'

'Well, let me frost the cupcake for you. All his coverage was term insurance, and there wasn't a single policy with a double-indemnity clause. Case closed.'

He was convincing, but I wasn't entirely convinced. I'd seen too many people do too many illogical things to rule out any act by a human being on the grounds that it didn't make sense.

Meanwhile, there was still Will to be considered. Even if Adrian Whitfield had died by his own hand, you had to give Will an assist at the very least. One columnist argued, perhaps facetiously, that the anonymous killer was getting more powerful every time. He'd had to get out there and kill his first three victims all by himself, but all he'd had to do was point a finger at numbers four and five. Once targeted by Will, they were struck down with no effort on his part, Rashid by an enemy within his gates, Whitfield by an even more intimate enemy, the one who lived within his own skin.

'Pretty soon he won't even have to write letters,' Denis Hamill concluded. 'He'll just think his powerful thoughts in private, and the bad guys'll be dropping like flies.'

Funny, I thought, that we hadn't heard from him.

★

Tuesday morning I was up before Elaine, and I had breakfast on the table when she got out of the shower. 'Great cantaloupe,' she pronounced. 'Much better than yesterday.'

'It's the other half of the one we had yesterday,' I said.

'Oh,' she said. 'I guess it's the preparation.'

'I put it on a plate,' I said, 'and I set it in front of you.'

'Yes, that's just what you did, you old bear. And nobody could have done it better, either.'

'It's all in the wrist.'

'Must be.'

'Combined with a sort of Zen approach,' I said. 'I was concentrating on something else while I just let breakfast happen.'

'Concentrating on what?'

'On a dream I can't remember.'

'You hardly ever remember your dreams.'

'I know,' I said, 'but I woke up with the feeling that there was something this dream was trying to tell me, and it seemed to me it was a dream I'd had before. In fact –'

'Yes?'

'Well, I have the sense of having been dreaming this dream a lot lately.'

'The same dream.'

'I think so.'

'Which you can't remember.'

'It had a familiarity to it,' I said, 'as if I'd been there before. I don't know if it's the same dream each time, but I think I keep dreaming about the same person each time. He's right there, and he's looking very earnest and trying to tell me something, and I wake up and he's gone.'

'Like a puff of smoke.'

'Sort of.'

'Like your lap when you stand up.'

'Well . . .'

'Who is he?'

'That's the problem,' I said. 'I don't remember who he is, and no matter how much I *try* to remember –'

'Quit trying.'

'Huh?'

She rose, moved to stand behind me. She smoothed my hair back with the tips of her fingers. 'There's nothing to remember,' she said. 'Just ease up. So don't try to remember. Just answer the question. Who'd you dream about?'

'I don't know.'

'That's okay. Imagine Adrian Whitfield.'

'It wasn't Adrian Whitfield.'

'Of course it wasn't. Imagine him anyway.'

'All right.'

'Now imagine Vollman.'

'Who?'

'The one who killed those kids.'

'Vollmer.'

'Fine, Vollmer. Imagine him.'

'It wasn't –'

'I know it wasn't. Humor me, okay? Imagine him.'

'All right.'

'Now imagine Ray Gruliow.'

'I didn't dream about Ray,' I said, 'and this isn't going to work. I appreciate what you're trying to do –'

'I know you do.'

'But it's not going to work.'

'I know. Can I ask you a couple of questions?'

'I suppose so.'

'What's your name?'

'Matthew Scudder.'

'What's your wife's name?'

'Elaine Mardell. Elaine Mardell Scudder.'

'Do you love her?'

'Do you have to ask?'

'Just answer the question. Do you love her?'

'Yes.'

'Who'd you dream about?'

'Nice try, but it's not going to . . .'

'Yes?'

'I'll be a son of a bitch.'

'So? Are you going to tell me?'

'Pleased with yourself, aren't you?'

'Pleased beyond measure, and – now stop that!'

'I just want to touch it for a minute.'

'Say the name, will you? Before it slips your mind again.'

'It won't,' I said. 'Now why in the hell would I dream about him?'

'Fine, keep me in suspense.'

'Glenn Holtzmann,' I said. 'How did you do that?'

'Ve haff vays of making you remember.'

'So it would seem. Glenn Holtzmann. Why Glenn Holtzmann, for Christ's sake?'

I was no closer to the answer an hour later when I went downstairs for the papers. Then I forgot Glenn Holtzmann for the time being.

There had been another letter from Will.

NINE

'An Open Letter to the People of New York.'

That's how Will headed it. He had addressed and mailed it, like all the others, to Marty McGraw at the *Daily News,* and they were the ones with the story. They gave it the front page headline and led with it, under McGraw's byline. His column, 'Since You Asked . . .', ran as a sidebar, and the full text of Will's letter appeared on the page opposite. It was a long letter for Will, running to just under eight hundred words, which made it just about the same length as McGraw's column.

He started out by claiming credit (or assuming responsibility) for the murder of Adrian Whitfield. His tone was boastful; he talked at first about the elaborate security set up to protect Whitfield, the burglar alarm, the three shifts of bodyguards, the armor-plated limousine with the bulletproof glass. 'But no man can prevail against the Will of the People,' he proclaimed. 'No man can run from it. No man can hide from it. Consider Roswell Berry, who fled to Omaha. Consider Julian Rashid, behind his fortified walls in St Albans. The Will of the People can reach across vast space, it can slip through the stoutest defenses. No man can resist it.'

Whitfield, Will went on, was by no means the worst lawyer in the world. It had simply been his lot to serve as representative of an ineradicable evil in the legal profession, an apparent willingness to do anything, however abhorrent and immoral, in the service of a client. 'We nod in approval when an attorney defends the indefensible, and even tolerate behavior in a client's interest which would earn the lawyer a horsewhipping were he so to act on his own behalf.'

Then Will launched into an evaluation of the legal system, questioning the value of the jury system. There was nothing startlingly original about any of the points he raised, though he argued them reasonably enough so that you found yourself ready to forget you were reading the words of a serial murderer.

He ended on a personal note. 'I find I'm tired of killing. I am grateful to have been the instrument selected to perform these several acts of social surgery. But there is a heavy toll taken on him who is called upon to do evil in the service of a greater good. I'll rest now, until the day comes when I'm once again called to act.'

I had a question, and I made half a dozen phone calls trying to get an answer. Eventually I got around to calling the *News*. I gave my name to the woman who answered and said I'd like to talk to Marty McGraw. She took my number, and within ten minutes the phone rang.

'Marty McGraw,' he said. 'Matthew Scudder, you're the detective Whitfield hired, right? I think we might have met once.'

'Years ago.'

'Most of my life is years ago. What have you got for me?'

'A question. Did the letter run verbatim?'

'Absolutely. Why?'

'No cuts at all? Nothing held back at the cops' request?'

'Now how could I tell you that?' He sounded aggrieved. 'For all I know, you could be Will yourself.'

'You're absolutely right,' I said. 'On the other hand, if I were Will, I'd probably know whether or not you cut my copy.'

'Jesus,' he said, 'I'd hate to be the one to do something like that. I know how I get when that mutt at the big desk cuts *my* copy, and I'm not a homicidal maniac.'

'Well, neither am I. Look, here's what I'm getting at. As far as I can tell, there's nothing in the letter to disprove the suicide theory.'

'There's Will's word on the subject. He says he did it.'

'And he's never lied to us in the past.'

'As far as I know,' he said, 'he hasn't. With Roswell Berry in Omaha he refused to confirm or deny, but he was being cute.'

'He mentioned that Berry'd been stabbed, if I remember correctly.'

'That's right, and that was information the police had held back, so that certainly suggested he'd had a hand in it.'

'Well, is there anything like that in the latest letter? Because I couldn't spot it. That's why I wondered if anything had been cut.'

'No, we ran it verbatim. I wasn't kidding when I said I'd hate to be the one to cut his copy. I'm already getting more attention than I want from the guy.'

'I can see where it must have cost you a lot of readers.'

His laugh was like a terrier's bark. 'In that respect,' he admitted, 'it's a fucking godsend. My only regret is he didn't get this rolling before my recent contract negotiations. Same time, a person gets nervous being

Will's window on the world. I have to figure he's reading me three times a week. Suppose he doesn't like what I write? Last thing I want to do is piss off an original thinker like him.'

'An original thinker?'

'Case in point. While I'm saying the sentence, the phrase I've got in mind is "nut job". And the thought strikes me that maybe he's got my phone tapped and he'll resent me for casting aspersions on his state of mind. So I do a spot edit in mid-sentence, strike out "nut job" and pencil in "original thinker".'

'The journalistic mind at work.'

'But on second thought I don't really believe he has my phone tapped, and what does he care what I call him? Names will never hurt him. I'm not sure sticks and stones will, either. What makes you think he's lying about getting Whitfield?'

'The amount of time it took him to write. It's been a full week since Whitfield died.'

He was silent for a moment. Then he said, 'That's what proves it.'

'Proves what? That he did it? Because I don't see how.'

'We just got this,' he said, 'or it would have run along with the rest of the story. So I don't want to say anything over the phone because we'd like to be first with it tomorrow. You right here in the city? You know where the *News* is, don't you?'

'Thirty-third between Ninth and Tenth. But if you hadn't asked I might have gone to the old place on East Forty-second. That's still the first thing that comes to mind when I think of the *News*.'

'What's the zip code?'

'The zip code? You want me to write to you?'

'No, not particularly. Look, you haven't got anything against tits, have you? There's a joint called Bunny's Topless on Ninth and Thirty-second that's quieter than a sulky Trappist this time of day. Why don't you meet me there in half an hour?'

'All right.'

'You won't have any trouble recognizing me,' he said. 'I'll be the guy with a shirt on.'

I don't know what Bunny's Topless is like at night. It would almost have to be livelier, with more young women displaying their breasts and more men staring at them. And it's probably sad at any hour, deeply sad in the manner of most emporia that cater to our less noble instincts. Gambling casinos are sad in that way, and the glitzier they are the more palpable is their sadness. The air has an ozone-tainted reek of base dreams and broken promises.

Early in the day, the place made no sense at all. It was a cave of a room, the door and windows painted matte black, the room within not so much decorated as thrown together, its furnishing a mix of what the previous owner had left and what had come cheap at auction. Two men occupied stools at either end of the bar, dividing their attention between the TV set (CNN with the sound off) and the bartender, whose breasts (medium size, with a slight droop) looked a good deal more authentic than her bright red hair.

There was a little stage, and they probably had dancers at night, but the stage was empty now and a Golden Oldies station on the radio provided the music. A waitress, clad like the bartender in cottontailed hot pants and rabbit ears and high heels and nothing else, worked the booths and tables. Maybe things would pick up some at lunchtime, but for now she had two men each at a pair of tables in front and one man all by himself in a corner booth.

The loner was Marty McGraw, and anybody would have recognized him. A little photo of him, head cocked and lip curled, ran three times a week with his column. There was gray in his hair that didn't show in the photo, but I knew about that for having seen him so many times on television since the Will story first broke. Aside from that, the years hadn't changed him much. If anything, time had treated him as a caricaturist would have done, accenting what was already there, making the eyebrows a little more prominent, pushing out the jaw.

He'd shucked his suit jacket and loosened his tie, and he had one hand wrapped around the base of a glass of beer. There was an empty rocks glass next to the beer glass, and the raw smell of cheap blended whisky rose straight to my nostrils.

'Scudder,' he said. 'McGraw. And this little darling' – he waved to summon the waitress – 'assures me her name is Darlene. She's never lied to me in the past, have you, sweetie?'

She smiled. I had the feeling she was called upon to do that a lot. She had dark hair, cut short, and full breasts.

'The bartender's name is Stacey,' he went on, 'but she'd probably answer to Spacey. You don't want to ask her to do anything terribly complicated. Order a pousse-café and you're taking your life in your hands. A shot and a beer's a safe choice here, and you want to make the shot some cheap blend, because that's what you're gonna get anyway, no matter what it says on the bottle.'

I said I'd have a Coke.

'Well, that's safe,' he said, 'if not terribly adventurous. Another of the same for me, Darlene. And don't ever change, understand?'

She walked off and he said, 'The zip code's one-oh-oh-oh-one, or should I say one-zero-zero-zero-one? You notice how they been doing that lately?'

'Doing what?'

'Saying zero. You give a credit card number over the phone, say "oh" for "zero", and they'll replace all your ohs with zeroes when they read it back to you for confirmation. You know what I think it is? Computers. You copy down a number by hand, what's it matter whether you make an oh or a zero on the page? They both look the same. But when it's keystrokes, you're hitting different keys. So they have to make sure.'

Our drinks came. He picked up the shot and tossed it off, took a small sip of the beer. 'Anyway, that's my theory, take it or leave it, and it's got nothing to do with Will's letter, anyway. He got the zip code wrong.'

'He put an oh for a zero?'

'No, no, no. He wrote down the wrong number entirely. The right address, 450 West Thirty-third Street, but for some goddam reason he put one-oh-oh-*one*-one instead of one-oh-oh-*oh*-one. One-oh-oh-eleven's the zip for Chelsea and part of the West Village.'

'I see,' I said, but I didn't. 'But what difference does it make? He did get the street number right, and you're the New York *Daily News*, for God's sake. You shouldn't be that hard to find.'

'You would think that,' he said, 'and I take back what I said before, because it's all of a piece with people saying zero instead of oh, and having to get the keystrokes right. It's fucking technology getting in everybody's face is what it is.'

I waited for him to explain.

'It delayed the letter,' he said, 'if you can believe it. I'd hate to guess how many pieces of mail a day get sent to the *News*, most of them written in crayon. So you'd think the dorks who sort the mail could figure out where we were, especially since it's no more than a long five-iron shot from the main post office. But all you have to do is put a one where an oh ought to be, pardon me all to hell, I mean a zero, and they're lost. They're fucking stymied.'

'There must have been a postmark,' I said.

'More than one,' he said. 'There was the original one, when it went through the machine at the intake station before it got shipped uptown to the Old Chelsea station on West Eighteenth, which is where they ship the mail for delivery to the one-oh-oh-one-one zips. Then it went out in somebody's route bag and came back again, and then it picked up a second postmark when they bounced it from Old Chelsea to the Farley building on Eighth Avenue, which is where the one-oh-oh-*oh*-one mail gets delivered out of. The second one was handwritten, which probably makes it a collector's item in this day and age, but what you're interested in, what anybody'd be interested in, is the first postmark.'

'Yes.'

He knocked back his glass of beer. 'I wish I had it to show it to you,' he said, 'but of course the cops took it. It tells you two things, the zip for the intake station and the date it went through the stamping machine. The zip was one-oh-oh-thirty-eight, indicating the station was Peck Slip.'

'And the date?'

'Same night Whitfield was killed.'

'What time?'

126

He shook his head. 'Just the date. Which escapes me at the moment, but it was that night, the night he died.'

'Thursday night.'

'Was it a Thursday? Yeah, of course it was, and we were on the street with it Friday morning.'

'But the postmark was Thursday.'

'Isn't that what I just said?'

'I just want to make sure I've got this right,' I said. 'It went through the stamping machine before midnight, and as a result it had Thursday's date on it and not Friday's.'

'You've got it right.' He pointed to my glass. 'What's that, Coca-Cola? You want a refill?' I shook my head. 'Well, I damn well do,' he said, and got Darlene's attention and signaled for another round.

I said, 'Whitfield died around eleven that night, and the first news flash was on New York One just before midnight. Unless I'm missing something, the letter went in the mail before Whitfield was dead.'

'Probably true.'

'Just probably?'

'Well, you're assuming the Post Office did everything right,' he said, 'and you already know how long it took them to deliver the fucking letter, so why should they be letter-perfect in any other area of operations? Meaning it's entirely possible somebody neglected to advance the date on the postmark at the stroke of midnight. But I'd certainly say it's odds-on that Adrian Whitfield still had a pulse when Will mailed the letter.'

'Peck Slip,' I said. 'That's down by the Fulton Fish Market, isn't it?'

'That's right. But the post office serves the whole three-eight zip code, and that includes a big chunk of downtown. One Police Plaza, City Hall –'

'And the Criminal Courts Building,' I said. 'He

could have been in court that afternoon, watching while Adrian entered a guilty plea for Irwin Atkins. He's already poisoned the whisky and written the letter, and now he drops it in the mail. Why doesn't he wait?'

'We already know he's cocky.'

'But not half-cocked. He's mailing the letter before his victim's dead. Suppose Adrian goes out and drinks a bottle of wine with dinner and doesn't want to mix the grape and the grain when he gets home? Suppose Adrian's still alive and kicking when Will's letter turns up on your desk? Then what?'

'Then I call the cops and they run over to Whitfield's apartment and grab the Scotch bottle before he can take a drink from it.'

'Does he ever say anything about the Scotch?' I'd clipped the piece from the *News* and I got it out now and scanned it. Our own drinks had come by this time, with Darlene setting them down and removing their predecessors without interrupting us. She didn't have to collect any money. Joints like that used to make you pay when they served you, but that was back before everyone paid for everything with a credit card. Now they run a tab, just like everybody else. 'There's a reference to poison,' I said, 'and he talks about the security set-up at Whitfield's apartment. He doesn't specifically say the poison's in the whisky.'

'Still, once he mentions poison and talks about the Park Avenue apartment –'

'They'd search everything until they found cyanide in the Scotch.'

'And Will winds up looking like a horse's ass.'

'So why take the chance? What's the big hurry that he has to get the letter in the mail?'

'Maybe he's leaving town.'

'Leaving town?'

'Take another look at the clipping,' he suggested. 'He's announcing his retirement. There won't be any more killing because he's done. He's saying goodbye. Isn't that what a fellow might do on his way to catch a slow boat to China?'

I thought about it.

'Matter of fact,' McGraw said, 'why else announce his retirement? He's got enough news for one letter, claiming credit for Whitfield. He could save the rest for another time. But not if he's pulling up stakes and relocating in Dallas or Dublin or, I don't know, Dakar? If he had a plane to catch, that'd be a good reason to put all the news in one letter and send it off right away.'

'And if it gets there before Whitfield takes the drink, then what?'

'Given that the son of a bitch is nuts,' he said, 'I'd be hard put to say just what he'd do, but I suppose he'd deal with it one way or the other. Either he'd come back and figure out some other way to get the job done or he'd decide fate had let Adrian off the hook. And maybe he'd write me one more letter about it and maybe he wouldn't.' He reached to tap the newspaper clipping. 'What I think,' he said, 'is there's no question in his mind that Whitfield's gonna go straight home and swallow the Scotch. You read what he wrote, he's talking about a *fait accompli*. Far as he's concerned, it's a done deal. Whitfield's already dead. If there's a word or phrase in his letter that suggests for a moment that the outcome's still up in the air, I sure as hell missed it.'

'No, you're right,' I said. 'He writes about it as though it already happened. But we're sure it didn't?'

'It's possible Whitfield was dead before this letter picked up its postmark. Barely possible. But the letter probably got dropped in a mailbox, and in order for it to get picked up and trucked to the Peck Slip post office and go through the machine that stamped it with a postmark —'

I scanned the clipping one more time. 'What I asked you over the phone,' I said, 'was whether there was anything in the letter that absolutely ruled out the possibility of suicide.'

'That's why I suggested a meeting. That's why we're sitting here. The letter doesn't rule out suicide, except for the fact that Will says he did it, and he's never lied to us in the past. But the postmark rules it out.'

'Because it was mailed before the death happened.'

'You got it. He might have decided to claim credit for Whitfield's suicide. But, good as he is, he couldn't read Whitfield's mind and know ahead of time that he was going to kill himself.'

TEN

It took me a while to get away from Marty McGraw. He looked around for the waitress, but she must have been on her break. He shrugged and walked over to the bar and came back with two bottles of Rolling Rock, announcing that he'd had enough whisky for the time being. He drank from one of the bottles, then pointed at the other. 'That's for you if you want it,' he said. I told him I'd pass, and he said he'd figured as much.

'I've been there,' he said.

'How's that?'

'Been there, done that. The rooms. The church basements. I went to a meeting every day for four months and didn't touch a drop all that time. It's a long fucking time to go without a drink, I'll tell you that much.'

'I guess it is.'

'I was having a bad time of it,' he said, 'and I thought it was the booze. So I cut out the booze and you know something? That made it worse.'

'Sometimes it works that way.'

'So I straightened out some things in my life,' he said, 'and then I picked up a drink, and guess what? Everything's fine.'

'That's great,' I said.

He narrowed his eyes. 'Sanctimonious prick,' he said. 'You got no right to patronize me.'

'You're absolutely right, Marty. My apologies.'

'Fuck you and your apology. Fuck you and the apology you rode in on, or should that be the

131

Appaloosa you rode in on? Sit down, for Christ's sake. Where the hell do you think you're going?'

'Catch some air.'

'The air's not going any place, you don't have to be in a rush to catch it. Jesus, don't tell me I insulted you.'

'I've got a busy day,' I said. 'That's all.'

'Busy day my ass. I'm a little drunk and it makes you uncomfortable. Admit it.'

'I admit it.'

'Well,' he said, and frowned, as if the admission was the last thing he'd expected from me. 'That case I apologize. That all right?'

'Of course.'

'You accept my apology?'

'You don't need to apologize,' I said, 'but yes, of course I accept it.'

'So we're okay then, you and me.'

'Absolutely.'

'You know what I wish? I wish you'd drink a fucking beer.'

'Not today, Marty.'

'"Not today." Listen, I know the jargon, all right? "Not today." You just do it a day at a time, don't you?'

'Like everything else.'

He frowned. 'I don't mean to bait you. It's the booze talking, you know that.'

'Yes.'

'It's not me wants you to drink, it's the drink wants you to drink. You know what I'm saying?'

'Sure.'

'What I found out, I learned it helps me more than it hurts me. It does more for me than it does to me. You know who else said that? Winston Churchill. A great man, wouldn't you say?'

'I'd say so, yes.'

'Fucking Limey drunk. No friend to the Irish either, the son of a bitch. More for me than to me, he was right about that though, you got to give him that much. I got the story of the year, you realize that?'

'I guess you do.'

'The story of the year. Locally, I mean. Overall scheme of things, what's Will in comparison to Bosnia, huh? You want to weigh 'em in the balance, Will's lighter than air. But who do you know that gives two shits about Bosnia? Will you tell me that? The only way Bosnia sells a newspaper's if you can manage to get "rape" in the headline.' He picked up the second bottle of Rolling Rock and took a sip. 'The story of the year,' he said.

After I finally got away from him, what I probably should have done was go to a meeting. When I first got sober I had found it unsettling to be around people who were drinking, but as I grew more comfortable with my own sobriety I gradually became less uneasy in the presence of drink. Many of my friends these days are sober, but quite a few are not, and some like Mick Ballou and Danny Boy Bell are heavy daily drinkers. Their drinking never seems to bother me. Now and then Mick and I make a night of it, sitting up until dawn in his saloon at Fiftieth and Tenth, sharing stories and silences. Never on those occasions do I find myself wishing that I were drinking, or that he were not.

But Marty McGraw was the kind of edgy drunk who made me uncomfortable. I can't say I wanted a drink by the time I got out of there, but neither did I much want to go on feeling the way I felt, as if I'd been up for days and had drunk far too much coffee.

I stopped at a diner for a hamburger and a piece of pie, then just started walking without paying too much attention to where I was headed. My mind was playing with what I'd learned about Will's letter and when it had been mailed, and I worried this piece of information like a dog with a bone; running it through my mind, then thinking of something else, then coming back to it and turning the thoughts this way and that, as if they were pieces of a jigsaw puzzle and I could fit them into place if I just held them at the right angle.

I was headed uptown when I started, and I suppose if I'd picked up a tailwind I might have walked clear to the Cloisters. But I didn't get that far. When I came out of my reverie I was only a block from my apartment. But it was a long block, a crosstown block, and it put me at a location that was significant in and of itself. I was at the northwest corner of Tenth Avenue and Fifty-seventh Street, standing directly in front of Jimmy Armstrong's saloon.

Why? It wasn't because I wanted a drink, was it? Because I certainly didn't think I wanted a drink, nor did I feel as though I wanted a drink. There is, to be sure, a part of me deep within my being that will always thirst for the ignorant bliss that is alcohol's promise. Some of us call that part of ourselves 'the disease', and tend to personify it. 'My disease is talking to me,' you'll hear them say at meetings. 'My disease wants me to drink. My disease is trying to destroy me.' Alcoholism, I once heard a woman explain, is like a monster sleeping inside you. Sometimes the monster begins to stir, and that's why we have to go to meetings. The meetings bore the monster and it dozes off again.

Still, I couldn't attribute my presence in front of Armstrong's to a talkative disease or a restless monster. As far as I knew, I'd never had a drink of anything stronger than cranberry juice on the northwest corner of Fifty-seventh and Tenth. I had stopped drinking by the time Jimmy moved from his original Ninth Avenue location. There had been other ginmills at Tenth and Fifty-seventh before his, including one I could remember called The Falling Rock. (It got the name when a neighborhood guy bought it and started remodeling the facade. While he was working on a ladder, a chunk of stone flaked off and fell, conking him on the head and almost knocking him cold. He figured it would be good luck to name the joint after the incident, but the luck didn't hold; a little while later he did something that irritated a couple of the Westies, and they hit him harder and more permanently than the rock had. The next owner changed the name to something else.)

I didn't want a drink, and I wasn't hungry, either. I shrugged it off and turned around, looking across the intersection at what I suppose I'll always think of as Lisa Holtzmann's building. Was that what I wanted? An hour or so with the Widow Holtzmann, sweeter than whisky and easier on the liver, and almost as certain a source of temporary oblivion?

No longer an option. Lisa, when I last spoke to her, had told me that she was seeing someone, that it looked serious, that she thought the relationship might have a future. I'd been surprised to discover that the news came as less of a blow than a relief. We agreed that we'd stay away from each other and give her new romance a chance to flower.

For all I knew it had gone to seed by now. The new man was by no means the first she'd dated since her husband's death. She'd grown up with a father who came to her bed at night, thrilling and disturbing her at once, always stopping short of intercourse because 'it wouldn't be right,' and she would be a while working her way out of the residue of those years. I didn't need a shrink to tell me that I was a component of that

135

process. It was not always clear, though, whether I was part of the problem or part of the solution.

In any case, Lisa's relationships did not tend to last, and there was no reason to believe the latest was still viable. I could without difficulty imagine her sitting by the phone now, wishing it would ring, hoping it would be me on the other end of it. I could make the call and find out if what I imagined was true. It was easy enough to check. I had a quarter handy, and I didn't need to look up the number.

I didn't make the call. Elaine has made it clear that she does not expect me to be strictly faithful. Her own professional experience has led her to believe that men are not monogamous by nature, and that extracurricular activity need not be either a cause or a symptom of marital disharmony.

For now, though, I chose not to exercise that freedom. Now and then I felt the urge, even as once in a while I felt the desire for a drink. There is, I have been taught, all the difference in the world between the desire and the act. The one is written on water, the other carved in stone.

Glenn Holtzmann.

Unaccountably pleased with myself for having resisted the slenderest of temptations, I marched east on Fifty-seventh and got almost to the corner of Ninth Avenue before the penny dropped. I had been dreaming a dream which I was somehow certain had some bearing on Adrian Whitfield's murder, and Elaine had somehow managed to coax and tease the subject of that dream out of some dark corner of my mind. It was Glenn Holtzmann I'd dreamed about, and I'd stood staring at the building he'd lived in without making the connection.

Glenn Holtzmann. Why was he disturbing my sleep, and what could he possibly be trying to tell me? I'd hardly had time to consider the point when Will's latest letter drove the question clear out of my mind.

I stopped at the Morning Star and sat at a window table with a cup of coffee. I took a sip and remembered one of the few meetings I'd had with Holtzmann. I'd been sitting in that very window, and perhaps at that very table, when he'd tapped on the glass to get my attention, then came inside and shared my table for a few minutes.

He'd wanted to be friends. Elaine and I had spent one evening with him and Lisa, and I hadn't liked him much. There was something off-putting about him, though I'd have had trouble defining it. I couldn't recall everything he'd said that time at the Morning Star, although it seemed to me that was when he'd informed me that Lisa had had a miscarriage. I'd felt sympathy for him then, but it hadn't made me want his friendship.

Not too long after that he was dead. Shot down on Eleventh Avenue while making a call from a pay phone. That had been a case of mine, and in its course, oddly enough, I'd found myself working for the brother of the chief suspect and the widow of the victim. I don't know how well I served either client, but by the time it was over I'd learned who killed Glenn Holtzmann. (It turned out he'd been killed by mistake, in what Elaine characterized as a perfect postmodern homicide. I'm not sure what she meant.)

Glenn Holtzmann, Glenn Holtzmann. He was a lawyer, in-house counsel for a publisher of large-print books. He'd floated the idea of my writing a book based on my experiences, but I'd been no more likely to write such a book than his firm would have been to

137

publish it. He'd been on a fishing expedition, perhaps in the hope that I'd drop some kernel of information that might prove profitable for him.

Because, as I was to learn, information meant profit to Holtzmann. He'd supplemented his income nicely as a bearer of tales, getting his start when he ratted out his uncle to the IRS. It was a profitable enterprise, if high in risk and low in prestige, and when he died on the sidewalk on Eleventh Avenue he left behind a two-bedroom high-rise apartment to which he had clear title and a metal strongbox in which he'd stowed something like $300,000 in cash.

Why the hell was I dreaming about him? I let the waiter refill my coffee cup, stirred it, stared out the window at my own apartment building, and tried to free-associate. Glenn Holtzmann. Lawyer. Publisher. Large-print. Failing vision. White cane, tap tap tap . . .

Glenn Holtzmann. Blackmail. Except it wasn't blackmail, not so far as I knew. He wasn't a black-mailer, he was an informer, a paid informer . . .

Glenn Holtzmann. Lisa. Legs, tits, ass. Stop it.

Glenn Holtzmann. Closet. Strongbox. Money. Too much money.

I sat up straight.

Too much money.

The phrase rang like a bell. Glenn Holtzmann had had too much money, and that was what had made his death look like something other than the act of random violence it appeared to be. It was the money that led his wife to call me, and it was the money that started me looking beneath the ordinary surface of his life for something that might explain his death.

I closed my eyes and tried to conjure up his face. I couldn't bring the image into focus.

Too much money. What the hell did that have to do

with Will? How could there be a money motive behind the murders? How, really, could there be any kind of motive for the killings, behind the particular mania which led the man to perceive himself as a righter of social wrongs?

Did anybody benefit from the deaths, singly or collectively? I considered the victims in turn. Richie Vollmer's death was good news for whatever children he would have otherwise gone on to kill, but they couldn't know who they were. It was, I suppose good news as well for all the rest of us, who were spared having to go on sharing a planet with Richie. But nobody made a dime out of his death, except the people with newspapers to sell. Richie died with nothing to leave and nobody to leave it to.

Patsy Salerno? Well, if you took a prominent mob guy off the board, it had to be good news to whoever wound up in his shoes. This particular fact of economic life had led the boys to kill each other right and left over the years, and it still applied even when someone else did the killing. But Patsy hadn't been on anybody else's list before he wound up on Will's, and when did his kind of people ever try to make their all-in-the-family hits look like somebody else's doing? For God's sake, they all but signed their work.

I didn't do any better with the rest of Will's list. I was willing to believe that somebody was making a dollar or two out of the anti-abortion movement, even as I supposed somebody had to be turning a buck on the other side, but I couldn't see a big financial payoff in wrapping a coathanger around Roswell Berry's neck. Somebody was richer for Julian Rashid's death, though I didn't know who or how much, but that particular case was cleared and Will hadn't done the killing, although he'd have gotten around to it if Scipio hadn't beaten him to the punch.

And Adrian Whitfield? No, and I was back to square one. Money's at the root of a lot of evil, but by no means all of it. Will, whoever he might be, wasn't getting rich off his actions. He wasn't even covering expenses – which, while not too considerable, had to include airfare to and from Kansas City, along with whatever he'd had to lay out for rope and wire and cyanide. (I figured the coathanger couldn't have cost him much.)

Once they caught him, one or more true-crime writers would publish books on the case, and just how fat they'd get on it would depend on how sensational the material was and how strong a hold Will still had on the public imagination. Until then, a lot of print and broadcast journalists were earning their salaries with Will's help, but without him they'd bring home the same money reporting on somebody else's misdeeds. Marty McGraw was on the top of the heap, glorying in his role in a story that was bigger than Bosnia, but his pay envelope hadn't gotten any thicker since Will went to work, and maybe he didn't care. All those moves from paper to paper had boosted his salary way up there already, and how much money did he need? You couldn't spend that much on blended whisky, even if the girls who brought it to you didn't have shirts on.

Too much money. That struck me as the ultimate irrelevance, because Will looked to be a pure idealist, however misguided. It was frustrating – I'd managed to remember who it was I'd dreamed about, and I'd ferreted out the message the dream had for me, and it didn't mean anything.

Well, why should it? A friend of Elaine's had attended a séance, in the course of which a dead uncle of hers had counseled her to buy a particular over-the-counter computer stock. She'd risked a couple of thousand dollars, whereupon the stock plummeted.

Elaine had not been surprised. 'I'm not saying it wasn't her Uncle Manny that spoke to her,' she said, 'but when he was alive nobody ever called him the Wizard of Wall Street. He was a furrier, so why should he suddenly be a financial genius now that he's dead? Where is it written that death raises your IQ?'

Same goes for dreaming. Just because the subconscious mind sends a cryptic message doesn't mean it knows what it's talking about.

Too much money. Maybe Glenn Holtzmann was talking to me, maybe he thought I should spread the wealth around. Well, a word to the wise and all that. I paid for my coffee, and left the waitress twice as much as usual. Matt Scudder, last of the big spenders.

After dinner that night I watched a little television with Elaine. There were a couple of cop shows on back to back, and I kept finding fault with their investigative procedure. Elaine had to remind me that it was only TV.

After the news at eleven I stood up and stretched. 'I think I'll go out for a while,' I said.

'Give Mick my love.'

'How do you know I'm not going to the midnight meeting?'

'How do you know you won't run into him there?'

'Do Jewish girls always answer a question with a question?'

'Is there something wrong with that?'

I walked south and west to Grogan's Open House, a Hell's Kitchen bar stubbornly holding its own in the face of neighborhood gentrification. Now and then a salesman will walk in and ask to speak to Grogan, which is a little like asking for Mr Stone at the Blarney Stone. 'There's no such person,' I heard the day barman tell one such visitor. 'And for all that, he's not in at the moment.'

Grogan's is the home turf of one Michael Ballou, although you won't find his name on the license or the deed. His criminal record would preclude his owning premises where liquor is sold, but Mick has extended the principle of non-ownership to all areas of his life. Another man's name appears on the ownership papers for his car, and the deed to his farm in Sullivan County. What a man takes care not to own, I have heard him say, they cannot take away from him.

We met some years ago when I walked into Grogan's and asked him some questions, feeling a little like Daniel in the lion's den. That was the start of our unlikely friendship, and it has broadened and deepened over time. We are two men of very different backgrounds leading vastly different lives, and I have ceased to grope for an explanation of the satisfaction we find in each other's company. He is a killer and a career criminal, and he is my friend, and you can make what you will of that. I don't know what to make of it myself.

Sometimes we make a long night of it, sitting up past closing with the door locked and all but one of the lights out, sharing stories and silences until dawn. Sometimes he'll finish up at the early Mass at St Bernard's on West Fourteenth Street, the Butchers' Mass, where he'll wear his late father's stained white apron and match the meatcutters who come there before they start work in the market down the street. Now and then I've stayed the course and gone with him, kneeling when they kneel, rising when they rise.

Male bonding, I guess they call it. Guy stuff, according to Elaine.

This was an early night, and I was out of there and on my way home well before closing. I don't remember too much of what we talked about, but it seems to me the conversation rambled all over the place. I know we talked about dreams, and he recalled a dream that had saved his life, alerting him to a danger of which he'd been unaware.

I said I supposed a dream was when you knew something on an unconscious level, and it came bubbling up to your consciousness. Sometimes it was that, he agreed, and sometimes it was one of God's angels whispering in your ear. I was not certain whether he was speaking metaphorically. He is a singular mix of brutal practicality and Celtic mysticism. His mother once told him he had the second sight, and he accordingly places more faith in feelings and hunches than you might expect.

I must have told him how I'd found myself standing in front of Armstrong's, because he talked some about the owner of The Falling Rock, and who'd killed him and why. We talked about other neighborhood homicides over the years, most of them old cases, with the killers themselves long since gone to the same hell or heaven as their victims. Mick remembered a whole string of men killed for no real reason at all, because someone was drunk and took a remark the wrong way.

'I wonder,' he said, 'if your man's grown to like the work.'

'My man?'

'Himself, that's killing men and writing letters to the newspaper about it. The People's Will, and do you suppose William's his true name?'

'No idea.'

'That might add to the fun,' he said, 'or not, as the case may be. He's full of himself, isn't he? Killing and claiming credit like a fucking terrorist.'

'It's like that,' I said. 'Like terrorism.'

'They all start with a cause,' he said, 'and it's noble or it's not, and along the way it fades and grows dim. For they fall in love with what they're doing, and why they're after doing it scarcely matters.' He looked off into the distance. 'It's a terrible thing,' he said, 'when a man develops a taste for killing.'

'You have a taste for it.'

'I have found joy in it,' he allowed. 'It's like drink, you know. It stirs the blood and quickens the heart. Before you know it you're dancing.'

'That's an interesting way to put it.'

'I have schooled myself,' he said deliberately, 'not to take life without good reason.'

'Will has his reasons.'

'He had them at the start. By now he may be caught up in the dance.'

'He says he's through.'

'Does he.'

'You don't believe him?'

He thought about it. 'I can't say,' he said at length, 'for not knowing him, or what drives him.'

'Maybe he's worked his way to the end of his list.'

'Or he's tired of the game. The work takes its toll. But if he's got a taste for it . . .'

'He may not be able to quit.'

'Ah,' he said. 'We'll see, won't we?'

I spent the rest of the week and most of the next one just getting through the days and enjoying the fall season. One offer of work came in, a negligence lawyer who needed someone to chase down witnesses to an accident, but I passed on it, pleading a heavy caseload. I didn't have a heavy caseload, I didn't have any kind of a caseload at all, and for the time being I wanted to keep it that way.

I read the paper every morning and went to a noon meeting every day, and an evening meeting too, more often than not. My attendance at AA wanes and waxes with the tides in my life. I go less often when I'm busier with other things, and seem to add meetings automatically in response to the prompting of stress, which I may or may not consciously feel.

Something evidently had me wanting to go to more meetings, and I didn't argue with it. The thought did come to me that I'd been sober for too many years to need so many meetings, and I told the thought to go to hell. The fucking disease almost killed me, and the last thing I ever want to do is give it another chance.

When I wasn't at a meeting I was walking around town, or at a concert or a museum with Elaine, or sitting in the park or in a coffee shop with TJ. I spent a certain amount of time thinking about Will and the people he'd killed, but there was nothing in the news to add fresh fuel to that particular fire, so it burned less brightly with every passing day. The tabloids did what they could to keep the story prominent, but there was only so much they could do, and yet another indiscretion in the British royal family helped nudge Will off the front page.

One afternoon I went into a church. Years ago, when I turned in my shield and left my wife and kids, I found myself dropping into churches all the time, though almost never when there was a service going on. I guess I found some measure of peace there. If nothing else I found silence, often an elusive commodity in New York. I got in the habit of lighting candles for people who'd died, and once you start that you're stuck, because it's a growth industry. People keep dying.

I got in another habit, too. I began tithing, giving a tenth of whatever money came my way to whatever poor box I saw next. I was ecumenical about it, but the Catholics got most of my trade because they worked longer hours. Their churches were more apt to be open when I was looking for a beneficiary for my largesse.

I've thought about it, and I can't say for sure what the tithing was all about. During those years I didn't keep records or pay taxes, or even file a return, so it's possible I thought of my tithe as a voluntary tax. It couldn't have amounted to very much, anyway, because I went long stretches without working, and when I worked I never made a great deal of money. My rent always got paid on time and my tab at Armstrong's got settled sooner or later, and when I could manage it I sent money to Anita and the boys. But the sums involved were small, and you wouldn't see any priests riding around in Lincolns on ten percent of my gross.

When I got sober I began spending my time not in the sanctuaries of churches but in their basements, where my contribution when they passed the basket was limited by tradition to a dollar. I rarely lit a candle, and I stopped tithing altogether, though I could no more tell you why than I could explain having begun the practice in the first place.

'You cleared up a little,' my sponsor suggested, 'and you realized you had more use for the money than the church did.'

I don't know that that's it. For a while I gave away a lot of money on the street, in essence tithing to the homeless population of New York. (Maybe I was just

146

cutting out the middleman, making a collective poor box of all those empty coffee cups and outstretched hands.) That habit, too, ran its course, perhaps because I was daunted by the ever-increasing profusion of cups and hands. Compassion fatigue set in. Unable to stuff a dollar bill into every beseeching cup or hand, I stopped it altogether; like most of my fellow New Yorkers, I got so I didn't even notice them anymore.

Things change. Sober, I found I had to do many of the chickenshit things that everybody else has to do. I had to keep records, had to pay taxes. For years I charged clients arbitrary flat fees and saved myself the aggravation of itemizing my expenses, but you can't work that way for attorneys, and now that I have a PI license much of my work comes from attorneys. I still work the old way for clients who are as casual as I am, but more often than not I save receipts and keep track of my expenses, just like everybody else.

And Elaine and I give away a tenth of our income. Mine comes from detective work, of course, and hers is primarily from her real estate investments, although her shop is beginning to turn a small profit. She keeps the books – thank God – and writes the checks, and our few dollars find their way to the dozen or so charities and cultural institutions on our list. It is, to be sure, a more regimented way of doing things. I feel more like a solid citizen and less like a free spirit, and I do not always prefer it this way. But neither do I spend much time chafing at the collar.

The church I went into on this occasion was on a side street in the West Forties. I didn't notice the name of it, and couldn't tell you if I'd ever dropped in there before.

I was lucky to find it open. While my own use of churches has diminished in recent years, so too has their accessibility. It seems to me that the Catholic churches, at least, used to be open the whole day long, from early in the morning until well into the evening. Now their sanctuaries are often locked up between services. I suppose that's a response to crime or homelessness or both. I suppose an unlocked church is an invitation, not only to the occasional citizen looking for a moment's peace, but to all of those who'd curl up and nap in the pews or steal the candlesticks from the altar.

This church was open and seemingly unattended, and it was a throwback in another way as well. The candles at the little side altars were real ones, actual wax candles that burned with an open flame. Lots of churches have switched over to electrified altars. You drop your quarter in the slot and a flame-shaped bulb goes on and stays on for your quarter's worth of time. It's like a parking meter, and if you stay too long they tow away your soul.

It's not my church, so I can't see that I've got any rights in the matter, but when did that sort of logic ever keep an alcoholic from nursing a resentment? I'm sure the electric candles are cost-efficient, and I don't imagine they're any harder for God to overlook than the real thing. And maybe I'm just a spiritual Luddite, hating change for its own sake, resisting an improvement in the candle-lighting dodge even as I resisted TJ's arguments for a computer. If I'd been alive at the time, I probably would have been every bit as pissed off when they switched from oil lamps to candles. 'Nothing's the same anymore,' you'd have heard me grumbling. 'What kind of results can you expect from melting wax?'

I wouldn't have wasted a quarter on an electric flame. But this church had the real thing, with three or four little candles lit. I looked at them, and my mind summoned up an image of Adrian Whitfield. I couldn't think what good it could do him to burn a candle on his behalf, but I found myself recalling Elaine's words. What could it hoit? So I slipped a dollar bill in the slot, lit one candle from the flame of another, and let myself think about the man.

I got a funny montage of images.

First I was seeing Adrian Whitfield at his apartment a few hours after he'd learned about Will's letter. He was pouring a drink even as he proclaimed himself a non-drinker, then explaining, talking about the drinks he'd had already that day.

Then I saw him sprawled on the carpet with Kevin Dahlgren hunkered down beside him, picking up the glass he'd dropped, sniffing at it. I hadn't been there to see it, had only heard Dahlgren's account of the moment, but the image came to me as clearly as if I'd witnessed it myself. I could even smell what Dahlgren had smelled, the odor of bitter almonds superimposed upon the aroma of good malt whisky. I'd never smelled that combination in my life, but my imagination was inventive enough to furnish it quite vividly.

The next flash I got was of Marty McGraw. He was sitting in the topless joint where I'd met him, a shot glass clutched in one hand, a beer glass in the other. There was a belligerent expression on his face, and he was saying something but I couldn't make it out. The reek of cheap whisky trailed up at me from the shot glass, the reek of stale beer from the other, and the two were united on his breath.

Adrian again, talking into a telephone. 'I'm going to let the genie out,' he said. 'First one today.'

Mick Ballou at Grogan's, on our most recent night together. It was what he thought of as a sober night, in that he was passing up the whisky and staying with beer. The beer in this instance was Guinness, and I could see his big fist wrapped around a pint of the black stuff. The smell of it came to me, dark and rich and grainy.

I got all of this in a rush, one image after another, and each overlaid heavily with scents, singly or in combination. Smell, they say, is the oldest and most primal sense, the sure trigger for memory. It bypasses the thought process and goes straight to the most primitive part of the brain. It doesn't pass Go, it doesn't collect its thoughts.

I stood there, letting it all come at me, taking in what I could of it. I don't want to make too much of this. I was not Saul of Tarsus, knocked off his horse en route to Damascus, nor was I AA's founder wrapped up in his famous white-light experience. All I did was remember – or imagine, or both – a whole slew of things one right after the other.

It couldn't have taken much time. Seconds, I would think. Dreams, are like that, I understand, extending over far less of the sleeper's time than it would require to recount them. At the end there was just the candle – the soft glow of it, the smell of the burning wax and wick.

I had to sit down again and think about what I'd just experienced. Then I had to walk around for a while, going over every frame in my memory like an assassination buff poring over the Zapruder film.

I couldn't blink it away or shrug it off. I knew something I hadn't known before.

ELEVEN

'The first night I went to Whitfield's place,' I told Elaine, 'TJ was over for dinner, we were watching the fights together —'

'In Spanish. I remember.'

'— and Whitfield called. And I went over there and talked with him.'

'And?'

'And I remembered something,' I said, and paused. After a long moment she asked me if I was planning on sharing it with her.

'I'm sorry,' I said. 'I guess I'm still sorting it out. And trying to think of a way to say it that won't sound ridiculous.'

'Why worry about that? There's nobody here but us chickens.'

There could have been. We were in her shop on Ninth Avenue, surrounded by the artwork and furnishings she dealt in. Anyone could have rung the bell and been buzzed in to look at the pictures and perhaps buy something, possibly one of the chairs we were sitting on. But it was a quiet afternoon, and for now we were alone and undisturbed.

I said, 'There was no liquor on his breath.'

'Whitfield, you're talking about.'

'Right.'

'You don't mean at the end, when he drank the poison and died. You mean the night you first met him.'

'Well, I'd met him before. I'd worked for the man.

But yes, I'm talking about the night I went to his apartment. He'd told me on the phone that he'd received a death threat from Will, and I went over there to suggest ways he might go about protecting himself.'

'And there was no liquor on his breath.'

'None. You know how it is with me. I'm a sober alcoholic, I can damn near smell a drink on the other side of a concrete wall. If I'm in a crowded elevator and the little guy in the far corner had a thimbleful of something alcoholic earlier in the day, I smell it as surely as if I just walked into a brewery. It doesn't bother me, it doesn't make me wish I were drinking or that the other person weren't, but I could no more fail to notice it than if somebody turned out the lights.'

'I remember when I had the chocolate.'

'The chocolate . . . oh, with the liquid centre.'

She nodded. 'Monica and I were visiting this friend of hers who was recovering from a mastectomy, and she passed around these chocolates someone had given her. And I got piggy, because these were very good chocolates, and I had four of them, and the last one had a cherry-brandy filling. And I had it half-swallowed before I realized what it was, and then I swallowed the rest of it, because what was I going to do, spit it out? That's what you'd have done, you'd have had reason to, but I'm not an alcoholic, I'm just a person who doesn't drink, so it wouldn't kill me to swallow it.'

'And it didn't make you take off all your clothes.'

'It didn't have any effect whatsoever, as far as I know. There couldn't have been very much brandy involved. There was a cherry in there, too, so that didn't leave much room for brandy.' She shrugged. 'Then I came home and gave you a kiss and you looked as startled as I've ever seen you.'

'It took me by surprise.'

'I thought you were going to sing me a chorus of "Lips That Touch Liquor Shall Never Touch Mine".'

'I don't even know the tune.'

'Do you want me to hum a little? But we're straying from the subject. The point is you're super-aware of the smell of booze and you didn't smell it on Adrian Whitfield. Could it be, Holmes, that the man hadn't been drinking?'

'But he said he had.'

'Oh?'

'It was a funny conversation,' I recalled. 'He started out by announcing that he didn't drink, and that got my attention because he was uncapping the Scotch bottle even as he said it. Then he qualified it by saying he didn't drink the way he used to, and that he pretty much limited himself to one drink a day.'

'That would be enough for anybody,' she said, 'if you had a big enough glass.'

'For some of us,' I said, 'you'd need a bathtub. Anyway, he went on to say that this particular day had been an exception, what with the letter from Will, and that he'd had a drink when he left the office and another when he got home to his apartment.'

'And you didn't smell them on his breath.'

'No.'

'If he brushed his teeth –'

'Wouldn't matter. I'd still smell the alcohol.'

'You're right, he'd just wind up smelling like crème de menthe. I notice alcohol on people's breath, too, because I don't drink. But I'm nowhere near as aware of it as you are.'

'All the years I drank,' I said, 'I never once smelled alcohol on anybody's breath, and it hardly ever occurred to me that anyone could smell it on mine.

Jesus, I must have gone around smelling of it all the time.'

'I kind of liked it.'

'Really?'

'But I like it better this way,' she said, and kissed me. After a few minutes she went back to her chair and said, 'Whew. If we were not in a semi-public place —'

'I know.'

'Where anyone could ring the bell at any moment, even though no one has in the longest time —' She heaved a sigh. 'What do you think it means?'

'I think we're still hot for each other,' I said, 'after all these years.'

'Well, I *know* that I mean the booze that wasn't on Whitfield's breath, which is uncannily like the dog that didn't bark in the night-time, isn't it? What do you make of it?'

'I don't know.'

'You're sure you noticed it at the time? Noticed the absence of it, I mean, and the contradiction between what he said and what you observed. It wasn't just something your imagination supplied when you were lighting candles and cursing the darkness?'

'I'm positive,' I said. 'I thought of it at the time, and then I just plain forgot about it because there were too many far more important things to think about. Here was a man sentenced to death by a killer who'd built up a pretty impressive track record. He wanted me to help him figure out a way to stay alive. That had more of a claim on my attention than the presence or absence of booze on his breath.'

'Of course.'

'I smelled the Scotch when he opened the bottle and poured the drink. And it struck me that I hadn't smelled it on his breath when he let me into the apartment. We shook hands, our faces weren't all that far apart. I'd have smelled it if it had been there to smell.'

'If the man hadn't been drinking,' she wondered, 'why would he say he had?'

'I have no idea.'

'I could understand if it was the other way around. People do that all the time, especially if they think the person they're talking to might have a judgment on the subject. He knew you didn't drink so he might assume you disapprove of others drinking. But you don't, do you?'

'Only when they throw up on my shoes.'

'Maybe he wanted to impress you with the gravity of the situation. "I'm not much of a drinker, I never have more than one a day, but this creep with the poisoned pen has me so rattled I've had a few already and I'm about to have another".'

'"And then I'll stop, because stress or not I'm no rummy." I thought of that.'

'And?'

'Why would he think he needed to do that? He just got a death threat from a guy with maximum credibility. Will's been all over the front pages for weeks, and so far he's batting a thousand. And here you've got Adrian Whitfield, a worldly man, certainly, and one professionally accustomed to the company of criminals, but all the same a far cry from a daredevil.'

'You wouldn't mistake him for Evel Knievel.'

'You wouldn't,' I said, 'because when all is said and done he's a lawyer in a three-piece suit, and the chances he takes tend not to be physical in nature. Of course he's going to take a letter from Will seriously. He doesn't have to prove it to me by pretending to have had drinks earlier.'

'You don't suppose . . .'

'What?'

'Could he have been a closet teetotaler?'

'Huh?'

'You said he poured a drink in front of you. Are you sure he actually drank it?'

I thought about it. 'Yes,' I said.

'You saw him drink it.'

'Not in a single swallow, but yes.'

'And it was whisky?'

'It came out of a Scotch bottle,' I said, 'and I got a whiff of it when he poured it. It smelled like booze. In fact it smelled like a single-malt Scotch, which is what it claimed to be on the label.'

'And you saw him drink it, and you smelled it on his breath.'

'Yes to the first part. Did I smell it on his breath afterward? I don't remember one way or the other. I didn't have occasion to notice.'

'You mean he didn't kiss you goodnight?'

'Not on the first date,' I said.

'Well, shame on him,' she said. '*I* kissed you goodnight, on *our* first date. I can even remember what you had on your breath.'

'You can, huh?'

'Whisky,' she said. 'And *moi*.'

'What a memory.'

'Well, it was memorable, you old bear. No, what I was getting at, I know there are people who drink but try to hide it. And I wondered if there might also be people who don't drink, and try to hide that.'

'Why?'

'I don't know. Why does anybody do anything?'

'I've often wondered.' I thought about it. 'A lot of us maintain our anonymity to one degree or another.

156

There's a longstanding tradition against going public about being a member of AA, though lately that's getting honored in the breach.'

'I know. All these Hollywood types go straight from Betty Ford to Barbara Walters.'

'They're not supposed to do that,' I said, 'but it's your own business to what extent you stay anonymous in your private life. I don't tell casual acquaintances unless I have a reason. And if I'm at a business meeting and the other fellow orders a drink, I'll just order a Coke. I won't issue an explanation.'

'And if he asks if you drink?'

'Sometimes I'll say "Not today," something like that. Or, "It's a little early for me," if I'm feeling particularly devious. But I can't imagine pouring a drink and pretending to drink it, or keeping colored water in a Scotch bottle.' I remembered something. 'Anyway,' I said, 'there were the liquor store records, the deliveries he'd had over the past months. They confirmed that he was just what he claimed to be, a guy who had one drink a day on the average.'

'He was ill,' she said. 'Some kind of lymphatic cancer, wasn't it?'

'It metastasized to the lymph system. I believe the original site was one of the adrenals.'

'Maybe he couldn't drink as much as he used to. Because of the cancer.'

'I suppose that's possible.'

'And he was in denial about his health, wasn't he? Or at least he wasn't telling people about it.'

'So?'

'So maybe that would lead him to pretend he was more of a drinker than he was.'

'But the first thing he did was tell me he wasn't much of a drinker.'

'You're right.' She frowned. 'I give up. I don't get it.'

'I don't get it, either.'

'But you don't give up, do you?'

'No,' I said. 'Not yet.'

Over dinner she said, 'Was Glenn Holtzmann a drinker?'

'Not that I ever noticed. And where did that question come from?'

'Your dreams.'

'You know,' I said, 'I'm having enough trouble making sense out of the thoughts I have while I'm awake. What was it Freud said about dreams?'

'"Sometimes it's only a cigar."'

'Right. If there's any connection between Glenn Holtzmann and the liquor Adrian Whitfield didn't have on his breath, I'm afraid it's too subtle for me.'

'I was just wondering.'

'Holtzmann was a phony,' I said. 'He betrayed people and sold them out.'

'Was Adrian a phony?'

'Did he have some secret life besides practicing criminal law? It doesn't seem very likely.'

'Maybe you sensed that he was hiding something about himself.'

'By pretending to be more of a drinker than he was. Or at least by pretending to have had more to drink on that one night than he had.'

'Right.'

'So my unconscious mind immediately made the leap from him to Glenn Holtzmann.'

'Why?'

'That was going to be my next question,' I said. 'Why indeed?' I put down my fork. 'Anyway,' I said, 'I think I figured out what Glenn Holtzmann was trying to tell me.'

'In the dream, you mean.'

'Right, in the dream.'

'Well?'

'"Too much money."'

'That's it?'

'What did we just say? Sometimes it's only a cigar?'

'Too much money,' she said. 'You mean like the line about a cocaine habit is God's way of telling you you've got too much money?'

'I don't think cocaine's got anything to do with it. Glenn Holtzmann had too much money, that's what made me dig deeper and find out about his secret life.'

'He had all that cash in the closet, didn't he? How does that apply to Adrian Whitfield?'

'It doesn't.'

'Then –'

'Sometimes it's only a cigar,' I said.

I don't remember any dreams that night, or even a sense of having dreamed. Elaine and I went home and finished what we'd started in her shop, and I slipped right off into a deep sleep and didn't stir until dawn.

But there had been a thought nagging at me before we went to bed, and it was still there when I woke up. I took it out and examined it, and I decided it wasn't something I had to devote my time to. I had a second cup of coffee after breakfast and considered the matter again, and this time I decided it wasn't as though there were too many other matters with a greater claim on my time. I had, as they say, nothing better to do.

And the only reason not to pursue it was for fear of what I might find out.

I made haste slowly. I went to the library first to check my memory against what the *Times* had run, noting down dates and times in my notebook. I spent a couple of hours at that, and then I went outside and sat on a bench in Bryant Park and went over my notes. It was a perfect fall day, and the air had the tang of a crisp apple. They'd been forecasting rain, but you didn't even have to look at the sky to know that it wasn't going to rain that day. It felt in fact as though it would never rain, or turn any colder than it was now. The days wouldn't get any shorter, either. It felt like eternal autumn, stretching out in front of us until the end of time.

Everybody's favorite season, and you always think it's going to last forever. And it never does.

Enough time had passed since Whitfield's death for them to have taken the NYPD seals off the door. All I had to do was find someone with authority to let me in. I don't know precisely where that authority was vested – Whitfield's heirs, the executor of his estate, or the co-op's board of directors. I'm sure it wasn't the building superintendent's decision to make, but he took it upon himself to make it, his resolution buttressed by the portrait of U S Grant I palmed him. He found a key and let me in and lingered at the door while I poked around in drawers and closets. After a while he coughed discreetly, and when I looked up he asked me how long I'd be. I told him that was hard to say.

'Because I'll have to let you out,' he said, 'and lock up after you, only I got a few things I have to be doing.'

He jotted down a phone number, and I agreed to call him. I felt a lot less pressed for time once he was out of there, and it's better if you're not in a hurry, especially when you don't know what you're looking for or where you're likely to find it.

It was close to two hours later when I used the phone in the bedroom to call the number he'd left me. He said he'd be up in a minute, and while I waited for him I retraced the route from the phone, the one Whitfield had used to call me that last night, into the room where he'd died. There were no bottles on or in the bar – guess they'd removed everything for lab tests – but the bar was there, and I stood where he'd have stood to make himself his last drink, then stepped over to where he was when he collapsed. There was nothing on the carpet to indicate where he had lain, no chalk outline, no yellow tape, no stains he'd left behind, but it seemed to me I knew just where he'd fallen.

When the super came I gave him an extra $20 along with an apology for having taken so long. The bonus surprised him, but only a little. It also seemed to reassure him that I hadn't appropriated any property of Whitfield's during his absence, although he still felt compelled to ask.

I hadn't taken a thing, I told him. Not even snapshots.

I didn't take anything from Whitfield's office, either, nor did I find anyone to let me in. Whitfield had shared an office suite and secretarial and paralegal staff with several other attorneys in an old eight-storey office building on Worth Street. I went to a noon meeting on Chambers Street the day after my visit to his apartment, then walked over to Worth and checked out his offices from the fifth-floor corridor. I weighed a few possible approaches and found them all unlikely to work on lawyers or legal secretaries, so I got out there and walked clear up to Houston Street and saw a movie at the Angelika. When it broke I called Elaine and told her I'd get dinner on my own.

'TJ called,' she said. 'He wants you to beep him.'

I would have if the phone I was using had a number on it. Most of them have had their numbers removed from the dials, and even if you manage to worm the number out of a cooperative operator, it won't do you any good; NYNEX has rigged the bulk of their pay phones so that they can no longer receive incoming calls. This is all part of the never-ending war on drugs, and its twin effects, as far as I can tell, have been a momentary inconvenience for the dealers, all of whom promptly went out and bought cellular phones, and a slight but irreversible decline in the quality of life for everybody else in town.

I had a plate of jerked chicken and peas and rice at a West Indian lunch counter on Chambers Street and went back to Whitfield's building on Worth. It was past five o'clock so I had to sign in with the guard downstairs. I scribbled something illegible on the sheet and rode up in the elevator. There were lights on in the law offices and a quick glance in passing showed me a man and two women seated at desks, two of them plugging away at computers, one talking on the phone.

I wasn't surprised. Lawyers keep late hours. I walked the length of the corridor and tried the men's room door. It was locked. The lock seemed unlikely to pose much of a challenge – it was designed, after all, to keep out the homeless, not to protect the crown jewels. On the other hand, if I was going to commit illegal entry I ought to be able to spend the next couple of hours in a pleasanter spot than a lavatory.

At the opposite end of the hall I found the one-room office of one Leland N Barish. His name was painted on the frosted glass, along with CONSULTANT. The lock looked to be the building's original equipment, shaped to take a skeleton key. I've carried a couple on my key ring for years, although I'd be hard put to tell you the last time I had occasion to use one of them. I didn't expect them to work now, but I tried the larger of the two and it turned the lock.

I let myself in. There was nothing to show who Barish was or who'd want to consult with him. The desk, its top uncluttered except for a couple of magazines, had a coating of dust that looked a good two weeks old. A stack of glassed-in bookshelves held only a few more magazines and eight or ten paperback science fiction novels. There was a wooden chair on casters that went with the desk, and an overstuffed armchair on which a cat had once sharpened its claws. The gray-beige walls showed rectangles and squares of a lighter shade, indicating where a previous tenant had displayed pictures or diplomas. Barish had neither repainted nor hung up anything of his own, not even a calendar.

I'd have gone through the desk drawers out of the idle curiosity that is an old cop's stock in trade. But the desk was locked, and I left it that way, unable to think of a reason to break in.

I'd switched the light on when I entered, and I left it on. No one could make out more than a silhouette through the frosted glass, but even if they could I had little to worry about, because it was odds-on nobody in the building had seen enough of Barish to remember what he looked like.

My guess was that 'consultant' was what it so often is, a euphemism for 'unemployed'. Leland Barish had lost a job and took this little office while he looked for another one. By now either he'd found something or he'd given up looking.

Maybe he'd found employment that took him to

Saudi Arabia or Singapore, and had left without bothering to clear out his office. Maybe he'd stopped paying rent months ago and his landlord hadn't gotten around to evicting him.

Whatever the actual circumstances, I didn't look to be running much of a risk cooping in his office for a couple of hours. I thought of TJ and decided to beep him, figuring it was perfectly safe for him to call me back, perfectly all right for Barish's phone to ring. I lifted the receiver and couldn't get a dial tone, which tended to confirm my guesses about Barish. I picked out the most recent magazine, a ten-week-old issue of the *New Yorker*, and settled myself in the easy chair. For a few minutes I tried to guess just what had become of Leland Barish, but then I got interested in an article about long-haul truckers and forgot all about him.

After an hour or so I noticed a key hanging from a hook on the wall next to the light switch. I guessed that it would unlock the door to the men's room, and it turned out I was right. I used the john, and checked Whitfield's office going and coming. It was still occupied.

I checked again an hour later, and an hour after that. Then I dozed off, and when I opened my eyes it was twenty minutes to twelve. The lights were out in the law office. I walked on past it and used the lavatory again, and the lights were still out when I returned.

The lock was better than the one on Barish's door, and I thought I might have to break the glass to get in. I was prepared to do that – I didn't think anyone was around to hear it, or inclined to pay attention – but first I used my pocket knife to gouge the door jamb enough so that I could get a purchase on the bolt and snick it back. I put on the lights, figuring that a lighted office would look less suspicious to someone across the street than a darkened office with someone moving around inside it.

I found Whitfield's office and got busy.

It was around one-thirty in the morning when I got out of there. I left the place looking as I'd found it, and wiped whatever surfaces I might have left prints on, more out of habit than because I thought anyone might dust the place for prints. I rubbed a little dirt into the gouges I'd made around the lock, so that the scar didn't look too new, and I drew the door shut and heard the bolt snick behind me.

I was too tired to think straight, and actually considered holing up in Barish's office and napping in his easy chair until dawn, all that in order to avoid having to sneak out past the guard. Instead I decided to bluff my way past him, and when I went downstairs the lobby was empty. A sign I'd missed on my way in announced that the building was locked from ten at night to six in the morning.

This didn't mean I couldn't get out, just that once out I couldn't get back in again. That was fine with me. I got out of there and had to walk three blocks before I could hail a cruising cab. Stickers on the windows in the passenger compartment warned me against smoking. In front, the Pakistani driver puffed away at one of those foul little Italian cigars. Di Nobili, I think they're called. Years and years ago I was partnered with a wise old cop named Vince Mahaffey, and he smoked the damn things day in and day out. I suppose they were no less appropriate for a Pakistani cabby than for an Irish cop, but I didn't let myself be transported on wings of nostalgia. I just rolled down the windows and tried to find something to breathe.

Elaine was asleep when I got in. She stirred when I slipped into bed beside her. I gave her a kiss and told her to go back to sleep.

'TJ called again,' she said. 'You didn't beep him.'

'I know. What did he want?'

'He didn't say.'

'I'll call him in the morning. Go to sleep, sweetie.'

'You all right?'

'I'm fine.'

'Find out anything?'

'I don't know. Go to sleep.'

'"Go to sleep, go to sleep." Is that all you can say?'

I tried to think of a response, but before I could come up with anything she had drifted off again. I closed my eyes and did the same.

TWELVE

Elaine was gone by the time I woke up. There was a note on the kitchen table explaining that she'd left early for an auction at Tepper Galleries on East Twenty-fifth, and reminding me to beep TJ. I had a shower first, and toasted an English muffin. There was coffee in the thermos, and I drank one cup and poured another before I picked up the phone and dialed his beeper number. When the tone sounded I punched in my own number and hung up.

Fifteen minutes later the phone rang and I picked it up. 'Who wants TJ?' he said, and went on without waiting for a response, ''Cept I know who it is, Diz, on account of I reckanize the number. You believe it took me this long to find a phone? Either they out of order or somebody be on them, talkin' like they gettin' paid by the word. You think I should get a cell phone?'

'I wouldn't want one.'

'You don't want a beeper,' he said, 'or a computer, neither. What you want's the nineteenth century back again.'

'Maybe the eighteenth,' I said, 'before the Industrial Revolution took the joy out of life.'

'Someday you can tell me how nice it was with horses and buggies. Why I don't want a cell phone, they cost too much. Cost when you call somebody, cost when somebody call you. Top of that, you got no privacy. Dude's chillin' with a Walkman, he's liable to pick up everything you sayin'. What makes it work like that?'

'How would I know?'

'Don't even need a Walkman. People be pickin' up your conversation on the fillings in their teeth. Next thing you know they think it's the CIA, tellin' 'em they supposed to go to the Post Office and shoot everybody.'

'You wouldn't want that on your conscience.'

'Damn, you right about that.' He laughed. 'I stick to my beeper. Hey, listen. I found that dude.'

'What dude is that?'

'Dude you had me lookin' for. Dude who was on the scene when the one dude shot the other dude.'

'There's too many dudes in that sentence,' I said. 'I don't know who you're talking about.'

'Talkin' 'bout Myron.'

'Myron.'

'Dude got shot in that little park? Dude had AIDS? Ring a little bell, Mel?'

'Byron,' I said.

'Byron Leopold. Wha'd I do, call him Myron? I been doin' that in my head all along. Thing is, see, I never heard of nobody named Byron . . . You still there?'

'I'm here.'

'You didn't say nothin', so I beginnin' to wonder.'

'I guess I was speechless,' I said. 'I didn't know you were still looking for the witness.'

'Ain't been nobody told me to stop.'

'No, but —'

'An' the man got me started in this detectin' business, everybody say he like a dog with a bone. Once he get his teeth in somethin', he ain't about to turn it loose.'

'Is that what they say?'

'So I gettin' to be the same my own self, like a dog with a bone. 'Sides, it be somethin' to do.'

'And you found the dude.'

'Took some doin',' he admitted. 'He wasn't exactly lookin' to be found. But he saw the whole thing, 'cept it was more hearin' than seein'. He wasn't lookin' at first, and when he did look he was seein' it from behind. So he saw the back of the dude who did the shooting, and he didn't see the gun, just heard, you know, pop pop.'

'That's what he heard? Pop pop?'

'What he heard was gunshots. What else you gone hear when somebody shoots a gun?'

'Everybody who was there heard the gunshots,' I said, 'and even if they hadn't the bullets in Leopold's body are fairly strong evidence that a couple of shots were fired. So if all this fellow did was hear the shots —'

'Ain't all he heard.'

'Oh.'

'That was all the man heard, you think I'd be botherin' you with it?'

'Sorry. What else did he hear?'

'Heard the dude say, "Mr Leopold?" Then he didn't hear nothin', so either Byron just nodded or his voice didn't carry. Then he heard the dude say, "Byron Leopold?" An' maybe he looked up an' maybe he didn't, but the next he heard the dude was bustin' caps.'

'Pop pop.'

'Like that.'

'When can I see this witness?'

'He might be pretty slow to talk to you. He already missed a few chances to talk to the police.'

'I don't suppose the gentleman's a vice president at IBM.'

'He's in the park sellin' product,' he said, 'an' soon as the dude commences to shoot, he ready to call it a day hisself. I can maybe put you 'cross a table from him, but

169

that don't mean he's gone talk to you. 'Sides, what you gonna axe him that I didn't axe him already?'

'"Mr Leopold? Byron Leopold?"'

'Don't sound to me like he's makin' it up.'

'No,' I said, 'it doesn't.'

An hour later I was watching him eat french fries at a Fourteenth Street coffee shop. His cheeseburger was but a memory. He was wearing baggy jeans and a denim jacket with a quilted lining. His railroader's cap was on the seat beside him.

I told him I had pretty much forgotten Byron Leopold.

'Why's that?' he wondered. 'You come to the conclusion he died of natural causes?'

'When I thought about it at all,' I said, 'which wasn't often, I suppose I figured he'd been taken for someone else and killed in error. Or that he'd unwittingly made an enemy in the neighborhood by sitting on the wrong bench or mouthing off at the wrong person. And he had AIDS, and he was far enough along so that the disease was visible. Maybe somebody had an AIDS phobia and decided the best cure lay in killing off the victims.'

'Like the dudes who set bums on fire.'

'As a quick cure for the problem of homelessness. That's the idea. I didn't think that was it, though, because that kind of killer doesn't act once and then go off and enter a monastery.'

'He repeats.'

'Usually.' The waitress came by and filled my coffee cup without asking. The coffee wasn't very good, but there was plenty of it. I said '"Mr Leopold? Byron Leopold?"'

'Like that.'

'Making sure he's got the right person.'

'Person he's supposed to shoot. Like he knows the name but he never met him before. We brainstormin', right? Battin' ideas back and forth?'

'Something like that,' I agreed. 'He sounds hired, doesn't he?'

'The killer? You mean like a pro?'

'Not like a pro,' I said. 'The whole thing's too raggedy-ass for a pro. Here's a man who's alone a lot, leads a very regular life, hasn't set up any security system to make himself hard to kill. It's easy to get close to him in private, so why would a professional hitman kill him in front of witnesses?'

'Only reason I said a pro, Joe, is you said hired.'

'An amateur,' I said, 'hired by another amateur. It pretty much takes a pro to hire a pro. You need to be connected, you can't look up Contract Killers in the Yellow Pages. Ordinary citizens hire killers all the time, but there's nothing terribly professional about the people who work for them.'

'An' it don't always work out the way it s'posed to,' he said. 'Like the other day in Washington Heights.'

I knew the one he was talking about. It had been all over the papers the past few days. A Dominican teenager, bridling at her father's strict discipline, had engaged a pair of local hard cases to kill the man, enticing them with the prospect of the $20,000 he kept in a strongbox in the closet, considering it ever so much safer than the bank.

So they showed up at the house one night and she let them in. She gave them the money, and then they were supposed to wait for Daddy to come home. But they got tired of waiting, and it occurred to them that he might be armed, and there was an easier way to close the account. So they took the girl who started the whole thing and shot her twice in the head, and they did the same for her sleeping mother and brother while they were at it, and then they went home. The father came home from work to find his family dead and his money gone. I bet his car wouldn't start, either.

'In Washington Heights,' I said, 'everybody had a reason. The girl was mad at her father, and the killers wanted the money.'

'So who had a reason to kill Byron?'

'That's what I was wondering.'

'Didn't have any money, did he?'

'Actually,' I remembered, 'he had more money than he should have. He cashed in his insurance and he died with something like forty thousand dollars in the bank.'

'Ain't that a motive?'

'He'd left it all to some AIDS charities. Some of those organizations are a little aggressive in their fund-raising, but I've never heard of them going out and killing for the money.'

'Besides, all they gotta do is wait, right? 'Cause the man already dyin'.' He frowned. 'You know what'd be nice? Piece of pie.' I beckoned the waitress over and he asked her what kind of pie she had, giving her response some careful attention. 'Pecan,' he decided, 'with some of that whatchacall à la mode on it. Say chocolate?' She looked at him, confused, and the street went right out of his speech. 'I'll have a piece of pecan pie,' he said, 'with a scoop of chocolate ice cream.' She nodded and went away, and he rolled his eyes. 'Now she be thinkin' I a doctor. She be after me to take out her appendix.'

'Tell her your doctorate's in botany.'

'That's just as bad, Tad. She'll have me talkin' to her plants. If killin' Byron didn't put no money in nobody's pocket, who'd hire somebody to do it?'

'I don't know.'

'He had AIDS, right? But he wasn't gay.'

'He got it from a needle.'

'He keep it all to himself? Or did he pass it on?' I must have looked puzzled. 'The virus, Cyrus. Who'd he go and infect?'

'He could have spread it around,' I said. 'Years ago, before he even knew he had it.'

'So he gives it to some woman, and then her husband or her boyfriend or her brother wants to know how she got it. "Couldn't be nobody but that no-account junkie Byron Leopold," she says.'

'Whereupon the husband or brother or whatever he is goes out and hires somebody to kill Byron.'

'Or does it his own self. Either way Byron'd be a stranger to him an' he might axe him his name to make sure he didn't kill the wrong person. "Mr Leopold? Byron Leopold?"'

'Pop pop.'

'All she wrote,' he agreed.

'What about "This is for Sheila, you dirty rat?" The way he did it, Byron wouldn't even know why he was dying.'

'If Sheila's brother was doin' it hisself, you'd 'spect him to say somethin'. If he only hired the shooter −'

'The shooter might not bother with the oratory. Even if the brother did it himself, he could have a speech planned and be too nervous to deliver it.' I drank some coffee. 'I don't buy any of it,' I said. 'Who takes that kind of revenge on a man with one foot in the grave? Byron Leopold was a bag of bones, his idea of a big day was sitting in the sun with his newspaper. No matter what he did to you, one long look at him and the resentment'd go right out of you.'

'What's that leave? Suicide?'

'I thought of that.'

'Huh?'

'Say he didn't want to live anymore but he couldn't bring himself to take action. So he hires somebody to do it for him.'

'He's afraid to stick his head in the oven, but he's cool with the idea of waitin' for somebody to sneak up and shoot him.'

'I said I thought of it. I never put it high up on the list.'

'Sides, how's he hire somebody who never met him face to face? You hire me to shoot you, I ain't gonna have to ask you your name.'

'Forget it,' I said. 'It never made any sense in the first place and it makes less sense now. Byron Leopold was murdered by someone who had a reason to kill him, and he himself was the only person in the world with a reason to want him dead. There ought to be a financial motive. That's what it feels like, but there's no money in it for anybody.'

'There's whatever he had. Forty kay? But you said some charity gets that.'

'And it's not enough anyway.'

'Not enough?'

'Not enough to kill for.'

'Dudes up on Washington Heights, they killed three people and only got half that much.'

'They were low-life dipshits,' I said. 'They probably killed for the hell of it. They already had the money. Why kill the girl? To keep her quiet? She couldn't tell anybody, and her mother and brother were asleep in their beds, for Christ's sake. They killed three people for no reason.'

'Guess you ain't likely to be a character witness for them. Anyway, wasn't no low-life shot Byron. Said,

174

"Mr Leopold." Polite, you know? Showed some respect.'

'It's little things that make all the difference.'

His pie had arrived while we were talking, and now it was mostly gone. He held a bite balanced on his fork and said, 'Funny about the forty kay. First it was too much and now it ain't enough.'

'He cashed in an insurance policy,' I said, 'and that would have brought him only a fraction of what he had in the bank. So in that sense the forty thousand was too much, but . . .'

'Somethin' wrong?'

'No.'

'Way you just broke off an' started starin'.'

'Too much money,' I said. 'Glenn Holtzmann had too much money. It was in his closet when he died. And I dreamed about him, and that's what the dream was trying to tell me. Too much money.' I looked across at TJ, who still had the last bite of pie on his fork. 'I thought the dream was about Will. But it wasn't. It was about Byron Leopold.'

THIRTEEN

It still didn't have to mean anything. It had been a dream, after all, and not a message from Glenn Holtzmann in the spirit world. (If his shade had indeed contacted me from beyond the beyond, he'd probably have had more on his mind than some guy who got himself shot on a park bench in the Village. 'Hey, Scudder,' he might have murmured, 'what's this I hear about you and Lisa?') The dream was my own self talking to me, and I wasn't necessarily all that much sharper while I slept.

Anyway, sometimes it's just a cigar.

'If,' TJ said, and stopped himself. 'No,' he said, holding up his hands as if to stop himself from running into a wall. 'No, I won't say it.'

'Good.'

'But if we did, be no stoppin' us.'

If we had a computer. That was the phrase he'd agreed not to say, and not a moment too soon, because those five little words played a key role in every sentence out of his mouth. I seemed to have two cases, the shooting death of Byron Leopold and Will's string of homicides. (What I didn't have was a client, unless you wanted to count Adrian Whitfield, who'd paid me some money a while back and encouraged me to extend the umbrella of my investigation to cover both cases.) Whichever one I wanted to fool with next, TJ seemed certain a computer would make all the difference.

Insurance records? Just boogie on into the insurance

company's data base. Airline records? Do the same for the airlines. The whole world was on-line these days, and a well-schooled hacker could reach out with ease and touch someone, anyone, and pick his brain while he was at it. All you needed was a computer and a modem and a phone line to plug into and the world would whisper all its secrets to you.

'You also need someone who knows what he's doing,' I said. 'It took the Kongs to crack the NYNEX computer. I'm willing to believe you could learn how to do all that, but not fast enough to do us any good now.'

'Take a while,' he admitted. 'Meantime, the Kongs could talk me through it.'

'If they happened to be in the neighborhood.'

'They ain't the only hackers could do it. Be easy to use them, though, an' they wouldn't have to come down from Boston to do it. All they'd have to be is near a phone.'

'How do you figure that?'

'Nothin' to it,' he said. 'I'd be on the computer, and be on the phone with them at the same time. You'd need two phone lines is all, one for the modem and one for the phone. Or you could use a cell phone to talk to them if you don't want to run a second line in.'

'In where?'

'In wherever you got the computer. Your apartment, most likely. Or the shop.'

'Elaine's shop?'

'So's she could use it for keepin' books an' takin' inventory. I could do all that for her.'

'If you took a course or two.'

'Well, it ain't rocket science. I could learn.'

'There's not a whole lot of spare room in the shop.'

He nodded. 'Be better off settin' up in the apartment.'

'We had to set up in a hotel room with the Kongs,' I remembered. 'Had to rent one, so that our little invasion of the phone company computer couldn't be traced back to us.'

'So?'

'Because what the Kongs did,' I went on, 'was illegal and traceable. If we pulled anything like that from the apartment, or from Elaine's shop, we'd have guys with badges knocking on the door.'

'Hackers has learned some tricks since then.'

'And what about the cyber cops? Don't you think they've learned anything?'

He shrugged. 'Way it works,' he said. 'Build a better mousetrap, somebody else gonna build a better mouse.'

'Anyway,' I said, 'technology only takes you so far, even if you're the Kongs. They couldn't get into the system, remember? No matter how many keys they punched, they couldn't find the combination.'

'They got in.'

'They *talked* their way in. They put technology on hold and called up a human being on the telephone.'

'Some girl, wasn't it?'

'And they sweet-talked her into giving up the password. They used that technique routinely enough to have a special phrase for it.' I groped around in my memory and came up with it. 'Social engineering, that's what they called it.'

'What you gettin' at?'

'I'll show you,' I said.

'Omaha,' Phyllis Bingham said. 'To think there was a time when I booked you and Elaine to London and Paris. And now it's Omaha?'

'How the mighty have fallen,' I said. 'But I don't want to go there. I just want to find out if somebody else did.'

'Ah,' she said. 'Detective work?'

'I'm afraid so.'

'And if he went there you have to chase after him?'

'I think he went and came back.' I handed her a slip of paper. 'Probably flew out there on either of these dates, and returned on either of these.'

'From New York to Omaha, and –'

'From Philadelphia.'

'From *Philadelphia*,' she said. 'I was just going to guess who flies non-stop from New York to Omaha, and I know America West used to, and I don't know if they still do, but it doesn't matter if he flew from Philadelphia. But who flies Philly to Omaha non-stop?' She flexed her fingers, frowned, tapped away at the keys. 'Nobody,' she announced. 'You can get there on USAir via Pittsburgh or you can fly Midwest Express through Milwaukee. Or United if you don't mind changing at O'Hare. Or any airline, just about, but those are the logical ones. I don't suppose you know which airline he used?'

'No.'

'And his name?'

'Arnold Wishniak.'

'Well, if we find him,' she said, 'we'll know it's him, won't we? Because how many Arnold Wishniaks could be going from Philadelphia to Omaha?'

'I'd say one at the most. I don't think he would have used his real name.'

'I don't blame him.'

'But he may have kept the initials.'

'Well, let's see.' She tapped away at the keys, periodically rolling her eyes while she waited for the machine to respond. 'Every computer's faster than the last one,' she said, 'and they're never fast enough. You get so you want it instantaneous. More than that, you want it to give you data before you can even think to ask for it.'

'Same with people.'

'Huh? Oh, right.' She giggled. 'At least computers keep improving. Do you see what I'm doing? I'm starting with USAir, and I'm asking if there's a Wishniak on Flight #1103 on the fifth, and there's not, and now I'll ask about Flight #179 the same day . . . No. Okay, the other date's the sixth, right? So we'll try #1103 . . . Nothing, and now we'll try #179. Is that the right number, #179? It is, so we'll try it. Nope.'

'I don't think he would have used his real name.'

'I know, but I wanted to rule it out because with the name I could access the records. With just the initials I can't.'

'Oh.'

'Let me try Midwest Express,' she said. She did, and United as well, and wound up shaking her head.

'There's another name you could try,' I said. 'He had a brother who anglicized the family name, and Arnold's borrowed the name in the past.'

I told her the name and she repeated it and frowned. 'Spell it?' I spelled it and she hit keys. 'It's a familiar name to me,' she mused. 'Where did I hear it recently?'

'No idea,' I said. 'Of course there's the ballplayer, Dave Winfield.'

She shook her head. 'Since the strike,' she said, 'I don't pay any attention. Flight #1103, on the fifth. No luck there. Flight #179, also on the fifth . . .'

Nothing on any of the flights in question.

'There's still a good chance he used the initials,' I said. 'But you can't access it that way. Suppose you just pull up the passenger manifests for each of those flights. Can you do that?'

'*I* can't.'

'Who can?'

'Some computer genius, probably. Or somebody at the airline who's got the access codes.' She frowned. 'This is important, huh?'

'Kind of.'

She picked up a phone, flipped through a Rolodex, dialed a number. She said, 'Hi, this is Phyllis at JMC. Who's this? Judy? Judy, I've got this very good customer of mine who happens to be a detective. He's on this case that involves a non-custodial parent . . . Right, you hear about stuff like this all the time. I know, it's amazing. They don't pay child support and then they come and kidnap the kids.'

She explained what I needed to know. 'He wasn't on any of those flights under his own name,' she said, 'but the detective thinks he may have kept the initials. No, I understand it's confidential, Judy. You would have to have a court order. Right.' She made a face, then forced a smile. 'Look, could you do this much? Without telling me the name, could you see if there's a male passenger on one of those flights with the initials AW? Yes, Philadelphia to Omaha.'

She covered the mouthpiece. 'She's not supposed to do this,' she said, 'but she'll bend a little. My guess, she's divorced and not on the best of terms with her ex.' She uncovered the mouthpiece. 'Hi, Judy. Rats. None at all, huh?'

'He probably paid cash,' I said.

She was quick. 'Judy,' she said, 'he probably made up a name, so he probably paid cash. If you could . . . uh-huh. Uh-huh. Right, I understand.'

She covered the mouthpiece again. 'She can't do it.'

'Can't or won't?'

'Won't. It's against the rules, she'd get in trouble, blah blah blah.'

TJ said, 'Could you do it? If you had the access codes?'

'But I don't.'

'But she does.'

She considered, shrugged, and uncovered the mouthpiece. 'Judy,' she said, 'last thing I want is for you to get in trouble. For curiosity, though, tell me something. Is that information there to be pulled up? Like whether a ticket was purchased cash or charge? I mean, suppose a customer comes in and pays me cash, and . . . Uh-huh. I see. So anybody could access it. I mean, I could get it myself if I had the access codes, is that right?' She grabbed up a pen, jotted down a phrase. 'Judy,' she said, 'you're a doll. Thanks.' She broke the connection, grinned fiercely, and held up a clenched fist in triumph. 'Yes!'

We still had a ways to go. What she managed to produce, after a lot of head-scratching and key-tapping, was a printout of passenger manifests for flights on the three airlines in question from Philadelphia to Omaha and as many return flights two days later. An asterisk next to a name indicated a non-credit card sale.

'Cash or check,' she explained. 'There's no distinction in the data bank. Also, these are just the cash and check sales made by the airline. Sales through travel agents are just listed that way, with no indication as to how payment was made. That's not what she told me, but if there's a way to separate it out, I can't figure it out.'

'That's all right.'

'It is? Because do you see the names coded with a C?

These are all customers who bought their ticket through another airline, probably because their trip originated with another flight segment on the issuing carrier. For all I know they paid for their ticket with Green Stamps.'

'I think the manifests are all I need.'

'You do?'

'If the same name turns up going and coming back, that's more significant than how he paid for the ticket.'

'I didn't even think of that. Let's check.'

I gathered up the sheets of paper. 'I've taken up enough of your time,' I said. 'The hard part's done. And, speaking of your time, I want to pay for it.'

'Oh, come on,' she said. 'You don't have to do that.'

I tucked the money into her hand. 'The client can afford it,' I said.

'Well . . .' She closed her fingers around the bills. 'Actually, that was fun. Not as much fun as booking you and your wife on a South Seas cruise, though. Be sure and call me when you're ready to go someplace wonderful.'

'I will.'

'Or even Omaha,' she said.

'The client can afford it,' TJ said. 'Thought we didn't have a client.'

'We don't.'

'"Social engineering." What you did is you used a computer. Only thing, it was somebody else's computer. And somebody else's fingers on the keys.'

'I suppose that's one way to put it.'

'Let's see the lists,' he said. 'See how many repeats we got.'

★

'Mr A Johnson,' I said. 'Flew Midwest Express from Philadelphia to Omaha on the fifth, changing planes in Milwaukee. He flew back to Philadelphia on the morning of the seventh. Paid by cash or check. My guess is cash.'

'You think it's him.'

'I do.'

'Whole lot of folks named Johnson. Right up there with Smith and Jones.'

'That's true.'

'"Cordin" to Phyllis, you got to show ID to get on a plane.'

'They've tightened up all their security measures.'

'Case you a terrorist,' he said, 'they want to make sure it's really you. They probably do the same when you buy the ticket, if you payin' cash. Ask for ID.'

I nodded. 'Same with a check, but then they always want proof of identity for a check. Of course, it's not that hard to get ID.'

'Store right on the Deuce, print up all kinds of shit. Student ID, Sheriff cards. Wouldn't make much of an impression on a cop, but you gonna look too hard at it if you're behind the counter at the airlines?'

'Especially if the customer's a prosperous-looking middle-aged white man in a Brooks Brothers suit.'

'The right front gets you through,' he agreed.

'And the ID may have been legitimate,' I said. 'Maybe he had a client named Johnson, maybe he hung onto a driver's license for some poor bastard who wouldn't need it while he was locked up in Green Haven.'

He scratched his head. 'We got a name of a dude flew to Omaha one day and back a couple days later. We got anything more than that?'

'Not yet,' I said.

'I'm glad you brought him in,' Joe Durkin said. 'This is the very mope we've been looking high and low for. I'll ask him a few questions soon as I remember where I put my rubber hose.'

'Bet I know where it's at,' TJ said. 'You want, I help you look for it.'

Durkin grinned and gave him a poke in the arm. 'What are you doing with my friend here?' he demanded. 'Why aren't you out on the street selling crack and mugging people?'

'My day off.'

'And here I thought you guys were dedicated. Seven days a week, fifty-two weeks a year, soothing the emotional pain of the public. Turns out you coast just like everybody else.'

'Hell, yes,' TJ said. 'I didn't want to do nothin' but work all the time, I be joinin' the po-leese.'

'Say that again for me, will you? Po-leese.'

'Po-leese.'

'Jesus, I love it when you talk dirty. Matt, I don't know what gives me the idea, but somehow I think you're here for a reason.'

We were in the squad room at Midtown North, on West Fifty-fourth Street. I took a chair and explained what I wanted while TJ went over to the board and thumbed through a sheaf of Wanted flyers.

'When you find one with your picture on it,' Joe advised him, 'bring it over and I'll get you to autograph it for me. Matt, let me see if I've got this straight. You want me to call the Omaha police and ask them to check hotel records for some zip named Johnson.'

'I'd appreciate it,' I said.

'You'd appreciate it. In a tangible way, do you suppose?'

'Tangible. Yes, I suppose –'

'I like that word,' he said. 'Tangible. It means you can touch it. You reach out and it's there. Which gives rise to a question. Why don't you reach out and touch someone?'

'Pardon me?'

'You know the hotel, right? The Hilton?'

'That's the place to start. I'm not positive that's where he stayed, but –'

'But you'd start there. Why didn't you? Use their 800 number and the call's free. Can't beat that for a bargain.'

'I called,' I said. 'I didn't get anywhere.'

'You identify yourself as a police officer?'

'That's illegal.' He gave me a look. 'I may have given that impression,' I admitted. 'It didn't do me any good.'

'Since when did you become incapable of calling a hotel and conning a little information out of a desk clerk?' He looked at the slip of paper in front of him. 'Omaha,' he said. 'What the hell ever happened in Omaha?' He looked at me. 'Jesus Christ,' he said.

'Not Him personally,' TJ put in, 'but this dude who said he was real tight with Him.'

'The abortion guy. What was his name?'

'How quickly we forget.'

'Roswell Berry. Will got him right in his hotel room, didn't he? I forget which hotel, but why is it something tells me it was the Hilton?'

'Why indeed?'

'You have reason to think our boy Will's a guy named Johnson?'

'It's a name he may have been using.'

'No wonder the Hilton wouldn't tell you anything. You wouldn't have been the first caller trying to get something out of them. All the tabloids, guarding the

186

public's right to know. The Omaha PD must have slammed the lid shut.'

'That would be my guess.'

'You know how many detectives are working on Will? I can't tell you the number, but what I do know is I'm not one of them. How do I justify sticking my nose in?'

'Maybe this doesn't have anything to do with Will,' I said. 'Maybe it's a simple investigation of a robbery suspect who pulled a series of holdups in this precinct and may have fled to Omaha.'

'Where he's got relatives. But instead of staying with them we think he holed up at the Hilton. We know the dates, and the name he used. That's some story, Matt.'

'You probably won't have to tell it,' he said. 'You're a New York police detective with a question that's easy to answer. Why should they give you a hard time?'

'People have never needed a reason in the past.' He picked up the phone. 'Here's a question that's *not* easy to answer. Why the hell am I doing this?'

'Allen W Johnson,' he said. 'That's Allen with two L's and an E. I don't know what the W stands for. I don't suppose it stands for Will.'

'I'm not sure it stands for anything.'

'Stayed two nights and paid cash. As a matter of fact, the Omaha cops checked on everybody staying at the hotel as part of their investigation of Berry's murder. Anybody paid cash, that was a red flag. So Mr Allen Johnson definitely had their attention.'

'Did they have a chance to talk to him?'

'He'd already checked out. Never used the phone or charged anything to his room.'

'I don't suppose they've got a description of him.'

'Yeah, they got a real useful one. He was a man and he was wearing a suit.'

'Narrows it down.'

'He checked out after Will got Berry with the coat hanger, but before the body was discovered. So why take a second look at him?'

'He paid cash.'

He shook his head. 'Not when he checked in. He gave them a credit card and they ran a slip..Then when he checked out he gave them cash. Apparently that's common. The card simplifies checking in, but you've got reasons for settling up in cash. Maybe the card's maxed out, or maybe you don't want the bill showing up at your house because you don't want your wife to know you were over at the Hilton humping your secretary.'

'And when you pay in cash −'

'They tear up the slip they took an imprint on. So nobody ever knows if the card's a phony, because they don't run it by the credit card company until you check out.'

'So we know he had a credit card,' I said, 'whether or not it was a good one. And he had a piece of photo ID in the same name.'

'Did I miss something? How do we know that?'

'He had to show it to get on the plane.'

'If he had the credit card for back up,' he said, 'the other could be any damn thing long as it had his picture on it. One of those pieces of shit they print for you on Forty-second Street, says you're a student at the School of Hard Knox.'

'Like I said,' TJ murmured.

'Tell me about this guy,' Joe said. 'Since you got my attention. How'd you get on to him?'

'From the airline records.'

'New York to Omaha?'

'Philadelphia to Omaha.'

'Where did Philadelphia come from?'

'I think the Quakers settled it.'

'I mean —'

'It's too complicated to go into,' I said, 'but I was looking for someone who flew Philly to Omaha and back again. He fit the time frame.'

'You mean he went out before Berry got killed and came back afterward.'

'It was a little tighter fit than that.'

'Uh-huh. Who is he, you want to tell me that?'

'Just a name,' I said. 'And a face, if he showed photo ID, but I haven't seen the face.'

'He's just a man in a suit, like the girl at the hotel remembered.'

'Right.'

'Help me out here, Matt. What have you got that I should be passing on to somebody?'

'I haven't got anything.'

'If Will's out there running around, looking for fresh names for his list —'

'Will's retired,' I said.

'Oh, right. We got his word for that, don't we?'

'And nobody's heard a peep out of him since.'

'Which makes the department look pretty stupid, wasting manpower and resources chasing a perpetrator who no longer represents a danger to the community. How's this your business, anyway? Who's your client?'

'That's confidential.'

'Oh, come on. Don't give me that shit.'

'As a matter of fact, it's privileged. I'm working for an attorney.'

'Jesus, I'm impressed. Wait a minute, it comes back

189

to me. Weren't you working for the last vic? Whit-field?'

'That's right. I wasn't doing much, I advised him on security and steered him to Wally Donn at Reliable.'

'Which did him a whole lot of good.'

'I think they did what they could.'

'I suppose so.'

'Whitfield hired me as an investigator,' I said. 'Not that there was much for me to investigate.'

'And you're still at it? That's the attorney you're working for? What are you, billing the estate?'

'He paid me a retainer.'

'And it covers what you're doing now?'

'It'll have to.'

'What have you got, Matt?'

'All I've got is Allen Johnson, and I told you how I got him.'

'Why'd you check those flights?'

'A hunch.'

'Yeah, right. You know what I do when I get a hunch?'

'You bet a bunch?'

He shook his head. 'I buy a lottery ticket,' he said, 'and I've never won yet, which shows how good my hunches are. You'd think I'd learn.'

'All it takes is a dollar and a dream.'

'That's catchy,' he said. 'I'll have to remember that. Now, if there's nothing else –'

'Actually . . .'

'This better be good.'

'I was just thinking,' I said, 'that it would be interesting to know if Allen W Johnson ever bought cyanide.'

He was silent for a long moment, thinking. Then he said, 'Somebody must have checked the records when

Whitfield got killed. Especially after the autopsy showed he was terminal and there was all that speculation that he killed himself. But Will's last letter scotched that line of thought.'

'It proved he killed Whitfield.'

'Uh-huh. It even mentioned cyanide, if I remember correctly. The cyanide had to come from somewhere, didn't it? It smells like almonds, but you can't make it out of almonds, can you?'

'I think you can extract minute quantities from peach pits,' I said, 'but somehow I don't think that's how Will got it.'

'And if he bought it where you had to sign for it, and had to show ID —'

'Maybe he signed in as Allen Johnson.'

He thought it over, straightened up in his seat. He said, 'You know what? I think you should find out who's in charge of the investigation into Will and his wacky ways and ask him to look it up for you. You're a nice fellow, make a good first impression, and a hundred years ago you used to be on the job yourself. I'm sure they'll be happy to cooperate with you.'

'I'd just hate to keep you from getting the credit.'

'Credit,' he said heavily. 'Is that how you remember it from your days on the force? Is that what you used to get for butting into somebody else's case? Credit?'

'It's a little different when the case is stalled.'

'This one? It can be stalled six different ways, it can have a dead battery and four flat tires, and it's still high-profile and high priority. You see Marty McGraw this morning?'

'The last time I saw him was around the time of Will's last letter.'

'I don't mean him, I mean his column. You read it today?' I hadn't. 'He had a hair up his ass about something, and I can't even remember what it was. Last line of the column – "Where's Will now that we need him?"'

'He didn't write that.'

'The hell he didn't. Hang on a minute, there must be a copy of the *News* around here somewhere.' He returned with a paper. 'I didn't have it word for word, but that's how it adds up. Here, read it yourself.'

I looked where he was pointing and read the final paragraph aloud. "'You find yourself thinking of a certain anonymous letter-writer of recent memory, and saying of him what some unfunny folks used to say of Lee Harvey Oswald. Where is he now that we need him?"'

'What did I tell you?'

'I can't believe he wrote that.'

'Why not? He wrote the first one, saying Richie Vollmer wasn't fit to live. Which, I have to say, was a hard position to find fault with. But it sure got Will's motor running.'

FOURTEEN

By the time we got out of there TJ was hungry again, and I realized I hadn't had anything but coffee since breakfast. We found a pizza place with tables and I got us a couple of Sicilian slices.

'I was at this one place,' he said, 'they had pizza with fruit on it. You ever heard of that?'

'I've heard of it.'

'Never tried it, though?'

'It never sounded like a good idea to me.'

'Me either,' he said. 'Had pineapple on it, an' somethin' else, but I disremember what. Wasn't peaches, though. Was that straight what you was sayin' before? Peach pits really got cyanide in them?'

'Traces of it.'

'How many of 'em you have to eat before you kill yourself?'

'You don't have to eat any of them before you kill yourself. You just put a gun in your mouth and –'

'You know what I mean, Dean. You couldn't poison somebody with peach pits 'cause he'd take one bite an' make a face an' spit it out. But could somebody lookin' to commit suicide choke down enough of them to do the job?'

'I have no idea,' I said. 'Of course if we had a computer I'm sure you could find out in no time.'

'You right, you know. All you gotta do is post the question on the Internet and some fool e-mail you the answer. How we gonna find out if Johnson bought the cyanide?'

'We'll wait.'

'For what?'

'For Joe Durkin to make a phone call.'

'Which he just said he ain't about to do.'

'That's what he said.'

'Said it like he meant it, too.'

I nodded. 'But it'll stick in his mind,' I said. 'And tomorrow or the next day he'll pick up the phone.'

'An' if he don't?'

'I'm not sure it matters. I know what happened. I'd need to fit a couple more things together in order to prove it, but I don't even know if I want to do that.'

'Why's that?'

'Because I'm not sure I see the point.'

'Biggest story all year,' he said. 'Man sells newspapers even when he don't do nothin'.'

'"Where is he now that we need him?"'

'Whole city's holdin' its breath, wants to know what he's gonna do next. Say he's retired, but maybe he bidin' his time. Everybody waitin' on his next move, wonderin' what's the next name on his list.'

'But we know better.'

'When you know the truth,' he said, 'don't you have to tell somebody? Isn't that what detectin' is, findin' out the truth an' tellin' somebody?'

'Not always. Sometimes it's finding out the truth and keeping it to yourself.'

He thought about it. 'Be a real big story,' he said.

'I suppose so.'

'Story of the year, what they'd be callin' it.'

'Every month there's another story of the year,' I said, 'and every year there's a story of the decade and a trial of the century. One thing we'll never have to worry about is a shortage of hype. But you're right, it would be a big story.'

'Get your name in all the papers.'

'And my face in front of a lot of TV cameras, if I wanted. Or even if I didn't. That's almost reason enough right there to keep the story quiet.'

'On account of you shy.'

'I'd just as soon stay out of the spotlight. I don't mind having my name in the paper once in a while. It draws clients, and while I don't necessarily want more business it's nice to be able to pick and choose. But this wouldn't be a little publicity. This would be a circus, and no, I wouldn't want to be the trained seal in the center ring.'

'So Will's secret be safe,' he mused, 'just because you don't want to go on "Geraldo".'

'I could duck most of the publicity. I could feed it to Joe and let him whisper it into the right ears. He'd find a way to make sure other people got the credit. That's probably what I'll do, if I do anything.'

'But you might not even do that much.'

'I might not.'

'Why?'

'Because he's a sleeping dog,' I said, 'and maybe the decent thing is to let him lie.'

'How you gonna decide?'

'By talking to people.'

'Like we doin' now?'

'Exactly like we're doing now,' I said. 'This is part of the process.'

'Glad I helpin'.'

'I'll go home and talk to Elaine,' I said, 'and later on I'll talk about it at a meeting. I won't be specific, and nobody will know what I'm talking about, but it'll help me clarify my own thoughts on the subject. And then there's somebody else I think I'll talk it over with.'

'Who's that?'

'An attorney I know.'

He nodded. 'Seems like don't nobody do nothin' without they first got to talk it over with a lawyer.'

Elaine and I had dinner at Paris Green, on Ninth Avenue, and our conversation stayed on a single topic from the Portobello mushroom appetizer clear through to the cappuccino. I walked her back to the Parc Vendôme and continued on up Ninth to St Paul's. I got there ten minutes late, and settled into my chair just as the speaker reached that point in the story where he took his first drink. I'd missed the history of the dysfunctional family, but I could probably get along without hearing it.

During the break I helped myself to coffee and chatted with a couple of people, and when the meeting resumed I got my hand up and talked about having to make a decision. I was wonderfully vague, and no one could have had a clue what I was getting at, but that's not atypical of AA shares. I talked about what was on my mind, and then a TV set designer talked about whether or not he was going home to Greenville for Thanksgiving, and then a woman talked about being on a date with a man who was drinking non-alcoholic beer, and how the whole thing had done a number on her head.

After we'd folded the chairs, I walked with some friends as far as the Flame, but turned down an invitation to join them for coffee, pleading a previous engagement. I headed over to Columbus Circle and rode the IRT local downtown to Christopher Street. By 10:30 I was standing on a stoop on Commerce Street, using a door knocker shaped like a lion's head.

Commerce Street is two blocks long and off the beaten path, and it can be hard to find. I'd put in

196

enough time at the Sixth Precinct so that I still knew my way around the Village, and I'd had occasion to get to this particular block several times in the past couple of years. Once Elaine and I had caught a play at the Cherry Lane Theater, just across the street. My other visits, like this one, were to Ray Gruliow's townhouse.

I didn't have to linger long on his stoop. He drew the door open and motioned me inside, his face bright with the smile that is his most winning feature. It was a smile that said the world was a great cosmic joke, and you and he were the only two people who were in on it.

'Matt,' he said, and clapped me on the shoulder. 'There's fresh coffee. Interested?'

'Why not?'

The coffee was strong and rich and dark, worlds removed from the bitter sludge I'd sipped out of a Styrofoam cup in the basement of St Paul's. I said as much and he beamed. 'When I go to St Luke's,' he said, 'I take my own coffee in a thermos jar. My sponsor says it's my way of distancing myself from the group. I say it's more a matter of distancing myself from a gastritis attack. What's your opinion?'

'I agree with both of you.'

'Ever the diplomat. Now. What brings you here besides the lure of my most excellent coffee?'

'The last time we spoke,' I said, 'you defended Adrian Whitfield against a charge of suicide. Do you remember?'

'Vividly. And shortly thereafter Will was good enough to send off a letter that validated my contention by claiming credit.'

I took another sip of the coffee. It was really something special.

I said, 'Adrian killed himself. He wrote the letter. He wrote all those letters, he killed all those people. He was Will.'

FIFTEEN

'It could have been murder,' I said, 'even if I couldn't figure out how Will had managed to pull it off. Assume he had his ways, assume he could scale the side of the building and get in through a window, or unlock the door and disarm the burglar alarm system and reset it afterward. It was a real locked-room puzzle, though, any way you looked at it.

'But if it was suicide, the hell, what's simpler than poisoning your own whisky? He could have done it whenever he had a few minutes alone, and that gave him plenty of opportunity. Just uncap the bottle, pour in the cyanide crystals, and put the cap back on.'

'And be sure not to drink from that particular bottle until you're ready to catch the bus.'

'That's right,' I said. 'But we're back to the points you raised earlier. Why, in the absence of any kind of a financial motive, go to all that trouble to make suicide look like murder? Why make it look like an impossible murder?'

'Why?'

'So that Will would get the credit, and look good in the process. This would be Will's last hurrah. Why not make it a good one and go out with a bang?'

He thought about it, nodded slowly. 'Makes a kind of sense if he's Will. But only if he's Will.'

'Granted.'

'So how did you get that part? Because if it's just a hypothesis that you dreamed up because it's the only way to make sense out of the locked–room–murder–that–has–to–be–suicide . . .'

'It's not. There's something else that got me suspicious.'

'Oh?'

'That first night at his apartment,' I said, 'he didn't have booze on his breath.'

'Well, for Christ's sake,' he said. 'Why didn't you say so earlier? Jesus, I'm surprised you didn't arrest the son of a bitch right then and there.'

But he listened without interrupting while I explained my recollection of that first visit to Whitfield's Park Avenue apartment. 'He made a point of saying he'd been drinking when he hadn't,' I explained. 'Now why the hell would he lie about something like that? He wasn't a heavy drinker, and he didn't claim to be a heavy drinker, but he did drink, and he even took a drink in front of me. So why the subterfuge, why pretend to have had a couple of drinks earlier in the evening?

'I didn't have to be able to answer that in order to conclude that he'd lied to me, and I didn't think he'd do that without a reason. Well, what did the lie accomplish? It underscored his claim of having been really rattled by Will's threat. What was he saying, really? Something along the lines of, "I'm truly and righteously scared, in fact I'm *so* scared that I've already had a couple of drinks today, and now I'm going to have another one and you can stand there and watch me do it."

'Why would he want me to think he was scared? I busted my head on that one. What I came up with was that the only reason he'd have for going out of his way to impress me with his fear was because it didn't exist.

That's why he had to lie about it. He wanted me to think he was afraid because he wasn't.'

'Why bother? Wouldn't you assume he was afraid, getting marked for death by some clown who was riding a hot streak? Wouldn't anybody?'

'You'd think so,' I said, 'but he knew something I didn't. He knew he wasn't afraid, and he knew he had nothing to be afraid of.'

'Because Will couldn't hurt him.'

'Not if he was Will.'

He frowned. 'That's a pretty big leap of logic, wouldn't you say? He's pretending to be afraid, therefore he's not afraid, therefore he's got nothing to fear. Therefore he's Will, master criminal and multiple murderer. I don't remember a whole lot from my freshman Logic class, but it strikes me there's a flaw in the ointment.'

'A flaw in the ointment?'

'The ointment, the woodpile. Maybe he's not afraid because he's got terminal cancer and he figures Will's just doing him a favor.'

'I thought of that.'

'And, since he's keeping his illness secret from the world, he puts on an innocent act in order to keep you from wondering why it doesn't upset him more to be Will's next headline.'

'I thought of that, too.'

'And?'

'I had to admit it was possible,' I said, 'but it just didn't ring true. The motive for subterfuge seemed pretty thin. So what if I didn't think he was afraid? I'd just figure him for a stoic. But if what he wanted to cover up was the fact that he was Will, well, you could understand why he'd be moved to keep that a secret.'

'Where did you go from there?'

'I took a look at the first murder.'

'Richie Vollmer.'

'Richie Vollmer. Adrian's client, now free to do it again.'

'Anybody would have gotten Richie off, Matt. It wasn't Adrian's doing. The state's case fell apart when the Neagley woman hanged herself. It's not as though Adrian handed her the rope.'

'No.'

'You think he felt responsible?'

'I wouldn't go that far. I think he saw Richie's release as a gross miscarriage of justice, and I think he read Marty McGraw's column and came to the conclusion that Marty was right. The world would be a better place without Richie in it.'

'How many people read that column? And what proportion of them found nothing in it to object to?'

'A whole lot of people read it,' I said, 'and most of them very likely agreed with it. Adrian had something most of the rest of us lacked. Two things, actually. He'd played a role in Richie's little dance through the halls of justice, and he could probably find a way to feel at least some responsibility for the outcome. Maybe he'd passed up a chance to get Richie to plead.'

'All right, it's speculative but I'll allow it. You said two things. What's the other one?'

'He had access.'

'To what, the blunt instrument he clubbed him with? Or the rope he used to hang him from the tree?'

'To Richie. Think about it, Ray. Here's a son of a bitch they caught dead to rights for killing children, and he walks, so now he's free but he's a pariah, a fucking moral leper. And you're Will, a public-spirited citizen determined to dispense rough justice. What do you do, look him up in the phone book? Call him up, tell him you want to talk to him about the advantages of investing in tax-free munis?'

'But Adrian would have known where to find him.'

'Of course he'd know. He was his lawyer. And do you think Richie would refuse a meeting with him? Or be on his guard?'

'You can never predict what a client will do,' he said. 'You're the next thing to a member of their family during the trial, and then it ends in an acquittal and they don't want to know you. I used to think it was ingratitude. Then for a while I decided it stemmed from a desire to put the experience behind them.'

'And now?'

'Now I'm back to ingratitude. God knows there's a lot of it going around.' He leaned back in his chair, his fingers interlaced behind his head. 'Let's say you're right,' he said, 'and Adrian had access. He could call Richie and Richie would meet him.'

'And not be on his guard.'

'And not be on his guard. Adrian wouldn't have to turn up on his doorstep disguised as a twelve-year-old girl. You have anything beside conjecture to place the two of them together?'

'The cops might have the manpower to turn up a witness who saw the two of them together,' I said. 'I didn't even try. What I looked for was the opposite, proof that Adrian was somewhere else when Richie was killed.'

'In court or out of town, for instance.'

'Anything that would give him an alibi. I checked his desk calendar and his time sheets at the office. I can't prove he didn't have an alibi, because he wasn't around to answer questions, but I couldn't find anything to establish one for him.'

'What about the others? Patsy Salerno was next. Another distinguished client?'

'Adrian never represented him. But a few years ago he had one of Patsy's soldiers for a client.'

'So?'

'Maybe it gave him a chance to take a strong dislike to the man. I don't know. Maybe it left him with a contact in Patsy's circle, someone who might let slip where Patsy was going to be having dinner and when.'

'So Adrian could get there first and hide in the toilet.' He shook his head. 'It's hard to picture him walking in there in the first place, this Waspy guy chasing up to Arthur Avenue for a plate of ziti and eggplant. And how does he hide in the can, and how can he be sure Patsy's going to answer a call of nature? I'll grant you Patsy was of an age where you wouldn't expect him to go too many hours between visits to the can, but you could still spend a long time waiting. And Adrian wasn't a guy who'd blend in there.'

'More conjecture,' I said.

'Go ahead.'

'Maybe he didn't try to blend in. Maybe he used who he was instead of trying to disguise it. Maybe he got Patsy's ear and set up a super-secret meeting.'

'On what pretext?'

'A traitor in Patsy's ranks. A leak in the US Attorney's office. A message from somebody highly placed in one of the other crime families. Who knows what he made up? Patsy'd have no reason to be suspicious. The only wire he'd worry about is the kind you wear, not the kind that goes around your neck.'

'He could even let Patsy pick the time and place,' Ray said. '"I'll make sure the back door's unlocked for you. Slip in, and the bathroom's along the hall on the right."'

'I don't even know if there's a rear entrance,' I said, 'but one way or another he'd let Patsy set up a meeting. And he'd make sure Patsy wouldn't mention it to anybody.'

'So his identity gives him access. Same as with Richie.'

'It strikes me as the best way for him to operate.'

He nodded. 'When you think of Will,' he said, 'you picture some Ninja gliding invisibly through the city streets. But the best cloak of invisibility might be a three-piece suit. I suppose you looked for an alibi for him for Salerno's murder? And I don't suppose he was fly-fishing in Montana?'

'As far as I can tell, he was right here in New York.'

'So were eight million other people,' he said, 'and I don't see you accusing them of murder. What about Julian Rashid? How was Adrian planning on getting into the compound in St Albans?'

'I don't know,' I admitted. 'Maybe he was working on a plan to lure Rashid out. I know he wasn't there when Rashid was killed. He spent the evening with –' I checked my notebook '– Henry Berghash and DeWitt Palmer.'

'A judge and a college president? I'd say it's a damn shame the Cardinal couldn't join them. I don't suppose the three of them wound up at a leather bar on West Street.'

'Dinner at Christ Cella's, fifth-row seats for the new Stoppard play, and drinks afterwards at Agincourt. A notation in his calendar, backed up with a credit-card receipt and a ticket stub.'

'That's just perfect,' he said. 'You managed to find him a rock-solid alibi for the one murder Will didn't commit.'

'I know.'

'You think he set it up that way? He knew Scipio was going to do it and made sure he covered himself?'

'I think it was coincidence.'

'Because it's hardly incriminating, having an alibi.'

'No.'

'Any more than it's incriminating *not* having an alibi for the other two murders.'

'True.'

'But we've left one out, haven't we? The abortion guy. Except he'd hate to be called that, wouldn't he? I'm sure he'd much rather be known as the anti-abortion guy.'

'Protector of the unborn,' I said.

'Roswell Berry. Killed not here in nasty old New York but halfway across the country in the telemarketing capital of America.'

'Omaha?'

'You didn't know that about Omaha? Whenever there's an ad on a cable channel, a 24-hour 800 number for you to order a Vegematic Pocket Fisherman CD of Roger Whittaker's greatest hits, nine times out of ten the person who takes your order is sitting in an office in Omaha. Did Adrian have an alibi when Berry got killed?'

'Yes, he did.'

His eyebrows went up. 'Really? That sinks your whole theory, doesn't it?'

'No,' I said, 'it's the closest thing I've got to hard evidence, and it's strong enough to have brought me here tonight. See, Adrian did have an alibi for Berry's murder. And it's full of holes.'

'He went to Philadelphia,' I said. 'Rode down and back on the Metroliner, had a seat reserved both ways in the club car. Charged the ticket to his American Express card.'

'Where'd he stay in Philly?'

'At the Sheraton near Independence Hall. He was there three nights, and again he used his Amex card.'

'And meanwhile Roswell Berry was being murdered in Omaha.'

'That's right.'

'Which is what, two thousand miles away?'

'More or less.'

'Don't make me dig,' he said. 'This would appear to clear Adrian. How does it implicate him?'

'Here's what I think he did,' I said. 'I think he went to Philly and checked into the hotel and unpacked a bag. Then I think he took his briefcase and caught a cab to the airport, where he paid cash and showed ID in the name of A Johnson. He flew to Omaha via Milwaukee on Midwest Express. He registered at the Hilton as Allen Johnson, showing a credit card in that name when he checked in but paying cash when he left. He got there in plenty of time to kill Berry and he got out before the body was found.'

'And flew back to Philadelphia,' Ray said. 'And packed his bag and paid his hotel bill and got on the train.'

'Right.'

'And you've got nothing that places him in Philadelphia during the time that our Mr Johnson was either in or en route to Omaha.'

'Nothing,' I said. 'No phone calls on his hotel bill, no meals charged, nothing at all to substantiate his presence in the city except that he was paying for a hotel room.'

'I don't suppose there was a maid who would remember if the bed had been slept in.'

'This long after the fact? The only way she'd remember is if she slept in it with him.'

'Matt, why'd he go to Philly? You'll say to set up an alibi, I understand that much, but what was his ostensible purpose?'

'To keep some appointments, evidently. He had four or five of them listed on his desk calendar.'

'Oh?'

'Times and last names. I don't think they were real appointments. I think they were there for show. I checked the names against his Rolodex and couldn't find them. More to the point, I checked his phone bills, home and office. The only call to Philly that fits the time frame was the one he made to the Sheraton to book his room.'

He thought about it. 'Suppose he was seeing somebody in Philadelphia. A married woman. He calls her from a pay phone because —'

'Because her husband might check Adrian's phone records?'

He started over. 'He can't call her at all,' he said. 'She has to call him, and that's why there are no calls to her on his phone bill. The appointments on his calendar are with her. The names are phony so no one can glance at his calendar and recognize her name. He goes there and never leaves his room, she visits him when she can, and somebody else named Johnson flies out to Omaha and back, not because he's Will but because he wants to discuss investments with Warren Buffet.'

'And Adrian stays in his room all that time and never orders a sandwich from Room Service? Or eats the mixed nuts from the mini bar?'

I went over it again, letting him raise objections, knocking them down as he raised them.

'Allen Johnson,' he said. 'Is that right? Allen?'

'Allen at the Hilt
counter.'

'If you'd found a w
name in the top drawe
had something.'

'He could have it tuck
'or stashed in a safe-deposi
of it once he knew he wo

'And when was that?
Omaha?'

'Or when he wrote the let   as
Will's last victim. Or later. It w   it showed
up on a list of recent cyanide   asers.'

'Where would you find a list like that?'

'You'd have to compile it, which is what someone
very likely did once the autopsy results confirmed
cyanide as the cause of Adrian's death. We can be sure
his own name didn't show up on the list, or we'd have
read headlines about it. He'd have thought of that. If he
needed to show ID in order to buy cyanide, he'd have
made sure it was in another name.'

'And he'd have felt safe enough using Allen Johnson
again.'

'Unless he'd already destroyed it, yes. I don't imagine
he'd be overly concerned about someone putting the
two Johnsons together, one from a hotel in Omaha and
the other from a poison-control ledger in New York.'

'No.'

He excused himself, and came back saying how
lucky he was – there had been no one lurking in the
bathroom with a garrote.

'Though I wouldn't have made his list,' he said, 'if
only because he already had a criminal lawyer on it.
Hell of an eclectic list he came up with, wouldn't you
say?'

ath, a Mafia boss, a Right-to-Lifer, e-rouser. All along everybody's been the common denominator. You'd think become apparent when you know who did it, s still hard to spot.'

He only really needed a reason for the first one,' I said, 'and he had that. There he was, brooding over his role in Richie Vollmer's release, and McGraw's column stirred him to action. At that point he very likely intended just to commit one single act of murder.'

'And then what happened?'

'My guess is he found out he liked it.'

'Got a thrill out of it, you mean? Middle-aged lawyer all of a sudden finds out he's got the soul of a psychopath?'

I shook my head. 'I don't imagine he suddenly blossomed as a thrill killer. But I think he found it satisfying.'

'Satisfying.'

'I think so, yes.'

'Killing people who had it coming, making the world a better place for it. That what you mean?'

'Something like that.'

'I suppose it could be satisfying,' he said. 'Especially for a man who's under a death sentence himself. "What can I do to improve the world before I leave it? Well, I can take that son of a bitch off the boards. There, I may not live forever, but at least I outlived you, you bastard".'

'That's the idea. The first one's Richie. The second one's because he wants to do it again, so he picks someone else the law can't lay a finger on. He's had some exposure to Patsy Salerno, enough to form a strong negative opinion of the man.'

'And after that?'

'I would think the motives thinned out as he went along. Numbers three and four were similarly untouchable. Roswell Berry had clearly incited acts that led to the deaths of physicians performing abortions, and the law couldn't lay a glove on him. I don't suppose there was a personal element in it, unless Adrian knew one of the doctors or had strong feelings on the subject of abortion rights.'

'His sister,' Ray said suddenly.

'His sister? I didn't think he had any brothers and sisters.'

'He told me about her once,' he said. 'A long time ago, back when he used to put away a lot more than one drink a day. He liked those single-malt Scotches even then, though I couldn't tell you the brand.' He grinned suddenly. 'I can remember the taste, though. Isn't that a surprise? We were both about half lit and he told me about his sister. She was two or three years older than Adrian. She was away at college when she died, and Adrian was in his last year of high school.'

I thought I knew the answer, but I asked the question anyway. 'What did she die of?'

'Blood poisoning,' he said. 'One of those infections that goes through you like wildfire. That was all they told him at the time. It was years later before he got the whole story from his mother. She wouldn't tell him until after his father died, and of course you can figure it out now.'

'Yes.'

'Septicemia following a back-street abortion. Did it transform Adrian into a crusader for abortion rights? Not that you'd notice. Maybe he wrote out a check once in a while, or voted for or against a candidate because of his stand on the issue, but he didn't sign a lot of petitions and open letters, and I never saw him out on Fifth Avenue picketing St Patrick's.'

'But when it came to draw up a little list –'

He nodded. 'Sure. Why not? "This one's for you, Sis."' He stifled a yawn. 'Funny,' he said. 'I never got tired when I drank. It was always the easiest thing in the world to talk the night away.'

'I'll go home and let you get some sleep.'

'Sit down,' he said. 'We're not through yet. Anyway, all we need is a little more coffee.'

'You don't even begin to have what you could call proof,' Ray Gruliow said. 'It's far too little for an indictment, let alone a conviction.'

'I realize that.'

'All of which is moot, admittedly, given that the defendant is no longer among the living.' He settled back in his seat. 'And you weren't trying to sell it to a jury anyway, were you? I'm the guy you want to buy it.'

'And?'

'And I suppose I'm sold.'

'You could turn up enough evidence,' I said, 'once you had a ton of guys with badges looking for it. Print up a few dozen photos of Adrian and show them to people at airports and hotels and you'll find someone who remembers him. Pull NYNEX's records of local calls made from his home and office phones. He probably made most of his calls from pay phones, but there may be some calls that tie in with some of Will's activities. Go through his apartment and his office with the kind of detailed search I didn't have the time or authority for and who knows what kind of hard evidence you'll find.'

'So what's the question?'

'The question is what do I do with this sleeping dog.'

'Traditionally, you're supposed to let them lie.'

'I know.'

'Adrian's dead, and Will's officially retired. He said so in his last letter. What did he do, drop that in the mail on his way out of the courtroom?'

'It looks like it.'

'Wrote the letter, put a stamp on it, carried it around with him. Then his trial's wrapped up, with his client conveniently copping a plea, and it's time to throw in the towel. So he mails the letter and goes home and plays out the last scene.'

'Calls me first,' I said.

'Calls you first and says he wishes he had more time. Then goes out and makes sure his bodyguard's watching when he takes his last drink and kisses the carpet. That business about the wrong zip code on the letter to the *News*. You think that was to delay the letter?'

I shook my head. 'I don't think so. You couldn't know it would work. With the volume of mail the paper gets, there's ample opportunity for some clerk somewhere along the way to spot the letter and redirect it into the right slot. I just think he got the zip wrong.'

'I guess he had things on his mind.' He turned to me, his eyes probing mine. 'You know what I think? I think you have to take what you've got and hand it to the cops.'

'What makes you say that?'

'Because otherwise they'll be running down false trails and barking up wrong trees for months on end. How many men do you suppose they've got assigned to Will?'

'No idea.'

'A substantial number, though.'

'Obviously.'

'Well, you could let them waste their time,' he said, 'on the assumption that it would keep them from making trouble for somebody else, but I don't even know if that's true. Who knows how many lives they're going to turn inside out looking for Will?' He yawned. 'But there's a more basic consideration. Who's your client? How do you best serve his interests?'

'The only client I've had has been Adrian.'

'Well, you haven't resigned and he hadn't fired you. I'd say he's still your client.'

'According to that line of reasoning, I ought to let it lie.'

He shook his head. 'You're missing something, Matt. Why did Adrian hire you?'

'I wouldn't take any payment for advising him on how to go about protecting himself. I suppose this was his way of paying me for my time.'

'What did he engage you to do?'

'To investigate the whole case. I told him I couldn't be expected to accomplish much.' I remembered something. 'He alluded to my tendency to stay with a case. Stubbornness, you could call it.'

'You could indeed. Don't you see? He wanted you to solve it. He didn't want to leave loose ends. He wanted to baffle everybody, he wanted the audience holding its breath when the curtain went down. But then, after a decent interval, he wants a chance to come out and take a bow. And that's where you come in.'

I thought about it. 'I don't know,' I said. 'Why not just leave a letter to be delivered a certain amount of time after his death? As far as that goes, let's remember that we're talking about a multiple murderer with delusions of grandeur. Do you really think you can read his mind?'

'Throw all that out, then. The hell with what he

wanted and what he didn't want. You're a detective. It's who you are and it's what you do. That's why you stayed with it and that's why you solved it.'

'If I've solved it.'

'And that's why you'll sit down with your friend Durkin tomorrow and tell him what you've got.'

'Because it's who I am and what I do.'

'Uh-huh. And I'm afraid you're stuck with it.'

SIXTEEN

The phone rang the next morning while we were having breakfast. Elaine answered it, and it was TJ, checking to see if she wanted him to spell her at the shop. She talked with him, then said, 'Hang on,' and passed me the phone.

'It ain't the peach pits,' he said. 'You got to crack the pits, and there's this kernel inside.'

'What are you talking about?'

'Talkin' 'bout cyanide, Clyde. Like he put in the Scotch bottle? I can't say if you could kill yourself eatin' peach kernels, but there was a dude did it with apricots. Didn't eat but fifteen or twenty of 'em, and that was enough.'

'Apricot kernels, you mean.'

There was a pause, and I could picture his eyes rolling. 'If you could die from eatin' fifteen or twenty apricots, don't you think they'd make 'em put a warnin' on the package? Dude cracked open the pits, ate the kernels, an' that was his last meal.'

'And it was suicide?'

'Couldn't find out for sure. Could be he was tryin' to cure cancer. There's this drug they make outta apricot kernels, and you've got people swearin' it works and people swearin' it don't. Laetrile? Might be I ain't pronouncin' it right.'

'I've heard of it.'

'So this dude who ate the kernels, could be he was on a do-it-yourself Laetrile project. But we was wonderin' if you could kill yourself that way, eatin'' peach pits, an' if fifteen or twenty's all it takes, I guess the answer's yes, at least with apricots. Assumin' you fool enough to try.'

'Somehow I don't think Adrian got cyanide from apricot kernels.'

'No, but that leaves a whole lot of other ways to get it. Turns out there's all kinds of industrial uses for that shit.' He went on to tell me some of them. 'So his name might turn up on a list,' he said, 'or Allen Johnson's might, but they might not. On account of there's so many different ways to get it.'

'How do you happen to know all this?'

'Computer.'

'You don't have a computer.'

'This girl does.'

'What girl?'

'Girl I know. Not like the Kongs, she ain't no hacker, don't know how to do anything tricky, sneakin' into networks an' data bases and all of that. She just use it to do her homework and balance her checkbook an' shit.'

'So you asked her computer about peach pits and cyanide and it spat out all that information?'

'You don't ask the computer nothin'. Computer just a machine.'

'Oh.'

'She got this on-line service, see, and you hook up to that and browse these different message boards. An' when you find somebody might know the answer to your question, you send him an e- mail. An' he e-mails you back. Like talkin', 'cept it on the screen.'

'Oh.'

'An' what else you can do, you can post a question on the message board, an' people post their answers an' you can pick 'em up later on. Or they'll e-mail it straight back to you. Anything you want to know, somebody out there got the answer.'

'Oh.'

'Course, sometimes what you get gonna be the *wrong* answer, 'cause people who don't know be just as apt to answer as people who do. So all of that about the apricot kernels ain't exactly somethin' you can take to the bank, Frank. Might be he got the details wrong.'

'I see.'

'Anyway,' he said, 'I learned all of that, so I thought I'd pass it on. I be at Elaine's shop later, case you need me.'

I finished my coffee, and I was on my way out the door when the phone rang.

It was Joe Durkin. 'We have to talk,' he said.

'I was on my way over.'

'Don't come here. There's that coffee shop I met you once, Greek place, Eighth between Forty-fourth and Forty-fifth. I forgot the name, they changed it when they redecorated, but it's the same place.'

'I know the one you mean. The east side of Eighth.'

'Right. Ten minutes?'

'Fine. I'll buy the coffee.'

'All I want is straight answers,' he said. 'I don't give a shit who buys the coffee.'

He was in a booth when I got there. He had a cup of coffee in front of him and an expression on his face that I couldn't read. He said, 'I want to know what you know about Will.'

'What brought this on?'

'What brought it on? I made a phone call this morning, just thought I'd ask if the Allen Johnson name

218

turned up on any lists they might have got from Poison Control.'

'I gather it rang a bell.'

'The name? It couldn't, because I didn't get that far. Before I knew it I was right in the middle of a Chinese fire drill. What did I know about Will? What did I have and where did it come from?'

'What did you tell them?'

'That I'd heard something from a source during an investigation of another matter. I don't remember exactly what I said. I didn't mention your name, if that's what you were wondering.'

'Good.'

'The only reason I kept you out of it,' he said, 'is before I give you to them I want to know what I'm giving. How did this Allen Johnson get to be Will, and how did you get on to him, and who the hell is he anyway?' When I hesitated he added, 'And don't hold out on me, Matt. If you're blowing smoke, blow it someplace else, will you? And if you've got something, well, the son of a bitch already murdered five people. Don't sit there with your thumb up your ass while he goes and kills somebody else.'

'He's not going to kill anybody else.'

'Why, because he gave us his word? He kills people but he draws the line at lying?'

'His killing days are over.'

'And you know for a fact he won't change his mind?'

'He can't.'

'Why's that?'

'Because he's dead,' I said. 'The last person he killed was himself. I'm not blowing smoke and I'm not holding out, either. Will was Adrian Whitfield. He killed three people and then he killed himself.'

He looked at me. 'In other words, case closed. Is that what you're saying?'

'It'll take some police work to wrap it up and tie off the loose ends, but –'

'But Will's history and the people of this great city can sleep safe in their beds. Is that it?'

'Evidently not,' I said, 'if your tone of voice is anything to go by. What have you got?'

'What have I got? I haven't got a thing. I could tell you what they've got downtown, except you can figure it out for yourself when I tell you who they got it from. Our old friend Martin J McGraw.' I looked at him and he nodded. 'Yeah, right,' he said. 'Another letter from Will.'

SEVENTEEN

The letter had obviously been written after its author had read Marty McGraw's most recent column, the one that ended in an oblique invitation to Will to deal harshly with the principal owner of the New York Yankees. 'An Open Letter to Marty McGraw,' was how he headed it, and he started with a reference to the last line of McGraw's column. 'You ask where I am now that you need me,' he said. 'The question answers itself if you will but remember what I am. The Will of the People is always present, even as it is always needed. The particular flesh and blood embodiment of that Will who writes these lines, and who has been called to action several times in recent months, is nothing more than a physical manifestation of that Will.'

He went on in that abstract vein for another paragraph or two, then turned specific. His letter's title notwithstanding, Marty McGraw was not his target. Neither was the Yankees' arrogant owner. Instead he named three New Yorkers whom he charged with acting in flagrant opposition to the public good. First was Peter Tully, head of the Transit Workers Union, who was already threatening to greet the new year with a bus and subway strike. Second on the list was Marvin Rome, a judge who'd never met a defendant he didn't like. The final name was that of Regis Kilbourne, for many years the theater critic of the *New York Times*.

Hours later, I finally got to see a copy of the letter. 'You keep shaking your head like that,' Joe Durkin said, 'you'll wind up suing yourself for whiplash.'

'Will never wrote this letter.'

'So you said. At great length, as I recall.'

We'd spent the day in a conference room at One Police Plaza, where I got to tell my story over and over to different teams of detectives. Some of them acted respectful while others were cynical and patronizing, but whatever attitude they struck it felt as though they were acting the part. They all seemed impossibly young to me, and I suppose they were. Their average age must have been around thirty-five, which gave me a good twenty years on them.

I don't know why they had to ask me the same questions quite as many times as they did. A certain amount of that was probably to see if I contradicted myself or offered any additional information, but eventually I guess they just settled into a routine. It was easier to go over my story a few more times than to think of something else to do.

Meanwhile, other people were off doing other things. They sent a crew to toss Adrian's apartment and another to disrupt things at his office. His photograph went out by wire to Omaha and Philadelphia, as well as to Midwest Express's hub city, Milwaukee. They weren't keeping me posted, but I guess some corroborating evidence began to turn up, because there was an attitudinal shift sometime around the middle of the afternoon. That was when it began to become clear that they knew the story I'd spun for them was more than smoke.

Joe was around for the whole thing. He wasn't always in the conference room, and at one point I thought he'd gone home, or back to his precinct. He came back, though, and he brought a sandwich and a container of coffee for me. He disappeared again after a while, but he was planted in a chair in the outer office when they finally told me to go home.

We walked a couple of blocks, passing up a few favorite cop watering holes, and wound up in the bar of a Vietnamese restaurant on Baxter Street. The place was the next thing to empty, with one man reading a newspaper at a table and another nursing a beer at the far end of the bar. The woman behind the bar looked exotic, and thoroughly bored. She fixed a martini for Joe and a Coke for me and left us alone.

Joe drank a third of his martini and held the glass aloft. 'I ordered this,' he said, 'not because I ever liked the taste of these things, but because after a day like today I wanted something that would hit me right between the eyes.'

'I know what you mean,' I said. 'That's why I ordered a Coke.'

'Is that a fact. Don't tell me you never get the urge for something stronger.'

'I get lots of urges,' I said. 'So?'

'So nothing.' He nodded in the direction of the bartender. 'Talk about urges,' he said.

'Oh?'

'What do you figure, black father and Vietnamese mother?'

'Something like that.'

'A lonely GI far from home. A girl, young in years, but filled with the ancient knowledge of the East. Listen to me, will you? It's funny, though. You see somebody looks exotic like that, you think it'd be special. But it's just in your mind.'

'You've looked at clouds from both sides now.'

'Oh, go fuck yourself,' he said.

'Everybody tells me that.'

'Yeah, and I can see why. Here, I got a copy of this.

223

I don't think I was supposed to, and I *know* I'm not supposed to show it to you, but I'll bet you anything it's in the paper by morning, so why should you be the last person in town to see it?'

And he handed me Will's letter.

'It's all wrong,' I said. 'Will didn't write this.'

'If Will was Whitfield,' he said, 'and assuming Whitfield's not playing possum, then all of that goes without saying, doesn't it? Of course he didn't write it. Dead men don't write letters.'

'They can write them before they die. He already did that once.'

He took the letter from me. 'He's got references to the column of McGraw's that ran yesterday, Matt. And he talks about Tully's threat of a TWU strike, and that's only been news in the past week or ten days.'

'I know that,' I said. 'There's plenty of evidence to disprove any theory that Adrian wrote this and arranged to have it mailed weeks after his death. But suppose I never even suspected Adrian. You could still take one look at this and know that the same person hadn't written it.'

'Oh? Style's pretty close.'

'Will Number Two is literate,' I said. 'He's got an ear for language, and I'd guess he made a conscious effort to mimic Will Number One. I haven't got the other letters handy to compare them, but it seems to me I can recognize phrases that I've read before.'

'I don't know about that. I'd agree it has a familiar ring to it. But wouldn't anybody copycatting Will make an effort to sound like the original?'

'Not everybody could pull it off.'

'No?' He shrugged. 'Maybe it's harder than it looks. You know, he didn't just copycat the style of the writing. He got the rest of it right, too. See the signature?'

'It's printed in script.'

He nodded. 'Same as the others. I was talking to a couple of the guys while the rest of them were in there trying to make your head spin. I asked about the forensic side.'

'I was wondering about that,' I said. 'It seems to me it shouldn't be much of a trick to prove that the new letter was typed on a different machine.'

'Well, sure,' he said. 'If it was typed.'

'If it wasn't, I said, 'he's got a funny kind of handwriting.'

'I mean typed on a typewriter, which it wasn't, and neither were any of the earlier letters. They were done on a computer and printed on a laser printer.'

'Can't they identify the computer and the printer forensically?'

He shook his head. 'With a typewriter the keys'll be worn differently, and this one'll be out of alignment, or the E and O's'll be filled in. Or the typeface is different. A typewriter's like a fingerprint, no two alike.'

'And a computer?'

'With a computer you can choose a different typeface everytime, you can make the type larger or smaller by touching this key or that one. You see how the signature's in script? You get that by switching to a script font.'

'So you can't tell if two letters came out of the same computer?'

'I'm not a hundred percent in the loop on this,' he said, 'but there's a certain amount you can tell. With Will's letters, the ones from Will Number One, they think there was more than one printer involved.'

He went on to tell me more than I could take in,

about ways in which you could compose a letter on one computer, copy it on a disk, and then print it out through another computer and printer. I didn't listen too carefully, and eventually I held up a hand to stop him.

'Please,' I said. 'I'm sick to death of computers. I can't have a conversation with TJ without hearing how wonderful they are. I don't care about the typeface or the paper, or if he composed it on the East Side and printed it out on the West Side. I don't even care about the writing style. What's so different it jumps off the page at you is what he's saying.'

'How do you mean?'

'His list.'

'The original Will wrote open letters to the vics,' he said. 'This one writes to McGraw. Plus he lists three at once.'

'Uh-huh. And look who's on the list.'

'Peter Tully, Marvin Rome, and Regis Kilbourne.'

'Adrian picked people society couldn't come to terms with. A child killer who got away with it. A Mafia don who got away with everything. A right-to-lifer who'd incited homicide and remained untouchable. A racist firebrand who, like the rest of them, had found a way around the system.'

'And a defense attorney.'

'Adrian didn't really belong on the list, did he? That should have been grounds for suspecting him in and of itself. Leave him out, though, and you've got four people who could certainly be viewed as public enemies out of the law's reach. You could argue that the small-W will of the people might very well be what big-W Will was carrying out.'

'And the new list?'

'A labor leader, a judge, and a critic. They're right up

there with Jack the Ripper and Attila the Hun, wouldn't you say?'

'Oh, I don't know,' he said. He knocked back the rest of his martini, caught the bartender's eye and pointed to his glass. 'I could probably think of a few people who might not break down crying if Send-'em-home Rome went to that great courtroom in the sky. The son of a bitch has made a career out of never giving a police officer the benefit of the doubt. He sets minimum bail or releases on own recognizance all the damn time, dismisses cases right and left.'

'He's a judge,' I said, 'and the people voted him into office, and they could vote him out if they really wanted to. And one of these days they probably will.'

'Not soon enough.'

'What about Peter Tully?'

'Well, he's an arrogant prick,' he said. 'What's Will have to say about him? "You hold an entire city hostage to your lust for power as you threaten to thrust a wrench into the machinery of urban transit." You know, maybe Will Number Two isn't such a great mimic after all. I can't see Number One coming up with a sentence like that.'

'Listen to his bill of goods against Regis Kilbourne. "Your power over the Broadway stage is near absolute, and it has absolutely corrupted you. Drunk with it, you unfailingly choose form over content, style over substance, promoting the willfully obscure at the expense of the well-made drama with a story to tell." There's more about how he'll criticize an actor for being physically unattractive, and how unfair it all is.'

He thought about it while the girl brought his drink. 'It's not just the exotic aspect,' he said once she was out of hearing range. 'It's also she happens to be gorgeous.'

'You and Regis Kilbourne,' I said, 'placing an undue premium on physical appeal.'

'We're both a couple of superficial bastards,' he agreed. 'Who the hell would want to kill a critic?'

'Anybody who ever wrote a play or appeared in one,' I said, 'which in this town would have to include half the waiters and a third of the bartenders. But they'd like to kill him the way you'd welcome a shot at Judge Send-'em-home Rome. You might relish the fantasy, and it might not break your heart if a piece of the cornice broke off a tall building and took him out when it landed. But you wouldn't actually want to kill him.'

'No, and I probably wouldn't jump for joy if somebody else did, either. It's not good for the system when people start taking out judges.'

'Or critics,' I said, 'or labor leaders, either. You know the difference between the two Wills? The first one objected to the invulnerability of his targets, the way they'd managed to subvert the system. But these three don't have that kind of invulnerability. Marvin Rome's not going to be riding the bench forever. The voters'll probably boot him next time he comes up for reelection.'

'Let's hope so.'

'And Peter Tully can shut down the city, but the governor can return the favor. Under the Taylor Law, he can lock up anybody who orders a work stoppage by public employees. Kilbourne's probably got a job for life at the *Times*, but he's likely to rotate off the theater desk sooner or later, like the man before him. These three are by no means invulnerable, and that's not what's got the new Will's motor running. What he resents is the power of the men on his list.'

'Power, huh?'

'Tully can throw a switch and plunge the city into

immobility. Rome can unlock the cell doors and put criminals back on the street.'

'And Regis Kilbourne can tell an actress her nose is too big and her tits are too small and send her running in tears to the nearest plastic surgeon. If you call that power.'

'He can pretty much decide which shows stay open and which ones close.'

'He's got that much clout?'

'Just about. It's not him personally, it's the position he holds. Whoever reviews plays for the *Times* has influence that comes with the territory. A bad notice from him won't guarantee a show's dead, and a rave won't necessarily keep one open if everybody else hates it. But that's usually what happens.'

'Which means he's the man.'

'Yes.'

'"What man?" "The man with the power." Remember that?'

'Vaguely.'

'"What power?" "The power of voodoo."'

'It come's back to me now.'

'"Who do?" "You do." They don't write 'em like that anymore, Matt.'

'No, and I can see why. He must feel powerless himself, don't you figure?'

'Who, the man with the power?'

'The man who wrote this.'

'Let's see.' He held the letter, scanned it. 'Powerless, huh?'

'Don't you think so?'

'I don't know,' he said. 'I suppose that's what the Feebies would say if they did a profile of him. He resents the power others have over him and seeks to redress the balance by threatening their lives. Plus he wet the bed when he was a kid.'

'Funny how they always tell you that.'

'Like it's going to help you find the son of a bitch. "Hey, the FBI says our guy used to wet the bed, so I want you guys out on the street looking for a grownup little pisspot." Useful bit of knowledge when you're mounting a manhunt, but they always toss it in.'

'I know.'

'Along with the information that he came from a dysfunctional family. Jesus, that's helpful, isn't it? A dysfunctional family, holy shit, whoever heard of such a thing?'

'If you came from a dysfunctional family,' I said solemnly, 'you'd wet the bed, too.'

'And probably kill a few people while I was at it. It's all part of the package.' He frowned at the letter. 'Powerless and resenting the power of others. Yeah, I suppose so. It's a hard theory to argue with. But you know what he reminds me of, Will Number Two?'

'What?'

'A list of pet peeves like you'd write up for the high school yearbook. "What really pisses me off is insincere people, snap quizzes in algebra class, and lumpy mashed potatoes."'

'Well, who likes lumpy mashed potatoes?'

'Not me. They make me want to kill the Pope. But isn't that how it reads? "Here's a list of the people who really piss me off."'

'You're right.'

'I am, aren't I?' He pushed his stool back. 'The son of a bitch doesn't sound like a homicidal maniac. He just sounds like a nut with a hair up his ass.'

EIGHTEEN

The next couple of days were a three-ring circus for the media. Marty McGraw broke the story of the new letter from Will, with WILL'S BAAAAACK! on his newspaper's front page. Reporters hurried around town interviewing his three prospective victims, each of whom seemed to take the distinction more as an insult than a threat.

Peter Tully chose to see Will not as a personal foe but as an enemy of organized labor as a whole. He issued a statement linking the anonymous letter-writer with the repressive anti-union forces as exemplified by the mayor and the governor. There was a wonderful cadence of old-fashioned lefty rhetoric to his words. You could almost hear the Almanac Singers in the background, harmonizing on 'Union Maid' and 'Miner's Lifeguard', songs to fan the flames of discontent.

Judge Marvin Rome managed to view Will's attack as an assault on civil liberties and the rights of the accused. The one time I saw him on the news, he was linking Will with prosecutors and police officers who were willing to call an end run around the Bill of Rights in order to railroad a defendant — 'invariably poor, and all too often black' — into a prison cell. Will's threat, he assured the public, would no more lead him to compromise his principles than had the vilification he'd received over the years from DAs and cops and their lackeys in the press. He would go on dispensing true justice and tempering it with mercy.

Regis Kilbourne turned the whole thing into a

free-speech issue, lamenting a world in which a critic might feel constrained in any way from the free expression of his views. He went on to say the worst constraints came not from government censorship or his newspaper's editorial policy, but from 'those very aspects of oneself one tends to regard as emblematic of one's better nature'. Friendship, compassion, and a sense of fair play seemed to be the worst offenders, tempting one to give a kinder, gentler review than the material might otherwise deserve. 'If I have dared to inflict pain, to destroy a cherished relationship, to crush a perhaps promising career, all for the sake of a higher truth, can simple physical fear possibly sway me from my course? Indeed, it cannot and it will not.'

They were all going to carry on bravely, but that didn't mean they were ready to make Will's work easier for him. Peter Tully declined police protection but went about guarded by a thuggish phalanx of husky well-armed union members. Judge Rome accepted the NYPD's offer and supplemented their ranks with some additional cops he hired as moonlighters. (This struck some people as curious, and a *Post* reporter quoted an unnamed source: 'If Will really wants to kill Marvin Rome, odds are he's a cop himself.') Regis Kilbourne also took the police protection, and, at each of the openings and previews he attended, his companion was not one of the dewy-eyed and pouting young women he favored, but a burly plainclothes cop with a five o'clock shadow and an expression of bored bemusement.

Will's letter, targeting three prominent New Yorkers at once, would have been enough all by itself to keep the story hot for a week or more. Long before it had a chance to die down, McGraw broke the news that Adrian Whitfield, already famous as Will's most recent victim, had now been definitely determined by police investigators to have been Will himself. (One of the TV news shows hit the air with a news flash hours before the *Daily News* was on the street with it, but Marty was the first to have all the details.)

While nobody knew quite what to make of it, everybody remained determined to make the most of it. I'd hoped the cops would keep me out of it, and they may have done what they could, but there was just too much media attention for anyone to slip by unnoticed. After the first phone call we learned to let the answering machine screen everything. I took to leaving my building via the service entrance, which kept to a minimum the number of reporters who caught up with me. I had to enter through the lobby, however, and that was when they were apt to corner me, sometimes with microphones and cameras, some-times with notebooks. I was poor fodder for either medium, though, shouldering wordlessly past them, giving them nothing, not even a smile or a frown.

I saw myself on TV one evening. I was visible for less time than it took an off-camera voice to identify me as the Manhattan-based private detective, formerly employed by Adrian Whitfield, whose investigation into his client's death had led to Whitfield's unmasking. 'It's great,' Elaine said. 'You could very easily look angry or impatient or guilty or embarrassed, the way people do when they won't talk to the press. But instead you manage to look sort of harried and oblivious, like a man trying to get off a crowded subway car before they close the doors.'

I've been in the limelight before over the years, though it's never shined that brightly on me, nor have I basked in it for very long. I've never cared for it and I didn't like it any better this time around. Fortunately it didn't seem to affect me much. A few people at AA meetings made veiled reference to my momentary fame. 'I've been reading about you in the papers,' they might say, or, 'Saw you on TV the other night.' I would deflect the remark with a smile and a shrug, and nobody pursued the subject. The greater portion of my AA acquaintances couldn't make a connection between the PI named Scudder who'd unmasked Will and that guy Matt who usually sat in the back row. They might know my story, but relatively few of them knew my last name. AA is like that.

I didn't stay that hot for that long, perhaps because I managed to avoid adding any fuel to the fire myself. The press didn't need me to build the case against Adrian Whitfield, which got a little stronger and solider day by day. If there'd been room for doubt, the police kept finding bits of hard evidence to fill it in. Airline and hotel employees had ID'd his photo, and NYNEX records had turned up some calls that didn't admit to a more innocent explanation, including two to a residential hotel on upper Broadway. There was no way to guess what hotel guest he'd talked to, but Richie Vollmer had been living there, registered under an alias, and both calls were logged the day before Richie's death.

The clearer it became that Adrian was the original Will, the murkier the waters grew around Will #2. A whole string of deaths had given the first Will a grim credibility. A threat, after all, has a certain undeniable authority when it's uttered by a man with blood on his hands.

But when the threat comes from a copycat, and when everybody damn well knows he's a copycat, how much weight do you attach to it? That was a question that was getting asked a lot, on TV and in the papers, and I can only assume the police were asking it themselves. As far as anyone could tell, the man (or woman, for all anyone knew) who'd written out a death sentence for the unlikely partnership of Tully, Rome and Kilbourne had never killed anything but time. That being the case, how much of a danger was he? And what did you do about it?

You had to do something. They still empty schools and office buildings when some joker phones in a bomb threat, even when they know it's almost certainly a hoax. The fire engines roll when the alarm goes off, notwithstanding the fact that most calls turn out to be false alarms. (The NYFD started taking down most of their red streetcorner callboxes when statistics showed that virtually all alarms called in from the street were the work of pranksters. But they had to physically dismantle the boxes. They couldn't leave them standing and ignore the alarms.)

Meanwhile, everybody waited to see what would happen next. The three men named in Will's letter probably waited with a little more urgency than the rest of the public, but even they probably found themselves paying a little less attention as the days passed and nothing untoward took place.

Like Benny the Suitcase, bored to tears with the job of starting Tony Furillo's car every morning. Complaining that nothing ever happened.

One day I caught a noon meeting at the Citicorp building and spent an hour or two in the stores, trying to get an early start on my Christmas shopping. I didn't find a thing to buy, and I just wound up feeling overwhelmed by the season.

It happens every year. Even before the Salvation

Army Santas can get out there and start competing with the homeless for handouts, I find myself haunted by all the ghosts of Christmas past.

I've largely come to terms with the failure of my first marriage, with my shortcomings as a husband and a father. 'Clearing up the wreckage of the past' is what they call that ritual in AA, and it's a process you neglect at your peril.

I'd done all that, making amends, forgiving others and forgiving myself, systematically laying the ghosts of my own history. I didn't rush into it the way some people do, but I kept working at it over time. There was a series of long talks with my sponsor, a lot of soulsearching, plenty of thought and a certain amount of action. And I would have to say it worked. Here was something that had haunted me for years, and now it doesn't.

Except when it does, and that is most apt to happen around the time November starts to bleed into December. The days get shorter and shorter, the sun gives less and less light, and I start to remember every present I didn't get around to buying, every argument I ever had, every nasty remark I ever made, and every night I found a reason to stay in the city instead of hauling my sad ass home to Syosset.

So when I'd walked home from my failed shopping spree I went not to the Parc Vendôme but to the hotel across the street. I told myself I couldn't face a media gauntlet in the lobby, but in fact I had no reason to expect to encounter one. The reporters had understandably lost interest in the fellow who walked through them as if he was trying to get off the subway.

I said hello to Jacob behind the desk and exchanged nods with a fellow who spends most of his waking hours in the Northwestern's faded lobby. The poor bastard moved into the hotel years before I did, and sooner or later he'll die there. I don't suppose he stands much chance of marrying a beautiful woman and moving across the street.

I went up to my room. I put the TV on, took a quick tour of the channels, and switched it off again. I pulled a chair over to the window and sat there, looking out at everything and nothing.

After a while I picked up the phone, made a call. Jim Faber answered the phone himself, saying 'Faber Printing' in the gruff voice in which I have come to find considerable reassurance over the years. It was good to hear his voice now, and I said as much.

'Matter of fact,' I said, 'just dialing your number made me feel better.'

'Well, hell,' he said. 'I can remember times I'd be getting to the bar for the first one of the day, and really needing it. You know, feeling like I was going to jump right out of my skin?'

'I remember the feeling.'

'And once the drink was poured I could relax. I hadn't had it yet, it wasn't in my bloodstream spreading peace and love to every cell in my body, but just knowing it was there had the same effect. But what can be so bad that you're actually driven to call your sponsor?'

'Oh, the joy of the season.'

'Uh-huh. Everybody's favorite time of year. I don't suppose you've been to a meeting within recent memory.'

'I left one about two hours ago.'

'That a fact. What's keeping you busy these days, besides guilt and self-pity? You hot on the trail of Will's replacement?'

237

'He's got half the cops in town after him,' I said, 'and all the reporters. He doesn't need me.'

'Seriously? You're not investigating the case?'

'Of course not. I'd just get in everybody's way.'

'So what is it you're doing, if you're not doing that?'

'Nothing, really.'

'Well, there's your answer,' he said. 'Get off your ass and do something.'

He rang off. I hung up the phone and looked out the window. The city was still out there. I went out to take another crack at it.

NINETEEN

I couldn't do much in what was left of that afternoon. All I really managed was to figure out which people to see and what questions to ask them.

That would have to wait until morning. Meanwhile Elaine and I caught the new Woody Allen movie and listened to a piano trio at Iridium. Walking home, I told her the season was getting to me.

'Well, I'm not an alcoholic,' she said, 'and I'm not even a Christian, and it gets to me. It gets to everybody. Why should you be different?'

'What drew me to you in the first place,' I said, 'was your wonderfully incisive mind.'

'Rats. All these years I thought it was my ass.'

'Your ass,' I said.

'You can't have forgotten it.'

'When we get home,' I said, 'I'll refresh my memory.'

In the morning I put on a suit and tie and went downtown to the Chase branch on Abingdon Square where Byron Leopold had done his banking. The bank officer I sat down with was a bright young woman named Nancy Chang. Early on she said, 'I can't help it, I have to ask. Does this have anything to do with the man who's writing those letters?' I assured her it didn't. 'Because I recognized your name right away from the newspaper stories. You're the man who broke the case.'

I said something appropriately modest, but for a change I wasn't sorry for the recognition. It certainly greased the wheels, and I walked out of there with a photocopy of a check payable to Byron Leopold in the amount of $56,650. It was drawn on a bank in Arlington, Texas, and the name of the account was Viaticom.

'Viaticom,' I said. 'Have you ever heard of an insurance company by that name?'

'No,' she said. 'Is that what this is supposed to be? An insurance payment?'

'He cashed in a policy,' I said. 'But this is more than the cash value would have amounted to, unless my source made a mistake in the amount. And Viaticom doesn't sound like any insurance company I ever heard of.'

'It doesn't, does it? You know what it sounds like? Some Silicon Valley outfit that makes software.'

I said, 'Maybe the insurance company has a separate unit for policy redemption.'

'Maybe.'

'You sound dubious.'

'Well, it doesn't look like any insurance company check that I ever saw,' she said, fingering the photocopy. 'They're all computer-generated these days, and usually machine-signed. This is all filled in by hand with a ballpoint pen. And it looks as though it was signed with the same pen, and by the same person.'

'Viaticom,' I said.

'Whatever that means. No address, just Arlington, Texas.'

'Wherever that is.'

'Well, I can tell you that much,' she said brightly. 'It's between Dallas and Fort Worth. Where the Rangers play?'

'Oh, of course.'

'See? You knew all along.' She grinned. 'Are you

going to have to fly down there? Or can you let your fingers do the walking?'

The 817 information operator had a listing for Viaticom. I'd have tried to wheedle the address out of her as well as the number, but before I could ask she'd shunted me to some digital recording that told, me, the, number, one, numeral, at, a, time. I can't figure out how those things work, but I know better than to try reasoning with them.

I wrote down the number and dialed it, and when a woman answered and said, 'Viaticom, good morning,' I had no trouble believing I was talking to somebody in Texas. It was all there in her voice – the boots, the big hair, the shirt with the pearl buttons.

'Good morning,' I said. 'I wonder if I could get some information on your company. Could you tell me –'

'One moment please,' she said, and put me on Hold before I could finish my sentence. At least I was spared the canned music. I held for a minute or two, and then a man said, 'Hi, this is Gary. What can I do for you?'

'My name's Scudder,' I said, 'and I'd like to know something about your company.'

'Well, Mr Scudder, what would you like to know?'

'For openers,' I said, 'I wonder if you could tell me what it is that you do.'

There was a short pause, and then he said, 'Sir, nothing would make me happier, but if there's one thing I've learned it's not to give interviews over the phone. If you want to come on over here I'll be more than happy to accommodate you. You can bring your notebook and your tape recorder and I'll kick back and tell you more than you maybe want to know.' He chuckled. 'See, we welcome publicity, but every phone interview we've ever done's turned into an unfortunate experience for us, so we just don't do them anymore.'

'I see.'

'Would it be hard for you to come on over and see us? You know where we are?'

'A hell of a long ways from where I am,' I said.

'And where would that be?'

'New York.'

'Is that right. Well, I wouldn't have said you sounded like a Texan, but I know you reporters move around a lot. I talked to a little old gal the other day, she was born in Chicago and worked on a paper in Oregon before she found her way to the *Star-Telegram*. You with one of the New York papers yourself?'

'No, I'm not.'

'Business paper? Not the *Wall Street Journal*?'

I might have tried fishing if I'd known what I was fishing for. But it seemed to me a more direct approach was called for.

'Gary,' I said, 'I'm not a reporter. I'm a private detective based here in New York.'

The silence stretched out long enough to make me wonder if the connection was still open. I said, 'Hello?'

'I didn't go anywhere. You're the one made the call. What do you want?'

I plunged right in. 'A man was killed here some weeks ago,' I said. 'Shot to death on a park bench while he was reading the morning paper.'

'I get the impression that happens a lot up there.'

'Probably not as much as you might think,' I said. 'Of course, there are people in New York who think folks in Texas are out robbing stagecoaches five days a week.'

'When we're not busy remembering the Alamo,' he said. 'Okay, I take your point. Myself, I haven't been in

New York City since our senior trip in high school. Lord, I thought I was hip slick and cool, and your town made me feel like I just fell off a hay wagon.' He chuckled at the memory. 'Haven't been back since, and I'm one Texan who doesn't wear a string tie *or* carry a gun, so I sure didn't shoot that fellow. How's Viaticom come into play?'

'That's what I'm trying to find out. The name of the deceased is Byron Leopold. Approximately four months before his death he deposited a check from you in excess of fifty thousand dollars. That was virtually his only income for the year. My original assumption was that he'd cashed in an insurance policy, but the amount seemed high in relation to the policy. And your check didn't look like an insurance company check.'

'Not hardly, no.'

'So,' I said, 'I was hoping you could enlighten me.'

Another long pause. The seconds ticked away, and I found myself thinking about my phone bill. You tend to be more aware of expenses when you haven't got a client to pick up the tab. I didn't mind paying to talk to Texas, but I found myself resenting the Pinteresque pauses.

I was at a pay phone, with the charges being billed to a credit card. I could have placed the call at a lower rate from my apartment, or gone across the street to my hotel room and talked for free; a few years ago the Kongs, my young hacker friends, had worked their magic to give me an unsolicited gift of free long-distance phone calls. (There'd been no graceful way to decline, but I eased my conscience by not going out of my way to take advantage of my curious perk.)

At length he said, 'Mr Scudder, I'm afraid I'm just going to have to cut this short. We've had unfortunate experiences with the press lately and I don't want to stir up more of the same. All we do is provide people with an opportunity to die with dignity and you people make the whole business of viatical transactions sound like a flock of hovering vultures.'

'Whole business of what? What was the phrase you just used?'

'I've said all I intend to say.'

'But —'

'You have a nice day now,' he said, and hung up on me.

When I met Carl Orcott a couple of years ago he had the habit of fussing with one of a half-dozen pipes in a rack on his desk, now and then bringing it to his nose and inhaling its bouquet. I'd told him he didn't have to refrain from smoking on my account, only to learn that he wasn't a smoker. The pipes were a legacy from a dead lover, their aroma a trigger for memory.

His office in Caritas, an AIDS hospice no more than a five-minute walk from Byron Leopold's apartment, was as I remembered it, except that the rack of pipes was gone. Carl looked the same, too. His face might have been a little more drawn, his hair and mustache showing more gray, but the years might have done all that themselves, unassisted by the virus.

'Viatical transactions,' he said. 'It's an interesting phrase.'

'I don't know what it means.'

'I looked up the word in the dictionary once. It means travel-related. A viaticum is a stipend given to a traveller.'

I asked him to spell it and said, 'That's just one letter away from the name of the firm. They call themselves Viaticom.'

He nodded. 'Sounds a little less like Dog Latin and a

244

good deal more high-tech. More appealing for the investors.'

'Investors?'

'Viatical transactions are a new vehicle for investment, and firms like your Viaticom are part of a new industry. If you thumb through gay publications like *The Advocate* and *New York Native* you'll find their ads, and I suppose they advertise as well in financial publications.'

'What are they selling?'

'They don't actually sell anything,' he said. 'They act as middlemen in the transaction.'

'What kind of transaction?'

He sat back in his chair, folded his hands. 'Say you've been diagnosed,' he said. 'And the disease has reached the point where you can no longer work, so your income has stopped. And even with insurance your medical expenses keep eating away at your savings. Your only asset is an insurance policy that's going to pay somebody a hundred thousand dollars as soon as you're dead. And you're gay, so you don't have a wife or kids who need the money, and your lover died a year ago, and the money's going to go to your aunt in Spokane, and she's a nice old thing but you're more concerned with being able to pay the light bill and buy the cat some of the smoked oysters she's crazy about than enriching Aunt Gretchen's golden years.'

'So you cash in the policy.'

He shook his head. 'The insurance companies are bastards,' he said. 'Some of them won't give you a dime more than the cash surrender value, which is nothing compared to the policy's face amount. Others nowadays will pay more to redeem a policy when it's undeniably evident that the insured doesn't have long

245

to live, but even then it's a rotten deal. You get a much more generous offer from companies like Viaticom.'

I asked him how it worked. A facilitator of viatical transactions, he explained, would bring together two interested parties, an AIDS patient whose illness had progressed medically to the point where a maximum survival time could be estimated with some degree of precision, and an investor who wanted a better return on his money than he could get from banks or government bonds, and about the same degree of security.

Typically, the investor would be sure of an annual return of around twenty to twenty-five percent on his money. It was like a zero-coupon bond in that all the money came at the end, when the insured party died and the insurance carrier paid off. Unlike a bond, of course, the term wasn't fixed. The AIDS sufferer could live longer than predicted, which would lessen the per annum return somewhat. Or, on the other hand, he could pop off before the ink was dry on the agreement, thus providing the investor with a much faster payoff on his investment.

And there was always the investor's nightmare. 'The lure of the cure,' Carl drawled. 'Imagine betting the kids' college funds on the lifespan of some poor set designer, and then one day medical science tells you your kids'll have their doctorates long before he's done crying over Judy Garland records.' He rolled his eyes. 'Except it won't happen that way, even if we get that long-awaited medical miracle. You might develop a vaccine to prevent future cases, you might come up with a magic bullet to knock out or arrest the virus, but how are you going to breathe life into a completely devastated immune system? Oh, doctors keep gradually extending the survival time, and that's all factored into the equation. But those of us who are accepted as parties to viatical transactions are past the point of no return. The kids can go to college after all. The investment's safe.'

'Some investment,' I said.

'Strikes you as ghoulish, doesn't it?'

'I just can't imagine writing out a check and then sitting back and waiting for some stranger to die so I can collect.'

'I know what you mean. There have been articles written about this, you know, and not just in the gay press.'

'I must have missed them. The man I spoke with did say something about negative publicity.'

'Some writers think it's just awful,' he said. 'Reprehensible to profit from the misfortunes of others, blah blah blah. Horrible to think of anyone making money from AIDS. Well, honey, what do you think the drug companies are doing? What do you think the researchers are doing?' He held up a hand. 'Don't tell me there's a difference. I know that. I also know it's not people with AIDS who get upset about viatical transactions, because for us it's a godsend.'

'Really.'

'Absolutely. Matt, once you've been diagnosed with full-blown AIDS you damn well know you're dying, and this many years into the epidemic you've got a fairly good idea what else the future holds. If somebody in Texas makes it possible for you to live decently and comfortably in the time you've got left, how are you going to think of him? As a bloodsucker or as a benefactor?'

'I see what you mean. But —'

'But even so you can't help seeing one party as a buzzard and the other as roadkill. It's a natural reaction.

247

One company even set up a sort of pool, like a mutual fund for viatical transactions. Instead of an individual buying a single policy, the investment funds are combined and the risk is spread out over a whole portfolio of policies.'

'The risk of longevity.'

He nodded. He toyed with a stapler on his desk, and I remembered his dead lover's pipes and wondered what he'd done with them, and when. 'But most policies are assigned to individual investors,' he said. 'I think the paperwork must be a lot simpler that way. And there's no great need to spread the risk, because there's not really very much risk to spread. "Viaticum, money given to a traveler." Everyone's a traveler, you know. And, sooner or later, everybody makes the trip.'

Back at the Chase branch, Nancy Chang went over Byron Leopold's records again, working backward from the date when he'd deposited the Viaticom check. Every three months there was a check drawn to the order of Illinois Sentinel Life. The checks had stopped two months before he got the Viaticom check.

'He transferred ownership of the policy,' I said, 'so he stopped paying the premiums, and that became the responsibility of the other party to the transaction.'

'And when he died —'

'The insurance company would have paid the money directly to the beneficiary. But who is he and how much did they pay him?'

'"Always the beautiful answer that asks the more beautiful question,"' she said, and laughed at my evident puzzlement. 'E E Cummings. Though I suppose it would be more appropriate to quote Wallace Stevens, wouldn't it?'

'Did he have something to say about questions and answers?'

'I'm not sure what he had to say,' she said, 'because I could never tell what he was getting at. But he worked all his life as an executive with an insurance company. And at the same time he was one of the leading American poets of his time. Can you imagine?'

I knew I was going to be spending some time on the phone, and I decided I might as well make free calls from my hotel room. If I could work pro bono, so could the phone company.

I called Illinois Sentinel Life, headquartered in Springfield, and got shunted around from one person to another. I didn't get the feeling that any of the men or women I spoke to were among the leading American poets of our time, but how could I be sure?

I finally wound up talking to a man named Louis Leeds who told me, after a certain amount of fencing, that Byron Wayne Leopold had indeed been an Illinois Sentinel Life policyholder, that the face amount of the policy had been $75,000, and that ownership of the policy had been transferred on such and such a date to a Mr William Havemeyer of Lakewood, Ohio.

'Not Texas,' I said.

No, he said, not Texas. Lakewood was in Ohio, and he wouldn't swear to it but it seemed to him that it was a suburb of Cleveland. The lake would be Erie, he said.

'And the wood?'

'I beg your pardon? Oh, the wood! Very funny. I suppose the wood would be oak or maple. Or maybe knotty pine, ha ha ha.'

Ha ha ha. Had the claim been processed? It had. And had a check been issued to Mr Havemeyer?

'Well, he's named as the beneficiary, so we could

hardly have paid the money to anyone else. And the policy has been retired and noted as paid in full.'

I asked if Mr Havemeyer was the beneficiary of any other policies. There was a pause, and he said he would have no way of knowing that.

'Ask your computer,' I said. 'I bet it knows. Feed it the name of William Havemeyer and see what it comes up with.'

'I'm afraid I couldn't do that.'

'Why not?'

'Because that would be confidential. Our records are by no means public information.'

I drew a breath. 'William Havemeyer was the beneficiary of Byron Leopold's insurance. He wasn't a friend or a relative of the insured. Leopold sold him the policy.'

'That's called a viatical transaction,' he said. 'It's perfectly legal. We don't entirely approve of them, but in most states the owner of an unencumbered insurance policy has the legal right to transfer ownership in return for a financial consideration.'

He talked about the company's requirement that prior beneficiaries be notified, and such complicating circumstances as insurance coverage stipulated in a divorce settlement. 'But I don't believe any of that applies in the present circumstances,' he said.

'Suppose William Havemeyer has participated in more than one viatical transaction.'

'It strikes me as an unpleasant way to seek a return on capital,' he said, 'but there's nothing illegal about it.'

'I understand. Suppose other persons of whose insurance he was the beneficiary also died violently?'

There was a pause almost worthy of Gary down in Arlington. Then, slowly, he said, 'Do you have reason to believe . . .'

'I'd like to rule it out,' I told him. 'And I should think you'd like to rule it out yourself. I understand there's an ethical line here, but it's certainly not unethical for you to check your records. After you've done that, you can decide whether or not to share your findings with me.'

I had to repeat that a couple of times, but eventually he decided it was safe to ask his computer for information, since I wasn't there to peek over his shoulder at the screen. He put me on hold, and I listened to elevator music interrupted at all-too-brief intervals with plugs for the peace of mind provided by coverage from Illinois Sentinel Life.

He came back right in the middle of one such announcement. Mr William Havemeyer, he was able to assure me, not without a tone of triumph, was known to Illinois Sentinel Life solely as the beneficiary of the late Byron Wayne Leopold. He was not insured himself by the company, nor was he either the policyholder or the beneficiary of any other ISL coverage.

'I feel it's all right for me to tell you this,' he said, 'because I'm not actually imparting any data. I'm simply confirming the absence of such data.'

That was true enough, and I thanked him and let it go at that. I didn't see any point in telling him that a failure to do as he had done would have confirmed the opposite; if he'd come back and refused to tell me anything, he'd have been telling me quite a bit.

Always the beautiful question . . .

'I don't get it,' I told Elaine.

'The appeal of viatical transactions? It's not hard to understand from a dollars-and-cents standpoint.' She jotted down numbers on a pad. 'The big plunger in Lakewood paid out just over fifty-six thousand, and in less than a year he collected on a seventy-five-thou-sand-dollar policy. What kind of return is that?' More numbers. 'Almost forty percent. Can that be right? Yes, it can, and actually it's more than that, because he didn't have to wait the full year.'

'He'd have paid more than fifty-six grand,' I pointed out. 'Viaticom had to make something for their troubles. They're the ones who put the whole thing together. My guess is that they must have taken a minimum of five thousand dollars off the top before they wrote out their check to Byron.'

'So if Mr Lakewood —'

'Mr Havemeyer.'

'If he paid sixty and got back seventy-five that's a return of what twenty-five percent per annum? And he got it in less than an annum, and even if he'd waited a full two annums that's still better than the banks give you.'

'Would you invest in something like this?'

'No.'

'It didn't take you long to answer that one.'

'Well, I don't have any moral objection to it,' she said. 'And the men at the hospice pointed out that it's a real boon to the people with AIDS. So I think it's a good thing that other people are doing it. But it turns my stomach.'

'The idea of sitting around and waiting for somebody to die.'

She nodded. 'And trying not to be irritated when they go on living, and trying not to jump for joy when they die. I mean, screw all that. Or don't you agree?'

'No, I agree completely.'

'It may be a great investment,' she said, 'but not for me. The higher the return, the worse I'd feel about the whole thing. I think I'll stick to real estate. And thrift-shop art.'

'I'm with you,' I said. 'But that's not the part I don't get. Say you're Havemeyer.'

'Okay. I'm Havemeyer.'

'You've bought a policy on a dying man. You paid, round numbers, sixty thousand dollars. According to medical science, you've got a max of two years to wait before you collect seventy-five thousand.'

'So?'

'Why rush things? Why would you come to New York and shoot down a man on a park bench? Why go through that to get the money a few months sooner, or even a whole year sooner?'

'Unless you needed the money right away . . .'

'It still doesn't make sense. If you need cash that urgently, the policy's an asset. There must be a way you can borrow against it, or sell it to one of Viaticom's other investors. And if you just want to increase your profit, well, I can't see it as a motive for the taking of a human life. You're still getting the same seventy-five grand. You're just getting it a little earlier than you would otherwise.'

'Time is money.'

'Yes, but it's not that much money. And people who want fast money bad enough to kill for it aren't investing in insurance policies, anyway. They're out there robbing banks or dealing coke.'

'Maybe Havemeyer didn't do it.'

I shook my head. 'It can't be a coincidence,' I said. 'He just looks too good for it. What do we know about the murder? It was an amateur effort committed by a stranger who knew the name of his victim and said it out loud to confirm his identity before shooting him.

That sounds to me like a perfect fit. There's even a motive.'

'Money, you mean.'

'Right. And all along this case felt to me like one with a financial motive.'

'Your dream,' she said. 'Remember? "Too much money."'

'Uh-huh. And now it's turned on its head, because as a motive it strikes me as too little money. It's just not enough to kill for.' She started to say something and I held up a hand to cut her off. 'I know, people get killed every day for chump change. Two guys buy a bottle of Night Train and argue over the change, and one stabs the other. A mugger shoots a guy who was trying to hang on to his wallet and takes five dollars off the corpse. But that's different. The people who commit crimes like that don't have sixty thousand dollars to invest. They don't live in suburbs in the Midwest and fly to New York to kill strangers.'

'That's not what I was going to say.'

'Oh.'

'I was going to say it's not enough to kill for if you just do it once. But if you take the proceeds and buy another policy – do you see what I mean? If you wait for nature to take its course, you get your twenty-five percent return in somewhere between one and two years. But if you speed things up and get it in four or five months, and then buy another policy and repeat the process –'

'You're making your money grow rapidly.'

'But you still can't see it.'

'Not really,' I said. 'Anyway, aside from that one policy, Illinois Sentinel Life never heard of Mr Havemeyer of Lakewood. So if he's done this before it's been with other companies, and I couldn't even begin to look for his traces. How many insurance companies are there in the country?'

'Too many.'

'TJ would tell me it's possible to hack your way into some insurance company computer network and learn everything you could possibly want to know without leaving your desk. And maybe it is, if you've got the Kongs' expertise and a few thousand dollars' worth of computer equipment to play with, and if you don't mind committing felonies left and right. In the mean-time —'

'He didn't purchase a policy issued by, what was it, Illinois Sentinel?'

'That's right. So?'

'But he may well have participated in other viatical transactions involving other insurers. Wouldn't he have gone through the same broker?'

'Oh, for God's sake,' I said. 'Why didn't I think of that?'

TWENTY

I called Viaticom a few minutes after nine the next morning and got a recording advising me that their office hours were from nine to five. I looked at my watch, frowned, and then remembered the time difference. It was an hour earlier in Texas. I waited an hour and called again, and the woman who answered was the same cowgirl who'd put me on Hold the day before. I asked for Gary and she wanted to know my name. I gave it to her, and she put me on Hold again.

I was there for a while. When she came back on the line to tell me that Gary was out, her voice was different, thick with suppressed anger. She didn't like having to lie, and she was irritated with me for putting her in such a position.

I asked when she expected him. 'I'm sure I don't know,' she said, angrier than ever.

I went through the motions, giving her my number although she hadn't bothered to ask for it, asking that she have Gary call me as soon as possible. I didn't think he would, and a little before noon I stopped waiting for his call.

Nancy Chang at the Chase had wondered if I'd have to go to Arlington. Or could I let my fingers do the walking? My fingers didn't seem equal to the task, but that didn't necessarily mean I had to get on an airplane.

I called Wally Donn at Reliable. We'd spoken briefly after the Whitfield-as-Will story broke, and he said now that he still couldn't get over it. 'The son of a bitch,' he said. 'You know what he did? He hired us to protect him from himself. And we wound up looking bad when we couldn't do it. And now we look worse than ever, because we were right next to him and didn't have a clue what was going on.'

'Look on the bright side,' I said. 'Now there's no reason in the world why you can't bill the estate.'

'Which I've already done, and don't think I didn't pad it just a little to cover the aggravation factor. Now the question is will they pay it, and I'm not holding my breath.'

I asked him to recommend a PI in the vicinity of Arlington, Texas, and he came up with a fellow named Guy Fordyce. He was based in Fort Worth, with an office on Hemphill.

'Wherever the hell that is,' Wally said.

I reached Fordyce. He sounded gruff and competent and said he had an open slot the following morning. 'I could try calling him this afternoon,' he said, 'but I can't see why I'd have any better luck than you did. Be more effective if I walk in unannounced.'

He called the next day around noon. I was out at the time and got back to find his message on my machine. I called his office and got someone who said he'd beep him. I waited, and a few minutes later the phone rang and it was him.

'Slippery little prick,' he said. 'I made a couple of calls yesterday just to find out who I was dealing with, and what I learned about Gary Garrison didn't make me yearn to go bass fishing with him. The consensus is that what he's doing with this viatical shit is legitimate enough, but there's something about the whole deal that makes the average citizen want to puke.'

'I know what you mean.'

'And Garrison himself has a checkered past. He sold

penny stocks for a while and got sued a few times and had to face criminal fraud charges on two occasions. Charges dropped both times, but that's not the same as saying he's squeaky clean.'

'No.'

'There's been some pressure locally to either outlaw these viaticals or regulate the shit out of them. Meanwhile, Garrison's doing a hell of a business, and his end of it's higher than a middleman's probably ought to be. That's one of the things they want to regulate.'

'I figured he was making out all right for himself.'

'You bet he is. So he's in a funny position, wanting publicity because it means more sales and looking to keep a low profile for fear that the regulators are going to regulate him right out of business. And even if this particular operation's honest, the man's used to being a crook, so it's second nature for him to weasel out of answering a direct question.'

'One of nature's noblemen,' I said.

'Oh, he's a prince. I let him start out thinking I was an investor, and then he just might have formed the impression that I was an investigator from a state agency I didn't get around to naming, and he got real cooperative. He's done business with your William Havemeyer three times in all. The transactions involved policies with three different insurance companies.'

He gave me names and addresses and dates and numbers. In addition to Byron Leopold, the men in whose lifespan William Havemeyer had a vested interest included a San Franciscan named Harlan Phillips and a Eugene, Oregon resident named John Wilbur Settle. Phillips was insured by Massachusetts Mutual, while Settle's coverage was with Integrity Life and Casualty.

'Life and casualty,' I said.

'Yeah, they go hand in hand, don't they? I regret to say I don't know what's become of either of these gentlemen. Garrison can't say if they're alive or dead. He doesn't follow up. Once the policy's changed ownership and the transaction's completed, it's out of his hands.'

'It won't be hard to find out the rest of it.'

'Just make a few calls.'

'Right.'

He told me what all of this was going to cost me, and said he'd put a bill in the mail. The price seemed reasonable enough, and certainly came to a good deal less than what I would have spent flying there myself. I told him as much and thanked him for his efforts.

'Any time,' he said. 'Mind if I ask what you think you're looking at here? Is your boy Havemeyer setting these people up and knocking them off?'

'That's the way it feels,' I said. 'But it all depends on what I learn from the insurance companies.'

'That's a point. If Phillips and Settle are still alive and taking nourishment, that'd weaken the theory some, wouldn't it!'

But they were both dead.

I got excited at first. I had a line on a serial murderer, I knew his name and where he lived, and nobody else in the world even suspected he existed. I got a rush right in the old ego. When I broke this one I'd have the media dogging me again, and this story would be national, not just local. Maybe, I thought, instead of slipping out the service entrance I ought to meet the onslaught head on. Maybe I should welcome the attention and make the most of it.

Amazing what a mind can do if you give it half a

chance. In less time than it takes to tell about it I had myself guesting on Letterman and doing a cameo on 'Law and Order'. I could see myself sitting across the table from Charlie Rose, explaining the workings of the criminal mind. I just about had myself racing around the country on a book tour before it struck me that the deaths of Harlan Phillips and John W Settle weren't quite enough to get William Havemeyer indicted for murder.

Because they were supposed to die. They'd had AIDS, both of them, and it had been sufficiently advanced as to meet the medical criteria established by the viatical transaction brokers. Just because they were dead didn't mean Havemeyer killed them. Mother Nature could have beaten him to the punch.

So I made some more phone calls, and what I learned saved me from having to make the tough choice between 'Inside Edition' and 'Hard Copy'. Harlan Phillips had died in a hospice in the Mission district, two years and eight months after having been diagnosed with AIDS, and just short of a year after assigning his Mass Mutual policy to William Havemeyer. John Wilbur Settle, treating himself to a trip abroad, no doubt with the windfall that blew his way when Havemeyer bought his policy, was one of eighty-four people drowned when a Norwegian passenger ferry caught fire, burned, capsized and sank in the Baltic Sea.

I remembered the incident, though I hadn't paid a great deal of attention to it at the time. I went to the library and determined that the fire had broken out as a result of a failure of the ship's electrical system, that the ship had been carrying a load of passengers slightly in excess of its legal capacity, and that many of them were described as holiday revelers, which is often a nonjudgmental way of saying everybody was drunk. Rescue efforts were delayed as a result of a communications snafu, but were nevertheless reasonably successful, with over 900 passengers and crew members surviving. Of an even dozen Americans aboard, three were casualties, and the paper of record dutifully supplied their names. They were Mr and Mrs D Carpenter, of Lafayette, Louisiana, and Mr J Settle, of Eugene, Oregon.

Somehow I couldn't see Bad Billy Havemeyer flying off to Oslo, then sneaking aboard the SS *Magnar Syversen* and crossing a couple of wires in the engine room. Nor could I picture him at Phillips's bedside in San Francisco, ripping out IVs, say, or pressing a pillow over a ravaged face.

I left the library and just walked for a while, not really paying much attention to where I was going. It was cold out and the wind had a nasty edge to it, but the air was fresh and clean, the way it gets when there's a north wind blowing.

When I got home there was a message on the machine. Marty McGraw had called and left a number. I called him back and he said he just wanted to keep in touch. What was I working on these days?

Just going around in circles, I said, and winding up back at square one.

'Be a good name for a restaurant,' he said.

'How's that?'

'Square One. A restaurant, a saloon, place on the order of the old Toots Shor's. Kind of joint where you can have a few pops and get a decent steak without worrying what kind of wine goes with it. Call it Square One because you know you're always going to wind up back at it. You getting anywhere with Will?'

'You must mean Will Number Two.'

'I mean the son of a bitch who wrote me a letter threatening three prominent New Yorkers, and nobody seems to give a shit. I don't suppose you've been looking into it by any chance.'

'I don't figure it's any business of mine.'

'Hey, when did that ever stop you in the past?' I didn't say anything right away, and he said, 'That sounded wrong, the way it came out. Don't take it the wrong way, will you, Matt?'

'Don't worry about it.'

'You read that crap in the competition this morning?'

'The competition?'

'The *New York Fucking Post*. That's close to the original name of that rag, as a matter of fact. The *New York* Evening *Post*, that's what used to grace that masthead.'

'Like the *Saturday Evening Post*?'

'That was a magazine, for Christ's sake.'

'I know that, I just —'

'Slight difference, one's a magazine, the other's a newspaper.' I could hear the drink in his voice now. I suppose it had been there all along, but I hadn't been aware of it before. 'There's a story about the *Post*,' he said. 'Years ago, before you were born or your father before you, they were in an ass-kicking and hair-pulling contest with the old *New York World*. The *Post* had the rag on one day and ran an editorial calling the *World* a yellow dog. Now this was considered quite the insult. You know, yellow journalism? You familiar with the term?'

'Not as well as you are.'

'What's that? Oh, a wiseass. You want to hear this or not?'

'I'd love to hear it.'

'So everybody was waiting to see what the *World* was going to come back with. And next day there's an editorial in the *World*. "The *New York Evening Post* calls us a yellow dog. Our reply is the reply of any dog to any post." You get it, or is the subtlety of a bygone age lost on you?'

'I get it.'

'In other words, piss on you.'

'When was this?'

'I dunno, eighty years ago? Maybe more. Nowadays a newspaper could come right out and say, "Piss on you," and nobody'd turn a hair, the way standards have fucking crumbled. How the hell did I get on this?'

'The *Post*.'

'Right, the *New York Fucking Post*. They've got an analysis of the latest letter, supposedly proves the guy's a phony, a talker and not a doer. Some expert, some college professor, needs to read the instructions on the roll of Charmin before he can figure out how to wipe his ass. What do you think of that?'

'What do I think of what?'

'Wouldn't you say it's irresponsible? They're calling the guy a liar to his face.'

'Only if he reads the *Post*.'

He laughed. 'And piss on them, huh? But you get what I mean, don't you? They're saying, "I dare you." Saying, "Go ahead, kill somebody, make my day." I call that irresponsible.'

'If you say so.'

'Why, you patronizing son of a bitch. Are you too much of a big shot now to have a conversation with me?'

I resisted the impulse to hang up. 'Of course not,' I said soothingly. 'I think you're probably right saying what you said, but it's no longer something I'm involved in, not even peripherally. And I'm going nuts enough without it.'

'Oh, yeah? Over what?'

'Another case that's not really any business of mine, but I seem to have taken it on. There's a man I'm just about certain committed murder, and I'm damned if I can figure out why.'

'Gotta be love or money,' he said. 'Unless he's a public-spirited son of a bitch like my guy.'

'It's money, but I can't make it make sense. Suppose you're insured and I'm the beneficiary. I gain if you die.'

'Why don't we make it the other way around?'

'Just let me —'

'No, really,' he said, his voice rising as he got into it. 'I know this is hypothetical, but why do I have to be the schmuck? Make it that *I* win if *you* die.'

'Fine. You gain if I die. So I jump out the window, and —'

'Why do a crazy thing like that?'

'And you shoot me on the way down. Why?'

'You jump out the window and I shoot you on the way down.'

'Right. Why?'

'Target practice? Is this some trick, you were wearing a parachute, some shit like that?'

'Jesus,' I said. 'No, it's not a trick question. It's an analogy.'

'Well, excuuuuse me. I shoot you on the way down?'

'Uh-huh.'

'And kill you.'

'Right.'

'But you would have died anyhow when you

264

landed. Because this is an analogy and not a trick question, so please tell me it's not a first-floor window you just jumped out of.'

'No, it's a high floor.'

'And no parachute.'

'No parachute.'

'Well, shit,' he said. 'I don't get the money if it's suicide. How's that for simple?'

'Doesn't apply.'

'Doesn't apply? What the fuck is that supposed to mean?'

'Suicide wouldn't invalidate the policy,' I said. 'Anyway, when I jump out the window it's not suicide.'

'No, it's an act of Christian charity. It's a response to overwhelming public demand. Why isn't it suicide when you jump out the window? You're not a bird or a plane, let alone Superman.'

'The analogy was imperfect,' I allowed. 'Let's just say I'm falling from a great height.'

'What did you do, lose your balance?'

'Wouldn't be the first time.'

'Ha! Tell me about it. So it's an accident, is that what you're saying? . . . Where'd you go? Hey, Earth to Matt. Are you there?'

'I'm here.'

'Well, you had me wondering. It's an accident, right?'

'Right,' I said. 'It's an accident.'

TWENTY-ONE

I stayed put over the weekend. I went to a couple of meetings, and Saturday afternoon Elaine and I took the #7 train out to Flushing and walked around the new Chinatown. She complained that it wasn't like Manhattan's Chinatown at all, feeling neither quaint nor sinister but disturbingly suburban. We wound up eating at a Taiwanese vegetarian restaurant, and after two bites she put down her chopsticks and said, 'I take back everything I said.'

'Not bad, huh?'

'Heaven,' she said.

Sunday I had dinner with Jim Faber for the first time in quite a few weeks, and that meant another Chinese meal, but in our own part of town, not way out in Queens. We talked about a lot of different things, including Marty McGraw's column in that morning's *News*, in which he'd essentially accused Will #2 of jerking us all around.

'I can't understand it,' I said. 'I talked to him a couple of days ago and he was pissed off at the *Post* for running a story suggesting that this Will is all hat and no cattle. And now he —'

'All hat and no cattle?'

'All talk and no action.'

'I know what it means. I'm just surprised to hear it coming out of your New York mouth.'

'I've been on the phone with a lot of Texans lately,' I said. 'Maybe some of it rubbed off. The point is he called them irresponsible for writing Will off, and now he's deliberately goading him himself, telling the guy to shit or get off the pot.'

'Maybe the police put him up to it.'

'Maybe.'

'But you don't think so.'

'I think they'd be more inclined to let sleeping dogs lie. That's more their style than using Marty as a cat's-paw.'

'Cats and dogs,' he said. 'Sounds like rain. McGraw's a drunk, isn't he? Didn't you tell me that?'

'I don't want to take his inventory.'

'Oh, go ahead and take his inventory. "We are not saints," remember?'

'Then I suppose he's a drunk.'

'And you're surprised he's not perfectly consistent? Maybe he doesn't remember objecting to the story in the *Post*. Maybe he doesn't even remember reading it.'

Monday I got on the phone right after breakfast and made half a dozen calls, some of them lengthy. I called from the apartment, not from my hotel room across the street, which meant I'd be charged for the calls. That allowed me to feel virtuous and stupid instead of shady and clever.

Tuesday morning Marty McGraw's column included a letter from Will. There was a teaser headline to that effect on the front page, but the main story was about a drug-related massacre in the Bushwick section of Brooklyn. Before I even saw the paper, the doorman rang upstairs during breakfast to announce a FedEx delivery. I said I'd be down to pick it up, and I was eager enough to get going that I skipped my second cup of coffee.

The delivery was what I was expecting, an overnight letter containing three photographs. They were all four-by-five color snaps of the same individual, a slightly built white man in his late forties or early fifties, clean-shaven, with small even features and eyes that were invisible behind wire-rimmed eyeglasses.

I beeped TJ and met him at a lunch counter in the Port Authority bus terminal. It was full of wary people, their eyes forever darting around the room. I suppose they had their reasons. It was hard to guess which they feared more, assault or arrest.

TJ spoke highly of the glazed doughnuts, and put away a couple of them. I let them toast a bagel for me and ate half of it. I knew better than to drink their coffee.

TJ squinted at the photos and announced that their subject looked like Clark Kent. ''Cept he'd need more than a costume change to turn hisself into Superman. This the dude chilled Myron?'

'Byron.'

'What I meant. This him?'

'I think so.'

'Don't look like no iceman. Look like he'd have to call in for back-up 'fore he'd step on a cockroach.'

'That witness you found,' I said. 'I was wondering if you could find him again.'

'The dude who was dealin'.'

'That's the one.'

'Might be I could find him. You sellin' product, you don't want to make yourself too hard to find. Or folks be buyin' from somebody else.' He tapped the picture. 'Dude saw the shooter from the back, Jack.'

'Didn't he get a glimpse of his face after the shooting?'

He tilted his head back, grabbing at the memory. 'Said he was white,' he recalled. 'Said he was ordinary-lookin'. Must be he saw him a little bit, but don't there be other witnesses got a better look at him?'

'Several of them,' I agreed.

'So what we doin', coverin' all the bases?'

I shook my head. 'The other witnesses might have to testify in court. That means their first look at Havemeyer ought to be in a police lineup. If his lawyer finds out some private cop showed them a picture ahead of time, then their ID is tainted and the judge won't allow it.'

'Dude I found ain't about to testify,' he said. 'So it don't matter how tainted he gets.'

'That's the idea.'

'Tainted,' he repeated, savoring the word. 'Only thing, I supposed to work for Elaine today. Mindin' the shop while she checks out this Salvation Army store somebody told her about.'

'I'll cover for you.'

'I don't know,' he said. 'Lotta stuff you got to know, Bo. How to write up sales, how to make out the charge slips, how to bargain with the customers. It ain't somethin' you can do just walkin' in off the street.'

I swung at him and he grinned and dodged the blow. 'Didn't I tell you?' he said. 'You got to work to establish the jab.' And he snatched up the photographs and headed for the door.

The photos had been taken by a third-year student at Western Reserve, in Cleveland. I'd started out with a name and phone number from Wally Donn, but the guy I reached was swamped with work and didn't know when he could get to it. He gave me two other numbers, and when each one led me no further than an answering machine I looked in my book and called a fellow I knew in Massillon, Ohio. Massillon's not exactly next door to Cleveland, but I didn't know anybody closer.

I'd met Tom Havlicek six or seven years ago when a man I'd locked up once killed an old friend of Elaine's, along with her husband and children. Havlicek was the cop in charge, a police lieutenant who liked his work and was good at it. We'd hit it off and stayed in touch. I'd managed to deflect his periodic invitations to come out to Ohio and hunt deer, but I'd seen him twice in New York. He came alone the first time, to attend a police products trade show at the Javits Center and I met him for lunch and showed him a little of the city. He liked what he saw enough to bring his wife a year or so later, and Elaine and I took them to dinner and arranged theater tickets. We joined them for the revival of *Carousel* at Lincoln Center, but they were on their own for *Cats*. Friendship, Elaine explained, only goes so far.

It didn't take long to determine, through a contact in the Cleveland Metropolitan PD, that William Havemeyer had skated thus far through life without getting into trouble. 'He hasn't got a yellow sheet,' he reported. 'Which means he hasn't been arrested. Not in Cuyahoga County, at any rate. Not under that name.'

I thanked him and got the name and phone number of his Cleveland contact.

'Now since they never arrested him,' he went on, *'they* sure don't have a photo of him, and Garvin' – his friend on the CMPD – 'gave me a number of a guy he knows who retired recently, but it turns out he's in Florida for the season. So I thought of my sister's boy.'

'He's a police officer?'

'A college student. He'll be a lawyer when he's through. Just what the world needs more of.'

'You can't have too many lawyers,' I said.

'That seems to be the Good Lord's view of the matter, the way he keeps making more of them. Won't be long before they've got nobody left to sue but each other. He's a bright young man, never mind who his uncle is, and photography's his hobby.'

'How is he at lurking?'

'Lurking? Oh, to get the photo. I'd say he's a devious cuss. Serve him in good stead in his chosen profession. Should I call him?' I said he should. 'And when are we going to shoot some deer, will you tell me that?'

'Probably never.'

'Never make a hunter out of you, will we? You know what? Why don't you come out here after the season's over and we'll just take a walk in the woods, which is the best part of hunting anyway. No guns to carry, and no risk of being mistaken for a twelve-point buck by somebody who had his breakfast out of a flask. Of course you don't get to bring home any venison that way.'

'Which spares you from having to pretend to enjoy it.'

'Not your favorite meal, eh? Nor mine either, truth be known, but there's something about going out and getting it that satisfies a man.'

I called him from Elaine's shop to tell him the photos had arrived and his nephew had done a good job.

'I'm glad to hear that,' he said, 'but I'm not surprised. He always took good pictures, even as a little kid. I spoke to him just last night, and I'll tell you what pleases me is how much fun he got out of doing the work. We could make a good police officer out of that boy.'

'I bet your sister would love to hear that.'

'Her and my brother-in-law both, and I guess I see

their point. No question but that lawyers get richer than cops. Who ever said the world's a fair place?'

'I don't know,' I said, 'but I swear it wasn't me.'

I spent a few hours minding the shop, and it's a good thing I don't have to do that too often. Someone – I think it was Pascal – wrote something to the effect that all of man's problems stem from his inability to sit alone in a room. I'm generally pretty good at sitting alone in a room, with or without the TV on, but that day I found it a trial. For one thing, I wanted to be out on the streets doing something. For another, people kept interrupting me, and to no purpose. They would call up, ask for Elaine, want to know when she would be coming back, and ring off without leaving a name. Or they would come to the door, stick their heads in, register a certain amount of dismay at seeing me instead of the lady of the house, and go somewhere else.

A couple of people did come in and browse, but I didn't have to talk price with them, or make out charge-card slips, because none of them tried to buy anything. One inquired about the price of several paintings – all the prices were clearly marked – and said that she would be back. That means about as much as saying 'I'll call you' to a woman after the two of you have seen a movie together. 'People who keep shops,' Elaine had told me, 'are more realistic than girls on dates. We know you won't be back.'

I had time to read the papers. Marty McGraw's column did indeed include Will's latest letter. Without naming names, the anonymous author made it clear that the three men on his list were just a starting point. Many more of us were candidates for his next list, unless we saw the light and mended our ways. The letter struck me as tired and unconvincing. I had the feeling Will #2 didn't even believe it himself.

TJ breezed in somewhere around the middle of the afternoon. He was wearing baggy jeans, with a down vest in hunter orange over his camo jacket. He was dressed for success, if your line of work happened to be street crime.

'Got to change,' he said, slipping past me to the back room. He came back wearing khakis and a button-down shirt. 'Don't want to scare the customers off,' he said, 'but if I went downtown like this, I'da scared the dude off.'

'You found him?'

He nodded. 'Says it's the man he saw.'

'How sure is he?'

'Sure enough to swear to it, 'cept he ain't about to swear to nothin'. Told him he wouldn't have to. That straight?'

'Probably. Can you take over now until Elaine gets back?'

'No problem. Where you goin', Owen?'

'Can't you guess?'

'I don't guess,' he said. 'I detect. Where I detect you's goin' is Cleveland.'

I told him he was a good detective.

I'd already called from the shop to book the flight, and I walked over to Phyllis Bingham's office to pick up the ticket, then back to the apartment to pack a bag with a clean shirt and a change of socks and underwear. I didn't know how long this was going to take, but I figured to be away overnight no matter what.

Phyllis had me flying Continental out of Newark. I beat the rush-hour traffic to the airport, and by the time we were on the ground in Cleveland most of the commuters were sitting down to dinner. There was a small group of people with hand-lettered cardboard signs waiting at the security gate, and one of the signs had my name on it. The kid holding it was tall and rangy, with close-cropped reddish blond hair and a narrow face.

'I'm Matthew Scudder,' I said, 'and you must be Jason Griffin. Your Uncle Tom said he'd try to reach you, and that you'd come if you had the time free.'

He grinned. 'He told me I'd better have the time free. "Meet his plane and drive him out to Lakewood, and anywhere else he wants to go." Is that where you want to go first? This man's house in Lakewood?'

I said it was, and we went to his car, a Japanese import a couple of years old. It sparkled, and I guessed that he'd taken it through a car wash on his way to the airport.

On the way, I asked him what he knew about the case. 'Nothing,' he said.

'Tom didn't tell you anything?'

'My uncle's a need-to-know kind of guy,' he said. 'He gave me a name and an address and told me to go take the guy's picture without being obvious about it. I told him I might have to buy a telephoto lens.'

'I'll reimburse you.'

He grinned. '"Borrow one," he said. 'So that's what I did. I parked across the street from Mr Havemeyer's house and waited for him to come home. When he did get home he drove straight into the garage. It's an attached garage, which is unusual in that neighborhood. They're mostly older homes there, but his is newer than the others and it's got a carport-type garage. So he went on in without giving me a look at him, let alone a chance to zoom in and take his picture.'

'What did you do, wait for him to come out again?'

'No, because he'd probably leave the same way, right? Uncle Tom hadn't told me how to cope with this sort of situation. As a matter of fact the only advice he gave me — well, can you guess what it was?'

'Bring a milk bottle.'

'He said a wide-mouthed jar. Same difference. I asked him what I was supposed to do with it, and he said after I sat there for a couple of hours the answer would come to me. At which point I figured out what the jar was for. You'll never guess what he told me next.'

'What's that?'

'"When the jar fills up, empty it in the gutter." I said, like, pour it out in the gutter? No one'll see you, he said, and it'll wash away. I told him thanks for the wise counsel, but I probably would have figured out how to empty the jar on my own. He said after all the rookies he's trained over the years he's learned to leave nothing to chance.'

'He's a wise man,' I said. 'But I'm on your side. I have a feeling you'd have worked out the part about emptying the jar all by yourself.'

'Maybe, but on the other hand I have to admit I never would have thought to bring the jar in the first place. You don't ever see them peeing in bottles in the movies.'

I agreed that you didn't. 'How'd you get the pictures?'

'There was this kid shooting baskets all by himself a few doors down the street. I told him I'd give him five bucks if he could ring the doorbell and get the man inside to come outside of his house. He went and rang it and ran off, and Mr Havemeyer opened the door a crack and then shut it again. I snapped a picture but it wasn't one of the ones I sent you because you couldn't see anything. Anyway, I told the kid that wasn't good enough, but if he did it again and got the guy to come out I'd pay him the five and another five on top of it.'

'And it worked.'

'He made it work. He went into his own house and got a paper bag about so big and filled it with crumpled newspaper. Then he put it on the stoop and set it on fire, and then he rang the bell again and pounded on the door and ran like a thief. Mr Havemeyer opened the door a crack again, and then he rushed outside and started stomping and kicking at the burning bag.' He grinned. 'It took me a minute to get focused because I was laughing too hard to hold the camera steady. It was pretty funny.'

'I can imagine.'

'It's an old Halloween trick, actually.'

'As I recall,' I said, 'there's a surprise in the bag.'

'Well, yeah. Dog crap, so when you stomp out the fire you're stepping in it. The kid skipped that part.'

'Just as well.'

'The pictures don't show what he's doing,' he said, 'because with the lens I was right in tight on his face. But I have to laugh when I look at them, because his expression brings it all back.'

'I thought he looked sort of beleaguered.'

'Well,' he said, 'that's why.'

Cleveland's airport is south and west of the city. Lakewood is situated on the lake, appropriately enough, and a little ways to the west of Cleveland, so we could get there without running into city traffic. Jason drove and kept up his end of the conversation, and I found myself comparing him with TJ. Jason was probably a year or two older, and looked on the surface to have had an easier time of it, blessed as he was with a white face and a middle-class upbringing. He'd had a good deal more in the way of formal education, although you could argue that TJ's street sense was as valuable, with a tuition every bit as pricey. By the time we got to Lakewood I'd decided that the two of them weren't as different as they seemed. They were both decent kids.

Lakewood turned out to be an older suburb, with big trees and pre-war houses. Here and there you'd see a lot that the builders had originally passed up, with a little ranch house perched on it looking like the new kid on the block. We parked across the street from one of these and Jason killed the engine.

'You can't see where the fire was,' he said. 'When I drove off he was going at it with a broom. I guess he did a pretty good job of cleaning up.'

'He could have hired that same kid to scrub it for him.'

'That would be something, wouldn't it? I don't know if he's home. With the garage door shut you can't tell if his car's there or not.'

'I don't think I'll have to set any fires to find out,' I said. 'I'll just ring his doorbell.'

'Do you want me to come with you?'

I considered it. 'No,' I said. 'I don't think so.'

'Then I'll wait here.'

'I'd appreciate that,' I said. 'I don't know how long I'll be. It may be a while.'

'No problem,' he said. 'I've still got that jar.'

I only had to ring the bell once. The eight-note chimes were still echoing when I heard his footsteps approaching. Then he opened the door a crack and saw me, and then he opened it the rest of the way.

The photos were a good likeness. He was a small and slender man, with some age showing in his pink face and some gray lightening his neatly combed hair. Close up, I could see his watery blue eyes behind his bifocal lenses.

He was wearing dark gabardine slacks and a plaid sportshirt. There were several pens in the breast pocket of the shirt. His shoes were brown oxfords, recently polished.

There was no fire raging on his stoop this time, just another middle-aged guy. But Havemeyer still sported his beleaguered expression, as if the world was just a little bit more than he could cope with. I knew the feeling.

I said, 'Mr Havemeyer?'

'Yes?'

'May I come in? I'd like to talk with you.'

'Are you a policeman?'

It's often a temptation to say yes to that question, or to leave it artfully unanswered. This time, though, I didn't feel the need.

'No,' I said. 'My name is Scudder, Mr Havemeyer. I'm a private investigator from New York.'

'From New York.'

'Yes.'

'How did you get here?'

'How did I . . .'

'Did you fly?'

'Yes.'

'Well,' he said, and his shoulders drooped. 'I guess you'd better come in, hadn't you?'

TWENTY-TWO

You'd have thought it was a social call. He led me to the front parlor, recommended a chair, and announced that he could do with a cup of tea. Would I have one? I said I would, and not just to be sociable. It sounded like a good idea.

I stayed there while he fussed in the kitchen, and it struck me that he might return brandishing a butcher knife, or holding the same gun he'd used to kill Byron Leopold. If he did, I wouldn't stand a chance. I wasn't wearing body armor, and the closest thing I had to a weapon was the nail clipper on my key ring.

Somehow, though, I knew I wasn't in any danger. There was a greater risk that he'd seize the opportunity to turn the knife or gun on himself, and I figured he had the right. But he didn't strike me as suicidal, either.

He came out carrying a silver-handled walnut tray bearing a china teapot flanked by a sugar bowl and a little milk pitcher. There were spoons and cups and saucers as well, and he set everything out on the coffee table. I drank my tea black, while he added milk and sugar to his. The tea was Lapsang Souchong. I can't ordinarily tell one kind of tea from another, but I recognized its smoky bouquet before I'd even taken a sip.

'There's nothing like a cup of tea,' he said.

I'd brought a pocket tape recorder along, and I took it out and set it on the table. 'I'd like to record this,' I said. 'If it's all right with you.'

'I suppose it's all right,' he said. 'Really, what difference does it make?'

I switched on the recorder. 'This is a conversation between Matthew Scudder and William Havemeyer,' I stated, and mentioned the date and time. Then I sat back and gave him a chance to say something.

'I guess you know everything,' he said.

'I know most of it.'

'I knew you'd come. Well, not *you*, not specifically. But someone. I don't know what made me think I could get away with it.' He raised his eyes to mine. 'I must have been crazy,' he said.

'How did it happen?'

'That boat,' he said. 'That awful, awful boat.'

'The ferry.'

'The *Magnar Syversen*. They had no business keeping the damnable boat in service, you know. It was manifestly unsafe. You wouldn't believe how many violations they uncovered. And do you know how many people were needlessly killed?'

'Eighty-four.'

'That's right.'

'And John Wilbur Settle was one of them.'

'Yes.'

'And you held a policy on his life,' I said. 'You'd bought it through a broker in Texas who specializes in viatical transactions. You'd already been a party to one such transaction, involving a man named Phillips.'

'Harlan Phillips.'

'You made money on Phillips,' I said, 'and invested it in Settle.'

'These were good investments,' he said.

'So I understand.'

'Good for all concerned. For the poor men who were horribly ill and had no money, and for those of us

280

seeking a safe investment with a generous return. I'm sorry, you told me your name but I don't remember it.'

'Matthew Scudder.'

'Yes, of course. Mr Scudder, I'm a widower. My wife had multiple sclerosis, she was ill for most of the years of our marriage and died almost seven years ago.'

'That must have been hard.'

'It was, I suppose. You get used to it, just as you get used to being alone. I worked for over twenty years for the same corporation. Five years ago they offered me early retirement. "You've been such a good and faithful employee for so many years that we'll pay you to quit." They didn't use those words, obviously, but that's what it amounted to. I accepted their offer. I didn't really have much of a choice in the matter.'

'And that gave you money to invest.'

'It gave me money that I had to invest if I was going to have sufficient income to see me through. Savings bank interest wouldn't be enough, and I've never been comfortable with risk. You flew here, didn't you? I've never flown anywhere in my life. I've always been afraid to fly. Isn't that ridiculous? I shot a man dead in the street, I murdered him in cold blood without turning a hair, but I'm afraid to get on an airplane. Did you ever hear anything so ridiculous in your life?'

I tried not to glance at the tape recorder. I just hoped it was getting all this.

I said, 'When the boat sank . . .'

'The *Magnar Syversen*. A floating death trap. You'd expect better than that from the Scandinavians, wouldn't you?'

'Well, it was an accident.'

'Yes, an accident.'

'And that was relevant, wasn't it? The policy you held on the life of John Wilbur Settle was for fifty thousand dollars, and if he'd stayed home and died of AIDS that's what you would have received in the course of time.'

'Yes.'

'But because his death was the result of an accident . . .'

'I got twice that much.'

'A hundred thousand dollars.'

'Yes.'

'Because the policy had a double-indemnity clause.'

'Which I didn't even know about,' he said. 'I had no idea whatsoever. When the insurance company check arrived I thought they'd made a mistake. I actually called them up, because I was sure that if I didn't they'd come around wanting the money back with interest. And they told me about double indemnity, and how I was getting twice the face amount of the policy because of the way Mr Settle died.'

'Quite a windfall.'

'I couldn't believe it. I'd paid thirty-eight thousand dollars for the policy, so I was already getting a very good return on my investment, but this was just remarkable. I had very nearly tripled my investment. I'd turned thirty-eight thousand dollars into a hundred thousand.'

'Just like that.'

'Yes.'

'So you entered into another viatical transaction.'

'Yes. I believed in it as an investment medium, you see.'

'I can understand why.'

'I put some of the proceeds in the bank and the rest in a viatical transaction. I bought a larger policy this time, seventy-five thousand dollars.'

282

'Did you first make sure there was a double-indemnity clause?'

'No! No, I swear I didn't.'

'I see.'

'I never asked. But when I received the policy –'

'You read it.'

'Yes. Just, you know, to see if there was such a clause.'

'And as it happened there was.'

'Yes.'

I let the silence stretch, drank some more of my tea. The red light glowed on the side of my little tape recorder. The tape advanced, recording the silence.

'Some commentators have been very critical of viatical transactions. Not as an investment, everyone agrees that they're a good investment, but the idea of waiting for a person to die so that you can benefit financially. There was a cartoon I saw, a man walking in the desert and vultures circling overhead. But it's not like that at all.'

'How is it different?'

'Because you just don't think about the person that much. If you think of him at all you wish him well. I'd certainly rather have a man enjoy one more month of life than that my investment mature one month sooner. After all, I know he's not going to live forever, that much is a medical fact, and both my principal and the interest on it are guaranteed by the irreversible biological progress of his condition. With both Harlan Phillips and John Settle, why, I knew they were going to die, and within a fairly certain period of time. But I didn't dwell on it, and I didn't wish it sooner.'

'But with Byron Leopold it was different.'

He looked at me. 'Do you know what it is to be obsessed?' he demanded.

'I'd have to say I do.'

'If the disease were to run its course and he to die of it, I would get seventy-five thousand dollars. If he should happen to be struck by a car, or slip and fall in the bathtub, or die in a fire, then I would receive twice that amount.' He took off his glasses, held them in both hands, and stared at me, defenseless. 'I could think of nothing else,' he said. 'I could not get the fact out of my mind.'

'I see.'

'Do you? I'll tell you something else that happened. I began to think of it as my money. The whole amount, one hundred fifty thousand. I began to feel entitled to it.'

I've heard certain thieves say something similar. You have something and the thief wants it, and in his mind a transfer of ownership occurs, and it becomes his – his money, his watch, his car. And he sees you still in possession of it and becomes seized by a near-righteous indignation. When he relieves you of it, he's not stealing it. He's reclaiming it.

'If he died of AIDS,' he was saying, 'half the money would be lost. I couldn't get over the idea of what a colossal waste it would be. It's not as though *he* would get the money, or his heirs, or anyone at all. It would be completely lost. But if he died accidentally, by misadventure –'

'It would be yours.'

'Yes, and at no cost to anyone. It wouldn't be his money, or anybody else's money. It would just come to me as a pure windfall.'

'What about the insurance company?'

'But they assumed that risk!' His voice rose, in pitch and in volume. 'They sold him a policy with a double-indemnity clause. I'm sure the salesman suggested it.

No one ever deliberately asks for it. And its presence would have made his annual premium a little bit higher than it would have been otherwise. So the money was already there. If it wasn't a windfall for me, it would be a windfall for the insurance company because they'd get to keep it.'

I was still digesting that when his voice dropped and he said, 'Of course the money wasn't going to come from out of thin air. It was the insurance company's, and I was in no sense entitled to it. But I began to see it that way. If he died accidentally it was mine, all of it. If he died of his disease, I'd be cheated out of half of it.'

'Cheated out of it.'

'That's how I began to see it, yes.' He lifted the tea pot, filled both our cups. 'I started imagining accidents,' he said.

'Imagining them?'

'Things that might happen. In this part of the country people are killed in auto accidents with awful frequency. I don't suppose that happens as often in New York.'

'It happens,' I said, 'but probably not as often.'

'When you think of New York,' he said, 'you think of people getting murdered. Although the actual murder rate's not particularly high there compared with the rest of the country, is it?'

'Not that high, no.'

'It's much higher in New Orleans,' he said, and went on to name a couple of other cities. 'But in the public mind,' he said, 'New York's streets are the most dangerous in the nation. In the world, even.'

'We have the reputation,' I agreed.

'So I imagined that happening to him. A knife or a gun, something swift and surgical. And do you know what I thought?'

'What?'

'I thought what a blessing it would be. To both of us.'

'Both you and Byron Leopold?'

'Yes.'

'How did you figure that?'

'A quick death.'

'Almost a mercy killing,' I said.

'You're being ironic, but is it less merciful than the disease? Nibbling away at your life, leaving you with less and less, finally taking away the will to live before it finally takes your life? Do you know what it's like to watch that happen to someone you love?'

'No.'

'Then you should be grateful.'

'I am.'

He took off his glasses again, wiped his eyes with the back of his hand. 'She died by inches,' he said.

I didn't say anything.

'My wife. It took her years to die. It put her on crutches and it put her in a wheelchair. It would take a bite of her life, and we would adjust to that and become accustomed to that. And then it would take another bite. And it never got better. And it always got worse.'

'It must have been very hard for you.'

'I suppose it was,' he said, as if that aspect hadn't occurred to him before. 'It was awful for her. I used to pray that she would die. I felt conflicted about that. How can you pray for the death of someone you love? You can pray for relief, but can you pray for death? "God, ease her pain," I would say. "God, give her the strength to bear her burden." And then I would find myself praying, "God, let it be over." ' He sighed, straightened up. 'Not that it made the slightest bit of difference. The disease had its own schedule, its own

286

pace. Prayer wouldn't slow it down or speed it up. It tortured her for as long as it wanted to, and then it killed her. And then it was over.'

The tape recorder had a sense of theater. It picked that moment to get to the end of side one. You want to open it up and turn the cassette over and start it recording again with as little fuss as possible, to keep from breaking the mood. So of course my fingers sabotaged the process, fumbling with the catch, fumbling with the cassette.

Maybe it was just as well. Maybe the mood needed breaking.

When he resumed talking, he returned to the subject of Byron Leopold. 'At first I just thought that someone might kill him,' he said. 'Some burglar breaking into his house, some mugger on the street. Anything, a stray bullet from a war between drug dealers, anything I'd read about in the newspaper or see on television. I'd recast it in my mind and imagine it happening to him. There was a program, I think it was based on a real case, this male nurse was smothering patients. They weren't all terminal, either, so I don't suppose it was strictly a case of mercy killing. I thought that might happen, and I realized if it did the death would probably be misdiagnosed and recorded as natural.'

'And you'd be cheated.'

'Yes, and never know it. For all I knew some thoughtful nurse had smothered Harlan Phillips on his death bed. There was a double-indemnity clause in that policy, too. So for all I knew —'

'Yes.'

'If Byron Leopold was going to be murdered, it couldn't look as though he'd died in his sleep, or succumbed to his disease. It wouldn't have to be disguised as an accident. I checked, and homicide fits the definition of accident for insurance purposes. By now, you see, I was contemplating doing it myself. I don't know when that happened, that the idea entered my mind, but once it was there it was always there. I couldn't think of anything else.'

He had never thought of taking an active part in ending his wife's agony. Even when he prayed for her death, it never occurred to him to do anything to bring it about. When he had reached the point that he was actively considering ways to kill Byron Leopold, it struck him that a knife or a bullet would have spared his wife a great deal of suffering.

'But I could never have done it,' he said.

'But you thought you could do it with Leopold.'

'I didn't know. The only way I could imagine doing it was with a gun. I couldn't possibly strike him or stab him, but maybe I could point a gun and pull a trigger. Or maybe not. I wasn't at all certain.'

'Where did you get the gun?'

'I'd had it for years. It belonged to an uncle of mine, and when he passed away my aunt didn't want it in the house. I put it in a trunk in the attic, along with a box of shells that came with it, and never thought of it again. And then I did think of it, and it was where I'd put it. I didn't even know if it would work. I thought it might blow up in my hand if I tried to fire it.'

'But you used it anyway?'

'I drove out into the country and test-fired it. I just shot a couple of bullets into a tree trunk. It seemed to work all right. So I went home, and I thought about it, and I couldn't eat and I couldn't sleep and I knew I had to do something. So I went to New York.'

'How did you get the gun through airport security?'

'How did I . . . But I didn't go to the airport. I didn't fly, I never fly.'

'You told me that,' I said. 'I'd forgotten.'

'I took the train,' he said. 'There's no security check, no metal detectors to pass through. I guess they're not afraid of hijackers.'

'Not since Jesse James.'

'I went to New York,' he said, 'and I found the building where he lived, and it turned out there was a bed-and-breakfast just a block and a half away. I didn't know how long I'd be there but I didn't think it could possibly take me more than a week. Assuming I would be able to do it.'

As it turned out, he could have done it the morning after his first night in the bed-and-breakfast. He'd gone to the little park so that he could watch the entrance to Leopold's building, and the minute he saw the man emerge on crutches and carrying a newspaper, he somehow knew it was the man he sought. AIDS showed in the man's face, and it was evident that the disease was in its later stages.

But he hadn't brought the gun with him. It was in his room, wrapped in a dishtowel and locked in his suitcase.

He brought it the following morning, and Byron Leopold was already on his bench in the park when he got there. It had occurred to him that there might be more than one AIDS victim living at that address, given that the neighborhood seemed to have a high concentration of homosexuals. While a quick death would undoubtedly constitute a blessed deliverance for this man, whoever he might be, it seemed prudent to make sure of his identity. This was, to be sure, murder for gain, however he chose to rationalize it, and it would profit him not at all to kill the wrong person.

'So I went up to him,' he said, 'and I called him by name, and he nodded, and I said his name again, and he said yes, that he was Byron Leopold, or whatever he said, I don't remember exactly. And I still wasn't sure I would do it, you see, because I hadn't committed myself. I could just walk away having made the identification, and then I could do it some other time. Or I could go back home and forget about it.

'"Mr Leopold?" "Yes." "Byron Leopold?" "Yes, what is it?" Something like that. And then I had the gun out and I was shooting him.'

He was vague on the details after that point. He started running, expecting pursuit, expecting capture. But no one came after him and no one caught him. By early evening he was back on the train, bound for Cleveland.

'I thought they would come for me,' he said.

'But no one did.'

'No. There were people in the park. Witnesses. I thought they'd furnish a description and one of those composite drawings would be in all the newspapers. I thought someone would make a connection between the insurance policy and myself. But there was nothing in the papers, nothing at all as far as I could see. And I kept waiting for someone to come to the door, but no one did.'

'It sounds as though you would have welcomed it.'

He nodded slowly. 'I've thought about it all the time,' he said, 'and I still can't explain it, not to myself and certainly not to anybody else. I had the illusion that I could go to New York and kill this man, and then I could come back here, and the only change in my life would be that I would have more money.'

'But that's not the way it was.'

'The instant I pulled the trigger,' he said, 'the illusion vanished like a portrait in smoke blown away by a gust of wind. You couldn't even see where it had been. And it was done, the man was dead, there was no reversing it.'

'There never is.'

'No, there never is, not one bit of the past. It's all etched in stone. You can't erase a word, not a syllable.' He sighed heavily. 'I thought . . . well, never mind what I thought.'

'Tell me.'

'I thought it didn't matter,' he said. 'I thought he was going to die anyway. And he was!'

'Yes.'

'And so are we all, every last one of us. We're all mortal. Does that mean it's no crime to kill us?'

No crime for God, I thought. He does it all the time.

'I told myself I was doing him a favor,' he went on bitterly. 'That I was giving him an easy out. What made me think that was what he wanted? If he'd been ready to die he could have taken pills, he could have put a plastic bag over his head. There are enough ways. For God's sake, he lived on a high floor, he could have gone out the window. If that's what he wanted.' He frowned. 'You can tell he wasn't eager to die. There was only one reason for him to sell that policy. It was to get money to live on. He wanted his life to be as comfortable as possible for as long as it lasted. So I provided the money,' he said, 'and then I took away the life.'

He'd removed his glasses in the course of that speech, and now he put them on again and peered through them at me. 'Well?' he said. 'Now what happens?'

★

Always the beautiful question.

'You have some choices,' I said. 'There's a Cleveland police officer, a friend of a friend, who's familiar with the situation. We can go to the stationhouse where you'll be placed under arrest and officially informed of your rights.'

'The Miranda warning,' he said.

'Yes, that's what they call it. Then of course you can have your attorney present, and he'll explain your options. He'd probably advise you to waive extradition, in which case you'll be escorted back to New York for arraignment.'

'I see.'

'Or you can accompany me voluntarily,' I said.

'To New York.'

'That's right. The advantage in that, as far as you're concerned, is chiefly that it cuts out a certain amount of delays and red tape. And there's another personal consideration.'

'What's that?'

'Well, I won't use handcuffs,' I said. 'If you're officially in custody you'll have to be cuffed through-out, and that can be both embarrassing and uncomfort-able on the plane. I don't have any official standing so I'm not bound by rules of that sort. All we'll have to do is get two seats together.'

'On a plane,' he said.

'Oh, that's right. You don't fly.'

'I suppose it strikes you as terribly silly. Especially now.'

'If it's a phobic condition the rules of logic don't apply. Mr Havemeyer, I don't want to talk you into anything, but I'll tell you this. If you're officially taken into custody and escorted to New York, they'll make you get on a plane.'

'But if I were to go with you —'

'How long does it take on the train?'

'Under twelve hours.'

'No kidding.'

'The Lake Shore Limited,' he said. 'It leaves Cleveland at three in the morning and arrives at ten minutes of two in the afternoon.'

'And that's how you went to New York?'

'It's not that bad,' he said. 'The seats recline. You can sleep. And there's a dining car.'

You can fly it in a little over an hour, but even if I left him in a holding cell in Cleveland, I wouldn't be able to catch a flight back until something the next morning.

'If you want,' I said, 'I'll take the train with you.'

He nodded. 'I suppose that would be best,' he said.

TWENTY-THREE

It was a long night.

I left Havemeyer alone long enough to duck across the street to the car and bring Jason Griffin up to speed. He had plans for the evening but insisted it was no problem to cancel them, and that he'd be glad to take me and my prisoner to the train station. I told him he might as well join us inside the house, and he agreed that it would be more convenient than sitting in the car with the wide-mouthed jar his uncle had recommended.

While he locked the car, I hurried back to the house myself, anxious about having left Havemeyer alone, I was afraid I might find him dead by his own hand, or on the phone with his lawyer. It was hard to say which of the two prospects was more troubling, but both fears proved groundless. I found him in the kitchen, rinsing out our tea cups.

I told him I'd invited my driver in to join us, and moments later there was a knock on the door and I opened it for Jason. I didn't know what the three of us were going to talk about, but that settled itself when Havemeyer determined that Jason was a student at Western Reserve. That led to a conversation about the college's football team, which turned easily enough into a spirited discussion of Cleveland's pro team, the Browns, and their perfidious owner's decision to pack the franchise off to Baltimore.

'The nicest thing I can find to say about that man,' Havemeyer said, 'is that he's an utter son of a bitch.'

That led me almost inevitably to an analysis of the character and probable ancestry of Walter O'Malley, and gave rise to a more theoretical discussion of just what a team was, and the extent to which athletes belonged to it, or it to its fans. This would have been interesting enough all by itself, but circumstance gave it a special spin. The room was thick with two conversations, the one we were having and the one we were choosing not to have. The former was about sport and its illusions, the latter about homicide and its consequences.

Jason made a couple of phone calls to cancel his plans for the evening. I called Amtrak to book two Cleveland-to-New York seats on the Lake Shore Limited, then called Elaine in New York and got to hear my own voice on our answering machine; I left word that I'd be back in the city sometime the following afternoon. When I got back to the living room, Jason and Havemeyer were weighing prospects for dinner. Jason offered to go out for pizza, and Havemeyer said it was quicker and simpler to have it delivered. He made the phone call himself, and the kid from Domino was there well within the statutory twenty-minute time limit. Havemeyer drank a bottle of Amstel Light with his pizza, while Jason and I had Cokes. I had the sense that Jason would have preferred a beer, and wondered what had kept him from taking one. Did he feel it was inappropriate to drink on duty? Or had his uncle described me as a sober alcoholic, leading him to assume it was bad form to drink in front of me?

After we'd eaten, Havemeyer remembered that he ought to pack for the trip. I went into the bedroom with him and leaned against the wall while he took his time selecting articles of clothing and arranging them in his suitcase. When he was done he closed it and hefted it and made a face. He said he'd been meaning to get one of those suitcases on wheels you saw everybody using these days, but he hadn't gotten around to it.

'But I don't suppose I'll be making many more trips,' he said.

I asked if the suitcase was heavy.

'It's not too bad,' he said. 'I've got more clothes in here than the last time I went, but I don't have the gun, and that was heavier than you'd think. That reminds me. What should I do about the gun?'

'You still have it?'

'I suppose that's foolish, isn't it? I was going to get rid of it. Drop it down a sewer, or heave it into the lake. But I kept it. I thought I might, oh, need it.'

'Where is it?'

'In the attic. Do you want me to get it? Or should I just leave it where it is?'

I considered the question. There was a time when the answer would have been obvious, but a lot of court decisions had changed the rules regarding admissibility of evidence. Would it be better to leave the gun where it was for the time being, so that it could be found in due course after a proper warrant had been obtained?

Probably, I decided, but I weighed that against the possibility that someone would break into the house and steal the gun in the meantime, and concluded it was better to have the weapon in my possession. Even if some judge disallowed it, along with his taped confession and a few other things, it seemed to me there ought to be more than enough hard evidence to make a case against him.

He climbed up into the attic crawl space and came down holding the gun wrapped in a red and white checkered cloth. A dish towel, I guess it must have been. He presented it to me like that, and I could smell the gun without unwrapping it. He hadn't cleaned it since firing it, and it smelled of the gunshots that had killed Byron Leopold.

I went out to Jason's car and locked it in my suitcase.

We killed time playing hearts, and Havemeyer made another pot of tea, and Jason drove us to the station early, getting us there almost an hour before train time. I gave him some money, and he told me he thought he ought to be paying me for the experience. I told him not to be silly and he put the money in his pocket.

Havemeyer insisted on buying our train tickets, even as he had insisted on paying for the pizza. 'Two one-way tickets,' he announced. 'You won't be coming back to Cleveland. And neither will I.'

The train was crowded and we couldn't get two seats together. I took the conductor aside and told him I was a private detective escorting a material witness back to New York. He got a fellow to switch his seat, and I gave Havemeyer the window and sat down next to him.

We talked for an hour or so. He wanted to know what to expect, and I told him as much as I knew. I told him he would want an attorney, even if all he was going to do was cooperate with the police and plead guilty. He said there was a man in Cleveland he'd used in the past, but the man didn't take criminal cases, and anyway he was in Cleveland. 'But I suppose he could recommend someone,' he said. I said that was very likely true, and that I could recommend several New York lawyers.

He said he supposed he'd be spending the rest of his life in prison. I said that wasn't necessarily true, that he could very likely plead to a lesser charge than murder two, that a lawyer could argue that the strain of his wife's death constituted some sort of mitigating circumstances, and that his previously unblemished record (not even a traffic violation, aside from a couple of parking tickets) would certainly work to his advantage.

'You'll have to go to prison,' I said, 'but it'll probably be minimum-security, and the bulk of the other cons will be white-collar criminals, not child molesters and strongarm thugs. I'm not saying you'll like it, but it won't be some hellhole out of *The Shawshank Redemption*. And I'd be surprised if you wound up serving more than five years.'

'That doesn't seem very long,' he said, 'for killing an innocent man.'

It would seem longer once he was doing it, I thought. And if it still didn't seem long enough, he could always re-enlist.

Some forty-five minutes out of Cleveland Havemeyer took a Valium, which was evidently his custom on long train trips. He offered me one but I passed. I would have liked one, but then I would have liked a pint of Early Times, as far as that goes. Havemeyer swallowed his Valium and put his seat back and closed his eyes, and that was the last I heard from him for the next five or six hours.

I'd picked up a paperback at Newark before they called my flight, and I'd never even opened it en route to Cleveland. I got it from my bag now and read for a while, pausing now and then to put the book down on my lap and look off into the distance, thinking long thoughts. Train travel lends itself to that sort of thing.

Sometime before dawn I closed my eyes, and when I opened them it was light outside and we were pulling into Rochester. I slipped off to the diner for a cup of coffee. Havemeyer was still sleeping when I got back.

He woke up not long after that and we got some breakfast and returned to our seats. He stayed awake the rest of the way but still seemed faintly tranquilized, not talking much. He read the Amtrak magazine, and when he'd exhausted its possibilities I gave him the paperback I'd given up on.

Around noon, shortly after we left Albany, I made a phone call. You could do that, they had a phone you could use, just running your credit card through a slot. I called the Sixth Precinct and managed to get Harris Conley. I told him I was on my way back from Cleveland with a suspect in the killing of Byron Leopold. I didn't even have to remind him who Byron Leopold was, but then it's a name that sticks in your mind.

He said, 'What did you do, arrest him? I'm not sure of the legal status of that.'

'He's with me voluntarily,' I said. 'I've got a full confession on tape. I'm not sure of the legal status of that, either, but I've got it, along with the gun he used.'

'That's pretty amazing,' he said. He offered to have the train met by a contingent of cops, but I didn't think that was necessary. Havemeyer was coming in voluntarily, and I thought he'd be more comfortable surrendering at the precinct. Besides, I'd promised to keep him out of handcuffs as long as possible.

I wanted to second-guess myself when we got to Grand Central. There was a light rain falling and it had the usual effect of making the taxis disappear. But before too long one pulled up to discharge a passenger and we grabbed it and headed downtown.

*

I didn't have to stick around too long at the Sixth. I turned over the gun (which, unwrapped, turned out to be .38 revolver, with live rounds in three of its six chambers) to Conley, along with the tape of Havemeyer's confession. I answered a battery of questions, then dictated a statement.

'I'm glad I was around when you called,' Conley told me, 'and lucky I even remembered what you were talking about. I don't suppose I have to tell you we weren't exactly pushing this one.'

'That's no surprise.'

'Triage,' he said. 'You put in your time on the ones you stand a chance of breaking. And the ones where there's a lot of heat from up top.'

'That's how it's always been.'

'And always will be, would be my guess. Point is, this wasn't a front-burner case, not after the first seventy-two hours. And the whole city's so nuts today, especially the department, it's a wonder I remember my own name, let alone yours and Byron Leopold's.'

'Why is the city so nuts?'

'You don't know? Where the hell did you spend the past twelve hours?'

'On a train.'

'Oh, right. But even so, didn't you see a newspaper? Listen to the radio? You came through Grand Central, you must have walked past a newsstand.'

'I had luggage to carry and a confessed murderer to escort,' I reminded him. 'I didn't have time to care what was happening in Bosnia.'

'Forget Bosnia. Bosnia didn't make the headlines today. It was all Will this morning.'

'Will?'

He nodded. 'Either it's Number One back from the

dead or Number Two's more dangerous than anybody thought. You know the theater critic?'

'Regis Kilbourne.'

'That's the one,' he said. 'Will got him last night.'

TWENTY-FOUR

You could almost say he'd been asking for it.

I'd somehow missed the column he wrote. It had appeared toward the end of the previous week, not in the Arts section where his reviews always ran, but on the *Times*'s op-ed page. I've since had a look at that issue of the paper, and it seems to me I read Safire's column that day, an inside-the-mind-of-piece on a pair of presidential hopefuls. So I very likely took a look at what Regis Kilbourne had to say, and probably stopped reading before I got to the payoff.

That would have been natural enough, because his brief essay started off as a spirited defense of freedom of the press. He'd said the same things before, in response to having been given a spot on Will's list, going on about a critic's profound responsibilities to his conscience and his public. I might very well have decided I didn't have to listen to all that again.

He'd used up the greater portion of his 850 words before he got to the point. The rest of his column was given over to a review of a dramatic production, but this particular show was staged neither on nor off Broadway but all over town. He reviewed Will, and he gave him a bad notice.

'It is customary but by no means imperative,' he wrote, 'to revisit a long-running show after a substantive change in the cast. When the original production was essentially a star vehicle, such revisits are almost always disappointing. And this is certainly true in the case of what, were it mounted as a Broadway musical, some producer would surely entitle *Will!* complete down to the now-obligatory exclamation point.

'In its first incarnation, *Will!* was unquestionably good theater. With the late Adrian Whitfield quietly elegant in the title role, the production had a powerful grip on its audience of eight million New Yorkers. But what succeeded initially as brilliant tragedy (albeit not unleavened by its comic moments) has come back to us as farce, and a farce with all the zest and sparkle of a fallen soufflé.

'With Whitfield's death and unmasking, his understudy has emerged from the wings – and has fallen flat on his face. Will #2, as we seem to be calling him, is a man of bombast and empty rage. We take this pale copy seriously only because we remember the original.

'No more. "You're only a pack of cards," Alice said, scattering her adversaries to the four corners of Wonderland. I say the same to this craven who drapes himself in the fallen Whitfield's garb. No longer will I go about guarded and live as if under siege. No longer will one seat of my two on the aisle be taken up by a burly chap who'd much rather be home watching "NYPD Blue". I'm taking my life back, and I can only recommend the same course of action to the current Will. Close the show, strike the set – and get a life.'

Kilbourne had made his decision on his own, but he'd let the cops know about it before his op-ed piece informed the rest of the world. While they'd advised against it, nobody tried very hard to talk him out of it. They'd reached much the same conclusion he had. Copycat killers can be as dangerous as the original, but it was beginning to look as though Will wasn't a copycat killer after all. He was a copycat letter-writer.

He would still be pursued, and eventually caught, but there was a lot less urgency attached to the matter.

So Tuesday night, while I was playing hearts with a college student and a confessed murderer in the kitchen of a ranch house in Lakewood, Ohio, Regis Kilbourne was watching a preview performance of the new P J Barry play, *Poor Little Rhode Island*. His companion was a young woman named Melba Rogin, who looked like a model but was in fact a fashion photographer. After the performance the two had drinks and a light supper at Joe Allen's, then took a taxi to the brownstone in Chelsea where he had a floor-through apartment on the parlor floor.

At 1:15 or thereabouts he suggested she stay over, but she had an early shoot and wanted to get home. (One of the tabloids had her speculating on what would have happened if she'd stayed the night. Would Kilbourne still be alive? Or would she have died along with him?) He walked to Seventh Avenue with her and put her in a cab headed downtown – her loft was on Crosby Street – and the last she saw of him he was on his way home.

He evidently went straight back to his apartment, and sometime within the next hour or two he had a visitor. It appeared that either Will had managed to get hold of a key or Kilbourne let him in, as there were no signs of forced entry. Nor did Kilbourne seem to have resisted his killer. He'd been struck on the head with some heavy object, the blow delivered with enough force to have very likely rendered him unconscious. He'd either fallen to the floor or been laid out there, face down. Then the killer stabbed him in the back with a Sabatier carbon-steel kitchen knife, which had been subsequently removed from the corpse, washed in the sink, and placed in the wire basket to dry.

('Will's probably not a chef,' Elaine told me. 'You have to hand-dry knives like that. They're not stainless, and they'll rust. A chef would have known that.' Maybe he knew, I said, and didn't care. A chef would have cared, she said.)

I don't know that the knife had time to rust, but I do know there were traces of blood still on it, which nailed it down as the murder weapon. There were no prints on it, though, or prints other than Kilbourne's and Melba Rogin's anywhere in the apartment.

Kilbourne was found fully dressed, wearing the slacks and sweater he'd donned to put Melba in a cab. (She said he'd worn a brown suede baseball jacket as well, and that garment had been found slung over the back of a chair.) Either Will had arrived before his victim had gone to bed, or Kilbourne had dressed again in the same clothes before answering the door. According to Melba, he'd been wide awake when she left him, so he might have stayed up to read or watch television, or even to write his review.

If he'd done any writing, he'd left no sign of it. He still used a typewriter, an ancient Royal portable that evidently had some sort of totemic status in his eyes. There was no work-in-progress in his typewriter, no notes alongside it. Some reporter asked Melba Rogin how he'd liked the play – he'd probably have asked the same question of Mary Lincoln – and she claimed not to know. According to her, he would never say anything about a play until he'd written his review. 'But I don't think he loved it,' she admitted.

That opened up a new vein of speculation. Some wit got his name in Liz Smith's column by theorizing that Kilbourne had hated the play and written a withering review, and that his late-night visitor was the play-wright himself, P J Barry, who'd struck down his tormentor before taking home the offending review and consigning it to the flames. 'But I know P J Barry,' Smith wrote, 'and I've seen *Poor Little Rhode Island*, and I can no more imagine PJ doing such a thing than I can believe *anyone* could find a bad word to say about his play.'

There were no calls to or from Kilbourne's apartment around the time the murder would have occurred, no reports of strangers entering or lurking around the brownstone. Sooner or later, though, they would turn up a witness, someone who'd seen someone coming or going, someone who'd heard a shout or a cry, someone who knew something.

It was just a matter of time.

Toward the end of the week, I got a call from Ray Gruliow. His had been one of the names I'd given to William Havemeyer, and Hard-Way Ray had agreed to represent him. 'The poor son of a bitch,' he said. 'He's the last person you'd figure to commit murder. It's not my kind of case at all, you know. He's not poor, he's not black, and he hasn't tried to blow up the Empire State building.'

'He'll ruin your image.'

'Right, he'll unbesmirch it. You know, if it weren't so clearly contrary to his own wishes, I'd kind of like to try the case. I think I could get him off.'

'How, for God's sake?'

'Oh, who knows? But you could start by putting the system on trial. Here's a poor mutt who works hard all his life, never saves a dime, and his company shows its gratitude by forcing him out. Then you've got his wife's death, years of pain and suffering, all of which can't help but impinge on his emotional state. Of course the first thing I do is get that confession ruled inadmissible.'

'Which one? After I got him on tape, he walked into the Sixth Precinct and told them the same story all over again. *After* they'd given him the Miranda warning. And they videotaped the whole thing, including Miranda.'

'Fruit of the poisoned tree. The first confession was improperly obtained –'

'The hell it was.'

'– so that makes all further confessions suspect.'

'That doesn't make any sense.'

'Well, probably not, but I'd think of something. The point is that's not what he wants, but I think I can carry on enough when I sit down with the DA's guy to strike a pretty good deal for him.' He speculated some about that, and then said, 'I wonder what happens to the money.'

'What money?'

'The hundred and fifty thousand. Integrity Life paid the claim, double indemnity and all, and the money's sitting in Havemeyer's savings account in Lakewood. He hasn't spent a penny of it.'

'I don't suppose he gets to use it to pay his attorney.'

'He doesn't get to do anything with it. You can't legally profit as the result of the commission of a crime. If I'm convicted of killing you, I can't inherit your property or collect on your life insurance. Basic principle of law.'

'And a reasonable one, from the sound of it.'

'I don't think anybody's likely to argue the point, though it's had a few unfortunate effects. There was that dame who killed the diet doctor a few years back. Her lawyer could have pleaded her guilty with extenuating circumstances, and just about got her off

307

with time served and community service, but she had no money of her own and she stood to inherit under the terms of the doc's will. But she had to be found not guilty for that to happen, so the lawyer gambled and lost, and his client wound up with long prison time. Now was his decision colored by the knowledge that she had to inherit for him to get paid? No, absolutely not, because we attorneys are never influenced by such considerations.'

'Thank God for that,' I said.

'Havemeyer's going to plead,' he said, 'so the money's not going to be his. But what happens to it?'

'The insurance company gets it back.'

'The hell they do. They collected premiums all those years, they accepted the risk, and they owe the money. The full amount, too, because murder fits the definition of accidental death. They've got to pay it to somebody, but to whom?'

'To Byron Leopold's estate, I guess. Which means a couple of AIDS charities.'

'That would be true,' he said, 'if Leopold still owned the policy. In that case Havemeyer would be excluded as beneficiary and Leopold's estate would receive the funds. But Leopold transferred ownership of the policy for value received. He's out of the picture.'

'What about Havemeyer's heirs?'

'Uh-uh. Havemeyer never had title to the money. He can't pass on what's never been his in the first place. Never mind the fact that nobody can inherit anything from him while he's still alive. But that does bring up a question. Havemeyer owned the policy and named himself as beneficiary. But did he name a secondary beneficiary, in the event that he might predecease Leopold? He might not have bothered, figuring that if he died before Leopold did, the money payable to him on Leopold's death would simply be paid to his estate.'

'Havemeyer's estate, you mean?'

'Right. In other words, why bother to designate a secondary beneficiary if the money'll go to him anyway? There are reasons, as it happens. The money doesn't have to wait until the estate goes through probate. But he might not have been so advised, or he might not have bothered. But if he did, can the secondary beneficiary benefit?'

'Why not? He wouldn't be excluded because he wasn't a party to the murder.'

'Ah, but did Havemeyer enter into the viatical transaction with the prior intent of killing Leopold?'

'He says not.'

'Good for him, but how do we know one way or the other? And if he did, can't we argue that his criminous intent in fact nullifies the viatical transaction, thereby restoring ownership of the policy to Byron Leopold?'

'So the charities would get the money.'

'Would they? Were they his designated beneficiary before the viatical transaction?'

'Jesus,' I said.

'I assume that was an interjection,' he said, 'and not the name of his beneficiary.'

'I know his beneficiary,' I said. 'She had to acknowledge that she knew she'd been removed as beneficiary before the viatical transaction could go through.'

'Sure, that's standard. How do you happen to know her?'

'She's a friend of mine, she's in the program. She got me started looking into his death in the first place.'

He laughed aloud. 'What do you know about that?

She didn't know it, but she was acting in her own self-interest.'

'You mean she's going to wind up with the money?'

'She's got a damn good claim,' he said. 'If Havemeyer had it in mind to commit murder, as his subsequent actions would strongly imply, the viatical transaction can be declared null and void. If it's void, and policy ownership thereby returns to Leopold, and if she was his beneficiary until such time as he deleted her in order to proceed with the transaction, I'd say she's effectively reinstated by the transaction's nullification. I'd certainly be happy to argue that point. Unless I was retained by the charities named in his will, in which case I'd be every bit as happy to argue that his failing to make the woman his heir was evidence of intent to benefit them and not her, and —'

The rest was too legalistic and convoluted for me, but the gist of it was that Ginny might ultimately come into $150,000. 'Tell her to call me,' he said. 'I can't represent her, but I'll find her somebody who can.'

Ginny was astonished, of course, and her first reaction was that she wasn't entitled to the money. Suppose she just let the charities have it? I pointed out that Byron's intent seemed clear to me, and that she could always ease her conscience down the line by giving part of the proceeds to the charities.

'Anyway,' I said, 'you earned it. If you hadn't got me started looking for Byron's killer, the money would never get out of Lakewood, Ohio. What Havemeyer didn't spend on pizza and tea bags he'd leave to his relatives.'

'If anybody earned it,' she said, 'you did. Suppose we split it.'

'What, you and I?'

'You, me, and the charities. Three-way split.'

'That's too much for me,' I said, 'and probably too much for the charities, but we can thrash that out later on. In the meantime, call the lawyer.'

I don't know if there was a connection, but the day after I had that conversation with Ginny I went out and did my Christmas shopping. I didn't know that she'd wind up with the insurance proceeds, nor could I presume on the basis of an impulsive remark of hers that she'd share what she got with me. But the prospect of a windfall, however slender and remote, evidently succeeded in infusing me with the Christmas spirit. I didn't empty my pockets into the Salvation Army kettles, I didn't sashay down the street whistling 'Away in the Manger', but I did somehow manage to brave the crowds in the midtown stores and buy enough presents to cover all the bases.

A shop on Madison Avenue was the source of gifts for my sons, Mike and Andy, and Mike's wife, June, and I was able to arrange to have everything shipped – the briefcase and woven-leather handbag to Michael and June in San José, the binoculars to Andy in Missoula, Montana, where he'd recently wound up after brief stints in Vancouver and Calgary.

I thought I'd have trouble with Elaine's present – always do but then I saw a pair of earrings in a shop window and knew instantly that they'd look great on her. Chunky little hearts in frosted glass, accented with deep blue stones. They were Lalique, the saleswoman informed me, and I nodded solemnly as if I knew what that meant. I gathered it was good.

The next morning, or the one after that, I went out after breakfast and read the paper across the street at the Morning Star. Then I walked on down to the main library at Fifth and Forty-second. I stayed there until I got hungry, had lunch on a bench in Bryant Park, eating quickly because it was a little too cold to sit there comfortably. When I was done I went back inside again and spent some more time looking things up and making notes.

Walking home, I stopped at a glitzy diner at Fifty-sixth and Sixth and had a cup of coffee and a piece of pie. I thought about what I knew, or thought I knew, and tried to figure out what I was going to do with it.

There was nothing about Will on the news that night, and nothing in the morning papers. Marty McGraw's column was given over to his thoughts on the latest tussle between the city's mayor and the state's junior senator. They were both Republicans, both Italian-Americans, and they couldn't have had more contempt for each other if one were a Serb and the other a Croat.

I picked up the phone and called a few cops, including Harris Conley and Joe Durkin. Then I tried Marty McGraw, but I couldn't reach him and nobody knew where he was.

I had an idea where I'd find him.

TWENTY-FIVE

'Well, look who's here,' he said. 'I'm flattered all to hell and back, because unless you turned into a pervert or developed a taste for low company, you must have come here just to see me.'

'I figured there was a chance I'd find you here.'

He tilted back his head, looked at me through half-lidded eyes. He had an empty shot glass and half a glass of beer in front of him, and I gathered it wasn't his first of the morning. But he looked and sounded entirely sober.

'You figured there was a chance you'd find me here,' he said. 'Well, I always said you were a great detective, Mattie. Tomorrow you'll show up with Judge Crater, and the day after that you'll tell the world who really snatched the Lindbergh baby. You figure there's a connection?'

'Anything's possible.'

'Sure. Those could even be real.'

I looked where he was gesturing, and saw a waitress in the standard Bunny's Topless getup – high heels, mesh panty hose, scarlet hot pants with white cotton-tail, and nothing above the waist but the rabbit ears and too much eye makeup. Her face, for all the makeup, was impossibly young, and her breasts had the gravity-defying insouciance of silicon.

'Clear up a point for me,' he said when she came over to our table. 'What's your order?'

'You've got it backwards. I'm supposed to take your order.'

'I don't want to take your order, I just want to know what it is. Are you a Carmelite or are you one of the Little Sisters of the Poor?' When she looked confused he said, 'I'm just joking, honey. Don't mind me. I know you're new here, but they must have told you I'm harmless.'

'Oh, I don't know,' she said. 'I bet you're armed and dangerous.'

He grinned, delighted. 'Hey, you're okay,' he said. 'You give as good as you get. I'll tell you what. Bring me another round, a double shot and a beer, but what you can do, you can make it *two* double shots, and *two* beers.' My face must have shown something, because he said, 'Relax, Mattie. I know you wouldn't touch a drop to save your soul, you self-righteous fuck. And please pardon my French, sweetheart, and whatever you do don't tell your Mother Superior what I just said. I want you to bring me two rounds at once so we won't have to disturb you later, and you can also bring my sobersided father here whatever he's having.'

'Club soda will be fine,' I told her.

'Bring him two club sodas,' he said, 'and the devil take the hindmost.' She walked off, her cottontail bobbing, and he said, 'I don't know how I feel about silicon. They all look perfect but they don't look real. And what's the effect on the next generation? Do teenage boys grow up expecting perfect tits?'

'When you're a teenage boy,' I said, 'all tits are perfect.'

'Not if all you ever see is silicon. Used to be girls would go out and get their tits done so they could get a guy. Now there's married men asking their wives to call the plastic surgeon, make an appointment. "What do I want for Christmas, Mona? Well, now that you mention it, big knockers'd be nice." Make sense to you?'

'Hardly anything does,' I said.

'Amen to that, brother.'

'And yet you come here,' I said.

'I like tawdry,' he said, 'and I like tacky, and I have a passion for paradox. And, even though I barely look at the tits, it's nice to know they're there if I get the urge. Plus this place is three blocks from the fucking office and yet no one from the paper would be caught dead here, so I don't get disturbed. That's my story, Monsieur Poirot. Now what's your excuse?'

'I came here to see you.'

She brought the drinks. 'On my tab,' he said, and gave her a five-dollar tip. 'I'm a class guy,' he said. 'You notice I just gave her the money. I didn't try to stuff it down the front of her Spandex shorts, as I've seen some of the customers do. I more or less assumed you came here to see me, O Great Detective. What I wondered is why.'

'To see what you could tell me about Will.'

'Ah, I see. You want the hat trick.'

'How's that?'

'You unmasked one killer and brought another back alive. What's it like in Lakewood, Ohio, anyway? Do the natives wear shoes?'

'For the most part.'

'Glad to hear it. You got Adrian, you got this Havemeyer, and now you want Will Number Two. Adrian's understudy, if you want to stay with the theatrical image Regis invoked so nicely in his op-ed piece.' His eyes widened. 'Wait a minute,' he said. 'Havemeyer's first name is William, isn't it? What do they call him?'

'When I called him anything,' I said, 'it was Mr Havemeyer.'

'So it could be Bill or Willie. Or even Will.'

'It could be anything at all,' I said. 'I told you what I called him.'

'I thought cops always call perps by their first names.'

'I guess I've been off the job too long.'

'Yeah, you've turned respectful. It's good you're not still wearing the uniform or you'd be a disgrace to it. If they call him Will, and who's to say they don't, that'd be the hat trick all right, wouldn't it? Three guys named Will, and Mattie gets 'em all.'

'I'm not chasing Will Number Two.'

'You're not?'

I shook my head. 'I'm just your average concerned citizen,' I said. 'All I know is what I read in the papers.'

'You and Will Rogers.'

'And I was wondering what you might know that they're not reporting. For instance, has there been another letter from the guy?'

'No.'

'He always sent a letter after each killing. Like a terrorist group claiming credit for a bombing.'

'So?'

'It's surprising he'd break the pattern.'

He rolled his eyes. 'It's Adrian's pattern,' he said, 'and Adrian's not writing letters these days. Why expect the new guy to operate the same way?'

'That's a point.'

'Adrian didn't threaten three guys at once, either. There's a lot of differences between them, including the psychological gobbledy-gook everybody's been spouting.' He had already thrown down one double shot, and now he took a dainty sip of the other and chased it

316

with an equally dainty sip of beer. 'That's why I wrote what I did,' he said.

'The column where you taunted him?'

'Uh-huh. I don't know. One day I was annoyed the way everybody else was calling him a paper tiger, and next thing I knew I was trying to bait him.'

'I was wondering about that.'

'I decided they were right,' he said, 'and I decided the guy was never gonna *do* anything, and I got the bright idea that if I stuck something through the bars of his cage and poked him he'd at least roar, and maybe that would give the cops something to go on. And I knew it was safe to provoke him because he wasn't about to get out of the cage.'

'But he did.'

'Yeah. I'm not saying it's my fault, because fucking Kilbourne was pretty provocative himself, telling Will to strike the set and get his ass off the stage. But I don't mind telling you it's pretty much ended my interest in the matter.'

'Oh?'

'I'm glad I haven't had another I-shot-the-sheriff letter from the son of a bitch. If he writes any more letters I hope he mails them to somebody else. I don't think he will, and I don't think he'll kill anybody else, either, although I'm not about to suggest they quit guarding Peter Tully and Judge Rome. But the point is I'm walking away from it. I can find other things to write about.'

'It's not hard in this town.'

'Not hard at all.'

I took a long drink of club soda. Out of the corner of my eye I watched our waitress take an order from a table of new arrivals, three men in their early thirties dressed in jackets and ties. One of them was stroking her bottom and patting her cottontail. She didn't even seem to notice.

'Maybe I shouldn't even bring this up,' I said, 'considering your lack of interest. But I wanted your input.'

'Go ahead.'

I dug out my notebook, flipped it open. 'My curse upon the withered hand that grips my nation's throat.'

He froze with the glass halfway to his lips, screwed up his face in a frown. 'What the hell is that?'

'Sound familiar?'

'It does but I can't think why. Help me out here, Mattie.'

'The first letter from Will Number Two, where he shared his little three-name list with us.'

'That's right,' he said. 'He was going on about Peter Tully, right after that crap about chucking a wrench into the machinery of the city, or whatever the hell it was. So?'

'Except he had it a little different. "A curse upon the withered hand that grips a city's throat." *A* curse instead of *my* curse, and *a city* instead of *my nation*.'

'So?'

'So Will was paraphrasing the original.'

'What original?' He frowned again, and then drew back his head and looked at me. 'Wait a minute,' he said.

'Take all the time you want, Marty.'

'I'll be sweetly and resoundingly fucked,' he said. 'You know who the cocksucker was quoting?'

'Who?'

'Me,' he said, eyebrows raised high in indignation. 'He was quoting me. Or paraphrasing me, or whatever the hell you want to call it.'

'No kidding?'

'You wouldn't know it,' he said, 'because nobody knows it, but once upon a time I had the bad taste and ill fortune to write a play.'

'*The Tumult in the Clouds.*'

'My God, how would you know that? It's from Yeats, the poem's "An Irish Airman Foresees His Death". Sweet Christ, it was awful.'

'I'm sure it was better than that.'

'No, it was a stinker, and you don't have to take my word for it. The reviews showed rare unanimity of opinion on that subject. Nobody objected to the title, though, even though it had nothing to do with flying. There was plenty of tumult, however. Short on clouds, long on tumult. But it was Irish as all get-out, my heartfelt autobiographical take on the Irish-American experience, and nothing gets an Irish book or play off to a better start than a title from Yeats. It's good the old boy wrote a lot.'

'And the line's from your play?'

'The line?'

'The one about the withered hand and the nation's throat.'

'Oh, that Will did a turn on. In the play the withered hand was Queen Victoria's, if I remember correctly. And the throat was that of Holy Ireland, you'll be unsurprised to learn. It was a tinker woman who delivered the line. Mother of Mercy, what did I know about tinker women? Or Ireland either, for that matter. I've never been to the poor benighted country, and never want to go, either.'

'You're pretty good,' I said.

'How's that, Mattie?'

'Not recognizing the line at first. Then realizing that I must know where it's from, and deciding to come up with it first yourself. And pretending that you're unaware that I know where the line's from, but how could you be? Because how would I know the original line if I didn't know about the play?'

'Hey, you lost me around the clubhouse turn.'

'Oh?'

He hefted his glass. 'You sober sons of bitches,' he said, 'you just don't understand how this stuff slows down the thought processes. You want to go over that again? You must have known because I had to know because you knew because I said you said – you see what I mean, Mattie? It's confusing.'

'I know.'

'So do you want to run it by me one more time?'

'I don't think so.'

'Hey, suit yourself. You're the one brought it up, so –'

'Give it up, Marty.'

'How's that?'

'I know you did it. You wrote the letters and you killed Regis Kilbourne.'

'That's fucking nuts.'

'I don't think so.'

'Why would I do any of that? You want to tell me that?'

'You wrote the letters to stay in the limelight.'

'Me? You're kidding, right?'

'Will made you really important,' I said. 'You wrote a column and the next thing anybody knew a killer was knocking off prominent people all over New York.'

'And Omaha. Don't forget Omaha.'

'Then Will killed himself, and it turned out the Wizard of Oz was just the little man behind the curtain. He was Adrian Whitfield, and he wasn't larger than life anymore. There was no more story, and that meant no more front-page headlines for you. And you couldn't stand that.'

'I got a column runs three times a week,' he said. 'You know how many people read what I write, Will or no Will?'

'Quite a few.'

'Millions. You know what I get paid to write what I write? Not millions, but close.'

'You never had a story like this one before.'

'I've had plenty of stories over the years. This town's up to here with stories. Stories are like assholes, everybody's got one and most of 'em stink.'

'This was different. You told me so yourself.'

'They're all different while you're writing them. You have to think they're special at the time. Then they run their course and you move on to something else and tell yourself it's special, and twice as special as the last one.'

'Will was your creation, Marty. You gave him the idea. And he addressed all his letters to you. Every time there was a new development, you were first with it. You showed what you got to the cops, and you were the first person they shared with.'

'So?'

'So you couldn't bear to see the story end. Regis Kilbourne was closer than he knew when he compared the case to a Broadway play. When the star left the stage, you couldn't stand the idea of closing the show. You put on his costume and tried to play the part yourself. You wrote letters to yourself and wound up giving yourself away, because you couldn't keep from quoting your own failed play.'

He just looked at me.

'Look at the three men you put on Will's list,' I said. 'A union boss who threatens to shut down the city and a judge who keeps unlocking the jailhouse door. Two fellows who manage to piss off a substantial portion of the population.'

'So?'

'So look at the third name on the list. The theater critic for the *New York Times*. Now who the hell puts a critic on that kind of list?'

'I wondered that myself, you know.'

'Don't insult my intelligence, Marty.'

'And don't you insult mine. And don't ride rough-shod over the facts or all you'll get for your troubles is saddle sores. You know when *The Tumult in the Clouds* opened? Fifteen years ago. You know when Regis Kilbourne started reviewing for the paper of record? *I* happen to know, because it was in all the obits. Just under twelve years ago. It was another guy reviewed *Tumult* for the *Times*, and he died of a heart attack five or six years ago himself, and I swear it wasn't because I jumped out of a closet and yelled "Boo!" at him.'

'I read the *Times* review.'

'Then you know.'

'I also read Regis's review. In *Gotham Magazine*.'

'Jesus, where'd you find that? I'm not even sure I read it myself.'

'Then how come you quoted it? In the same letter where you talked about Peter Tully's withered hand having the city by the throat, you had this to say about Send-'em-Home Rome.' I found it in my notebook. '"You have not the slightest sensitivity to the feelings of the public, and no concern for their wishes." That's what you wrote. And here's what Kilbourne wrote about you: "As a journalist, Mr McGraw presents himself as one who would rather keep the common touch than walk with kings. Yet as a playwright he has

322

not the slightest sensitivity to the feelings of the theater-going public, and no concern for their wishes."'

'I remember the review.'

'No kidding.'

'Now that you read it to me, I remember it. But I swear I didn't recognize the line in Will's letter. The hell, he quoted my play, he could quote my reviews while he was at it. Maybe the son of a bitch was obsessed with me. Maybe he thought throwing some quotes around, which *I* didn't even happen to recognize, maybe he thought that was a way to curry favor with me.' He looked at me, then shrugged. 'Hey, I'm not saying it makes sense, but the guy's a nut. Who can figure someone like that?'

'Give it up, Marty.'

'The fuck's that supposed to mean? "Give it up, Marty." You sound like some fucking TV show, anybody ever tell you that?'

'Kilbourne's review in *Gotham* was scathing. The play got negative notices all around, but Kilbourne was vicious, and all of his venom was directed against the play itself and the man who wrote it. It amounted to a personal attack, as if he resented a columnist presuming to write a play and wanted to make sure you never tried it again.'

'So? That was fifteen years ago. I had a couple of drinks, I kicked a chair and punched a wall and said a couple of words I never learned from the nuns, and I forgot about it. Why the hell are you shaking your head at me?'

'Because you quoted the review.'

'That was Will quoted the review, remember? Will Number Two, and I don't know who he is but he ain't me.'

'You quoted the review in your column, Marty.' I

opened the notebook again and cited chapter and verse, quoting lines from Kilbourne's review that had found their way into various columns Marty had written both before and after the death of Adrian Whitfield. When I finished I closed the notebook and looked at him. His eyes were lowered and a full minute passed without a word from him.

Then, still not looking at me, he said, 'Maybe I wrote the letters.'

'And?'

'What harm could it do? Keep a good story alive and throw the fear of God into three sons of bitches while you're at it. Don't tell me there's laws against it.' He sighed. 'I don't mind breaking a law when I've got a good reason. And I don't mind upsetting the emotional equilibrium of three assholes who never gave a rat's ass how many emotional equilibriums they knocked to hell and gone. Or do I mean equilibria? You a Latin scholar, Mattie?'

'Not since high school.'

'The kids don't take Latin anymore. Or maybe it's back in again, for all I know. *Amo, amas, amat. Amamus, amatis, amant.* You remember?'

'Vaguely.'

'*Vox populi, vox dei.* The voice of the people is the voice of God. And I suppose the will of the people is the will of God, wouldn't you say?'

'I'm no expert.'

'On Latin?'

'Or on the will of God.'

'Yeah. I'll tell you something, Mr Expert. That first column I wrote? When I more or less told Richie Vollmer to kill himself and do the world a favor?'

'What about it?'

'I meant what I wrote in that column. I never

thought it would inspire anyone to homicide, but if the thought had crossed my mind I might have gone ahead and written it anyhow.' He leaned forward, looked into my eyes. 'But if I ever had the slightest notion that writing more letters from Will would lead to the murder of anyone, Tully or Rome or Kilbourne, I never would have done it.'

'And that's what happened? You put the idea in someone's head?'

He nodded. 'Unintentionally, I swear it. I gave Adrian the idea and I gave it to this idiot as well.'

'You know,' I said, 'the cops'll break you. You won't have an alibi for the night of Kilbourne's death, or if you do it won't hold up. And they'll find witnesses who can place you on the scene, and they'll find carpet fibers or blood traces or some goddamn thing or other, and they won't even need that because before all the evidence is in hand you'll cave in and confess.'

'You think so, huh?'

'I'm sure of it.'

'So what do you want me to do?'

'Give it up now,' I said.

'Why? So you can have the hat trick, is that it?'

'I've already had more publicity than I want. I'd just as soon stay out of it.'

'Then what's the point?'

'I'm representing a client,' I said.

'Who? You can't mean Whitfield.'

'I think he'd want me to see this through.'

'And what's in it for me, Mattie? Mind telling me that?'

'You'll feel better.'

'I'll *feel* better?'

'Havemeyer did. He thought he could commit murder and then go right back to his life. But he found out he couldn't. It was eating him up and he didn't know what to do with it. He was ready to give it up the minute I walked in the door, and he told me he felt relieved.'

'You know, he handled the killing part neatly enough,' he said. 'Havemeyer, I mean. Shot him, ran down the street, got away clean.'

'Nobody ever gets away clean.'

He closed his eyes for a moment. When he opened them he said he could certainly use another drink. He caught the waitress's eye, held up two fingers, and made a circular motion. Neither of us said anything until she came to the table with another double round, two double shots with beer chasers for Marty, two more glasses of club soda for me. I still had a glass and a half of soda from the round before, but she took them away, along with Marty's empty glasses.

'Oh, fuck it,' he said, when she was out of hearing range. 'You're right about one thing, you know. Nobody ever gets away with anything. What do you want me to say? I wrote the letters and I killed the son of a bitch. You happy now? What the hell's that?'

I put the tape recorder on the table. 'I'd like to record this,' I said.

'And if I say no it turns out you're wearing a wire, right? I think I saw that program.'

'No wire. If you say no I'll leave it turned off.'

'But you'd prefer to record it.'

'If you don't object.'

'Fuck it,' he said. 'What do I care?'

TWENTY-SIX

Scudder: Please state your name for the record.

McGraw: What bullshit ... My name is Martin Joseph McGraw.

S: You want to tell me what happened?

M: You know what happened. You already told *me* what happened ... Oh, all right. After the death of Adrian Whitfield I desired as a journalist to maintain the momentum of the story. I sought to do this by writing additional letters.

S: From the person who called himself Will.

M: Yes.

S: Whitfield's last letter wasn't really misaddressed, was it?

M: He got the zip code wrong. That happens a lot but it doesn't delay the mail. We're the *Daily News*, for God's sake. Even the geniuses at the Post Office can find us.

S: So his letter arrived —

M: First thing Friday morning. Body was barely cold and there's a letter on my desk claiming credit for it. I took a good look at the postmark, wanting to know when it was mailed and where from, and while I was at it I happened to notice the zip code.

S: And?

M: First thing I thought was it wasn't from Will, because he never made that mistake. Then I read the letter and I knew it was from Will, it couldn't be from anybody else. And he said he was through. There

327

wouldn't be any more letters, there wouldn't be any more victims. He was done.

S: Did you suspect Whitfield wrote the letter?

M: Not at the time. Remember, I'm reading this before there's any speculation about suicide. I don't know the autopsy's going to show he was dying of cancer. I just got the thought that I ought to hang on to this letter and see what happens. What the hell, it could have been delivered late the way it was addressed, so why not give myself time to think it through?

S: And you turned the letter over finally –

M: To spike the suicide theory. It proved Will was the killer. I thought about addressing a new envelope and mailing it to myself, but that could constitute sabotaging the investigation.

S: Hadn't you already done that?

M: I'd delayed it slightly, but a new envelope would establish that the letter had been mailed at a later date than it actually had, and suppose they finally catch up with Will and he can prove he's in Saudi Arabia at the date the letter's postmarked? I wanted to cover my ass without kicking sand over any bona fide clues. And then I remembered the zip code and decided to take advantage of it. So I took the envelope and circled the zip code in red and scribbled 'delayed – wrong zip code' alongside of it. I made the writing illegible enough so you'd believe some postal employee actually wrote it. Anybody examining it would be able to determine when it was actually mailed, and would simply assume it had been delayed somewhere in the system.

S: That was clever.

M: It was clever but it was stupid, because it was the first step in fucking around with the case.

S: And the next step was writing your own letter.

328

M: I just wanted to keep it alive.

S: The story.

M: That's right. Even if Whitfield killed himself, which I didn't think he did, that still left Will out there, with a couple of other killings to his credit. Now he's lying low, but what's it gonna do to him to see someone else pretending to be him? He has to respond, doesn't he? And even if he doesn't, he's back in the news.

S: So you wrote the letter . . .

M: So I wrote the letter, and then you broke the case and got Adrian tagged as Whitfield. And now I'm out here with this stupid phony letter from some fucking copycat, with everybody in a rush to demonstrate that only a punk with cheese where his guts ought to be would write such a chickenshit letter. I thought it was a pretty good letter. Remember, it wasn't supposed to be Will. It was supposed to pry Will out of the woodwork.

S: But that was impossible . . .

M: Because Adrian was Will, and the poor fuck was dead. And the story goes about quietly dying, and I try to fan the flames a little, and then that asshole Regis Kilbourne isn't content with stinking up the Arts section, he's got to piss all over the op-ed page. And he couldn't just say, hey, look at me world, I'm braver than the characters Errol Flynn used to play. Instead the dirty little cocksucker has the nerve to review me.

S: He gave you another bad notice.

M: He killed *Tumult*, you know. Most of the other notices were gentle, even if they weren't going to sell any tickets. But he was vicious. He had a line toward the end, how he was speaking this candidly in the hope that it would dissuade me from ever writing another play. Can you imagine reviewing a first play that way?

S: It must have been painful.

M: Of course it was. And I have to say it worked. I never wrote a second play. Oh, I tried, I wanted nothing more than to prove the cocksucker wrong, but I couldn't do it. I'd type 'Act One, Scene One,' and then I'd fucking freeze. He put me out of business as a playwright, the bastard. He stabbed me in the back.

S: And you returned the favor.

M: Funny, huh? That wasn't planned. Except it's hard to say what was planned and what wasn't.

S: What happened?

M: He reviewed me a second time, told me to strike the set and get a life. And I thought, Jesus, he's asking for it, isn't he? I found out what play he was going to that night, and when the curtain came down I was waiting outside. I followed him right into Allen's. I got to look at the poster.

S: The poster?

M: For *Tumult*. All the posters on the walls in there are for shows that didn't make it. *Kelly*. *Christine*. If you close within a few days of your opening night, you're sure of a place of honor in Joe Allen's.

S: I knew that, but I never noticed your poster there.

M: Oh, it's there, right alongside the men's room door. *The Tumult in the Clouds*, a new play by Martin Joseph McGraw. And there's the man who killed it, stepping out with this hot-looking broad while he gets ready to piss all over somebody else's life's work. I had a few at the bar while Kilbourne and the photographer stuffed their faces, then went outside when they did. I didn't have to do a 'follow that cab' routine. I was close enough to hear what he said to the cabby, so I got my own cab and wound up standing across the street from his house. I almost went in while she was there.

S: Oh?

M: Because I thought maybe he's alone, maybe she

dropped him and kept the cab. If I'd gone and she'd been there –

S: You'd have killed them both?

M: No, never. First place he wouldn't have let me in. 'Go way, I've got somebody here.' You know what? I'd have gone home and slept it off and that would have been the end of it.

S: Instead . . .

M: Instead I stayed where I was. I had a pint in my coat pocket and I kept warm nipping at it, and then the two of them came out and walked down to the corner. I thought, fuck it, am I gonna follow them to her place now? Or are they off to some after-hours to party until dawn? They could do it without me. But instead he put her in a cab and came home.

S: And?

M: And went in his fucking house.

S: And what did you do?

M: Finished the pint. Stood there for a while with my thumb up my ass. And then I went over and rang his bell. He buzzed me in but kept me standing in the hallway. I told him who I was and that there'd been a new development in the Will case. Even then he didn't much want to let me in, but he did, and I went in and started babbling, the cops this and Will that, I didn't know what I was saying, and I don't suppose he knew what to make of it. Long story short, I got behind him and crowned him with an engraved cut-glass paperweight. Fancy fucking thing, weighed a ton, he got it for making a speech somewhere. I hit him as hard as I ever hit anybody in my life and he went down like the good ship *Titanic*.

S: And you went into the kitchen . . .

M: Yeah.

S: And got the knife?

M: And got the knife, yeah. And stabbed him in the back. I thought, teach you to turn your back on me, you little fuck. I thought, you stabbed me in the back, now we're even. Who knows what I thought? I was too drunk for whatever I thought to make much sense.

S: You washed the knife.

M: I washed the knife, and do me a big favor and don't ask me why. If I was worried about prints all I had to do was wipe it, right? But I washed it, and then I put the paperweight in my pocket and took it home with me. And then I went to bed.

S: And you remembered everything when you woke up?

M: Everything. You used to have blackouts?

S: Lots of them.

M: I never had one in my life. I remembered every fucking thing. The only thing, I tried to tell myself maybe I dreamed it. But the fucking paperweight's sitting on the bedside table, so it's no dream. I killed him. Can you believe it?

S: I guess I have to.

M: Yeah, and so do I. I killed a human being because he gave my play a bad review fifteen years ago. I can't fucking believe it. But I believe it.

TWENTY-SEVEN

The week before Christmas was about as social as it gets for us. We were out just about every night. We had dinner one night with Jim and Beverly Faber, and another night with Elaine's friend Monica and her married boyfriend. (Monica, according to Elaine, figures if a guy's not married there must be something wrong with him.)

One afternoon we stopped in at a reception at Chance Coulter's art gallery on upper Madison Avenue, then had dinner with Ray Gruliow and his wife. We ended the night at Danny Boy Bell's table at a new cellar jazz club in the West Nineties, listening to a young man who'd listened a lot to Coltrane when he wasn't listening to Sonny Rollins. The following afternoon Mick called to say someone had given him a good pair of seats for the Knicks game, and could Elaine and I use them? Elaine, who feels about basketball the way Mick feels about ballet, insisted that I go with Mick. We watched them lose to the Hornets in overtime, and she met the two of us afterward for dinner at Paris Green.

The night before Christmas we had dinner at home. She made pasta and a salad and we thought about having a fire in the fireplace and decided it was more trouble than it was worth. Besides, she said, Santa might sue. During the evening the phone rang a few times, with the usual round of holiday greetings. One of the callers was Tom Havlicek, telling me I'd once again managed to miss the opening day of deer season.

'Damn,' I said. 'I'd marked it on my calendar, too.' He asked for an update on Havemeyer, and I filled him in and told him his fellow Ohioan had a good lawyer and would probably wind up with a relatively light sentence.

Jason would be interested, he said. The boy had been buying the New York papers and clipping the stories. And he'd spent a long afternoon with Tom in Massillon, getting a little career advice. He was talking about taking a couple of undergraduate courses in police science, then getting his law degree and passing the bar exam, and then going into some form of police work.

'My guess is he'll land in the DA's office,' he said, 'but the way he's talking now he wants to wear blue and carry a badge. You ever hear of a working cop with a law school diploma on his wall?' I said he'd probably wind up being Massillon's next chief of police, and Tom made a rude noise. 'For that,' he said, 'you need two things I hope he'll never have, a fat ass and a foul disposition. And you never heard me say that.'

Shortly before midnight the two of us walked up to St Paul's. It was a clear night, and not too cold, and it looked as though they were having a decent turnout for midnight mass. Our destination, however, was not the sanctuary but the basement, where my AA group was having our annual midnight meeting. It's an open meeting, not limited to self-declared alcoholics, so Elaine was welcome. For the occasion, candles provided the illumination, and there was a better-than-usual selection of cookies laid out by the coffee urns, but in every other respect it was a typical meeting, with the speaker's drinking story taking up the first twenty minutes or so and round-robin sharing filling out the hour.

At one o'clock we said the serenity prayer and put the chairs away and walked home, and by the time we got there we decided not to wait until morning to open our presents. I got a cardigan sweater from Barney's and a silk shirt from Bergdorf's, along with firm instructions to take them back and exchange them if I didn't think I was likely to wear them. I also got a hat from Worth & Worth – 'Because you got the hat trick,' she said, 'so I figured you earned it.'

'It's a different style for me.'

'It's a homburg. Does it fit? It should, it's the same size as your fedora. Try it on. What do you think?'

'Well, it fits. I think I like it. It's dressier than the fedora, isn't it?'

'A little bit. Let's see. Oh, I really like it.'

'It's me, huh?'

'Not every man could wear a hat like that.'

'But I can?'

'They should use you in their ads,' she said. 'You old bear.'

She seemed to like her presents. I made her open the earrings last, and the light that came into her eyes told me I'd chosen well. 'You wait here,' she said. 'I want to try them on. Give me the homburg.'

'What for?'

'Just gimme.'

She went into the bathroom and emerged a few minutes later wearing the hat and the earrings and nothing else. 'Well?' she said. 'What do you think?'

'I think the earrings really make the outfit.'

'Yeah? What else do you think?'

'Come here,' I said, 'and I'll show you.'

We slept late Christmas morning, and were in the middle of breakfast when the doorman called on the intercom to tell us we had a visitor who gave his name as TJ. Send him up, I said.

'I gave my name as TJ,' he said, "cause that be who I am, Sam.'

He'd brought presents, wrapped and tied with ribbon. Elaine's was an antique dresser set, a brush and comb and hand mirror and scissors, all backed in mother of pearl. 'This is beautiful,' she said. 'How did you know to buy me this?'

'Saw you lookin' at one the time we went to the Twenty-sixth Street flea market. Only it wasn't in good shape so you put it back. So I figured I might find one in better condition.'

'You're amazing,' she said.

'Yeah, well, Merry Christmas, you know?'

'Merry Christmas, TJ.'

To me he said, 'What you waitin' for? Ain't you gonna open yours?'

It was a card case covered in ostrich skin. It was quite elegant, and I told him so.

'Figured you could use it. For your business cards, you know? Open it up, this here's the best part. See? Two compartments. What *they* say is one's for your cards and one's for cards people give to you, but what *I* figured is one's for your cards and the other's for the fake ones you use when you's representin' yourself to be somebody you ain't.'

'The perfect gift,' Elaine said, 'for the man who has everything except integrity.'

He unwrapped his presents, which included a sweater she'd picked out for him and a new wallet. "Cause yours was lookin' a little shabby, Abby,' she said, and he rolled his eyes. She told him to look inside, and he found the gift certificate.

'Because it's bad luck to give a wallet with nothing in it,' she explained.

'Brooks Brothers,' he said. 'Buy me somethin' slick to wear on the Deuce.'

'God help the Deuce,' I said, and stood up and stretched. 'Well, so much for Christmas.'

'It be over already?'

'Just about. Right now there's something I need your help with across the street.'

'What, in the hotel? Can't be movin' furniture. You ain't hardly got none.'

'No heavy lifting,' I said. 'That's a promise.'

TJ's face is expressive, but only when he wants it to be. I guess you learn to mask your emotions on the street. I've seen him receive information that astounded him without any of his surprise showing in his eyes.

But when I opened the door to my hotel room I was able to get a good look at his face, and the mask slipped. His eyes widened and his jaw dropped.

'You got one,' he said, approaching the desk reverently. 'Never thought you would. Told you an' told you, but I never thought you would. Elaine bought it for you, didn't she?'

I shook my head. 'I picked it out myself.'

'It's a Mac,' he announced. 'They easier to learn, what everybody says. That girl helped me learn all that shit about cyanide? She's got a Mac. Probably teach me how to use it. Not to do like the Kongs can do, but regular stuff. An' there's courses I can take, an' other people can teach me things. Shit, you got everything here. Got a printer, got a modem. Don't tell me you hooked this up all by yourself?'

'The fellow who sold it to me helped set it up. He also installed all the software he assured me I couldn't

337

live without. The disks and boxes are in the closet, and there's a stack of manuals on the chair.'

'Takes up space,' he said. 'That why you set it up here 'stead of 'cross the street?'

'That's one reason.'

He picked up a thick instruction manual, riffled the pages, returned it to the stack. 'Keep us both readin' for months,' he said. 'Man, you really did it. Bought yourself a real present.'

'No.'

'No?'

'It's for you,' I said. 'Merry Christmas.'

'It's for me?'

'That's right.'

'No it ain't', he said. 'I likely to be the one uses it the most, but that don't make it mine.'

'I bought it for you,' I said, 'and I'm giving it to you. *That's* what makes it yours.'

'You serious?'

'Of course I'm serious,' I said. 'Merry Christmas.'

He was a moment taking it all in. 'That be why it's over here,' he said. 'So I can fool with it an' not be disturbin' you an' Elaine. You be able to fix it up with them downstairs so I can come up anytime I want?'

'How could they stop you?'

'What you mean? They own the hotel, they stop anybody they want.'

'Not if it's your room.'

'Say what?'

I tossed him the key and he snatched it out of the air. I said, 'I've had this place for twenty years, and the rent's so low I'd be crazy to give it up. But I never use it. I come here maybe once a month to sulk and make free phone calls. What do I need it for?'

'So you givin' it to me?'

'I'll go on paying the rent,' I said, 'and I'll be the tenant of record, so that it stays rent-controlled. But they'll know at the desk that I'm letting you stay here, and Santa Claus was nice enough to them this year so that they won't give you a hard time.' I shrugged. 'I may drop by now and then to make long-distance calls, or to watch you perform miracles on the computer, but I won't show up without calling first. Because it's your place now.'

He turned toward the computer, rested his fingers on the keyboard. 'Guess you figure I ain't got no place of my own,' he said.

'As a matter of fact,' I said, 'I'm personally convinced you've got six homes of your own, including a penthouse on Sutton Place and a beachfront cottage in Barbados. But I'm a selfish son of a bitch, and I wanted to manipulate you into living right across the street from us.'

'Figured you had a reason.' He was still looking at the computer. He was silent for a moment, and then he said, 'You know, I ain't cried in years. Last time was when my grandmother came home from the doctor's an' said she was gonna die. Then when she did die I was real sad, you know, but I was cool with it. I didn't part with no tears. An' I ain't cried since.'

I didn't say anything.

'An' I don't *want* to cry,' he said. 'So there's stuff I'd be sayin' now, 'bout you an' Elaine, an' how, you know, how I feel an' all. But I ain't gonna say it.'

'I understand.'

''Cause if I was to try to say it . . .'

'I understand.'

'But that don't mean it don't be real, 'cause it do.'

'I understand that, too.'

'Yeah, well you real understandin', Brandon.' He

turned toward me, under control now. 'Merry Christmas,' he said.

'Merry Christmas.'